bel canto

Ann Patchett was born in Los Angeles in 1963. She is the author of *The Patron Saint of Liars*, *Taft* and *The Magician's Assistant* (shortlisted for the Orange Prize), and is the recipient of a Guggenheim Fellowship and the Nashville Banner Tennessee Writer of the Year Award in 1994. She has also written for numerous publications including, the *New York Times Sunday Magazine*, the *Chicago Tribune*, the *Boston Globe*, *Vogue*, *GQ*, *Elle*, and *Gourmet*. Ann Patchett lives in Nashville, Tennessee.

bel canto

a novel

Ann Patchett

This paperback edition first published in 2002
First published in Great Britain in 2001 by
Fourth Estate
A Division of HarperCollins*Publishers*
77–85 Fulham Palace Road,
London W6 8JB
www.4thestate.com

20 19 18 17 16

A catalogue record for this book is available from the British Library

ISBN 1-84115-583-7

Printed in Great Britain by
Clays Ltd, St Ives plc

For
Karl VanDevender

Fonti e colline chiesi agli Dei;
m 'udiro alfine,
pago io vovro,
ne mai quel fonte co 'desir miei,
ne mai quel monte trapassero

"I asked the Gods for hills and springs;
They listened to me at last.
I shall live contented.
And I shall never desire to go beyond that spring,
nor shall I desire to cross that mountain."

—Sei Ariette I: Malinconia, ninfa gentile
Vincenzo Bellini

Sprecher: Ihr Fremdlinge! was sucht oder fordert ihn von uns?
Tamino: Freundschaft und Liebe.
Sprecher: Bist du bereit, es mit deinem Leben zu erkämpfen?
Tamino: Ja.

Speaker: Stranger, what do you seek or ask from us?
Tamino: Friendship and love.
Speaker: And are you prepared even if it costs you your life?
Tamino: I am.

bel canto

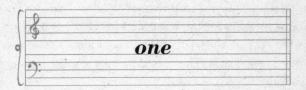

one

When the lights went off the accompanist kissed her. Maybe he had been turning towards her just before it was completely dark, maybe he was lifting his hands. There must have been some movement, a gesture, because every person in the living room would later remember a kiss. They did not *see* a kiss, that would have been impossible. The darkness that came on them was startling and complete. Not only was everyone there certain of a kiss, they claimed they could identify the type of kiss: it was strong and passionate, and it took her by surprise. They were all looking right at her when the lights went out. They were still applauding, each on his or her feet, still in the fullest throes of hands slapping together, elbows up. Not one person had come anywhere close to tiring. The Italians and the French were yelling, *"Brava! Brava!"* and the Japanese turned away from them. Would he have kissed her like that had the room been lit? Was his mind so full of her that in the very instant of darkness he reached for her, did he think so quickly? Or was it that they wanted her too, all of the men and women in the room, and so they imagined it collectively. They were so taken by the beauty of her voice that they wanted to cover her mouth with their mouth, drink in. Maybe music could be transferred, devoured, owned. What would it mean to kiss the lips that had held such a sound?

Some of them had loved her for years. They had every recording she had ever made. They kept a notebook and wrote down every place they had seen her, listing the music, the names of the cast, the conductor. There were others there that night who had not heard her name, who would have said, if asked, that opera was a collection of nonsensical cat screechings, that they would much rather pass three hours in a dentist's chair. These were the ones who wept openly now, the ones who had been so mistaken.

No one was frightened of the darkness. They barely noticed. They kept applauding. The people who lived in other countries assumed that things like this must happen here all the time. Lights go on, go off. People from the host country knew it to be true. Besides, the timing of the electrical failure seemed dramatic and perfectly correct, as if the lights had said, *You have no need for sight. Listen.* What no one stopped to think about was why the candles on every table went out as well, perhaps at that very moment or the moment before. The room was filled with the pleasant smell of candles just snuffed, a smoke that was sweet and wholly unthreatening. A smell that meant it was late now, time to go to bed.

They continued the applause. They assumed she continued her kiss.

Roxane Coss, lyric soprano, was the only reason Mr. Hosokawa had come to this country. Mr. Hosokawa was the reason everyone else had come to the party. It was not the kind of place one was likely to visit. The reason the host country (a poor country) was throwing a birthday party of unreasonable expense for a foreigner who had to be all but bribed into attending was that this foreigner was the founder and chairman of Nansei, the largest electronics corporation in Japan. It was the fondest wish of the host country that Mr. Hosokawa would smile on them, help them in some of the hundred different ways they needed helping. That could be achieved through training or trade. A factory (and this was the dream so dear its name could hardly be spoken) could be built here, where cheap labor could mean a profit for everyone involved. Industry could move the economy away from the farming of coca leaves and blackhearted poppies, creating the illusion of a country moving away from the base matter of cocaine and heroin, so as to promote foreign aid and make trafficking of those very drugs less conspicuous. But the plan had never taken root in the past, as the Japanese, by nature, erred on the side of caution. They believed in the danger and the rumors of danger countries such as this presented, so to have Mr. Hosokawa himself, not an executive vice president, not a politician, come and sit at the table was proof that a hand might be extended. And maybe that hand would have to be coaxed and begged. Maybe it would have to be pulled from its own deep pocket. But this visit, with its glorious birthday dinner replete with opera star, with several meetings planned and trips to possible factory sites tomorrow, was a full world closer than they had ever come before and the air in the room was sugared with promise. Representatives from more than a dozen countries who had been misled as to the nature of Mr. Hosokawa's intentions were present at the party, investors and ambassadors who might not encourage their governments to put a dime into the host country but would certainly support Nansei's every endeavor, now circled the room in black tie and evening gown, making toasts and laughing.

As far as Mr. Hosokawa was concerned, his trip was not for the purposes of business, diplomacy, or a friendship with the President, as later would be reported. Mr. Hosokawa disliked travel and did not know the President. He had made his intentions, or lack of intentions, abundantly clear. He did not plan to build a plant. He would never have agreed to a trip to a strange country to celebrate his birthday with people he did not know. He was not much for celebrating his birthday with people he did know, and certainly not his fifty-third, which he considered to be a number entirely without note. He had turned down half a dozen strong requests from these very people, for this exact party, until the promised gift was the presence of Roxane Coss.

And if she was the present, who would decline? No matter how far away, how inappropriate, how misleading it might prove to be, who would say no?

But first remember another birthday, his eleventh, the birthday on which Katsumi Hosokawa first heard opera, Verdi's *Rigoletto*. His father had taken him to Tokyo by train and together they walked to the theater in a steady downpour. It was October 22 and so it was a cold autumn rain and the streets were waxed in a paper-thin layer of wet red leaves. When they arrived at the Tokyo Metropolitan Festival Hall, their undershirts were wet beneath coats and sweaters. The tickets waiting inside Katsumi Hosokawa's father's billfold were wet and discolored. They did not have especially good seats, but their view was unobstructed. In 1954, money was precious; train tickets and operas were unimaginable things. In a different time, such a production would have seemed too complicated for a child, but this was only a handful of years after the war and children then were much more likely to understand a whole host of things that might seem impossible for children now. They climbed the long set of stairs to their row, careful not to look down into the dizzying void beneath them. They bowed and begged to be excused by every person who stood to let them pass into their seats, and then they unfolded their seats and slipped inside. They were early, but other people were earlier, as part of the luxury that came with the ticket price was the right to sit quietly in this beautiful place and wait. They waited, father and son, without speaking, until finally the darkness fell and the first breath of music stirred from someplace far below them. Tiny people, insects, really, slipped out from behind the curtains, opened their mouths, and with their voices gilded the walls with their yearning, their grief, their boundless, reckless love that would lead each one to separate ruin.

It was during that performance of *Rigoletto* that opera imprinted itself on Katsumi Hosokawa, a message written on the pink undersides of his eyelids that he read to himself while he slept. Many years later, when everything was business, when he worked harder than anyone in a country whose values are structured on hard work, he believed that life, true life, was something that was stored in music. True life was kept safe in the lines of Tchaikovsky's *Eugene Onegin* while you went out into the world and met the obligations required of you. Certainly he knew (though did not completely understand) that opera wasn't for everyone, but for everyone he hoped there was something. The records he cherished, the rare opportunities to see a live performance, those were the marks by which he gauged his ability to love. Not his wife, his daughters, or his work. He never thought that he had somehow transferred what should have filled his daily life into opera. Instead he knew that without opera, this part of himself would have vanished altogether. It was early in the second act, when Rigoletto and Gilda sang together, their voices twining, leaping, that he reached out for his father's hand. He had no idea what they were saying, nor did he know that they played the parts of father and daughter, he only knew that he needed to hold to something. The pull they had on him was so strong he could feel himself falling forward out of the high and distant seats.

Such love breeds loyalty, and Mr. Hosokawa was a loyal man. He never forgot the importance of Verdi in his life. He became attached to certain singers, as everyone does. He made special collections of Schwarzkopf and Sutherland. He believed in the genius of Callas above all others. There was never a great deal of time in his days, not the kind of time such interest clearly merited. Custom was that after having dinner with clients and completing paperwork, he would spend thirty minutes listening to music and reading librettos before falling asleep. It was impossibly rare, maybe five Sundays a year, that he found three consecutive hours to listen to one opera start to finish. Once, in his late forties, he ate a spoiled oyster and suffered a vicious bout of food poisoning that kept him home for three days. He remembered this time as happily as any vacation because he played Handel's *Alcina* continually, even while he slept.

It was his eldest daughter, Kiyomi, who bought him his first recording of Roxane Coss for his birthday. Her father was a nearly impossible man to buy gifts for, and so when she saw the disc and a name she did not recognize, she thought she would take a chance. But it wasn't the unknown name that drew her, it was the woman's face. Kiyomi found the pictures of sopranos irritating. They were always peering over the tops of fans or gazing through veils of soft netting. But Roxane Coss looked at her directly, even her chin was straight, her eyes were wide open. Kiyomi reached for her before she even noticed it was a recording of *Lucia di Lammermoor*. How many recordings of *Lucia di Lammermoor* did her father own? It didn't matter. She gave her money to the girl at the counter.

When Mr. Hosokawa put the CD in the player and sat down in his chair to listen, he did not go back to work that night. It was as if he was a boy in those high seats in Tokyo again, his father's hand large and warm around his own. He set the disc to play over and over, skipping impatiently past anything that was not her voice. It was soaring, that voice, warm and complicated, utterly fearless. How could it be at once controlled and so reckless? He called Kiyomi's name and she came and stood in the doorway of his study. She started to say something—yes? or, what? or, sir?—but before she could make out the words she heard that voice, the straight-ahead woman from the picture. Her father didn't even say it, he simply gestured towards one speaker with his open hand. She was enormously pleased to have done something so right. The music praised her. Mr. Hosokawa closed his eyes. He dreamed.

In the five years since then he had seen eighteen performances featuring Roxane Coss. The first was a lucky coincidence, the other times he went to the city where she would be, creating business to take him there. He saw *La Sonnambula* three nights in a row. He had never sought her out or made himself to be anything more than any other member of the audience. He did not assume his appreciation for her talent exceeded anyone else's. He was more inclined to believe that only a fool would not feel about her exactly how he felt. There was nothing more to want than the privilege to sit and listen.

Read a profile of Katsumi Hosokawa in any business magazine. He would not talk in terms of passion, as passion was a private matter, but opera was always there, the human interest angle to make him appear more accessible. Other CEOs were shown fly-fishing in Scottish rivers or piloting their own Learjets into Helsinki. Mr. Hosokawa was photographed at home in the leather chair he sat in when he listened, a Nansei EX-12 stereo system behind him. There were the inevitable questions about favorites. There was the inevitable answer.

For a price that was considerably more than the entire cost of the rest of evening (food, service, transportation, flowers, security) Roxane Coss was persuaded to come to the party, as it fell in between the end of her season at La Scala and the beginning of her appearance at Teatro Colón in Argentina. She would not attend the dinner (she did not eat before she sang) but would arrive at the end of the meal and perform six arias with her accompanist. Mr. Hosokawa was told by letter that he could make a request upon accepting the invitation, and while the hosts could make no promises, the request would be given to Miss Coss for her consideration. It was Mr. Hosokawa's selection, the aria from *Rusalka*, which she had just completed when the lights went out. It was to be the end of the program, though who is to say if she might have sung an encore or even two had the lights remained on?

Mr. Hosokawa chose *Rusalka* as a measure of his respect for Miss Coss. It was the centerpiece of her repertoire and would require no extra preparation on her behalf, a piece that surely would have been included in the program had he not requested it. He did not seek something achingly obscure, an aria from *Partenope* perhaps, so as to prove himself an aficionado. He simply wanted to hear her sing *Rusalka* while standing close to her in a room. *If a human soul should dream of me, may he still remember me on awaking!* His translator had written it out for him from the Czech years ago.

The lights stayed off. The applause began to show the slightest downward sweep. People blinked and strained to see her again. A minute passed, then two, and still the group remained comfortably unconcerned. Then Simon Thibault, the French Ambassador, who had, before coming to this country, been promised the much more desirable post of Spain (which had been unfairly given to another man as a payoff for a complicated political favor while Thibault and his family were packing) noticed the lights beneath the kitchen door were still on. He was the first to understand. He felt like he had been startled from a deep sleep, drunk from liquor and pork and Dvořák. He took his wife's hand, reached up for it in the darkness as she was still applauding, and pulled her into the crowd, dark bodies he could not see but pushed himself into. He went towards the direction of the glass doors he remembered being at the far end of the room, craning his head to try and catch a glimpse of starlight for orientation. What he saw was the narrow beam of a flashlight, one and then another, and he felt his heart cave down inside his chest, a feeling that could only be described as sadness.

"Simon?" his wife whispered.

It was already in place, without him seeing any of it, the web was spun and snug around the house, and while his first impulse, the natural impulse, was to press ahead anyway and see if he might beat out the odds, clear logic held him. Better not to draw attention to yourself. Better not to be an example. Somewhere in the front of the room the accompanist was kissing the opera singer, and so Ambassador Thibault drew his wife, Edith, into his arms.

"I'll sing in the dark," Roxane Coss called out, "if someone will get me a candle."

With these words the room stiffened and the final moment of applause turned to silence as it was noted that the candles, too, were dark. It was the end of the evening. By now the bodyguards napped inside limousines like great, overfed dogs. All across the room men slipped their hands into pockets and found only neatly pressed handkerchiefs and folding money. A surge of voices went up, there was some shuffling, and then, as if by magic, the lights came on.

* * *

It had been a beautiful party, though no one would remember that. White asparagus in hollandaise, a fish course of turbot with crispy sweet onions, tiny chops, only three or four bites apiece, in a cranberry demiglaze. Usually struggling countries longing to impress the heads of important foreign corporations chose Russian caviar and French champagne. Russian and French, Russian and French, as if that was the only way to prove prosperity. On every table sprays of yellow orchids, each flower no bigger than a thumbnail, all locally grown, trembled and balanced like mobiles, rearranging themselves with every exhalation of a guest. The effort that had gone into the evening, the positioning of each stem, the sweeping calligraphy of the place cards, had been lost without a moment's appreciation. Paintings had been borrowed from the national museum: a dark-eyed Madonna presenting a tiny Christ on her fingertips, his face oddly knowing and adult, was placed over the mantel. The garden, which the guests would see only for a moment when they walked the short distance from their cars to the front door or if they happened to glance out the window while it was still light enough, was polished and composed, birds of paradise and tightly wrapped canna lilies, banks of lamb's ear and emerald fern. They were not far from the jungle, and even in the most domesticated garden the flowers strained to overtake the dull stretch of neat Bermuda grass. From early in the morning young men had worked, wiping the dust from the leathery leaves with damp cloths, picking up the fallen blossoms of bougainvillea that rotted beneath the hedges. Three days before they had put a fresh coat of whitewash on the high stucco wall that surrounded the home of the Vice President, careful that none of the paint should fall on the grass. Every element was planned: crystal saltcellars, lemon mousse, American bourbon. There was no dancing, no band. The only music would be after dinner, Roxane Coss and her accompanist, a man in his thirties from Sweden or Norway with fine yellow hair and beautiful, tapering fingers.

*   *   *

Two hours before the beginning of Mr. Hosokawa's birthday party, President Masuda, a native of this country born of Japanese parents, had sent a note of regret saying that important matters beyond his control would prevent him from attending the evening's event.

There was great speculation about this decision after the evening turned bad. Was it the President's good luck? God's divine will? A tip-off, conspiracy, plot? Sadly, it was nothing so random. The party was scheduled to begin at eight o'clock and should have lasted past midnight. The President's soap opera began at nine. Among the President's cabinet members and advisers it was an open secret that matters of state could not be held Monday through Friday for one hour beginning at two in the afternoon or Tuesday evening for one hour beginning at nine. Mr. Hosokawa's birthday fell on a Tuesday this year. There was nothing that could be done about that. Nor could anyone conceive how to have a party that commenced at ten o'clock at night or had concluded by eight-thirty and which allowed time for the President to return home. It was suggested that the program could be taped, but the President abhorred taping. There was enough taping to endure when he was out of the country. All he asked of anyone was that certain hours of his week remain unquestionably open. The discussion of the problem of Mr. Hosokawa's ill-timed birthday party lasted for days. After a great deal of negotiating, the President relented and said he would attend. Hours before the party began, for an obvious and unstated reason, he firmly, irrevocably, changed his mind.

While President Masuda's commitment to his programs was completely known and acknowledged by his political inner circle, this commitment somehow managed to remain utterly unknown to the press or the people. The host country was mad for soap operas, and yet the President's unwavering devotion to his television set was so potentially embarrassing his cabinet would have gladly traded it in for an indiscreet mistress. Even members of the government who were themselves known to follow certain programs could not bear to see the obsession played out so rigidly in their head of state. So for many of the people at the party who worked with the President, his absence was noted with disappointment and no real surprise. Everyone else inquired, Has there been an emergency? Is President Masuda unwell?

"Matters in Israel," they were told confidentially.

"Israel," they whispered. They were impressed, never dreaming that President Masuda would be consulted on matters in Israel.

There was a clear division among the almost two hundred guests that night: those who knew where the President was and those who didn't, and so it remained until both sides forgot about him altogether. Mr. Hosokawa barely noticed the absence. He cared very little about meeting the President. What could a president possibly mean on the evening one would meet Roxane Coss?

Into the presidential void, the Vice President, Ruben Iglesias, stepped forward to host the party. This was not so difficult to imagine. The dinner was being given in his home. Throughout the cocktails and hors d'oeuvres, the sit-down dinner and the creamy singing, his mind stayed on the President. How easy it was to picture his running mate now as Iglesias had seen him a hundred times before, sitting in the dark on the edge of the bed in the master suite of the presidential palace, his suit jacket folded over the arm of a chair, his hands folded and pressed between his knees. He would be watching a small television that sat on his dresser while his wife watched the same program on a large screen in the den downstairs. A picture of a beautiful girl tied to a chair reflected in his glasses. She twisted her wrists back and forth, over and over again, until suddenly she found some slack in the rope and slid one hand free. Maria was free! President Masuda rocked back and clapped his hands silently. To think he had almost missed this, after waiting for weeks! The girl glanced quickly around the storeroom and then leaned forward to untie the coarse rope that bound her ankles.

Then in an instant the picture of Maria was gone and Ruben Iglesias lifted his face to the lights which were suddenly restored to his living room. He had just begun to register that a bulb was burned out on a side table lamp when men burst into the party from every window and wall. Everywhere the Vice President turned the edges of the room seemed to push forward, yelling. Heavy boots and gun butts pounded through vents, stormed in through doors. People were thrown together and then just as quickly broke apart in a state of animal panic. The house seemed to rise up like a boat caught inside the wide arm of a wave and flip onto its side. Silverware flew into the air, the tines of forks twisting against knife blades, vases smashed into walls. People slipped, fell, ran, but only for an instant, only until their eyes readjusted to the light and they saw the utter uselessness of their fight.

It was easy to see who was in charge—the older men, the ones shouting orders. They did not introduce themselves at the time and so, for a while, they were thought of not by their names but by their most distinctive features. Benjamin: raging shingles. Alfredo: mustache, first and second fingers missing on left hand. Hector: gold wire glasses that had lost one arm. With the Generals came fifteen soldiers who ranged in age from twenty to fourteen. There were now an additional eighteen people at the party. No one there could count them at the time. They moved and spread. They doubled and tripled as they pulsed around the room, appeared from behind curtains, came down from upstairs, disappeared into the kitchen. They were impossible to count because they seemed to be everywhere, because they were so similar, like trying to count bees in a swarm around your head. They wore faded clothing in dark colors, many in the dull green of shallow, sludgy ponds, a handful in denim or black. Over their clothing they wore a second layer of weapons, sashes of bullets, flashy knives in back pockets, all manner of guns, smaller guns holstered to thighs or sticking up hopefully from belts, larger guns cradled like infants, brandished like sticks. They wore caps with the bills pulled down, but no one was interested in their eyes, only their guns, only their shark-toothed knives. A man with three guns was recorded subconsciously as three men. There were other similarities between the men: they were thin, either from the wanting of food or just the business of growing, their shoulders and knees poked at their clothing. They were also dirty, noticeably so. Even in the confusion of the moment everyone could see that they were smudged and streaked, arms and faces and hands mottled in dirt as if they had arrived at the party by digging up through the gardens and dislodging a panel in the floor.

This entrance could not have taken more than a minute, and yet it seemed to last longer than all four courses of dinner. There was time for every guest to consider a strategy, revise it thoroughly, and abandon it. Husbands found wives who had drifted to the other side of the room, countrymen sought out their own and stood in blocks, speaking rapidly to one another. It was the consensus of the party that they had been kidnapped not by La Familia de Martin Suarez (so named for a boy of ten who had been shot dead by the government's army while passing out flyers for a political rally) but by the much more famous terrorists, La Dirección Auténtica, a revolutionary group of murderers whose reputation had been built over five years of wide-ranging brutality. It was the unspoken belief of everyone who was familiar with this organization and with the host country that they were all as good as dead, when in fact it was the terrorists who would not survive the ordeal. Then the terrorist missing two fingers who was wearing wrinkled green pants and a mismatched jacket raised the large .45-caliber auto and fired two rounds into the ceiling. A splattering of plaster dislodged and dusted a portion of the guests, at which point several of the women screamed, either from the firing of the gun or the touch of something unexpected on their bare shoulders.

"Attention," the man with the gun said in Spanish. "This is an arrest. We demand absolute cooperation and attention."

Roughly two-thirds of the guests looked frightened, but a scattered third looked both frightened and puzzled. These were the ones leaning towards the man with the gun, instead of away from him.

These were the ones that did not speak Spanish. They whispered quickly to their neighbors. The word *atención* was repeated in several languages. That word was clear enough.

General Alfredo had anticipated his announcement bringing about a sort of pricked, waiting silence, but no silence came. The whispering caused him to fire into the ceiling again, carelessly this time, hitting a light fixture, which exploded. The room was dimmer, and slivers of glass settled into shirt collars and rested on hair. *"Arresto,"* he repeated. *"Detengase!"*

It may seem surprising at first, such a large number of people unable to speak the language of the host country, but then you remember it was a gathering to promote foreign interest and the two guests of honor did not know ten words of Spanish between them, although *arresto* made logical sense to Roxane Coss and meant nothing to Mr. Hosokawa. They leaned forward as if it might make understanding easier. Miss Coss was not leaning far, as the accompanist had wrapped himself around her like a security wall, his body ready, anxious, to step in front of any bullet that might stray in her direction.

Gen Watanabe, the young man who worked as Mr. Hosokawa's translator, leaned over and spoke the words in Japanese to his employer.

Not that it would have done him any good in these present circumstances, but Mr. Hosokawa had once tried to learn Italian from a set of tapes he listened to on airplanes. For business purposes he should have learned English, but he was more interested in improving his understanding of opera. *"Il bigliettaio mi fece il biglietto,"* the tape said. *"Il bigliettaio mi fece il biglietto,"* he mouthed back silently, not wanting to disturb the other passengers. But his efforts were minimal at best and in the end he made no progress. The sound of the language spoken made him long for the sound of the language sung and soon he was slipping *Madama Butterfly* into the CD player instead.

When he was younger, Mr. Hosokawa saw the great advantage of languages. When he was older he wished he had made the commitment to learn them. The translators! They were ever-changing, some good, some full of schoolboy stiffness, some utterly, hopelessly stupid. Some could hardly speak their native Japanese and continually halted conversations to look up a word in a dictionary. There were those who could perform their job well enough, but were not the sort of people one wished to travel with. Some would abandon him the moment the final sentence of a meeting was completed, leaving him stranded and mute if further negotiations were necessary. Others were dependent, wanting to stay with him through every meal, wanting to accompany him on his walks and recount for him every moment of their own lusterless childhoods. What he went through just for a mouthful of French, a few clear sentences of English. What he went through before Gen.

Gen Watanabe had been assigned to him at a conference on the worldwide distribution of goods in Greece. Normally, Mr. Hosokawa tried to avoid the surprise element local translators so often provided, but his secretary had been unable to locate a Greek translator who could travel on short notice. During the plane ride to Athens, Mr. Hosokawa did not talk with the two senior vice presidents and three sales managers who accompanied him on the trip. Instead, he listened to Maria Callas sing a collection of Greek songs on his Nansei headset, thinking philosophically if the meeting was unintelligible to him, at least he would have seen the country she considered her home. After waiting in line to have his passport stamped and his luggage rifled through, Mr. Hosokawa saw a young man holding a sign, *Hosokawa*, neatly lettered. The young man was Japanese, which, frankly, was a relief. It was easier to deal with a countryman who knew a little Greek than a Greek who knew a little Japanese. This translator was tall for being Japanese. His hair was heavy and long in the front and it brushed across the top rims of his small round glasses even as he tried to keep it parted to one side. He appeared to be quite young. It was the hair. The hair denoted to Mr. Hosokawa a lack of seriousness, or perhaps it was just the fact that the young man was in

Athens rather than Tokyo that made him seem less serious. Mr. Hosokawa approached him, gave the slightest bow of acknowledgment that only included his neck and upper shoulders, a gesture that said, You have found me.

The young man reached forward and took Mr. Hosokawa's briefcase, bowing as he did so to the waist. He bowed seriously, though somewhat less deeply, to both of the vice presidents and the three sales managers. He introduced himself as the translator, inquired after the comfort of the flight, gave the estimated driving time to the hotel and the starting time of the first meeting. In the crowded Athens airport, where every second man seemed to sport a mustache and an Uzi, among the jostling of bags and the din of shouting and overhead announcements, Mr. Hosokawa heard something in this young man's voice, something familiar and soothing. It was not a musical voice, and yet it affected him like music. Speak again.

"Where are you from?" Mr. Hosokawa asked.

"Nagano city, sir."

"Very beautiful, and the Olympics—"

Gen nodded, contributing no information about the Olympics.

Mr. Hosokawa struggled to come up with something else. It had been a long flight and it seemed that in the time he had been on the plane he had forgotten how to make conversation. He felt it should be incumbent upon Gen to attempt to draw him out. "And your family, are they still there?"

Gen Watanabe paused for a moment as if he were remembering. A swarm of Australian teenagers passed them, each with a knapsack strapped to her back. Their shouts and laughter filled the concourse. "Wombat!" one girl cried out, and the others answered, "Wombat! Wombat! Wombat!" They stumbled in their laughter and clung to each other's arms. "They are all there," Gen said, eyeing the backs of the teenagers with cautious suspicion. "My father, mother, and two sisters."

"And your sisters, are they married?" Mr. Hosokawa did not care about the sisters, but the voice was something he could almost place, like the notes opening the first act of, what?

Gen looked at him directly. "Married, sir."

Suddenly this dull question took on the edge of something inappropriate. Mr. Hosokawa looked away while Gen took his luggage and led his party through the sliding glass doors into the blasting heat of Greece at noon. The limousine waited, cool and idling, and the men climbed inside.

Over the next two days, everything Gen touched became a smooth surface. He typed up Mr. Hosokawa's handwritten notes, took care of scheduling, found tickets to a performance of *Orfeo ed Euridice* that had been sold out for six weeks. At the conference he spoke in Greek for Mr. Hosokawa and his associates, spoke in Japanese to them, and was, in all matters, intelligent, quick, and professional. But it was not his presence that Mr. Hosokawa was drawn to, it was his lack of presence. Gen was an extension, an invisible self that was constantly anticipating his needs. He felt Gen would remember whatever had been forgotten. One afternoon during a private meeting concerning shipping interests, as Gen translated into Greek what he had just that moment said himself, Mr. Hosokawa finally recognized the voice. Something so familiar, that's what he had thought. It was his own voice.

"I don't do a great deal of business in Greece," Mr. Hosokawa said to Gen that night over drinks in the bar of the Athens Hilton. The bar was on top of the hotel and looked out over the Acropolis, and yet it seemed that the Acropolis, small and chalky in the distance, had been built there for just this reason, to provide a pleasant visual diversion for the drinking guests. "I was wondering about your other languages." Mr. Hosokawa had heard him speaking English on the phone.

Gen made a list, stopping from time to time to see what had been left out. He divided into categories the languages in which he felt he was extremely fluent, very fluent, fluent, passable, and could read. He knew more languages than there were specialty cocktails listed in the Plexiglas holder on the table. They each ordered a drink called an Areopagus. They toasted.

His Spanish was extremely fluent.

Half a world away, in a country twice as foreign, Mr. Hosokawa was remembering the Athens airport, all the men with mustaches and Uzis who called to mind the man who held the gun now. That was the day he met Gen, four years ago, five? After that, Gen came back to Tokyo to work for him full-time. When there was nothing that needed translating, Gen simply seemed to take care of things before anyone knew they needed taking care of. Gen was so central to the way he thought now that Mr. Hosokawa forgot sometimes he didn't know the languages himself, that the voice people listened to was not his voice. He had not understood what the man with the gun was saying and yet it was perfectly clear to him. At worst, they were dead. At best, they were looking at the beginning of a long ordeal. Mr. Hosokawa had gone someplace he never should have gone, let strangers believe something that was not true, all to hear a woman sing. He looked across the room at Roxane Coss. He could barely see her, her accompanist had her so neatly wedged between himself and the piano.

"President Masuda," the man with the mustache and the gun said.

There was an uneasy shifting among the well-dressed guests, no one wanting to be the one to break the news.

"President Masuda, come forward."

People kept their eyes blank, waiting, until the man with the gun brought the gun down so that now it faced the crowd, though in particular it appeared to be pointed at a blonde woman in her fifties named Elise, who was a Swiss banker. She blinked a few times and then crossed her wide-open hands one on top of the other to cover her heart, as if this was the place she was most likely to be shot. She would offer up her hands if they might afford her heart a millisecond of protection. While this elicited a few gasps from the audience, it did little else. There was an embarrassing wait that ruled out all notions of heroics or even chivalry, and then finally the Vice President of the host country took a small step forward and introduced himself.

"I am Vice President Ruben Iglesias," he said to the man with the gun. The Vice President appeared to be extremely tired. He was a very small man, both in stature and girth, who had been chosen as a running mate as much for his size as for his political beliefs. The pervasive thinking in government was that a taller vice president would make the President appear weak, replaceable. "President Masuda was unable to attend this evening. He is not here." The Vice President's voice was heavy. Too much of this burden was falling to him.

"Lies," the man with the gun corrected.

Ruben Iglesias shook his head sadly. No one wished more than he that President Masuda were in attendance right now, instead of lying in his own bed, happily playing over the plot of tonight's soap opera in his mind. General Alfredo quickly turned the gun in his hand so that he now held the muzzle rather than the handle. He brought the gun back in the air and hit the Vice President on the flat bone of his cheek beside the right eye. There was a soft thump, a sound considerably less violent than the action, as the handle of the gun hit the skin over the bone and the small man was knocked to the ground. His blood wasted no time in making its exit, spilling out the three-centimeter gash near his hairline. Some of it made its way into his ear and started the journey back into his head. Still, everyone, including the Vice President (now lying half conscious on his own living-room rug where not ten hours before he had rolled in a mock wrestling match with his three-year-old son) was pleased and surprised that he had not been shot dead.

The man with the gun looked at the Vice President on the floor and then, as if liking the sight of him there, instructed the rest of the party to lie down. For those who didn't speak the language this was clear enough, as one by one the other guests sank to their knees and then stretched out on the floor.

"Faceup," he added.

The few who had done it wrong rolled over now. Two of the Germans and a man from Argentina would not lie down at all until the soldiers went and poked them sharply in the backs of their knees with rifles. The guests took up considerably more room lying down than they had standing up, and to accommodate the need for space some lay down in the foyer and others in the dining room. One hundred and ninety-one guests lay down, twenty waiters lay down, seven prep cooks and chefs lay down. The Vice President's three children and their governess were brought from the upstairs bedroom, where, despite the late hour, they had yet to go to sleep because they had been watching Roxane Coss sing from the top of the stairs, and they, too, lay down. Scattered across the floor like area rugs lay some important men and women and a few extremely important men and women, ambassadors and various diplomats, cabinet members, bank presidents, corporation heads, a monseigneur, and one opera star, who appeared to be much smaller now that she was on the floor. Bit by bit the accompanist was moving on top of her, trying to bury her beneath his own broad back. She squirmed a bit. The women who believed that this would all be over shortly and they would be home in their own beds by two A.M. were careful to adjust their full skirts beneath them in a way that would minimize wrinkling. The ones who believed they would be shot presently let the silk wad and crease. When everyone had settled to the floor the room was left remarkably quiet.

Now the people were clearly divided into two groups: those who were standing and those who were lying down. Instructions were given, those lying down were to remain quiet and still, those standing up should check those lying down for weapons and for secretly being the president.

One would think that being on the floor would make one feel more vulnerable, more afraid. They could be stepped on or kicked. They could be shot without even the chance to run. Yet to a person everyone on the floor felt better. They could no longer plot to overpower a terrorist or consider a desperate run at the door. They were considerably less likely to be accused of doing something they did not do. They were like small dogs trying to avoid a fight, their necks and bellies turned willfully towards sharp teeth, *take me*. Even the Russians, who had been whispering a plot to make a run for it a few minutes before, experienced the relief of resignation. Not a few of the guests closed their eyes. It was late. There had been wine and turbot and a very nice small chop, and as much as they were terrified, they were tired. The boots that stepped around them, over them, were old and caked in mud that flaked off into trails across the elaborately patterned Savonnière carpet (which, mercifully, lay on a good pad). There were holes in the boots and the edges of toes could be seen, toes being now so close to eyes. Some of the boots had fallen apart and were held together by silver electrical tape that was itself filthy and rolled back at the edges. The young people crouched down over the guests. They did not smile but there was nothing particularly threatening in their faces either. It was easy to imagine how this might have gone if everyone had been standing, a smaller boy with several knives needing to establish his authority over a taller, older man wearing an expensive tuxedo. But now the boys' hands moved quickly, fluttering in and out of pockets, smoothing down pants legs with their fingers spread. For the women there was just the slightest tapping around the skirts. Sometimes a boy would lean over, hesitate, and pull away altogether. They found very little of interest, as this was a dinner party.

The following items were recorded in a notebook by the very quiet General Hector: six silver pen knives in trouser pockets and four cigar cutters on watch chains, one pearl-handled pistol scarcely larger than a comb in an evening bag. At first they thought it was a cigarette lighter and accidentally popped off a round trying to find the flame, leaving a narrow gouge in the dining-room table. A letter opener with a cloisonné handle from the desk and all manner of knives and meat forks from the kitchen, the poker and the shovel from the stand by the fireplace, and a snub-nosed .38 Smith & Wesson revolver from the Vice President's bedside table, a gun which the Vice President freely admitted to having when questioned. All of this they locked into an upstairs linen closet. They left the watches, wallets, and jewelry. One boy took a peppermint from a woman's satin evening clutch but first held it up discreetly for consent. She moved her head down and back, just a quarter of an inch, and he smiled and slipped off the cellophane.

One boy peered intently at Gen and Mr. Hosokawa, looking once and then again at their faces. He stared at Mr. Hosokawa and then backed up, stepping on the hand of one of the waiters, who winced and pulled it quickly away. "General," the boy said, too loudly for such a quiet room. Gen moved closer to his employer, as if to say by the position of his body that this was a package deal, they went together.

Over the warm and breathing guests stepped General Benjamin. At first glance one might have thought he had the unlucky draw of a large port wine birthmark, but with another look it was clear that what was on his face was a living, raging thing. The bright red river of shingles began somewhere deep beneath his black hair and cut a swath across his left temple, stopping just short of his eye. The very sight of them made the viewer weak from sympathetic pain. General Benjamin followed the path of the boy's pointing finger and he, too, stared at Mr. Hosokawa for a long time. "No," he said to the boy. He began to turn away, but then he stopped, said to Mr. Hosokawa in a conversational manner, "He thought you were the President."

"He thought you were the President," Gen said quietly, and Mr. Hosokawa nodded. A Japanese man in his fifties wearing glasses, there were another half-dozen lying around.

General Benjamin dropped his rifle down to Gen's chest and rested the muzzle there like a walking stick. The round opening was barely bigger than one of the studs on his shirtfront and it made a small and distinct point of pressure. "No talking."

Gen mouthed the word *traductor* to him. The General considered this for a moment, as if he had just been told the man he had spoken to was deaf or blind. Then he picked up his gun and walked away. Surely, Gen thought, there must be some medication that man could take that would help him. When he inhaled he felt a small, piercing ache where the point of the gun had been.

Not so far away, near the piano, two boys took their guns and poked at the accompanist until he was more beside Roxane Coss than on top of her. Her hair, which had been pulled up into an elaborate twist on the back of her head, was nearly impossible to lie on. She had surreptitiously removed the pins and put them in a neat pile on her stomach, where they could be collected as weapons if anyone was so inclined to take them. Now her hair, long and curled, spread out around her head and every young terrorist made a point of coming by to see it, some being bold enough to touch it, not the deep satisfaction of a stroke, but the smallest of taps with one finger near its curling ends. Leaning over this way, they could smell her perfume, which was different from the perfumes of the other women they had inspected. The opera singer had somehow replicated the scent of the tiny white flowers they had passed in the garden on their way to the air ducts. Even on this night, with the possibilities of their own deaths and the possibilities of liberation weighing heavily on their minds, they had noticed the smell of such a tiny, bell-shaped flower that grew near the high stucco wall, and now to find it here again so soon in the hair of the beautiful woman, it felt like an omen, like good luck. They had heard her sing while they waited crouched inside the air-conditioning vents. They each had a task, extremely specific instructions. The lights were to be cut off after the sixth song, no one ever having explained in their lives the concept of an encore. No one having explained opera, or what it was to sing other than the singing that was done in a careless way, under one's breath, while carrying wood into the house or water up from the well. No one having explained anything. Even the generals, who had been to the capital city before, who had had educations, held their breath so as to better hear her. The young terrorists waiting in the air-conditioning vents were simple people and they believed simple things. When a girl in their village had a pretty voice, one of the old women would say she had swallowed a bird, and this was what they tried to say to themselves as they looked at the pile of hair-pins resting on the pistachio chiffon of her gown: *she has swallowed a bird*. But they knew it wasn't true. In all their ignorance, in all their unworldliness, they knew there had never been such a bird.

In the steady river of approaching boys, one crouched down beside her and picked up her hand. He held it lightly, hardly more than rested her palm against his own, so that she could have taken it back from him at any minute, but she did not. Roxane Coss knew the longer he held her hand, the more he would love her, and if he loved her he was more likely to try and protect her from the others, from himself. This particular boy looked impossibly young and fine-boned beneath the bill of his cap, his eyelids burdened by the weight of a thousand silky black lashes. Across his narrow chest was a bandolier of bullets and his body curved beneath their weight. The rough wooden handle of a primitive kitchen knife stuck up from the top of one boot and a pistol was half falling from his pocket. Roxane Coss thought of Chicago and the frigid nights of late October. If this boy had been living in another country, in an entirely different life, he might still have gone out trick-or-treating next week, even if he had been too old. He might have dressed as a terrorist, worn old boots from a gardening shed, fashioned a bandolier from strips of corrugated cardboard, and filled each loop with a tube of his mother's lipstick. The boy would not look at her, only her hand. He studied it as if it were something completely separate from her. Under any other circumstances she would have pulled it away from him, but due to the remarkable course of the evening's events, she kept her hand still and allowed it to be studied.

The accompanist raised his head and glowered at the boy, who then settled Roxane Coss's hand back against her dress and walked away.

*   *   *

Two facts: none of the guests was armed; none of the guests was President Masuda. Groups of boys with guns drawn were dispatched to different corners of the house, down to the basement, up to the attic, out around the edges of the high stucco wall, to see if he had hidden himself in the confusion. But the word came back again and again that no one was there. Through the open windows came the raucous sawing of insect life. In the living room of the vice-presidential home, everything was still. General Benjamin sat down on his heels next to the Vice President, who was bleeding heartily into the dinner napkin which his wife, who lay beside him, pressed against his head. A more sinister edge of purple was now ringing his eye. It looked nowhere near as painful as the inflammation of his own face. "Where is President Masuda?" the General asked, as if it was the first moment they had noticed him gone.

"At home." He took the bloody cloth from his wife and motioned for her to scoot away.

"Why did he not come this evening?"

What the General was asking was, did he have a mole in his organization, did the President receive word of an attack? But the Vice President was dazed from the blow and feeling bitter besides, bitterness being a first cousin to the truth. "He wanted to watch his soap opera," Ruben Iglesias said, and in the hushed and obedient room his voice traveled to every ear. "He wanted to see if Maria would be freed tonight."

"Why were we told he would be here?"

The Vice President gave it up without hesitation or remorse. "He had agreed to attend and then he changed his mind." There was an uneasy shifting of bodies on the floor. The people who didn't know were as appalled to hear it as the ones who had known all along. Ruben Iglesias had at that exact moment ended his own political career. There had been no great love between him and Masuda to begin with, and now Masuda would ruin him. A vice president worked hard because he believed someday the office would be handed down, like property passed from father to son. In the meantime he bit his lip, took the dirty jobs, the ceremonial funerals, visits to earth-quake sites. He nodded appreciatively through each of the President's interminable speeches. But on this night he no longer believed he would someday be the President. Tonight he believed he would be shot along with some of his guests, possibly all of his guests, possibly his children, and if that was the case, he wanted the world to know that Eduardo Masuda, a man barely one centimeter taller than him-self, was home watching television.

The Catholic priests, sons of those murdering Spanish missionar-ies, loved to tell the people that the truth would set them free, and in this case they were exactly correct. The General named Benjamin had cocked his gun and was prepared to make an example by dispatching the Vice President into the next world, but the soap opera story stopped him. As much as he was sick to know that five months of planning for this one evening to kidnap the President and possibly overthrow the entire government were worthless and he was now sad-dled with two hundred and twenty-two hostages lying before him on the floor, he believed the Vice President's story completely. No one could make it up. It was too petty and small-minded. General Benjamin had no qualms about killing, believing from his own experi-ence that life was nothing more than excruciating suffering. If the Vice President had said the President had the flu, he would have shot him. If he had said the President was called away on urgent matters of national security, he would have shot him. If he had said it was all a ruse and the President had never planned on attending the party at all, *bang*. But Maria, even in the jungle where televisions were rare, electricity sketchy, and reception nonexistent, people spoke of this Maria. Even Benjamin, who cared for nothing but the freedom of the oppressed, knew something of Maria. Her program came on in the afternoons from Monday to Friday, with a special episode on Tuesday nights which more or less summarized the week for those who had to work during the day. If Maria was to be freed, it was not surprising that it should happen on a Tuesday night.

There was a plan, and that plan had been to take the President and be gone inside of seven minutes. They should be out of the city by now, speeding their way over the dangerous roads that led back to the jungle.

Through the windows, bright red strobe lights flashed across the walls accompanied by a high-pitched wailing. The sound was nagging and accusatory. It was nothing, nothing like song.

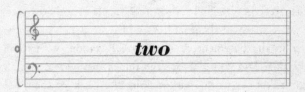

two

*a*ll night long the outside world bellowed. Cars skidded and sped. Sirens arrived, departed, flicked off and on and off again. Wooden barricades were dragged into place, people were herded behind. It was surprising how much more they could hear now that they were lying down. They had the time to concentrate—yes, there went the shuffling of feet, that was the sound of a baton being smacked into an open palm. The ceiling had been memorized (light blue with crown molding that was elaborate to the point of being tasteless, scrolling and spiraling and every inch of it leafed in gold, the three chipped holes left by bullets) and so guests closed their eyes to settle into the serious business of listening. Voices, exaggerated and mangled through the bullhorn's amplification, shouted instructions towards the street, made demands towards the house. They would settle for nothing short of unqualified, immediate surrender.

"You will put your guns down outside the door," the voice raged, loud and distorted as if it had bubbled up from the ocean floor. "You will open the door and exit before the hostages, hands on the backs of your heads. Next, the hostages will proceed through the front door. For the purposes of safety, hostages should keep their hands on the top of their heads."

When one voice had completed its pitch the bullhorn was handed off to another, who began it all over again with subtle variations of the threats. There were a series of loud clicks and then an artificial blue-white light spilled through the living-room window like cold milk and made everyone squint. At what point had their problems been discovered? Who had called these people in and how was it possible that so many of them had assembled so quickly? Did they wait together in the basement of some police station, wait for a night just like this? Did they practice the things they would say, shouting through bullhorns to no one, making the pitch of their voices go higher and higher. Even the guests knew that no one would put down his guns and walk out the door simply because he was told to do so. Even they understood that every time the demand was issued the chances of it being answered favorably receded. Each of the guests dreamed that he or she was in possession of a secret gun, and if they had such a gun they would certainly never throw it down the front porch steps. After a while they were so tired they forgot to wish that this had never happened, or to wish that they had never come to the party. All they wished was for the men outside to go home, turn off the bullhorns, and let them all have a night's sleep on the floor. Every now and then there would be a few free moments when no one was speaking, and in that false and temporary quiet a different kind of noise would come forward, tree frogs and locusts and the metallic clicking of guns being loaded and cocked.

Mr. Hosokawa later claimed he did not close his eyes all night, but Gen heard him snoring sometime after four A.M.. It was a soft, whistling snore like wind coming in beneath a doorjamb, and it gave Gen comfort. There was other snoring in the room as people fell asleep for ten minutes or twenty, but even asleep they remained obedient and stayed flat on their backs. The accompanist had worked his way out of his suit jacket so slowly he never appeared to move at all and he made a little balled-up pillow on which Roxane Coss could lay her head. All night long the muddy boots stepped over them, between them.

When the guests lay down the night before there had been a great deal of drama, which served as a distraction to what might happen, but by morning fear had coated the inside of every mouth. They had been awake thinking over the alternatives, which did not seem good. The rough brush of beards had sprung up during the night and eye makeup had been smeared from crying. Dinner jackets and dresses were crumpled, shoes were tight. Backs and hips ached from the hard floor and necks were locked straight ahead. Without exception, every last person on the floor needed to use the facilities.

In addition to suffering what the others suffered, Mr. Hosokawa bore the terrible burden of responsibility. All of these people had come for his birthday. By agreeing to a party under what he knew to be false pretense, he had contributed to the endangerment of every life in the room. Several employees of Nansei had come, including Akira Yamamoto, the director of project development, and Tetsuya Kato, senior vice president. Vice presidents from Sumitomo Bank and the Bank of Japan, Satoshi Ogawa and Yoshiki Aoi, respectively, had also come, despite Mr. Hosokawa's personal and repeated requests that they not attend. The host country had called them as well, explaining that it was a birthday party for their most valued customer and of course they wouldn't want to miss a birthday party. The ambassador from Japan had made the call. He was lying on the doormat now in the entry way.

But the hostage that pained Mr. Hosokawa the most (and even as he felt this he knew it was wrong, to place a higher value on one life over another) was Roxane Coss. She had been brought to this dismal jungle to sing for him. What vanity on his part to think this was an appropriate gift. It was enough to listen to her recordings. It had been more than enough to see her at Covent Garden, the Metropolitan. Why did he think it would be any better if he could stand close enough to smell her perfume? It was not better. Her voice, if he could be very honest, was not flattered by the acoustics in the living room. It made him uncomfortable to notice the supreme athleticism of her mouth, to see so clearly her damp pink tongue when she opened up wide and wider still. The lower teeth were not straight. It had been an honor but nothing that would be worth the harm that could come to her, to all of them. He tried to raise his head just a half an inch to see her. She was almost near him, since he had been standing in the front of the room when she was singing. Her eyes were closed now, though he imagined she was not sleeping. It was not that she was a very beautiful woman, if one could see her objectively, lying on a living-room floor. Each of her features seemed a bit too large for her face, her nose was too long, her mouth was too wide. Her eyes, certainly, were bigger, rounder, than average eyes, but no one could complain about her eyes. They reminded him of the blue of the rindo flowers that grew near Lake Nagano. He smiled to think of that, and wanted to turn and tell his thought to Gen. He looked instead to Roxane Coss, whose face he had tirelessly studied in program notes and CD inserts. Her shoulders were sloping. Her neck, perhaps, could be longer. A longer neck? He cursed himself. What was he thinking? None of it mattered. No one could see her objectively anyway. Even those who saw her for the first time, before she had opened her mouth to sing, found her radiant, as if her talent could not be contained in her voice and so poured like light through her skin. Then all that could be seen was the weight and the gloss of her hair and the pale pink of her cheeks and her beautiful hands. The accompanist caught sight of Mr. Hosokawa's raised head and Mr. Hosokawa quickly returned it to the floor. The terrorists were beginning to tap some of the guests and motion them to stand and follow. It was easy for Mr. Hosokawa to pretend he had only raised his head to see about that.

By ten in the morning a certain amount of whispering had begun. It wasn't so difficult to sneak in a word or two with all the noise that blasted in through the windows and the constant up and down of the guests being led into the hall. That was what had started the whispering. At first they all believed they were to be taken away and shot a handful at a time, probably in the garden behind the house. Victor Fyodorov fingered the package of cigarettes in his jacket pocket and wondered if they would let him smoke for a minute before gunning him down. He could feel the rivulets of sweat combing back his hair. It would almost be worth getting shot if he could have a cigarette now. The room was painfully still as they waited for the report, but when that first group returned, smiling, nodding, they whispered to the ones next to them, "Toilet, bathroom, WC." The word spread.

Everyone was led away with one escort: for every guest, a dirt-smeared young terrorist sporting several weapons. Some of the young men merely walked beside the guests, while others held the upper arm with varying degrees of aggression. The boy who came for Roxane Coss took her hand rather than her arm and held it in the manner of sweethearts looking for a deserted stretch of beach. He wasn't pretty the way the boy who held her hand earlier had been.

There were those who believed they would be killed, who over and over again saw the movie of themselves being led out the door at night and shot in the back of the head, but Roxane Coss thought no such thing. Maybe there would be a bad outcome for some of the others, but no one was going to shoot a soprano. She was prepared to be nice, to let her hand be held, but when the time was right she would be the one to get away. She was sure of it. She smiled at the boy when he opened the door to the bathroom for her. She half expected he would follow her inside. When he didn't she locked the door, sat down on the toilet, and cried, great, gulping sobs. She wrapped her hair around her hands and covered her eyes. Goddamn her agent who said this was worth all the money! Her neck was stiff and she felt like she might be getting a cold, but who wouldn't catch a cold sleeping on a floor. Wasn't she Tosca? Hadn't she jumped off the back of the Castle Sant' Angelo night after night? Tosca was harder than this. After this she would only play in Italy, England, and America. Italy, England, and America. She said the three words over and over again until she could regulate her breathing and was able to stop the crying.

Cesar, the boy with the gun who waited in the hallway, did not rap on the door to hurry her along as was done with other guests. He leaned against the wall outside and imagined her bending down towards the gold faucet to rinse out her mouth. He pictured her washing her face and hands with the little shell-shaped soaps. He could still hear the songs that she sang in his head and very quietly he hummed the parts that he remembered to pass the time, *Vissi d'arte, vissi d'amore, non feci mai male ad anima viva!* Strange how those sounds stayed so clearly in his mind. She was not quick in the bathroom, but what could you ask of such a woman? She was a masterpiece. Nothing about her could be rushed. When she finally came out her hand was slightly damp and thrilling-cool to the touch. *Vissi d'arte,* he wanted to say to her, but he didn't know what it meant. When he returned her to her spot near the piano, the accompanist was gone, and then, in a moment, he was returned as well. He looked considerably worse than the other guests. The accompanist was a troubling moon shade of white and his eyes were rimmed in bloody red. He was held tightly on either side by Gilbert and Francisco, two of the bigger boys. They used both of their hands to drag him forward. At first it appeared that the accompanist had tried to make a run for a window or door and had been overpowered, but when they went to return him to his spot, his knees folded beneath him as if they were two sheets of notebook paper asked to support his entire body weight. He slipped to the floor in a crumpling faint. The terrorists gave Roxane a piece of advice or information in Spanish, but she did not speak Spanish.

She sat up a bit, unsure whether or not she was allowed to sit up, and pulled his legs out straight. He was a large man, not heavy, but tall, and she struggled against the unnatural arrangement of his limbs. At first she had thought he was playing possum. She had heard of hostages pretending to be blind to facilitate their release, but no one could pretend their skin into that color. His head wagged dully from side to side when she shook him. One of the waiters who was near her leaned over and tugged the accompanist's arms down to his sides from where they had been pinned beneath him.

"What's happened to you?" she whispered. A set of muddy boots walked past. She stretched out beside the accompanist and took his wrist between her fingers.

Finally, the accompanist stirred and sighed and turned to face her, blinking rapidly as if he were trying to rouse himself from a deep and wonderful sleep. "Nothing will happen to you," he told Roxane Coss, but even with his bluish lips pressed against the side of her head, his voice was distant, exhausted.

"There will be a request for ransom," Mr. Hosokawa told Gen. They were both watching Roxane and her accompanist now, thinking at several points that the accompanist was dead, but then he would shift or sigh. "It is Nansei's policy to pay ransom, any ransom. They'll pay it for both of us." He could speak in his smallest voice, a sound too minimal to ever be called a whisper, and still Gen understood him perfectly. "They will pay it for her as well. It would only be fitting. She is here on my account." And the accompanist, especially if he were sick, he should not be forced to stay. Mr. Hosokawa sighed. Actually, in some sense, everyone in the room was here on his account and he wondered what such a ransom could add up to. "I feel that I have brought this on us."

"You are not holding a gun," Gen said. The sound of their own Japanese spoken so softly it could not have been heard twelve centimeters away, comforted them. "It was the President they meant to take last night."

"I wish they had him," Mr. Hosokawa said.

On the other side of the room near the bottom edge of a gold brocade sofa, Simon and Edith Thibault held each other's hand. They didn't settle in with the rest of the French but kept to themselves. They looked very much a pair, nearly brother and sister, with their dark straight hair and blue eyes. They lay on the floor of the dinner party with so much dignity and ease they looked not like two people forced to the floor at gunpoint, but like two people who had simply grown tired of standing. While everyone else lay rigid and trembling, the

Thibaults leaned in, her head on his shoulder, his cheek pressed to the crown of her head. He was thinking less of the terrorists and more of the remarkable fact that his wife's hair smelled of lilacs.

In Paris, Simon Thibault had loved his wife, though not always faithfully or with a great deal of attention. They had been married for twenty-five years. There had been two children, a summer month spent every year at the sea with friends, various jobs, various family dogs, large family Christmases that included many elderly relatives. Edith Thibault was an elegant woman in a city of so many thousands of elegant women that often over the course of years he forgot about her. Entire days would pass when she never once crossed his mind. He did not stop to think what she might be doing or wonder if she was happy, at least not Edith by herself, Edith as his wife.

Then, in a wave of government promises made and retracted, they were sent to this country, which, between the two of them was always referred to as *ce pays maudit,* "this godforsaken country." Both of them faced the appointment with dread and stoic practicality, but within a matter of days after their arrival a most remarkable thing happened: he found her again, like something he never knew was missing, like a song he had memorized in his youth and had then forgotten. Suddenly, clearly, he could see her, the way he had been able to see her at twenty, not her physical self at twenty, because in every sense she was more beautiful to him now, but he felt that old sensation, the leaping of his heart, the reckless flush of desire. He would find her in the house, cutting fresh paper to line the shelves or lying across their bed on her stomach writing letters to their daughters who were attending university in Paris, and he was breathless. Had she always been like this, had he never known? Had he known and then somehow, carelessly, forgotten? In this country with its dirt roads and yellow rice he discovered he loved her, he *was* her. Perhaps this would not have been true if he had been the ambassador to Spain. Without these particular circumstances, this specific and horrible place, he might never have realized that the only true love of his life was his wife.

"They don't seem to be in any hurry to kill anyone," Edith Thibault whispered to her husband, her lips touching his ear.

For as far as the eye can see there is nothing but white sand and bright blue water. Edith walking into the ocean for a swim turns back to him, the water lapping at her thighs. "Shall I bring you a fish?" she calls, and then she is gone, diving under a wave.

"They'll separate us later," Simon said.

She wrapped her arm tightly around his and took his hand again. "Let them try."

There had been a mandatory seminar last year in Switzerland, protocol for the capture of an embassy. He assumed that the rules would apply for overthrown dinner parties as well. They would take the women away. They would— He stopped. He honestly didn't remember what came after that. He wondered if when they took Edith, if she might have something with her, something of hers he could keep, an earring? How quickly we settle for less! thought Simon Thibault.

What had been a few pockets of careful whispering at first was now a steady hum as people returned from the bathrooms. Having stood up and stretched their legs, they didn't feel as obedient on the floor. Quietly, people began to have tentative conversations, a murmur and then a dialogue rose up from the floor, until the room became a cocktail party in which everyone was lying prone. Finally, General Alfredo was driven to shoot another hole in the ceiling, which put an end to that. A few high-pitched yelps and then silence. Not a minute after the gun went off, there was a knock on the door.

Everyone turned to look at the door. With all of the demands, the shuffle of crowds, barking of dogs, chop of helicopters dipping overhead, no one had knocked, and everyone in the house tensed, as one tenses when one does not wish to be disturbed at home. The young terrorists looked nervously at one another, taking deep breaths and slipping their fingers into the empty loop of the trigger guards as if to say that they were ready to kill someone now. The three Generals conferred with one another, did a bit of pointing until there was a line of young men on either side of the door. Then General Benjamin drew his own gun and, nudging the Vice President's shoulder with the rounded edge of his boot, made him get up and answer the door.

It only stood to reason that whoever was on the other side of the door had every intention of coming in firing and better they serve up Ruben Iglesias to this mistake. He got up from the nest he had made by the empty fireplace with his wife and three children, two bright-eyed girls and one small boy, whose face was sweaty and red from the work of such deep sleep. The governess, Esmeralda, stayed with them. She was from the north and did not hesitate to glare openly at the terrorists. The Vice President kept looking at the ceiling, afraid that last bullet might have nicked a pipe. That would be a hell of a thing to deal with now. The right side of his face, which changed and grew hourly, was now swollen into a meaty yellow red and his right eye was shut tight. Still the wound bled and bled. Twice he had had to get a new dinner napkin. As a boy, Ruben Iglesias prayed long hours on his knees in the Catholic church that God would grant him the gift of height, a gift He had not seen fit to grant a single member of his extended family. "God will know what to give you," the priests had told him without a hint of interest, and they were right. Being short had made him the second-most-important man in his government, and now it had very probably saved him from serious injury as the blow had landed more on the strong plane of his skull than the comparatively delicate hinge of his jaw. His face served as a reminder that everything had not gone smoothly the night before, another good message to those outside. When the Vice President stood, stiff and aching, General Benjamin put the slender broomstick of the rifle's barrel between his shoulder blades and steered him forward. His own condition, always exacerbated by stress, had begun to bloom one tiny pustule at the end of every nerve and he longed for a hot compress almost as much as he longed for revolution. The knock repeated itself.

"I'm coming," Ruben Iglesias said, not to the door but to the armed man behind him. "I know where my door is." He knew his life was probably over, and the knowledge of this fact gave him a temerity that he found useful.

"Slowly," General Benjamin instructed.

"Slowly, slowly, yes, tell me, please. I've never opened a door," the Vice President said under his breath, and then opened the door at his own pace, which was neither slow nor fast.

The man waiting on the front porch was extremely fair, and he wore his white-yellow hair neatly parted and combed back. His white shirt with a black tie and black trousers made him look very much like an earnest representative of an American religion. One imagined there was a suit jacket that had been surrendered to the heat, or perhaps it was off to show the red-cross armband that he wore. Ruben Iglesias wanted to bring the man in out of the harsh sun. Already his forehead and the tops of his cheeks had begun to burn red. The Vice President looked past him, down the path through his own front yard, or what he had come to think of as his own front yard. The house, in fact, was not his, nor was the lawn, the staff, the soft beds or fluffy towels. Everything came with the job and would be inventoried upon their departure. Their own possessions were in storage and there was a time he had thought hopefully that their things would stay exactly where they were while he and his family made their inevitable transition into the presidential mansion. Through the narrow opening of the front gate he saw an angry knot of police officers, military personnel, and reporters. Somewhere in a tree a camera flash popped a bright light.

"Joachim Messner," the man said, extending his hand. "I am with the International Red Cross." He spoke in French, and when the Vice President squinted at him he repeated his statement in mediocre Spanish.

His manner was so calm, so seemingly unaware of the chaos that surrounded them, that he could have been taking a Sunday morning collection. The Red Cross was always there to help the victims of earthquakes and floods, the very ones Vice President Iglesias was sent to comfort and assess. Ruben Iglesias shook hands with the man and then held up a finger, indicating that he should wait. "The Red Cross," he said to the bank of guns behind him.

Again there was a conference between the three Generals and it was agreed that this could be allowed. "Are you sure you want to come in?" the Vice President asked quietly in English. His English was imperfect, perhaps on par with Messner's Spanish. "There's no saying that they'll let you out."

"They'll let me out," he said, stepping inside. "The problem is that there are too many hostages. More hostages is not what they're look- ing for now." He looked around at the terrorists and then back to the Vice President. "Your face is not well."

Ruben Iglesias shrugged to indicate that he was philosophical about it all, having received the kinder end of the gun, but Messner took it to mean that he had not understood the question.

"I speak English, French, German, and Italian," he said in English. "I'm Swiss. I speak a little Spanish." He held up two fingers and placed them about a centimeter apart, as if to say that the amount of Spanish he spoke would fit into this space. "This isn't my region. I was on vacation, can you imagine that? I am fascinated by your ruins. I am a tourist and they call me into work." Joachim Messner seemed inordinately casual, like a neighbor stopping in to borrow eggs and staying too long to chat. "I should bring in a translator if I'm going to work in Spanish. I have one outside."

The Vice President nodded but frankly hadn't caught half of what Messner had said. He knew a little English but only when the words were spoken one at a time and he hadn't recently been clubbed in the head with a gun. He thought there was something in there about a translator. Even if there wasn't, he'd like one anyway. "*Traductor*," he told the General.

"*Traductor*," General Benjamin said, and scanned the floor, work- ing off a dim memory from the night before. "*Traductor?*"

Gen, who was helpful but not heroic by nature, lay still for a moment remembering the sharp point of pressure the gun had made against his chest. Even if he said nothing they would remember sooner or later that he was the translator. "Would you mind?" he whispered to Mr. Hosokawa.

"Go on," he said, and touched Gen's shoulder.

There was a moment of quiet and then Gen Watanabe raised a tentative hand.

General Alfredo waved him up. Gen, like most of the men, had taken off his shoes and he stooped down now to put them back on, but the General snapped at him impatiently. Gen, embarrassed, worked a path around the guests in his sock feet. He thought it would be rude to step over someone. He apologized quietly as he walked. *Perdon, perdonare, pardon me.*

"Joachim Messner," the Red Cross man said in English, shaking Gen's hand. "English, French, do you have a preference?"

Gen shook his head.

"French, then, if it's all the same. Are you all right?" Messner asked in French. His face was such a remarkable assemblage of colors. The very blue of his eyes, the very white of his skin, red where the sun had burned his cheeks and lips, the yellow hair which was the color of the white corn Gen had seen once in America. He was all primary colors, Gen thought. From such a face any beginning was possible.

"We are well."

"Have you been mistreated?"

"Spanish," General Alfredo said.

Gen explained and then said again, cutting his eyes to the Vice President, that they were well. The Vice President did not look well at all.

"Tell them I will act as their liaison." Messner thought for a minute, repeated the sentence fairly well in Spanish himself. Then smiled at Gen and said in French, "I shouldn't try. I'll get something terribly wrong and then we'll all be in trouble."

"Spanish," General Alfredo said.

"He says he struggles with Spanish."

Alfredo nodded.

"What we want, of course, is the unconditional release of all the hostages, unharmed. What we will settle for at present are some of the extras." Messner glanced around at his feet, the carpet of well-dressed guests and white-jacketed waiters who craned their heads towards him. The whole picture was extremely unnatural. "This is too many people. You're probably out of food now or you will be by tonight. There's no need for this many. I say release the women, the staff, anyone who is sick, anyone you can do without. We'll start there."

"In return?" the General said.

"In return, enough food, pillows, blankets, cigarettes. What do you need?"

"We have demands."

Messner nodded. He was serious yet weary, as if this were a conversation he had ten times a day before breakfast, as if every other birthday party ended up in just such a knot. "I'm sure you do and I'm sure they'll be heard. What I'm telling you is that this"—he spread his arm forward to make clear he meant the people on the floor—"is untenable to everyone. Release the extras now, the ones you don't need, and it will be taken as a goodwill gesture. You establish yourself as reasonable people."

"Who is to say we are reasonable?" General Benjamin asked Gen, who passed it on.

"You've had control of the property for twelve hours and no one is dead. No one is dead, are they?" Messner said to Gen. Gen shook his head once and translated the first half of the statement. "That makes you reasonable in my book."

"Tell them to send us President Masuda. We came here for the President and for him we will let everyone go." He gestured expansively across the room. "Look at these people! I don't even know how many people there are. Two hundred? More? You tell me one man for two hundred is not a reasonable exchange."

"They won't give you the President," Messner said.

"That's who we came for."

Messner sighed and nodded seriously. "Well, I came here on vacation. It seems that no one is going to get what they want."

All the time Ruben Iglesias stood beside Gen, passively listening to the conversation as if he had no real interest in its outcome. He was the highest-ranking political official in the room and yet no one was looking to him to be either the leader or the valuable, near-presidential hostage replacement. Ask the average citizen in this beautiful country so bereft of mass communication who the Vice President was and chances are they would shrug and turn away. Vice presidents were merely calling cards, things sent in lieu of things desired. They were replaceable, exchangeable. No war was fought or won over the inspiring words of a vice president, and no one understood this more clearly than the Vice President of the host country.

"Give them up," Ruben told the Generals calmly. "This man is right. Masuda would never come in here." Funny, but at that moment he was thinking, *come in here,* as in—this house, my house. Masuda had always excluded Ruben. He did not know his children. He never asked to dance with Ruben's wife at state dinners. It was one thing to want a common man on your ticket, it was something else entirely to want him at your dinner table. "I know how these things go. Give them the women, the extras, and it sends them a message that you are people they can work with." When the First Federal Bank was taken over two years ago they gave up nothing, not a single customer or teller. They hanged the bank's manager in the front portico for the media to photograph. Everyone remembered how that one ended: every last terrorist shot against the marble walls. What Ruben wanted to tell them was that these things never worked out. No demands were ever met, or were ever honestly met. No one got away with the money and a handful of comrades liberated from some high-security prison. The question was only how much time it would take to wear them down, and how many people would be killed in the process.

General Benjamin lifted one finger and poked at the bloodstained dinner napkin the Vice President held against his face. Ruben took it fairly well. "Did we ask you?"

"It is my house," he said, feeling slightly nauseated from a wave of pain.

"Go back to the floor."

Ruben wanted to lie down, and so he turned away without remark. He felt nearly sad when Messner took his arm and stopped him.

"Someone needs to sew up that cut," Messner said. "I'm going to call in a medic."

"No medics, no sewing," General Alfredo said. "It was never a pretty face."

"You can't leave him bleeding like that."

The General shrugged. "I can."

The Vice President listened. He could not plead his own case. And really, the thought of a needle now that this great soreness had settled in, the headache and hot pressure behind his eyes, well, he wasn't entirely sure he wasn't pulling for the terrorists to win this particular argument.

"Nothing will proceed if this man bleeds to death." Messner's voice was calm to balance out the seriousness of his statement.

To death? the Vice President thought.

General Hector, who did not make much in the way of contributions, told the governess to go upstairs and find her sewing kit. He clapped twice, like a schoolteacher calling the children to attention, and she was up and stumbling, her left foot having fallen asleep. As soon as she was gone, his son, Marco, who was just a little boy of four, cried in agony, as he believed the hired girl to be his own mother. "Settle this now," General Hector said gravely.

Ruben Iglesias turned his swollen face to Joachim Messner. A sewing kit was not what he had in mind. He was not a loose button, a hem in need of shortening. This was not the jungle and he was not a primitive man. Twice in his life he had had stitches before and they were neatly done in a hospital, sterile instruments waiting in flat silver pans.

"Is there a doctor here?" Messner asked Gen.

Gen did not know but he sent the question out across the room in one language after another.

"We must have invited at least one doctor," Ruben Iglesias said, though with the building pressure in his head he could not remember anything.

The girl, Esmeralda, was coming down the stairs now with a square wicker box held under one arm. She would not have stood out among so many woman dressed in evening wear. She was a country girl in a uniform, a black skirt and blouse, a white collar and cuffs, her dark, long braid, as big around as a child's fist, sliding across her back with every step. But now everyone in the room looked at her, the way she moved so easily, the way she seemed completely comfortable, as if this was any other day in her life and she had a moment to finish some mending. Her eyes were smart, and she kept her chin up. Suddenly, the whole room saw her as beautiful and the marble staircase she walked on shimmered in her light. Gen repeated his call, doctor, doctor, while the Vice President was moved to say the girl's name, "Esmeralda."

No one on the floor raised a hand and the conclusion was that no doctors were present. But that wasn't true. Dr. Gomez was lying in the back, almost to the dining room, and his wife was stabbing him sharply in the ribs with two red lacquered fingernails. He had given up his practice years ago to become a hospital administrator. When was the last time he had sewn a man up? In his days of practice he had been a pulmonologist. Certainly he had not run a needle through skin since his residency. He was probably no more qualified to do a decent job than his wife, who at least kept a canvas of petit point going all the time. Without taking a single stitch he saw how the whole thing would unravel: there would be an infection, certainly; they would not bring in the necessary antibiotics; later the wound would have to be opened, drained, resewn. Right there on the Vice President's face. He shuddered at the thought of it. It would not go well. People would blame him. There would be publicity later. A doctor, the head of the hospital, killing a man perhaps, even though no one could say it was his fault. He felt his hands shaking. He was only lying there and still his hands trembled against his chest. What hands were these to sew a man's face, to leave a scar for which they would both become known? And then there was this girl descending the staircase with her basket, looking so much like hope itself. She was an angel! He had never been able to find such intelligent-looking girls to work on the hospital floors, such pretty girls who could keep their uniforms so clean.

"Get up there!" his wife hissed. "Or I'll raise your arm for you."

The doctor closed his eyes and gently wagged his head from side to side in a way that would attract no attention to himself. Whatever would happen would happen. The stitches would neither save the man nor kill him. That card was already played and there was nothing to do but wait and see the outcome.

Esmeralda handed the basket to Joachim Messner but she did not step away. Instead, she lifted the lid, which was lined in a padded rose-covered print, took a needle from the tomato-shaped cushion and a spool of black thread, and threaded the needle. She bit off the thread with a delicate snap and made a neat little knot at the end. All of the men, even the Generals, watched her as if she was doing something quite miraculous, something far beyond needles and thread that they could never have managed themselves. Then she reached into her skirt pocket and took out a bottle of rubbing alcohol into which she lowered the needle and bounced it up and down several times. Sterilization. And here she was a simple country girl. Nothing could have been as thoughtful. She pulled the needle up holding only the knot on the thread and extended it to Joachim Messner.

"Ah," he said, taking the knot between his forefinger and thumb.

There was some discussion. First it was thought that they could both stand and then it seemed better for the Vice President to sit down and then best of all for him to lie down near a table lamp where the light was best. The two men were stalling, each dreading it more than the other. Messner rubbed his hands in alcohol three times. Iglesias was thinking he would rather be hit by the gun again. He lay down on the carpet away from his wife and children and Messner bent over him, leaning in and then blocking his own light, leaning back and turning the Vice President's head one way and then the other. The Vice President tried to make himself think of something pleasant and so he thought of Esmeralda. It was really quite remarkable how she managed things. Perhaps his wife had taught her that, the concept of bacteria, the need to keep things clean. How lucky he was to have such a girl looking after his children. The blood no longer pulsed but it continued to seep, and Messner stopped to blot it away with a napkin. Considering the circumstances, the blaring messages pouring in through the windows, the constant on and off of sirens, the hostages stretched across the floor, the terrorists sleepy with their guns and knives, you would have thought that no one would care what became of Ruben Iglesias's cheek, and yet the people craned their necks up like turtles to see what would happen next, to see the needle go down for that first stick.

"Five minutes is what you have left," General Alfredo said.

Joachim Messner pinched the skin closed with his left hand and with his right put the needle in. Thinking that a quick movement would be kinder, he misjudged the thickness of the material at hand and drove the needle hard into the bone. Both men made a noise that was less than a scream, sharp but small, and Messner jerked the needle out again with some effort, leaving them exactly where they had started. Except that now the little hole was working up a drop of blood itself.

No one had asked for her but there was Esmeralda cleaning her hands. She had a look on her face the Vice President had seen her use with his children. They had tried at something and failed and she had let things go far enough. She took the needle and thread from Joachim Messner and bobbed it again in the alcohol. It was with great relief that he moved aside. He did not care about her intentions or qualifications, he only watched her as she bent beside the light.

Ruben Iglesias thought her face was kind in the beatific manner of saints, even though she was not exactly smiling. He was grateful for her serious brown eyes, which were now just inches from his own. He would not close his eyes, no matter how great the temptation. He knew that he would never again see such concentration and compassion focused on his face even if he were to survive this ordeal and live to be a hundred. When the needle came towards him he held still and breathed in the grassy smell of her hair. He did feel like a button that had come undone, a pair of child's trousers spread across her warm lap that she sewed in the evening. It was not so bad. He was simply one more thing for Esmeralda to put together again, something else in need of repair. It hurt, the little needle. He did not like to see it pass before his eye. He did not like the small tug at the end of every stitch that made him feel like a trout, caught. But he was grateful to be so close to this girl he saw every day. There she was on the lawn with his children, sitting on a sheet beneath a tree, pouring them tea in chipped cups, Marco on her lap, his daughters, Rosa and Imelda, holding dolls. There she was backing into the hallway, good night, good night, she says, no more water, go to sleep, close your eyes, good night. She was silent in her concentration and still the very thought of her voice made him relax, and though it hurt he knew he would be sorry when it was over, when her hip was no longer pressed against his waist. Then she was finished and she made another knot. Like a kiss she leaned down to him and bit the thread, her lips having no choice but to brush the seam her hands had made. He could hear the quick cutting of her teeth, the disconnection of what bound them, and then she sat up again. She ran her hand across the top of his head, a gift for what he had suffered. Pretty Esmeralda.

"Very brave," she said.

Anyone who was close enough to see them smiled and sighed. She had done such nice work, laid down a neat train track of even black stitches along the side of his head. It was what one would expect from a girl who had been raised to sew. Marco shinnied back into Esmeralda's arms when she went to rejoin them. He pressed his head against her breasts and breathed her in. The Vice President himself did not move, the pain and the pleasure of it were all colliding and he released himself into the moment. He closed his eyes as if he had been given a proper anesthetic.

"Both of you," the General said to Messner and Gen. "Go lie down. We'll discuss this." He used his gun to point to the floor, someplace not too close by.

Messner did not try to resume negotiations. "I don't lie down," he said, but his voice was tired enough that one might have thought he would have liked to. "I wait outside. I'll come back again in one hour." With that he gave a courteous nod to Gen and simply opened the door and let himself out. Gen wondered if he might do the same, explain that he would be waiting outside. But Gen knew he was not Messner. There was no putting one's finger on it exactly, but it was as if there would be no point in shooting Messner. He seemed like someone who had been shot every day of his life and had simply had enough of it. Gen, on the other hand, his mind still full of stitches, was feeling decidedly mortal. Mortal and loyal, and he went to take his place beside Mr. Hosokawa.

"What did they say?" Mr. Hosokawa whispered.

"I think they'll let the women go. It isn't decided yet, but they seem to want to. They say there are too many of us." On every side of him was a person, some not six centimeters away. He felt like he was taking the Yamanote line into the Tokyo station at eight in the morning. He reached up and loosened his tie.

Mr. Hosokawa closed his eyes and felt a calmness spread over him like a soft blanket. "Good," he said. Roxane Coss would be released, safely off in time to sing in Argentina. Within a few days the scare of this event would leave her. She would follow their fate through the safety of the newspaper. She would tell the story at cocktail parties and people would be amazed. But people were always amazed. In Buenos Aires she would be singing Gilda the first week. It seemed to him the perfect coincidence. She is singing Gilda and he is still a boy with his father in Tokyo. He watches her from the high seats, from so far away and yet still her voice is as clear and delicate as it had been when he was standing close enough to touch her. Her bold gestures, her stage makeup, are perfect from a distance. She sings with her father, Rigoletto. She tells her father she loves him while in the high stands the boy Katsumi Hosokawa takes his father's hand. The opera pulls up from the tapestry rugs and the half-empty glasses of pisco sours in the living room, it moves away from specific birthdays and factory plans. It rises and turns above the host country until, gently, it lands on the stage, where it becomes its whole self, something distant and beautiful. All of the orchestra supports her now, it reaches with the voices, lifts the voices up, the beautiful voice of Roxane Coss is singing her Gilda to the young Katsumi Hosokawa. Her voice vibrating the tiny bones deep inside his ear. Her voice stays inside him, becomes him. She is singing her part to him, and to a thousand other people. He is anonymous, equal, loved.

Lying on the floor at opposite ends of the room were two priests of the Holy Roman Catholic Church. Monsignor Rolland was behind the sofa the Thibaults were in front of, having thought it would be better to stay away from the windows in case a shooting were to occur. As a leader of his people he had a responsibility to protect himself. Catholic priests had often been targets in political uprisings, you only needed to look at the papers. His vestments were damp with sweat. Death was a holy mystery. Its timing was for God alone to decide. But there were vital reasons for him to live. It was thought that the Monsignor was virtually guaranteed the spot of bishop if and when the present, ancient Bishop Romero completed his tenure through death. It was Monsignor Rolland, after all, who attended the functions and brokered the deals that made a wider path for the church. Nothing in the world was absolutely certain, not even Catholicism in these poverty-stricken jungles. Just look at the encroaching tide of Mormons, with their money and their missionaries. The gall of sending missionaries into a Catholic country! As if they were savages ready for conversion. Lying with his head on a small sofa pillow that he had managed to discreetly pilfer on his way to the floor, his hips still gave him pain and he thought of how, when this was over, there would be a long, hot bath and then he would take at the very least three days in his own soft bed. Of course, there was a positive way of looking at things, assuming there was no overt madness and he was released in the first wave of hostages, the kidnapping could be just the thing to seal the Monsignor's fate. The publicity of being kidnapped could make a holy martyr even of a man who had escaped unhurt.

And this would have been exactly the case, were it not for a young priest who was lying on the cold marble floor in the front hallway. Monsignor Rolland had met Father Arguedas, had been present when he received holy orders two years ago, but of this he had no memory. This country did not suffer from a lack of young men wanting to sign up for the priesthood. With their short dark hair and stiff black shirts these priests were as indistinguishable from one another as the children in their first communion whites. The Monsignor had no idea that Father Arguedas was even in the room, never once having set eyes on him during the course of the evening. So how did a young priest come to be invited to a party at the home of the Vice President?

Father Arguedas was twenty-six years old and worked as a third-tier parish priest on the other side of the capital city, lighting candles, serving communion, and maintaining duties no higher than those of a well-established altar boy. In the few moments of his day that were not consumed by loving God through prayer and serving the flock through deeds, he went to the library at the university and listened to opera. He sat in the basement, protected by the wings of an old wooden carrel, and listened to recordings through a set of giant black headphones that were too tight and made his head ache. The university was hardly wealthy and opera was not a priority for spending, so the collection was still on heavy records instead of compact discs. Although there were some pieces he liked better than others, Father Arguedas listened without discrimination, everything from *Die Zauberflöte* to *Trouble in Tahiti*. He closed his eyes and silently mouthed along the words he did not understand. At first he cursed the ones before him, the ones who left their fingerprints on the records, or scratched them or, worse, simply took one record away, so that there was no third act for *Lulu*. Then he remembered himself as a priest and went to his knees on the cement floor of the library basement.

Too often in these moments of listening he had felt his soul fill with a kind of rapture, a feeling he could not name but was disquieted by—longing? Love? Early in his seminary training he had set his mind to giving up opera as other young men had set their minds to giving up women. He thought there must be a darkness in such passion, especially for a priest. Lacking any real or interesting sins to confess, he offered up the imagined sin of opera one Wednesday afternoon as his greatest sacrifice to Christ.

"Verdi or Wagner?" said the voice from the other side of the screen.

"Both," Father Arguedas said, but when he recovered himself from the surprise of the question he changed his answer. "Verdi."

"You are young," the voice replied. "Come back and tell me again in twenty years, if God allows that I am here."

The young priest strained to recognize the voice. Certainly he knew all the priests at the San Pedro Church. "Is it not a sin?"

"Art is not sin. It's not always good. But it is not a sin." The voice paused for a minute and Father Arguedas slipped a finger into the black band of his collar, trying to move some of the thick warm air into his shirt. "Then again, some of the libretti . . . well, try to concentrate on the music. The music is the truth of opera."

Father Arguedas took his small, perfunctory penance and said each prayer three times as an offering of joy. He did not have to give up his love. In fact, after that he changed his mind completely and decided that such beauty would have to be one with God. The music gave praise, he was sure of that, and if the words too often focused on the sins of man, well, did Jesus himself not explore this subject exactly? When he suffered from any feelings of questionable discomfort, he simply rectified the situation by not reading the libretti. He had studied Latin in seminary, but he refused to make the connection to Italian. Tchaikovsky was especially good in these cases, as Russian escaped him completely. Sadly, there were times when the lust came through the music rather than the words. Having no understanding of French did not keep a priest safe from *Carmen*. *Carmen* gave him dreams. In most instances, though, he was able to pretend that every man and woman in every opera sang with so much grace and splendor because they sang about the love for God in their hearts.

Once freed by his confessor, Father Arguedas did not try to hide his love for music. No one seemed to care about his interests one way or the other so long as it did not take away from the duties of his life. Perhaps it was not a particularly modern country or a modern religion, but it was a modern age. People in the parish had a fondness for this young priest, the tireless vigor with which he polished the pews, the way he knelt in front of the candles for an hour every morning before first mass began. Among the people who noticed his good works was a woman named Ana Loya, the favorite cousin of the wife of the Vice President. She, too, had an interest in music and was generous in loaning Father Arguedas recordings. When she heard a rumor that Roxane Coss was coming to sing at a party, Ana telephoned her cousin to ask if a certain young priest could attend. He wouldn't have to be invited to dinner, of course, he could wait in the kitchen during the dinner. He could wait in the kitchen while Roxane Coss sang, for all it mattered, but if he could be in the house, even in the garden, she would be very grateful. Father Arguedas had once confided in Ana after a particularly mediocre rehearsal of the church choir that he had never heard opera sung live. The great love of his life, after God, lived only in dark vinyl. Ana had once lost a son, more than twenty years before. The boy was three when he drowned in an irrigation ditch. There were many other children and she loved them well and did not speak of the one who was lost. In fact, the only time she ever thought of that child now was when she saw Father Arguedas. She repeated her question to her cousin by telephone: "Could Father Arguedas come to hear the soprano?"

*   *   *

It was different in ways he never could have imagined, as if the voice were something that could be seen. Certainly it could be felt, even where he stood in the very back of the room. It trembled inside the folds of his cassock, brushed against the skin of his cheeks. Never had he thought, never once, that such a woman existed, one who stood so close to God that God's own voice poured from her. How far she must have gone inside herself to call up that voice. It was as if the voice came from the center part of the earth and by the sheer effort and diligence of her will she had pulled it up through the dirt and rock and through the floorboards of the house, up into her feet, where it pulled through her, reaching, lifting, warmed by her, and then out of the white lily of her throat and straight to God in heaven. It was a miracle and he wept for the gift of bearing witness.

Even now, after more than a dozen hours spent on the floor of the marble entryway, the cold having permeated into his bone marrow, the voice of Roxane Coss was making large, swooping circles through his head. If he had not been told to lie down, he might have been forced to ask if he might be allowed to. He needed all this time to rest, and better that it was on a marble floor. The floor kept him mindful of God. Had he been stretched out on a soft rug he might have forgotten himself altogether. He was glad to have spent the night in the sea of bullhorns and sirens because it kept him awake and thinking, glad (and for this he asked forgiveness) to have missed the morning's mass and communion because then he could stay there longer. The longer he stayed where he was, the longer the moment continued, as if her voice were still echoing against these papered walls. She was still there, after all, lying someplace where he could not see her but not so terribly far away. He said a prayer that she had had a comfortable night, that someone would have thought to offer her one of the couches.

In addition to his concern for Roxane Coss, Father Arguedas was worried about the young bandits. Many of them were propped upright against the walls, their feet apart, leaning on their rifles like walking sticks. Then their heads would drop back and they would fall asleep for ten seconds before their knees buckled and they slumped into their guns. Father Arguedas had often gone with the police to collect the bodies of suicides and often they looked like they must have begun in exactly such a position, their toes pressed down on the trigger.

"Son," he whispered to one of the boys who was guarding the people in the entry hall, mostly waiters and cooks laid on the hard floor, people of the lowest ranking. Being young himself, he often felt uncomfortable calling a parishioner "son," but this child, he felt, was his own. He looked like his cousins. He looked like every boy who ran from the church as soon as they had taken communion, the host still white and round on their tongues. "Come here."

The boy squinted towards the ceiling as if he was hearing the voice in his sleep. He pretended not to notice the priest. "Son," Father Arguedas said again. "Come here."

Now the boy looked down and a puzzlement crossed his face. How did one not answer a priest? How was it possible not to go if called? "Father?" he whispered.

"Come here," the priest mouthed, and patted his hand on the floor, nothing more than a little fluttering movement of his fingers beside him. It was not crowded on the marble floor. Unlike the carpeted living room, there was plenty of space to stretch here, and when one had been leaning against a rifle all night, an open expanse of marble floor would seem as inviting as a feather bed.

The boy looked nervously around the corner to the place where the Generals were in conference. "I'm not allowed," he mouthed. He was an Indian, this boy. He spoke the language from the north that Father Arguedas's grandmother spoke to his mother and aunts.

"I say you are allowed," he said, not with authority, but with compassion.

The boy considered this for a moment and then turned his head up as if he was studying the intricate crown molding that ringed the ceiling. His eyes filled up with tears and he had to blink madly to hold them back. He had been awake for such a long time and his fingertips trembled around the cool barrel of his gun. He could no longer exactly tell where his fingers stopped and the green-blue metal began.

Father Arguedas sighed and let it go for now. He would ask the boy again later just to let him know there was a place to rest and forgiveness for any sin.

The crowd on the floor pulsed with needs. Some had to go to the bathroom again. There were murmurings about medications. People wanted to stand up, to be fed, to have a drink of water to wash the taste from their mouths. Their restlessness emboldened them, but there was this as well: nearly eighteen hours had passed and still no one was dead. The hostages had begun to believe that they might not be killed. If what a person wants is his life, he tends to be quiet about wanting anything else. Once the life begins to seem secure, one feels the freedom to complain.

Victor Fyodorov, a Muscovite, finally gave in to himself and lit up a cigarette, even though all lighters and matches were to have been surrendered. He blew his smoke straight up to the ceiling. He was forty-seven years old and had been smoking regularly since he was twelve, even in hard times, even when decisions had to be made between cigarettes and food.

The General Benjamin snapped his fingers and one of the minions rushed forward to take Fyodorov's cigarette away, but Fyodorov only inhaled. He was a big man, even lying down, even with no weapon save the cigarette itself. He looked like the one who would win the fight. "Just try," he said to the soldier in Russian.

The boy, having no idea what had been said, was unsure of how to proceed. He tried to steady his hand when he withdrew his gun and pointed it at Fyodorov's middle in a halfhearted way.

"This is it!" Yegor Ledbed, another Russian and a friend to Fyodorov, said. "You will shoot us for smoking!"

What a dream it was, that cigarette. How much more delightful it was to smoke when one had not smoked in a day. Then one could notice the flavor, the blue tint of the smoke. One could relax into the pleasant light-headedness one remembered from boyhood. It was almost enough to make a man quit, so that he could know the pleasures of starting again. Fyodorov was almost down to the point of burning his fingers. What a pity. He sat up, startling the gunman with his girth, and crushed the cigarette against the sole of his shoe.

To the great pleasure of the Vice President, Fyodorov put the butt in the pocket of his tuxedo and the boy stuffed the gun awkwardly back into the waistband of his pants and slunk away.

"I will not take this another minute!" a woman shouted, but when they looked around no one could be sure who had spoken.

Two hours after Joachim Messner had left, General Benjamin summoned the Vice President up from the floor and had him open the door and wave Messner back in.

Was it possible that Messner had spent all this time waiting just outside the door? His delicate cheeks looked even more scorched than before.

"Everything all right?" Messner said to the Vice President in Spanish, as if he had spent the last two hours standing in the sun working on his language skills.

"Very little changes," the Vice President said in English, in an attempt to be thoughtful. He still had some vestiges of feeling like the host.

"Your face, it isn't bad. She did a very good job with the"—he struggled for the word—"sew," he said finally.

The Vice President lifted his fingers to his cheek but Messner held his hand down. "Don't touch it." He looked around the room. "The Japanese man, is he still here?"

"Where would he go?" Ruben asked.

Messner glanced around at the bodies at his feet, all of them warm and taking even breaths. Really, he had seen worse.

"I'm going to call for the translator," the Vice President told the

Generals, who looked away from them as if they had not noticed that Messner had arrived. Then finally one of them glanced up and gave some sort of brief, sideways gesture with his eyebrows that Ruben Iglesias took to mean, fine, go ahead.

He did not call for Gen, but walked the long way around the room to get to him. It was both an opportunity to stretch his legs and to take inventory of his guests. Most people gave something between a wince and a smile upon seeing him. The side of his face really was swelling horribly without ice. The stitches already strained against the burden of keeping his face together. Ice. It wasn't like he was looking for penicillin. There was plenty of ice in the house. There were two freezers, one side by side with the refrigerator in the kitchen and one in the basement just for storage. There was also a machine in the kitchen that stood separately and did nothing but pour forth ice all day into a plastic cabinet. And yet he knew he was not a favorite with these Generals, and to request so much as a cube might mean the closing of his other eye. How lovely it would be just to stand with his cheek resting lightly against the cool white metal of the freezer door. He didn't even need the ice, that would be enough. "Monsignor," he said, stepping around Monsignor Rolland on the floor. "I am so sorry. Are you comfortable? Yes? Good, good."

It was a beautiful house, a beautiful rug on which his guests crowded together. Who would have thought that he would one day live in such a house with two freezers and a machine that made only ice? It had been a spectacular piece of luck. His father lifted baggage onto flatbed carts, first for the trains and then for the airlines. His mother raised eight children, sold vegetables, took in needlework. How many times had that story been told? Ruben Iglesias working his way up. The first in his family to finish high school! Worked as a janitor to put himself through college. Worked as a janitor and a judge's clerk to put himself through law school. After that there was a successful career in the law, the correct steps on the unstable ladder of politics. It made him as attractive a running mate as his height. Never in the story did they mention how he had married well, the daughter of a senior partner he had made pregnant during a festive Christmas party, how the ambitions of his wife and her parents pushed him forward. That was a decidedly less interesting story.

A man on the floor near the tapestry wing-backed chair asked him a question in a language Ruben believed was German. The Vice President told him he did not know.

Gen the translator was lying very close to Mr. Hosokawa. He whispered something in Mr. Hosokawa's ear and the older man closed his eyes and nodded his head almost imperceptibly. Ruben had forgotten all about Mr. Hosokawa. Happy birthday, sir, he thought to himself. I don't suppose there will be any factories built this year. Not too far from them was Roxane Coss and her accompanist. She looked, if this was possible, even better than she had the night before. Her hair was loose and her skin glowed as if she had been waiting for this opportunity to rest. "How are you?" she mouthed in English, and touched her hand to her own cheek to indicate her concern for his injury. Perhaps it was the fact that he had had nothing to eat, maybe it was exhaustion or blood loss or the onset of an infection, but at that moment he was quite sure he would faint. The way she touched her face, did it because she could not stand and put her hand to his own cheek, the image of her standing and touching his cheek, he sank down to the floor, balancing on his toes, putting his hands down in front of him, and dropped his head forward until the feeling passed. Slowly he raised his eyes to hers, which now looked panicked. "I'm well," he whispered. At that moment he noticed her accompanist, who frankly did not look well at all. It seemed that if Roxane Coss was able to extend such compassion to him she should take a look at the man lying next to her. His paleness had a decidedly gray cast, and while his eyes were open and his chest moved in a shallow way, there was a stillness about him that the vice president thought was not good at all. "Him?" he said softly, and pointed.

She looked at the body beside her as if she was noticing it for the first time. "He says he has the flu. I think he's very nervous."

Speaking in the very smallest of whispers, the sound of her voice was thrilling, even if he wasn't exactly sure what she was saying.

"Translator!" General Alfredo called out.

Ruben had meant to stand and extend his hand to Gen, but Gen, younger, made it to his feet more quickly and reached down to help the Vice President. He took Ruben's arm, as if the Vice President had been struck suddenly blind, and led him forward through the room. How quickly one could form attachments under circumstances like these, what bold conclusions a man could come to: Roxane Coss was the woman he had always loved; Gen Watanabe was his son; his house was no longer his own; his life as he knew it, his political life, was dead. Ruben Iglesias wondered if all hostages, all over the world, felt more or less the same way.

"Gen," Messner said, and shook his hand somberly, as if offering condolences. "The Vice President should have medicine." He said this in French for Gen to translate.

"Too much time is spent discussing the needs of a foolish man," General Benjamin said.

"Ice?" Ruben offered himself, as suddenly his mind was filled with the pleasures of ice, of the snow on the tops of the Andes, of those sweet Olympic skaters on television, young girls wearing handkerchiefs of diaphanous gauze around their doll-like waists. He was burning alive now and the silver blades of their skates shot up arches of blue-white chips. He wanted to be buried in ice.

"Ishmael," the General said impatiently to one of the boys. "Into the kitchen. Get him a towel and ice."

Ishmael, one of the young boys holding up the wall, a small one with the worst shoes of all, looked pleased. Maybe he was proud of having been chosen for the task, maybe he wanted to help the Vice President, maybe he wanted a shot at the kitchen, where surely trays of leftover crackers and melted canapés were waiting. "No one gives my people ice when they need ice," General Alfredo said bitterly.

"Certainly," Messner said, half listening to Gen's translation. "Have you reached some kind of compromise here?"

"We'll let you have the women," General Alfredo said. "We have no interest in harming women. The workers can go, the priests, anyone who is sick. After that we'll review the list of who we have. There may be a few more to go after that. In return we'll want supplies." He produced a piece of paper, neatly folded, from his front pocket and clamped it between the three remaining fingers of his left hand. "These are the things we'll need. The second page is to be read to the press. Our demands." Alfredo had been so certain their plan would turn out better than this. It had been his cousin, after all, who had once worked on the air-conditioning system of this house and had managed to steal a copy of the blueprints.

Messner took the papers and scanned them for a minute and then asked Gen to read them. Gen was surprised to find his hands trembling. He could never remember an instance when what he was translating had actually affected him. "On behalf of the people, La Familia de Martin Suarez has taken hostage—"

Messner raised his hand for Gen to stop. "La Familia de Martin Suarez?"

The General nodded.

"Not La Dirección Auténtica?" Messner kept his voice down.

"You said we were *reasonable* men," General Alfredo said, his voice swelling with the insult. "What do you think? Do you think La Dirección Auténtica would be talking to you? Do you think we would be letting the women go? I know LDA. In LDA, the ones who are not useful are shot. Who have we shot? We are trying to do something for the people, can you understand that?" He took a step towards Messner, who knew how it was intended, but Gen moved quietly between them.

"We are trying to do something for the people," Gen said, keeping his tone deliberate and slow. The second part of the sentence, "Can you understand that?" was irrelevant and so he left it off.

Messner apologized for his mistake. An honest mistake. They were not LDA. He had to concentrate to keep the corners of his mouth from bending up. "How long before the first group can be released?"

General Alfredo could not speak to him. He ground down on his teeth. Even General Hector, who had the least to say, spat on the Savonnière carpet. Ishmael returned with two dishtowels full of ice cubes, a sign of the great abundance the kitchen held. General Benjamin batted one of the sacks from his hand, sending the clear diamond ice tripping and bouncing across the carpet. Anyone close enough scooped up the extra cubes and slipped them into their mouths. Ishmael, frightened now, quickly gave the remaining bag to the Vice President with a slight bow of the head. Ruben returned the nod, thinking it best not to draw any more attention to himself than was absolutely necessary, as clearly it would take little to provoke another gun butt to the side of the head. He touched the ice to his face and winced with the pain and the deep, deep pleasure of the cold.

General Benjamin cleared his throat and pulled himself together. "We'll divide them up now," he said. First he spoke to his troops. "Look alert. On your guard." The boys against the wall straightened out their legs and lifted their guns to their chests. "Everyone on your feet," he said.

"I beg for your attention," Gen said in Japanese. "It is now time to stand." If the terrorists minded speaking, they made an exception for Gen. He repeated the sentence again in as many languages as he could think of. He said it in languages he knew he need not include, Serbo-Croatian and Cantonese, just because there was comfort in speaking and no one tried to stop him. "Stand up," is not a message that needed translation in the first place. People are sheep about certain things. When some begin to stand, the rest will follow.

They were stiff and awkward. Some people tried to work their way back into their shoes and others just forgot them. Some people stomped lightly on one foot, trying to wrestle it from sleep. They were nervous. As much as they had been thinking that all they wanted was to stand, now that they were on their feet they felt insecure. It seemed so much more likely that transitions would be bad rather than good, that standing increased the likelihood of being shot.

"The women will stand to the far right of the room and the men to the far left."

Gen churned the sentence through the different languages with no clear idea of which countries were represented or who was in need of a translator. His voice was full of the soothing monotony of the overhead announcements heard in train stations and airports.

But the men and women did not part quickly. Instead they clung to one another, arms around necks. Couples who had not held each other this way for years, who had perhaps never held each other this way in public, embraced deeply. It was a party that had simply gone on too long. The music had stopped and the dancing had stopped and still the couples stood, each enveloped in the other, waiting. The only awkward pairing was between Roxane Coss and the accompanist. She looked so small in his arms she seemed almost a child. She didn't appear to want to be held by him, but on closer inspection she was actually shoring him up. He draped himself on her, and the grimace on her face was that of a woman unequal to the weight that had been given her. Mr. Hosokawa, recognizing her distress (because he had been watching, having no one to embrace himself, his own wife safely home in Tokyo), took the accompanist in his arms, wrapping the much larger man across his shoulders like a coat in warmer weather. Mr. Hosokawa staggered a bit himself, but it was nothing compared with the relief that flooded her face.

"Thank you," she said.

"Thank you," he repeated.

"You'll look after him?" At this point the accompanist raised his head and took some of his weight onto his own feet.

"Thank you," Mr. Hosokawa repeated tenderly.

Other men, single men, mostly waiters, all of whom wished that they had been the one to peel this dying gringo from her shoulders, moved forward to help Mr. Hosokawa, and together they shuffled to the left side of the room with the sour-smelling man, his blond head swinging as if his neck had been snapped. Mr. Hosokawa turned to look at her, so heartsick to think she would be alone. He might have thought that she was watching him, but really she was looking at her accompanist, who was slumped in Mr. Hosokawa's arms. Once he was away from her it was much easier to see how ill he looked.

Now, in the face of so many passionate good-byes, it struck Mr. Hosokawa that he had never even considered bringing his wife to this country. He did not tell her that she had been invited. He told her he was attending a business meeting, not a birthday party to be held in his honor. Their unspoken agreement was that Mrs. Hosokawa always stayed home with their daughters. They did not travel together. Now he could see how smart this decision was. He had kept his wife from discomfort and possibly harm. He had protected her. But still, he couldn't help but wonder what it would have been like for the two of them to stand together now. Would they have felt so much sadness when they were told to step away from one another?

For what seemed like a long time but could not have been a whole minute, Edith and Simon Thibault said nothing to each other. Then she kissed him and he said, "I like to think of you outside." He could have said anything, it made no difference. He was thinking of those first twenty years they were married, years when he had loved her without any kind of real understanding. This would be his punishment now, for all his time wasted. Dear Edith. She took off the light silk wrapper she was wearing. He had forgotten to ask for it. It was a wonderful blue, the blue used on the dinner plates of kings and the underbreasts of the birds in this very godforsaken jungle. She crumpled it up into a surprisingly small ball and pressed it into the waiting cup of his hands.

"Don't do anything stupid," she said, and because it was the last thing she asked of him, he swore he would not.

For the most part the separation of hostages was civil. No two had to be pried apart with a gun. When they knew their time was really up the men and the women separated, as if a complicated dancing reel were about to begin and soon they would join and split and change, passing their partners off only to receive them back into their arms again.

Messner took a stack of business cards out of his wallet and handed one to each of the Generals and one to Gen and one, thoughtfully, to the Vice President, and then left the rest in a dish on the coffee table. "This has my cell phone number," he said. "That's just me. You want to talk to me, you call this number. They're keeping the phone lines open to the house for now."

Each of them looked at the cards feeling puzzled. It was as if he was asking them to lunch, as if he didn't understand the gravity of the situation.

"You may need something," Messner said. "You may want to talk to someone out there."

Gen made a slight bow. He should have bowed to the waist for Messner, to show him respect for coming into this place, for risking his life for theirs, but he knew that no one would understand. Then Mr. Hosokawa came up and took a card from the dish, shook Messner's hand, and bowed deeply, his face turned down to the floor.

After that the Generals Benjamin, Alfredo, and Hector went to the men and from that pack cut out the workers, the waiters and cooks and cleaning staff, and placed them with the women. It was their ultimate intention to free the workers through revolution and they would not keep them hostage. Then they asked if anyone was very ill and had Gen repeat the question several times. Where one would think that every member would claim a faint heart, the crowd was remarkably quiet. A handful of very old men shuffled forward, a handsome Italian man showed a medical identification bracelet and was reunited to the arms of his wife. Only one man lied and his lie was not discovered: Dr. Gomez explained that his kidneys had failed years before and he was late for dialysis already. His wife turned away from him, ashamed. The sickest among them, the accompanist, appeared too confused to make the request for himself and so was placed into a chair at the side where they would be certain not to forget him. The priests were given leave as well. Monsignor Rolland made the sign of the cross over those who remained, a lovely gesture, and then walked away, but Father Arguedas, who really had no pressing duties to attend to, requested permission to stay.

"Stay?" General Alfredo said.

"You'll need a priest," he said.

Alfredo smiled slightly, and this was a first. "Really, you'll want to go."

"If the people are here through Sunday, you'll need someone to say mass."

"We will pray on our own."

"Respectfully, sir," said the priest, his eyes cast down. "I will stay."

And with that the matter was closed. Monsignor Rolland could do nothing but helplessly watch the whole thing. He was already standing with the women and the shame of it filled him with murderous rage. He could have choked the young priest to death with one hand, but it was too late. He had already been saved.

The Vice President should have been given medical leave but didn't even bother asking. Instead, sick with fever and holding a melted ice pack to his face, he was told to go out the door and down to the heavy gate in the wall to announce the release to the press. He barely had a second with his own wife, a decent woman who made the work of her life the well-being of his career and never said a word as she watched him throw her work away. He didn't have a minute with his two daughters, Imelda and Rosa, who had been so good, lying all day on their sides playing some complicated finger game with each other that he could not recognize. He said nothing to Esmeralda because there were no words to thank her. He was worried about her. If he was killed, would they keep her on? He hoped so. She had such a lovely straight back and was patient with the children. She had taught them to paint pictures of animals on small rocks and from those rocks elaborate worlds were made. There were plenty of them upstairs. Sooner or later he would be able to get away and go and find them. His wife clutched at their son until he cried out from the pressure of her hands. She was afraid they would try and take him to the side with the men, but Ruben stroked her fingers and reassured her. "No one will count him," he said. He kissed Marco on the head, kissed his silky, deeply boyish-smelling hair. Then he went to the door.

He was a better man for the job than President Masuda. The President couldn't say anything unless it was written down. He was not a stupid man, but he lacked spontaneity. Besides, he had a temper and false pride and would not stand being ordered from the floor to the door and back again. He would say something unscripted and get himself shot, which would eventually lead to everyone getting shot. For the first time he thought it was better that Masuda had stayed home to watch his soap opera because Ruben could be the servant, the straight man, and in doing so he could save the lives of his wife and his children and their pretty governess and the famous Roxane Coss. The particular job he had been given this time was in fact more suited to the talents of a Vice President. Messner came out and joined him on the front steps. The day had clouded over but the air was marvelous. The people at the end of the walkway lowered their guns and out came the women, their dresses shimmering in the late afternoon light. Were it not for all the police and photographers, a person walking by might have thought it was a party where every couple had fought and the women all took it upon themselves to leave early and alone. They were crying, and their hair fell into tangled knots. Their makeup was ruined and their skirts were held up in their fists. Most of them carried their shoes or had left their shoes behind and their stockings were torn on the flat shale stones of the front walk, though none of them noticed. There should have been a sinking ship behind them, a burning building. The farther they got from the house the harder they cried. The few men, the servants, the infirm, came out behind them, looking helpless in the face of so much sadness for which they were not responsible.

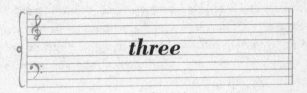

three

a clarification: all of the women were released except one.

She was somewhere in the middle of the line. Like the other women, she was looking back into the living room rather than out the open door, looking back to the floor on which she'd slept like it hadn't been a night but several years. She was looking back at the men who wouldn't be coming outside, none of whom she actually knew. Except the Japanese gentleman whose party this had been, and she certainly didn't *know* him, but he had been helpful with her accompanist, and for that she searched him out and smiled at him. The men shifted from foot to foot in their pack, all of them sad-eyed and nervous from the far side of the room. Mr. Hosokawa returned her smile, a small, dignified acknowledgment, and bowed his head. With the exception of Mr. Hosokawa, the men were not thinking about Roxane Coss then. They had forgotten her and the dizzying heights of her arias. They were watching their wives file out into the bright afternoon, knowing it was a probability that they would never see them again. The love they felt rose up into their throats and blocked the air. There went Edith Thibault, the Vice President's wife, the beautiful Esmeralda.

Roxane Coss was very nearly at the door, perhaps half a dozen women away, when General Hector stepped forward and took her arm. It was not a particularly aggressive gesture. He might have only been trying to escort her someplace, perhaps he had wanted her at the front of the line. *"Espera,"* he said, and pointed over to the wall, where she should stand alone near a large Matisse painting of pears and peaches in a bowl. It was one of only two works by Matisse in the entire country and it had been borrowed from the art museum for the party. Roxane, confused, looked at that moment to the translator.

"Wait," Gen said softly in English, trying to make the one word sound as benign as possible. *Wait,* after all, did not mean that she would never go, only that her leaving would be delayed.

She took the word in, thought about it for a moment. She still doubted that's what he had meant even when she heard it in English. As a child she had waited. She had waited at school in line for auditions. But the truth was that in the last several years no one had asked her to wait at all. People waited for her. She did not wait. And all of this, the birthday party, the ridiculous country, the guns, the danger, the *waiting* involved in all of it was a mockery. She pulled her arm back sharply and the jolt caused the General's glasses to slip from his nose. "Look," she said to General Hector, no longer willing to tolerate his hand on her skin. "Enough is enough." Gen opened his mouth to translate and then thought better of it. Besides, she was still speaking. "I came here to do a job, to sing for a party, and I did that. I was told to sleep on the floor with all of these people you have some reason to keep, and I did that, too. But now it's over." She pointed towards the chair where her accompanist sat hunched over. "He's sick. I have to be with him," she said, though it came off as the least convincing of her arguments. Slumped forward in his chair, his arms hanging from his sides like flags on an especially windless day, the accompanist looked more dead than sick. He did not raise his head when she spoke. The line had stopped moving, even the women who were free to go now stopped to watch her, regardless of whether or not they had any idea of what she was saying. It was in this moment of uncertainty, the inevitable pause that comes before the translation, that Roxane Coss saw the moment of her exit. She made a clean move towards the front door, which was open, waiting. General Hector reached up to catch her and, missing her arm, took her firmly by the hair. Such hair made a woman an easy target. It was like being attached to several long soft ropes.

Three things happened in close succession: first, Roxane Coss, lyric soprano, made a clear, high-pitched sound that came from what appeared to be some combination of surprise and actual pain as the tug caused her neck to snap backwards; second, every guest invited to the party (with the exception of her accompanist) stepped forward, making it clear that this was the moment for insurrection; third, every terrorist, ranging from the ages of fourteen to forty-one, cocked the weapon he had been holding and the great metallic click stilled them all like a film spliced into one single frame. And there the room waited, time suspended, until Roxane Coss, without so much as smoothing her dress or touching her hair, turned to go and stand beside a painting that was, in all honesty, a minor work.

After that the Generals began arguing quietly among themselves and even the foot soldiers, the little bandits, were leaning in, trying to hear. Their voices blurred together. The word *woman* was heard and then the words *never* and *agreement*. And then one of them said in a voice that was low and confused, "She could sing." With their heads together there was no telling who said it. It may well have been all of them, all of us.

There were worse reasons to keep a person hostage. You keep someone always for what he or she is worth to you, for what you can trade her for, money or freedom or somebody else you want more. Any person can be a kind of trading chip when you find a way to hold her. So to hold someone for song, because the thing longed for was the sound of her voice, wasn't it all the same? The terrorists, having no chance to get what they came for, decided to take something else instead, something that they never in their lives knew that they wanted until they crouched in the low, dark shaft of the air-conditioning vents: opera. They decided to take that very thing for which Mr. Hosokawa lived.

Roxane waited alone against the wall near the bright, tumbling fruit and cried from frustration. The Generals began to raise their voices while the rest of the women and then the servants filed out. The men glowered and the young terrorists kept their weapons raised. The accompanist, who had momentarily fallen asleep in his chair, roused himself enough to stand and walked out of the room with the help of the kitchen staff, never having realized that his companion was now behind him.

"This is better," General Benjamin said, walking a wide circle on the floor that had previously been covered in hostages. "Now a man can breathe."

From inside they could hear the extraneous hostages being met with great applause and celebration. The bright pop of camera flashes raised up over the other side of the garden wall. In the midst of the confusion, the accompanist walked right back in the front door, which no one had bothered to lock. He threw it open with such force that it slammed back against the wall, the doorknob leaving a mark in the wood. They would have shot him but they knew him. "Roxane Coss is not outside," he said in Swedish. His voice was thick, his consonants catching between his teeth. "She is not outside!"

So slurred was the accompanist's speech that it took even Gen a minute to recognize the language. The Swedish he knew was mostly from Bergman films. He had learned it as a college student, matching the subtitles to the sounds. In Swedish, he could only converse on the darkest of subjects. "She's here," Gen said.

The accompanist's health seemed temporarily revived by his fury and for a moment the blood rushed back into his gray cheeks. "All women are released!" He shook his hands in the air as if he were trying to rush crows from a cornfield, his quickly blueing lips were bright with the foam of his spit. Gen relayed the information in Spanish.

"Christopf, here," Roxane said, and gave a small wave as if they had only been briefly separated at a party.

"Take me instead," the accompanist howled, his knees swaying dangerously towards another buckle. It was a delightfully old-fashioned offer, though every person in the room knew that no one wanted him and everyone wanted her.

"Put him outside," General Alfredo said.

Two of the boys stepped forward, but the accompanist, who no one thought was capable of escape in his state of rapid and mysterious deterioration, darted past them and sat down hard on the floor beside Roxane Coss. One of the boys pointed his gun towards the center of his big blond head.

"Don't shoot her accidentally," General Alfredo said.

"What is he saying!" Roxane Coss wailed.

Reluctantly, Gen told her.

Accidentally. That was how people got shot at these things. No real malice, just a bullet a few inches out of place. Roxane Coss cursed every last person in the room as she held her breath. To die because an underskilled terrorist had poor aim was hardly how she had meant to go. The accompanist's breathing was insanely rapid and thin. He closed his eyes and put his head against her leg. His final burst of passion had been enough for him. Just that quickly he was asleep.

"For the sake of God," said General Benjamin, making one of the largest mistakes in a takeover that had been nothing but a series of mistakes, "just leave him there."

As soon as the words were spoken, the accompanist fell forward and vomited up a mouthful of pale yellow foam. Roxane was trying to straighten his legs out again, this time with no one to help her. "At least drag him back outside," she said viciously. "Can't you see there's something wrong with him?" Anyone could see there was something terribly, terribly wrong with him. His skin was wet and cold, the color of the inner flesh of fish gone bad.

Gen put in the request but it was ignored. "No President, one opera singer," General Benjamin said. "It's a rotten exchange if you ask me."

"She's worth more with the piano player," General Alfredo said.

"You couldn't get a dollar for him."

"We keep her," General Hector said quietly, and the subject of opera singers was closed. Though Hector was the least likely to speak, all of the soldiers were most afraid of him. Even the other two Generals exercised caution.

All of the hostages, even Gen, were on the other side of the room from where Roxane and her accompanist were pressed against the wall. Father Arguedas said a prayer quietly and then went to help her. When General Benjamin told him to return to his side of the room he smiled and nodded as if the General was making a little joke and in that sense was not committing a sin. The priest was amazed by the rushing of his heart, by the fear that swept through his legs and made them weak. It was not a fear of being shot, of course, he did not believe they would shoot him, and if they did, well, that would be that. The fear came from the smell of the little bell-shaped lilies and the warm yellow light of her hair. Not since he was fourteen, the year he gave his heart to Christ and put all of those worries behind him, had such things moved him. And why did he feel, in the midst of all this fear and confusion, in the mortal danger of so many lives, the wild giddiness of good luck? What unimaginable good luck! That he had been befriended by Ana Loya, cousin of the Vice President's wife, that she had made such an extravagant request on his behalf, that the request had been graciously granted so that he was allowed to stand in the very back of the room to hear, for the first time in his life, the living opera, and not just sung but sung by Roxane Coss, who was by anyone's account the greatest soprano of our time. That she would have come to such a country to begin with would have been enough. The honor he would have felt lying on his single cot in the basement of the rectory just knowing that she was for one night in the same city in which he lived would have been a miraculous gift. But that he had been allowed to see her and then, by fate (which may well portend awful things, but was still, as was all fate, *God's will*, His wish) he was here now, coming forward to help her with the cumbersome arrangement of her accompanist's gangly limbs, coming close enough to smell the lilies and see her smooth white skin disappearing into the neck of her pistachio-colored gown. He could see that a few of her hairpins remained in place on the crown of her head so that her hair did not fall in her eyes. What a gift, he could not think of it otherwise. Because he believed that such a voice must come from God, then it was God's love he was standing next to now. And the trembling in his chest, his shaking hands, that was only fitting. How could his heart not be filled with love to be so close to God?

She smiled at him, a smile that was kind but utterly in keeping with the circumstances at hand. "Do you know why they're detaining me?" she whispered.

At the sound of her voice he felt his first wave of disappointment. Not in her, never, but in himself. English. Everyone said it would be important to learn English. What was it the tourists said? "Have a nice way?" But what if that was an inappropriate response? What if it was in some way hurtful? It could be asking for something, camera film or directions or *money*. He prayed. Finally, sadly, he said the only word he was sure of, "English."

"Ah," she said, nodding in sympathy and turning her attention back to her work.

When they had settled the accompanist so that he at least appeared comfortable, Father Arguedas took his own handkerchief and wiped the pale sheen of vomit away. He would in no way pretend to have any real medical knowledge, but certainly he spent a great deal of time visiting the sick and the sacrament he had most often performed was viaticum, and given those two experiences he had to say that this man who had played the piano so beautifully looked closer to viaticum than he did to the anointing of the sick. "Catholic?" he asked Roxane Coss, touching the accompanist's chest.

She had no idea whether or not the man who played the piano for her had a relationship with God, much less what church that relationship might be conducted through. She shrugged. At least she could communicate with the priest this much.

"*Católica?*" he said, strictly for his own curiosity, and pointed, politely, to her.

"Me?" she said, touching the front of her dress. "Yes." Then she nodded. *"Sí, Católica."* Two simple words but she was proud of herself for answering in Spanish.

He smiled at that. As for the accompanist, if he was dying, if he was Catholic, those were two fairly big ifs. But where the matter of the soul's everlasting rest was concerned, it was better to err on the side of caution. If he mistakenly gave last rites to a Jew who then recovered, what harm had he done but taken up a little bit of his time, the time of an unconscious political hostage at that. He patted Roxane's hand. It was like a child's hand! So pale and soft, rounded on the top. On one finger she wore a dark green stone the size of a quail's egg that was surrounded in a fiery ring of diamonds. Normally, when he saw women wearing rings like that he wished they would make them contributions to the poor, but today found himself imagining the pleasure of gently sliding such a ring onto her finger. This thought, he was sure, was inappropriate, and he felt a nervous dampness creep across his forehead. And he without a handkerchief. He excused himself to go and speak to the Generals.

"That man there," Father Arguedas said, lowering his voice, "I believe he is dying."

"He isn't dying," General Alfredo said. "He's trying to get her out. He is pretending to die."

"I don't believe so. The pulse, the color of the skin." He looked back over his shoulder, past the grand piano and huge bouquets of lilies and roses arranged for a party long since over, to the spot where the accompanist lay on the edge of carpet like something large and spilled. "Some things one can't pretend."

"He chose to stay. We put him out the door and he came back. Those are not the actions of a dying man." General Alfredo turned his head away. He rubbed his hand. Ten years those fingers had been gone and still they ached.

"Go back to where you were told to wait," General Benjamin said to the priest. He was enjoying a breath of false relief seeing half of the people gone, as if half of his problems were solved. He knew it to be false but he wanted some quiet time in which to enjoy it. The room looked wide open.

"I would like some oil from the kitchen to perform last rites."

"No kitchen," General Benjamin said, wagging his head. He lit a cigarette in order to be rude to the young priest. He wanted the priest and the accompanist to have left when they were told to leave. People shouldn't be allowed to decide that they wished to remain a hostage. He had very little experience being rude to priests and he needed the cigarette as a prop. He shook out the match and dropped it on the carpet. He wanted to blow the smoke forward but could not.

"I can do it without the oil," Father Arguedas said.

"No last rites," General Alfredo said. "He isn't dying."

"I was only asking for the oil," the priest said respectfully. "I wasn't asking about the last rites."

Each of the Generals meant to stop him, to slap him, to have one of the soldiers march him back in line with a gun in his back, but none felt able to do so. That was either the power of the Church or the power of the opera singer leaning over the man they took to be her lover. Father Arguedas returned to Roxane Coss and her accompanist. She had unbuttoned the top of his shirt and was listening to his chest. Her hair spilled over his neck and shoulders in a way that would have thrilled the accompanist immeasurably if he had been conscious, but she could not wake him. Nor could the priest. Father Arguedas knelt beside him and began the prayer of last rites. Perhaps it was grander when one had the vestments and robes, when there was oil to work with, the beauty of candles, but a simple prayer felt in some ways closer to God. He hoped the accompanist was a Catholic. He hoped that his soul would speed towards the open arms of Christ.

"God the father of mercies, through the death and resurrection of His Son has reconciled the world to Himself and sent the Holy Spirit among us for the forgiveness of sins; through the ministry of the Church may God give you pardon and peace." Father Arguedas felt a rush of tenderness for this man, an almost choking bond of love. He had played for her. He had heard her voice day after day and been shaped by it. With great sincerity he whispered, "I absolve you from your sins," into the chalk-white ear. And truly, he did forgive the accompanist for everything he might have done, "in the name of the Father, and the Son, and of the Holy Spirit."

"Last rites?" Roxane Coss said, taking the cold, damp hand that had worked so tirelessly on her behalf. She didn't know the language, but the rituals of Catholicism were recognizable anywhere. This could not be a good sign.

"Through the holy mysteries of our redemption, may almighty God release you from all punishments in this life and in the life to come. May He open to you the gates of paradise and welcome you to everlasting joy."

Roxane Coss looked dazed, as if the hypnotist had swung his watch but had not yet snapped his fingers. "He was a very good pianist," she said. She wanted to join in, but frankly, no longer remembered the prayers. She added, "He was punctual."

"Let us ask the Lord to come to our brother with His merciful love, and grant him relief through this holy anointing." Father Arguedas touched his thumb to his tongue because he needed something wet and could think of nothing else. He marked the accompanist's forehead, saying, "Through this holy anointing may the Lord in His love and mercy help you with the grace of the Holy Spirit."

Roxane could see the nuns standing over her as she memorized her prayers. She could see the dark rosewood rosaries hanging from their waists, she could smell the coffee on their breath and a faint odor of perspiration in the fabric of their dresses, Sister Joan and Sister Mary Joseph and Sister Serena. She could remember each of them but not a single word of prayer. "Sometimes we ordered sandwiches and coffee after rehearsal," she said, though the priest could not understand her and the accompanist no longer heard her voice. "We talked some then." He had told her about his childhood. He was from Sweden, or Norway? He talked about how cold it was in the winters but how he never really noticed, growing up there. His mother wouldn't let him play any sort of ball games because she was so worried about his hands. Not after all the money she had spent on piano lessons.

Father Arguedas anointed the accompanist's hands, saying, "May the Lord who frees you from sin save you and raise you up."

Roxane picked up some of his fine blond hair and held it over her fingers. It looked anemic. It looked like it belonged to a person who wasn't long for this world. The truth was, she had hated the accompanist a little. For months they had worked together amicably. He knew his music. He played with passion but never tried to overshadow her. He was quiet and reserved and she liked that about him. She did not try to draw him out. She never thought about him enough to wonder if she should. Then it was decided that he would come with her on this trip. No sooner had the wheels of the plane lifted up from the tarmac than the accompanist grabbed her hand and told her about the impossible burden of love he had been living with. Didn't she know? All those days of being next to her, of hearing her sing. He leaned into her seat and tried to press his ear against her chest but she pushed him away. It was like that every minute of the eighteen-hour flight. It was like that in the limousine to the hotel. He pleaded and wept like a child. He cataloged every outfit she had worn to every rehearsal. Outside the car window an impenetrable wall of leaves and vines sped past. Where was she going? He crept one finger over to touch her skirt and she knocked it away with the back of her hand.

Roxane bowed her head and closed her eyes, pressed her hands together with the strands of his hair caught in between. "A prayer can just be something nice," Sister Joan had said. Sister Joan was her favorite, young and nearly pretty. She kept chocolate in her desk. "It isn't always the things you want. It can be the things you appreciate." Sister Joan would often ask Roxane to sing for the children before assembly, "Oh Mary We Crown Thee with Flowers Today," even in the dead of a Chicago winter.

"He always wanted to hear about Chicago, I grew up in Chicago," she whispered. "He wanted to know what it was like to grow up near an opera house. He said, now that he was in Italy he could never leave. He said he couldn't bear those cold northern winters now."

Father Arguedas looked up at her, desperate to know what she was saying. Was it confession, prayer?

"Maybe it was something he ate," she said. "There could be a food he was allergic to. Maybe he was sick before we got here." Certainly, he was not the man she had known.

They were all three quiet for a while, the accompanist with his eyes closed, the opera singer and the priest both staring down at those closed eyes. Then something occurred to Roxane Coss and without hesitation she reached into his pockets and pulled out his wallet and handkerchief and a roll of mints. She flipped through the wallet and put it down. His passport was there: Sweden. She slipped her hands deep into his pants pockets, at which point Father Arguedas stopped his prayers to watch her. There she found a hypodermic needle, used and capped, and a small glass vile with a rubber top, empty but for a drop or two circling the bottom. Insulin. All out of insulin. They would be back at the hotel by midnight, they had been promised. There was no reason to bring more than one shot along. She scrambled to her feet, the necessary proof in her upturned palms. Father Arguedas raised his head as she rushed to the Generals. "Diabetic!" she cried, a word that had to be more or less the same in any language. Those medical terms came off Latin roots, the single tree they should all understand. She turned her head towards the men's wall, where they were all watching, like this was any other night at the opera and tonight's performance was the tragic death of the accompanist, *Il Pianoforte Triste.*

"Diabetic," she said to Gen.

Gen, who had wanted to give the priest his chance, came forward now and explained what the Generals must, without benefit of translation, have understood: the man was in a diabetic coma, which meant that somewhere out there was the medicine needed to save him if he was still alive. They went over to see, General Benjamin dropping his cigarette into the marble fireplace which was big enough to hold three good-sized children. In fact, the Vice President's own three children had crowded in there together after it had been emptied of ashes and scrubbed down, and pretended to be cooked by witches. Father Arguedas had finished the formal prayer and now simply knelt beside the accompanist, his hands wrapped together, his head bowed, praying silently that the man would find solace and joy in God's eternal love now that he was dead.

When the priest opened his eyes he saw that he and the accompanist were no longer alone. Father Arguedas smiled gently at the assembled crowd. "Who can separate us from the love of Christ?" he said by way of explanation.

When Roxane Coss sank to the floor it was a lovely sight, the pale green chiffon of her dress billowing out like a canopy of new spring leaves caught in a sweep of April wind. She took in her hands the hand that his mother had been so careful with, the hand she had watched play Schumann lieder hour after hour without tiring. The hand was cold already, and the colors of his face, which hadn't seemed right for hours, were quickly becoming very wrong, yellow around the eyes, a pale lavender creeping up near his lips. His tie was gone, as were the studs from his shirtfront, but he still wore his black tails and white waistcoat. He was still dressed for performance. Never for a minute had she thought he was a bad man. And he had been a brilliant pianist. It was just that he shouldn't have waited until they were sealed up in that plane to tell her how he felt about her, and now that he was dead she wouldn't even hold that against him.

All the men had left their wall and come to the other side of the room, where they stood, more or less shoulder to shoulder with the band of terrorists. Every one of them had resented the accompanist, thought he was too lucky for being able to play the piano so well, thought he was too forward, the way he had shielded her from the rest of them. But when he was dead they felt the loss of him. He had died for her after all. Even from across the room in languages they may not have understood, they could follow the story clearly. He had never told her he was a diabetic. He had chosen to stay with her rather than ask for the insulin that could save his life. The poor accompanist, their friend. He was one of them.

"Now a man is dead!" General Benjamin said, throwing up his hands. His own illness flared at the thought of it and the pain was like hot needles sewing together the nerve endings of his face.

"It isn't as if men haven't died," General Alfredo answered coolly. He had nearly died himself more times than he could remember: a bullet in his stomach, that nearly killed him! Two fingers shot off not six months after that, then last year a bullet passing cleanly through the side of his neck.

"We are not here to kill these people. We are here to take the President and to go."

"No President," Alfredo reminded him.

General Hector, trusting no one, reached down and pressed his own thin fingers against the dead man's jugular. "Perhaps we should shoot him, put his body outside. Let them know who they're dealing with."

Father Arguedas, who had been keeping to his prayers, looked up and stared at the Generals pointedly. The idea of shooting their new-dead friend made the Spanish-speaking hostages recoil. Those who had not previously known that Roxane Coss did not speak the language were now sure of it because she remained in the same position, her head in her hands, her skirt circled out around her, while the Generals spoke of desecration.

A German named Lothar Falken, who knew just enough Spanish to get the vaguest idea of what was going on, sidled up to Gen in the crowd and asked him to translate.

"Tell them it won't work," he said. "The wound won't bleed. You could shoot him straight through the head now and they'd still figure out soon enough that he didn't die of a gunshot wound." Lothar was the vice president of Hoechst, a pharmaceutical company, and had been a biology major at university many years before. He was feeling especially bad about the death, as insulin represented the vast majority of the company's sales. They were, in fact, Germany's leading manufacturer of the drug. They had it everywhere back at the office, free samples of every variety of insulin just waiting to be given away, refrigerators full of endless, clinking glass vials there for the taking. He had come to the party because he felt if Nansei was considering an electronics plant in the host country, he might consider manufacturing there as well. Now he was staring at a man who died wanting insulin. He couldn't save the man's life, but at least he could spare him the indignity of being killed again.

Gen related the information, trying to choose words that would make the whole thing sound more gruesome rather than less, as he, too, did not want to see the poor accompanist shot.

General Hector took out his gun and stared thoughtfully down the sight. "That's ridiculous," he said.

Roxane Coss looked up then. "Who's he going to shoot?" she asked Gen.

"No one," Gen assured her.

She wiped her fingers in a straight line beneath her eyes. "Well, he isn't going to clean his gun. Are they going to start killing us now?" Her voice was tired, practical, as if to say she had a schedule and she needed to know where things stood.

"You might as well tell her the truth," the Vice President whispered to Gen in Spanish. "If anyone can stop this I would think it would be her."

It should not be Gen's responsibility, deciding what was best for her, what to tell and what not to tell. He did not know her. He did not know how she would take such a thing. But then she grabbed his ankle in the same way a standing person might have grabbed a wrist in an argument. He looked down at this famous hand touching his pant's leg and felt confused.

"English!" she said.

"They're considering shooting him," Gen confessed.

"He's dead," she said, in case they had missed the point. "How do you say dead in Spanish? *Dead.*"

"*Difunto,*" Gen said.

"*Difunto!*" Her voice was sliding up into the higher registers now. She stood up. At some point she had made the mistake of taking off her shoes, and in a room full of men this small woman seemed especially small. Even the Vice President had several inches on her. But when she put her shoulders back and raised her head it was as if she was willing herself to grow, as if from years of appearing far away on a stage she had learned how to project not just her voice but her entire person, and the rage that was in her lifted her up until she seemed to tower over them. "You understand this," she said to the Generals. "Any bullet that goes into that man goes through me first." She was feeling very bad about the accompanist. She had demanded that the flight attendant find her another seat but the flight was full. She had been quite cruel to him on the plane in an attempt to make him be quiet.

She pointed a finger at Gen, who reluctantly told them what she had said.

The men who circled them like a gallery approved of this. Such love! He had died for her, she would die for him!

"You've kept one woman, one American, and the one person that anyone in the world has ever heard of before, and if you kill me, and make no mistake, you will have to—are you getting all this?" she said to the translator. "The very wrath of God will come down on you and your people."

Even though Gen translated, a clear and simple word-for-word translation, every person in the room understood what she was saying without him, in the same way they would have understood her singing Puccini in Italian.

"Take him out of here. Drag him to the front steps if you have to, but you let the people out there send him home in one piece." A light perspiration had come up on Roxane Coss's forehead, making her glow like Joan of Arc before the fire. When she was completely finished she took a breath, fully reinflating her massive lungs, and then sat down again. Her back was to the Generals and she bent forward to lean her head against the chest of her accompanist. Resting on this still chest, she drew herself back into composure. She was surprised to find his body comforting and she wondered if it was just that she could like him now that he was dead. Once she felt she was herself again she kissed him to reinforce her point. His lips were slack and cool above the hard resistance of his teeth.

From somewhere in the middle of the crowd, Mr. Hosokawa stepped forward, reached into his pocket, and extended to her his handkerchief, clean and pressed. It was odd, he thought, to have been so reduced, to have so little to offer, and yet she took it as if his handkerchief were the thing she had most been hoping for and pressed it beneath her eyes.

"All of you go back," General Benjamin said, not wanting to watch another touching exchange. He went and sat down in one of the large wing-backed chairs near the fireplace and lit a cigarette. There was nothing to do. He couldn't strike her the way he should have, surely there would have been an insurrection in the living room and he wasn't certain that the younger members of his army would not shoot in her defense. What he didn't understand was why he felt grief for the accompanist. Alfredo was right, it wasn't as if this was the first person to die. Most days it seemed like half the people he knew were dead. The thing was the people he knew had been murdered, slaughtered in a host of ways that prevented him from sleeping well at night, and this man, the accompanist, had simply died. Somehow, those two things did not seem exactly the same. He thought of his brother in prison, his brother, as good as dead, sitting day after day in a cold, dark hole. He wondered if his brother could stay alive a little while longer, maybe just a day or two, until their demands were met and he could be released. The accompanist's death had worried him. People could simply die if no one got to them in time. He looked up from his cigarette. "Get away from here," he said to the crowd, and with that they all stepped away. Even Roxane got up and left her corpse as she was told. She seemed tired now. He commanded his troops to resume their positions. The guests were to go and sit and wait.

Alfredo went to the phone and picked it up hesitantly, as if he wasn't exactly sure what it could do. Warfare should not include cellular phones, it made everything seem less serious. He reached into one of the many pockets on his green fatigue pants and pulled out a business card and dialed Messner. He told him there had been an illness, no, a death, and that they needed to negotiate the retrieval of the body.

Without the accompanist, everything was different. One would think the sentence should read: *Without the extra one hundred and seventeen hostages, everything was different,* or *Now that terrorists had said they were not there to kill them, everything seemed different.* But that wasn't true. It was the accompanist they felt the loss of, even all the men who had so recently sent their wives and lovers outside, watched them walk away in the full splendor of their evening dress, they were thinking of the dead man. They had not known him at all. Many assumed he was an American. There they were, steadily producing insulin as a matter of course while another man died without it so that he could stay with the woman he loved. Each asked himself if he would have done the same and each decided the chances were good that he would not. The accompanist embodied a certain recklessness of love that they had not possessed since their youth. What they did not understand was that Roxane Coss, who now sat in the corner of one of the large down sofas, weeping quietly into Mr. Hosokawa's handkerchief, had never been in love with her accompanist, that she had hardly known him at all except in a professional capacity, and that when he had tried to express his feelings to her it turned out to be a disastrous mistake. The kind of love that offers its life so easily, so stupidly, is always the love that is not returned. Simon Thibault would never die in a foolish gesture for Edith. On the contrary, he would take every cowardly recourse available to him to ensure that their lives were spent together. But without all the necessary facts, no one understood what had happened, and all they could think was that the accompanist had been a better, braver man, that he had loved more fully than they were capable of loving.

Everything was slack now. The huge arrangements of flowers that were placed around the room were already wilting, the smallest edge of brown trimmed the petals of the white roses. The half-empty glasses of champagne that sat on end tables and sideboards were flat and warm. The young guards were so exhausted that some fell asleep against the wall and slid down to the floor without waking. The guests stayed in the living room, whispering a little but mostly being quiet. They curled into overstuffed chairs and slept. They did not test the patience of their guards. They took cushions off the sofa and stretched out on the floor in a way that was reminiscent of the night before but much better. They knew they were to stay in the living room, be mostly quiet, avoid sudden moves. No one considered slipping out of the bathroom window when they took themselves to the lavatory unattended, maybe out of some unspoken gentleman's agreement. A certain forced respect had been shown to the body of the accompanist, *their* accompanist, and now they had to try to live up to the standards he had set.

When Messner came in he asked first to see Roxane Coss. His lips seemed thinner now, stern, and he thoughtlessly spoke in German. Gen pushed up heavily from his chair and went to tell them what was being said. The Generals pointed to the woman on the couch, whose face was still pressed into a handkerchief.

"And she will be coming out now," Messner said, not as a question.

"The President is coming over?" General Alfredo said.

"You do expect to let her ride home with the body." It was not the Messner they had seen before. The sight of a room full of hostages forced to lie on the floor, the battered Vice President, the boys with their weapons, all of that had only made him tired, but he was angry now. Angry with nothing but a small red plus sign strapped over his upper arm to protect himself from a roomful of guns.

His anger seemed to inspire an extraordinary patience in the Generals. "The dead," Hector explained, "know nothing of who is sitting beside them."

"You said *all* women."

"We came up through the air-conditioning vents," General Benjamin said, and then after a pause he added a descriptive phrase. "Like moles."

"I need to know if I can trust you," Messner said. Gen only wished he could parody the weight of his voice, the way he struck every word like a soft mallet against a drum. "If you tell me something, am I to believe you?"

"We set free the servants, the ill, and all of the women but one. Perhaps there is something about this one that interests you. Perhaps if we had kept another it wouldn't have mattered so much to you."

"Am I to believe you?"

General Benjamin thought about this for a moment. He lifted his hand as if to stroke his cheek but then thought better of it. "We are not on the same side."

"The Swiss never take sides," Messner said. "We are only on the side of the Swiss."

None of the Generals had anything more to say to Messner, who needed no confirmation that the accompanist lying at his feet was, indeed, dead. The priest had covered the body with a tablecloth and the tablecloth stayed in place. Messner went out the door without pleasantries and returned an hour later with a helper. They brought in a rolling gurney of the type that comes from an ambulance, covered in boxes and sacks, and when they were unloaded Messner and his helper lowered the gurney and tried to tug the large man up. They ultimately had to be assisted by several of the younger terrorists. Death had made the body dense, as if every recital performed, each day's never-ending practice, came back in those final moments and balanced like lead bars across his chest. When he was in place and strapped down, his fine hands dangling from beneath the cutwork tablecloth, they took him away. Roxane Coss turned her head as if to study the couch pillows. Mr. Hosokawa wondered if she was thinking about Brunhilde, if she was wishing for a horse that would take her into the fire after her lover's corpse.

"I don't think they should have brought the food in like that," the Vice President said to a stranger sitting beside him, although he was hungry and curious as to what was in the bags. "I think they could have made two separate trips, out of respect." The late afternoon light was slanting through the tall windows of the living room, making heavy gold strokes across the floor. It was a lovely room, Ruben thought, a lovely time of day to be in the room. He very rarely was home before dark and often he wasn't home at all, out representing the President on one trip or another. The ice in his towel had almost completely melted and the sleeve of his starched dress shirt was soaked from where the water had trickled steadily down his arm. Still, the cool wet towel felt good on his swollen face. He wondered where his wife and children would sleep tonight, if the President and his wife would invite them into their home as a matter of good publicity or if they would go to a guarded room in a hotel. He hoped she would go to her cousin Ana's. At least Ana would comfort her, at least she would make some fun for the children and listen to the girls tell their stories about being kidnapped. They would have to double up in extra beds and sleep on pull-out sofas, but that would be all right. That would be better than the Masudas' chilly guest suite, where certainly Esmeralda would be made to sleep in the servants' quarters.

On the other side of the room near a large bank of windows, Gen and Mr. Hosokawa sat away from the rest of their countrymen. It was a complicated form of politeness in which the other men would not have joined them unless invited. Even in these uncharted circumstances the social order stood firm. Mr. Hosokawa was not much in the mood for company. "He was a magnificent accompanist," he said to Gen. "I've heard my share of them." Of all the men in the room, Mr. Hosokawa was the only one who continued to wear his jacket and tie. His suit had somehow remained remarkably uncreased.

"Would you like me to tell her?"

"What?"

"About the accompanist," Gen said.

Mr. Hosokawa looked to Roxane Coss, whose face was still turned behind the curtain of her own hair. Even though there were men sitting on the sofa where she sat, she was clearly alone. The priest was near her but not with her. His eyes were closed and his lips shaped small, silent words of prayer. "Oh, I'm sure she knows it." Then he added doubtfully, "I'm sure everyone has told her."

Gen did not press his point. He waited. It was not his role to advise Mr. Hosokawa. He knew the secret was to wait and let him come to his own conclusions.

"If it doesn't appear to be disturbing her," he said, "perhaps you could give my condolences. Tell her I thought her accompanist was a brave and talented man." He looked at Gen directly, something that was uncommon between them.

"What if I am responsible for this death?" he said.

"How could that be possible?"

"It was my birthday. They came here for me."

"They came here to work," Gen said. "They don't know you."

Mr. Hosokawa, the day after his fifty-third birthday, looked suddenly old. He had made a mistake, accepting such a gift, and now it seemed to be pulling the years from his life. "Tell her, though, tell her I am especially grieved."

Gen nodded, stood up, and crossed the room. It was a huge room. Even if you didn't count the grand entry hall on one end and dining room on the other, the living room was cavernous, with three separate areas set up with couches and chairs, living rooms within living rooms. The furniture had been moved aside for the recital and then had slowly been dragged back into mismatched configurations as the remaining guests made themselves comfortable. If there had been a reception desk it would have seemed very much like an enormous hotel lobby. If there had been a piano player, Gen thought, but then stopped himself. Roxane Coss was alone, but not too far away a young terrorist stood behind her, his rifle held close to his chest. Gen had seen this boy before. He was the one who had held Roxane Coss's hand when they were first on the floor. Why did he remember it was this one when all the others blurred together? It was something about his face, which was delicate, intelligent somehow, and it set him apart. Gen felt uncomfortable for having noticed this at all. Then the boy raised his eyes from the floor and saw Gen looking. They stared at one another for an instant and then both just as quickly looked away. There was a strange sensation low in Gen's stomach. It made it easier to speak to Roxane Coss. She did not frighten him the way this boy did.

"Forgive me," he said to the opera singer. He shook the boy from his mind. Never in a lifetime would Gen have come to her on his own. Never would he find the courage to express his own sympathies and remorse, in the same way that Mr. Hosokawa would not have the courage to speak to her even if his English had been perfect. But together they moved through the world quite easily, two small halves of courage making a brave whole.

"Gen," she said. She smiled sadly, her eyes still red and damp. She reached up from the couch and took his hand. Of all the people in the room, his was the only name she was sure of and it gave her comfort to say it aloud. "Gen, thank you for before, for stopping them."

"I didn't stop anyone." He shook his head. He was surprised to hear his name come out of her mouth. Surprised by the way it sounded. Surprised by the touch of her hand.

"Well, it would have all been pretty meaningless if you hadn't been there to tell them what I was saying. I would have been just another woman screaming."

"You made things very clear."

"To think they wanted to shoot him." She let go of his hand.

"I am glad," Gen said, but then he stopped, trying to think of what there was to be glad about. "I am glad that your friend had some peace. I'm sure they will send him home soon."

"Yes," she said.

Gen and Roxane each imagined the accompanist going home, as in sitting up in a seat by the window of a plane, looking out at the clouds that pooled over the host country.

"My employer, Mr. Hosokawa, asks me to offer you his condolences. He wanted me to tell you that your accompanist was very talented. We were honored to hear him play."

She nodded. "He's right, you know," she said. "Christopf was very good. I don't suppose people notice the accompanist very often. That's kind of him to say. Your employer." She raised up her open hand to Gen. "He gave me his handkerchief." It was a small white flag crushed into her palm. "I'm afraid I've ruined it. I don't think he'd want it back now."

"Of course he would want you to have it."

"Say his name again for me."

"Ho-so-kawa."

"Hosokawa," she said, nodding. "It was his birthday."

"Yes. He is feeling very sorry about that as well. He has a great sense of responsibility."

"That it was his birthday?"

"That you and your friend came here to perform for him. He feels that you are trapped here because of him, that perhaps your friend—" Again Gen stopped. There was no point in being so explicit. From this close, her face looked very young, very much like a girl's, with her clear eyes and long hair. But he knew she was at least ten years older than he was, somewhere in her late thirties.

"You tell Mr. Hosokawa for me," she said. She stopped to pin some of her hair back away from her face. "What the hell. It isn't like I'm so busy I can't tell him myself. Does he not speak English? Well, you'll translate. You're the only one of us around here who has a job now. Are there any languages you don't speak?"

Gen smiled at the very thought of such a thing, the towering list of languages he didn't speak. "Most of them I don't speak a word of," he said. He stood up and Roxane Coss put her hand on his arm to walk across the room as if she might faint. It was a possibility. She had had a very hard day. All around the room the men raised their heads and ended their conversations to watch them, the tall young Japanese translator navigating the wide expanse of living room with the soprano on his arm. How strange and lovely it was to see her hand resting on the top of his sleeve, her pale fingers nearly reaching his wrist.

When Mr. Hosokawa, who had been trying to look the other way, realized that Gen was bringing Roxane Coss to him, he felt a deep blush coming up from the collar of his shirt and he stood to wait for her arrival.

"Mr. Hosokawa," Roxane said, and held out her hand to him.

"Miss Coss," he said, and bowed.

Roxane took one chair and Mr. Hosokawa took the other. Gen pulled up a third, smaller chair and waited.

"Gen has told me you feel in some way responsible for this," she said.

Mr. Hosokawa nodded. He spoke to her with great honesty, the kind two people use after a lifetime of knowing one another. But what was a lifetime? This afternoon? This evening? The kidnappers had reset the clocks and no one knew a thing about time anymore. Better this once to be inappropriate and honest as the burden of his guilt was tightening a string around his throat. He told her he had declined many invitations from the host country but then agreed to come once they told him she would be there. He told her he had never had any plans of helping this country. He told her he was a great admirer of her work and named the cities he had seen her in. He told her he must be in some part responsible for the death of her accompanist.

"No," she said. "No. I sing in so many places. It's rare that I would sing for a private party like this. To tell you the truth, most people don't have the money, but I've done it before. I didn't come here for your birthday. With all respect, I didn't even remember whose birthday it was. Besides, from what I understand, these people didn't even want you, they wanted the President."

"But I was the one who set this thing in motion," Mr. Hosokawa said.

"Or did I?" she said. "I thought about declining. I declined several times until they came up with more money." She leaned forward, and when she did, Gen and Mr. Hosokawa ducked their heads down as well. "Don't get me wrong. I am very capable of blame. This is an event ripe for blame if ever I saw one. I just don't blame you."

The members of LFDMS could have opened all the doors at that moment, thrown down their guns and told everyone to go, and Mr. Hosokawa would not have experienced any greater sense of relief than the one he had knowing Roxane Coss forgave him.

Several of the foot soldiers came around with the bags that Messner had brought in on the accompanist's gurney and distributed sandwiches and cans of soda, wrapped slices of dark cake and bottled water. If nothing else, the food seemed to be in great abundance and when they took one sandwich each the boy shook the bag at them, urging them wordlessly to reach in for more. Or maybe there was simply more for them because they were sitting with Roxane Coss.

"It looks like I'll stay for supper," she said, unwrapping the white paper like a present. Inside the heavy slabs of bread there was a piece of meat, orangish-red with sauce or watery peppers. Its juice dripped into the paper which she spread across her lap. The two men waited for her to begin, but they didn't have to wait for long. She ate like she was starving. "There are people who would like to have a picture of this," she said, lifting up the sandwich. "I'm very particular about my food."

"We make exceptions in extraordinary times," Mr. Hosokawa said, and Gen translated. He was pleased to see her eating, pleased that her grief had not overwhelmed her in any way that could endanger her health.

For Gen, the oily piece of meat (which animal?) inside stained bread made him stop and consider exactly how hungry he was. He was hungry. He turned his head away from Roxane Coss and Mr. Hosokawa, afraid of the orange grease on his lips. But before he had the chance to eat even half of his sandwich, one of the boys wearing a green baseball cap came for him. They were just starting to become distinguishable, these boys. This one had a cap with a photo button of Che Guevara on it, another wore a knife on his chest, one more had a cheap scapula of the Sacred Heart tied high up on his throat with a string. Some of the boys were very big or very small, a few had a handful of whiskers sprouting on their chins, others had acne. The boy that Gen had noticed with Roxane had a face like a fine-boned Madonna. The boy that came for him now told Gen in a Spanish so rudimentary that it was a struggle to understand, that the Generals would see him now.

"Forgive me," he said in English and Japanese, wrapping up what was left of his meal and putting it discreetly beneath a chair in hopes it would still be there when he returned. He had especially wanted the cake.

General Hector used a pencil to take notes on a yellow tablet. He was extremely meticulous about his writing.

"Name?" General Alfredo asked a man sitting on a red ottoman near the fireplace.

"Oscar Mendoza." The man took his handkerchief out of his pocket and wiped his mouth. He was finishing off a piece of cake.

"Any identification?"

Mr. Mendoza took out his wallet, found a driver's license, a credit card, pictures of his five daughters. General Hector copied down the information. He wrote down his address. General Benjamin picked up the pictures and studied them. "Occupation?" he said.

"Contractor." Mr. Mendoza did not like them having his address. He lived only five miles from here. He had planned on bidding to build the factory that he had been told Mr. Hosokawa had come to his country to develop. Instead he had slept on a floor, said good-bye to his wife and his grand string of girls for who knew how long, and had to consider the possibility that he might be shot.

"Your health?"

Mr. Mendoza shrugged. "Good enough I would think. I'm here."

"But do you know?" General Benjamin said, trying to remember the tone that the doctor had taken with him when he had gone to the city years before to see about his shingles. "Do you have any conditions?"

Mr. Mendoza looked as if he were being asked about the internal workings of his wristwatch. "I wouldn't know."

Gen came along behind them and waited while they asked a few more questions, all of them remarkable only in what unhelpful answers they engendered. They were trying to get rid of more hostages. They were trying to discern who else might be dying. The death of the accompanist had made them nervous. The crowd outside, which had quieted for a while, had begun to bellow again once they saw the body tucked inside its white tablecloth. "*Mur*-der! *Mur*-der!" they chanted. From the street there came a constant barrage of bull-horned messages and demands. The phone rang and rang and rang with would-be negotiators. Soon, all of the terrorists were going to have to be allowed to sleep. The Generals were bickering in some shorthand nonsense that Gen couldn't follow. General Hector stopped the argument by taking out his pistol and shooting the clock on the mantel. There were too many people to watch, even with the crowd cut in half. They went from man to man, asking, printing down the answers and names. Gen served in the cases where Spanish was not understood. It was the foreigners they placed their hopes on anyway. Foreign governments willing to pay foreign ransoms. The Generals were having to rethink their failed mission. If they couldn't get the President, then there should still be something in it for their troubles. They planned to talk to every hostage in the room, to assess and rank them to see who would be most beneficial in getting comrades released from high-altitude prisons, for getting money for the cause. But the polling process lacked science. The guests played down their own importance when questioned.

"No, I don't run the company, not exactly."

"I am only one member on a board of many."

"This diplomatic post is not as it seems. It was arranged by my brother-in-law."

No one was quite willing to lie, but they tugged down the edges of the truth. The note-taking made them nervous.

"All of this information will be checked by our people on the outside," Alfredo said again and again, and Gen translated it into French and German, Greek and Portuguese, each time careful to say *their* people outside. Something a translator should never do.

In the middle of an interview with a Dane who was thought to be a potential backer for the nonexistent Nansei project, General Benjamin, the upper right portion of his faces in flames, turned to Gen. "How did you get to be so smart?" he said in an accusatory tone, as if there was a secret cache of intelligence hidden somewhere in the house that Gen was hoarding all for himself.

Gen felt tired, not smart. He felt hungry. Sleep was singing him lullabies. He longed for what was left of his sandwich. "Sir?" he said. He could see Mr. Hosokawa and Roxane Coss sitting quietly together, unable to speak because their translator was busy with the terrorists' footwork.

"Where did you learn so many languages?"

Gen had no interest in telling his story. Was his sandwich still beneath the chair? The cake? He was wondering whether or not they would qualify for release and feeling a sad resignation in the knowledge they would not. "University," he said simply, and turned his eyes back to the man they were questioning.

When they made their lists of those to keep and those to send away, Gen should have been on the top of the list to go. He was worth no money, he had no leverage. He was as much an employee, a working-man, as the ones who had fine-sliced the onions for dinner. But when the lists were drawn up his name did not appear anywhere. He was somehow beneath their thought altogether. Not that he would have gone without Mr. Hosokawa. He would have chosen to stay like that young priest, but everyone likes to be asked. Once the interviews were completed and the final decisions were made it was late in the evening. All around the room lamps were clicked on. Gen was given the task of making copies of the lists. He had somehow become the secretary to the whole event.

In the end, counting the translator (he added his own name), it was decided that thirty-nine hostages would be kept. The final number was forty, because Father Arguedas again refused to leave. With fifteen soldiers and three generals, it gave them very nearly the two-hostages-for-every-one-captor ratio that they had decided upon as being reasonable. Considering that the original plan was for eighteen terrorists to take one president, the recalculation felt to be as much as they could reasonably handle. What they wanted, what would have been best, would be to tease out the release of the extras, to keep them all for another week and then let them dribble out, a few here and there in exchange for demands that were met. But the terrorists were tired. The hostages had needs and complaints. They took on the weight of a roomful of restless children all needing to be shushed and petted and entertained. They wanted them gone.

The Vice President could not help himself. He was picking up glasses and putting them on a large silver tray he knew the maid kept in the sideboard in the dining room. When he went to the kitchen he was followed but not stopped and he took a minute to rest his cheek against the freezer door. He came back with a dark green plastic garbage bag and began to pick up the wrappers from the sandwiches. There were no crusts of bread left in the papers, only small pools of orange oil. They had all been hungry. He picked up the soda cans from the tables and rugs, even though the tables and rugs did not technically belong to him. He had been happy in this house. It had always been such a bright place when he came home, his children laughing, running down the hallways with their friends, the pretty Indian maids who waxed the floors down on their hands and knees despite the presence of an electric polisher in the broom closet, the smell of his wife's perfume as she sat at the dressing table brushing her hair. It was his home. He had to make some attempt to put it back towards the familiar so as to keep things bearable.

"Are you comfortable?" he would say to his guests as he swept some tender crumbs into the palm of his hand. "Are you holding up all right?" He wanted to nose their shoes under the sofa. He wanted to drag the blue silk chair down to the other end of the room where it belonged, but decorum prohibited that.

He made another trip to the kitchen for a wet cloth, hoping to blot up something that looked like grape juice out of the tight knots of the Savonnière rug. At the far end of the room he saw the opera singer sitting with the Japanese man whose birthday was yesterday. Funny, but with the pain in his head now he could think of neither of their names. They were leaning towards one another and from time to time she would laugh and then he would nod happily. Was it her husband who had just died? The Japanese man would hum something and she would listen and nod and then, in a very quiet voice, she would sing it back to him. What a sweet sound. Over the constant ruckus of the messages being boomed in through the window it was hard to make out what it was she was singing. He could only hear the notes, the clear resonance of her voice, like when he was a boy and would run down the hill past the convent, how he could hear just a moment of the nuns' singing, and how it was better that way, to fly past it rather than to stop and wait and listen. Running, the music flew into him, became the wind that pushed back his hair and the slap of his own feet on the pavement. Hearing her sing now, softly, as he sponged at the carpet, was like that. It was like hearing one bird answer another when you can only hear the reply and not the plaintive, original call.

When Messner was called again he came quickly. Ruben Iglesias, Vice President, houseboy, was sent to the door to let him in. Poor Messner looked more exhausted, more sunburned as the day went on. How long were these days? Had it been today that the accompanist had died? Had it only been last night that their clothes were fresh and they ate the little chops and listened to the aria of Dvořák? Or was Dvořák something they drank in small glasses after dinner? Had it been so recently that the room was still full of women and the sweet chiffon of their gowns, their jewelry and jeweled hair combs and tiny satin evening bags fashioned to look like peonies? Had it been just yesterday that the house was cleaned, the windowpanes and windowsills, the sheer curtains and heavy drapes washed and rehung, everything in immaculate order because the President and the famous Mr. Hosokawa, who might want to build a factory in their country, were coming to dinner? It was then that it struck the Vice President for the first time: why had Masuda asked him to have the party at his house? If this birthday was so important, why not the presidential palace? Why, if not because he knew all along that he had no intention of coming?

"I think you're getting an infection," Messner said, and touched the tips of his pale fingers to Ruben's burning forehead. He flipped open his cellular phone and made a request for antibiotics in a combination of English and Spanish. "I don't know what kind," he said. "Whatever they give to people with smashed-up faces." He put his hand over the bottom of the phone and said to Ruben, "Any—" He turned to Gen. "What is the word *allergies*?"

"*Alergia.*"

Ruben nodded his tender head. "Peanuts."

"What is he calling about?" General Benjamin said to Gen.

Gen told him it was for medication for the Vice President.

"No medication. I haven't given authorization for any medication," General Alfredo said. What did this Vice President know about infection? The bullet in his stomach, now that was an infection to talk about.

"Certainly not insulin," Messner said, flipping shut his phone.

Alfredo appeared not to hear him. He was shuffling his papers. "Here are the lists. This is who we are keeping. This is who we are letting go." He put the yellow tablet pages on the table in front of Messner. "These are our demands. They've been updated. There will be no more releases until the demands are completely and fully met. We have been, as you say, very reasonable. Now is the time for the government to be reasonable."

"I'll tell them that," Messner said, picking up the papers and folding them into his pocket.

"We've been very conscientious in matters of health," Alfredo said.

Gen, suddenly tired, held up his hand for a moment to stop the dialogue, trying to remember the word for *concienzudo* in English. It came to him.

"Anyone needing medical attention will be released."

"Including him?" Messner tipped his head toward the Vice President, who, lost inside the intricate world of his own fever, paid no attention to what was being said.

"Him we keep," General Alfredo said shortly. "We didn't get the President. We have to have something."

* * *

There was another list, aside from The Demands (money, prisoners released, a plane, transportation to the plane, etc. . . .) This was the list that slowed things down, the list of Small and Immediate Needs. The details were not interesting, certain things had to come in before the excess of hostages could go out: pillows (58), blankets (58), toothbrushes (58), fruit (mangoes, bananas), cigarettes (20 cartons filtered, 20 cartons unfiltered), bags of candy (all types, excluding licorice), bars of chocolate, sticks of butter, newspapers, a heating pad, the list went on and on. Inside, they imagined the people on the outside being dispatched on a great scavenger hunt, trying to come up with what was needed in the middle of the night. People would be banging on glass doors, waking up shopkeepers who would be forced to flick on the bright overhead lights. No one wanted to wait until morning and risk the possibility of someone changing his mind.

When all the remaining guests were herded together into the dining room to hear the hostage list and release list, there was a great sense of excitement. It was a cakewalk, a game of musical chairs in which people were randomly rewarded or punished and they were each one glad to take their chance at the wheel, even those like Mr. Hosokawa and Simon Thibault, who must have known they didn't have a chance of going home, stood with the rest of the men, their hearts beating wildly. The men all thought that Roxane Coss was sure to be let go now, the idea of keeping one woman would become cumbersome and embarrassing. They would miss her, they were missing her already, but everyone wanted to see her go.

They called through the names and told them to go to either the left or the right, and while they didn't say which side was to be released, it was clear enough. One could almost tell from the cut of the tuxedo who would be staying. A great wall of darkness came from those who could now reasonably assume their fate and it pulled them away from the lucky hilarity of the others. On one side, men deemed less important were going back to their wives, would sleep in the familiar sheets of their own beds, would be greeted by children and dogs, the wet and reckless affection of their unconditional love. But thirty-nine men and one woman on the other side were just beginning to understand that they were digging in, that this was the house where they lived now, that they had been kidnapped.

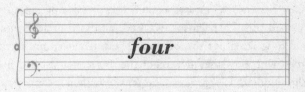

four

*f*ather Arguedas explained to Gen, who explained to Mr. Hosokawa, that what they were looking at in the hours they spent staring out the window was called *garúa*, which was more than mist and less than drizzle and hung woolly and gray over the city in which they were now compelled to stay. Not that they could see the city, they could not see anything. They could have been in London or Paris or New York or Tokyo. They could have been looking at a field of blue-tipped grass or a gridlock of traffic. They couldn't see. No defining hints of culture or local color. They could have been anyplace where the weather was capable of staying bad for indeterminate amounts of time. From time to time, instructions came blasting over the wall, but even that seemed to be diminishing, as if the voices couldn't always permeate the fog. The *garúa* maintained a dull, irregular presence from April through November and Father Arguedas said to take heart since October was very nearly over and then the sun would return. The young priest smiled at them. He was almost handsome until he smiled, but his smile was too big and his teeth turned and crossed at awkward angles, making his appearance suddenly loopy. Despite the circumstances of their internment, Father Arguedas remained sanguine and found cause to smile often. He did not seem to be a hostage, but someone hired to make the hostages feel better. It was a job he carried out with great earnestness. He opened his arms and put one hand on Mr. Hosokawa's shoulder and the other on Gen's, then he dipped his head down slightly and closed his eyes. It might have been to pray but if it was he did not force the others to join him. "Take heart," he said again before pressing on in his rounds.

"A good boy," Mr. Hosokawa said, and Gen nodded and both returned to looking out the window. The priest need not have been concerned with how they felt about the weather. They had no issue with the weather. The *garúa* made sense, while atmospheric clarity would not. When one looked out the window now it was impossible to see as far as the wall which cut off the garden from the street. It was difficult to make out the shapes of the trees, to tell a tree from a shrub. It made the daylight seem like dusk in much the same way the floodlights that had been set up on the other side of the wall almost made night into day, the kind of false, electric day of an evening baseball game. In short, when one looked out the window during the *garúa* all one really saw was the *garúa* itself, not day or night or season or place. The day no longer progressed in its normal, linear fashion but instead every hour circled back to its beginning, every moment was lived over and over again. Time, in the manner in which they had all understood it, was over.

So to rejoin the story a week after Mr. Hosokawa's birthday party ended seems as good a place as any. That first week was only details anyway, the tedium of learning a new life. Things were very strict in the beginning. Guns were pointed, commands were given and obeyed, people slept in rows on the living-room carpet and asked for permission in the most personal of matters. And then, very slowly, the details began to fall away. People stood on their own. They brushed their teeth without asking, had a conversation that was not interrupted. Eventually they went to the kitchen and made a sandwich when they were hungry, using the backs of spoons to spread the butter onto bread because all of the knives had been confiscated. The Generals had a peculiar fondness for Joachim Messner (even if they did not demonstrate this fondness to him) and insisted that not only was he in charge of negotiations but that he must be the one to bring all supplies to the house, to lug every box alone through the gate and up the endless walkway. So it was Messner, his vacation long since over, who brought their bread and butter to the door.

Time could barely pull the second hand forward on the clock and yet look at all that had been accomplished—could it only have been a week? To have gone from guns being pushed into backs to most of the guns being locked up in a broom closet should have taken no less than a year, but already the captors knew the hostages would not mount an insurrection and in return the hostages knew, or almost knew, they would not be shot by the terrorists. Of course there were still guards. Two boys patrolled outside in the garden and three circled the rooms of the house, their weapons pointed out like canes for the blind. The Generals continued to give them orders. One of the boys, from time to time, would take a little poke at one of the guests with the muzzle of his gun and tell him to go to the other side of the room for no reason at all other than the pleasure of seeing them move. At night there were sentries, but by twelve o'clock they had always fallen asleep. They did not wake when their weapons slipped from their fingers and clattered on the floor.

For the guests of Mr. Hosokawa's birthday party, most of the day was spent wandering from window to window, maybe playing a hand of cards or looking at a magazine, as if the world had become a giant train station in which everything was delayed until further notice. It was this absence of time that had everyone confused. General Benjamin had found a heavy crayon that belonged to Marco, the young son of the Vice President, and every day he made a thick blue slash on the wall in the dining room, six slashes down and then one across to indicate a week had passed. He imagined his brother in solitary confinement, Luis, forced to make scratches against the brick with his fingernail in order to remember the days. Of course, in a house there were more traditional ways of keeping track of time. There were several calendars, a date book and planner in the kitchen by the phone, and many of the men wore watches which gave the date as well as the time. And if any of those methods were to fail they could easily turn on the radio or television and hear what day it was while listening to news of themselves. But still General Benjamin thought that the old-fashioned way was the best. He sharpened his crayon with a gutting knife and added another slash to his collection on the wall. It galled Ruben Iglesias no end. He would have punished his children sharply were they to do such a barbaric thing.

Without exception, these were men who were largely unfamiliar with the concept of free time. The ones who were very rich stayed at their offices late into the evening. They sat in the backseats of cars and dictated letters while their drivers shepherded them home. The ones who were young and very poor worked just as hard, albeit at a different kind of work. There was wood to be cut or sweet potatoes to be dug out of the ground. There were drills to be learned with the guns, how to run, how to hide. Now a great, unfamiliar idleness had fallen on them and they sat and they stared at one another, their fingers drumming incessantly on the arms of chairs.

But in this vast ocean of time Mr. Hosokawa could not seem to startle up any concern for Nansei. While he stared at the weather he never wondered if his abduction had affected stock prices. He did not care who was making his decisions, sitting at his desk. The company that had been his life, his son, had fallen away from him as thoughtlessly as a coin is dropped. He took a small spiral notebook from the pocket of his tuxedo jacket and, after inquiring as to the correct spelling from Gen, added the word *garúa* to his list. Incentive was key. No matter how many times Mr. Hosokawa had listened to his Italian tapes in Japan he could remember nothing that was on them. No sooner had he heard the beautiful words, *dimora*, *patrono*, than they vanished from memory. But after only one week of captivity look at all the Spanish he had learned! *Ahora* was now; *sentarse*, sit; *ponerse de pie*, stand up; *sueño*, sleep, and *requetebueno* was very good, but it was always spoken with a certain coarseness and condescension that told the listener not that he had done well but that he was too stupid to merit high expectations. And it wasn't just the language that had to be overcome, there were all the names to learn as well, those of the hostages, those of the captors when you could get one of them to tell you his name. The people were from so many different countries that there were no easy tricks of association, no familiar toehold from which to pull oneself up. The room was full of men he did not know and should know, though they all smiled and nodded to one another. He would have to work harder to introduce himself. At Nansei he had made a point of learning the names of as many of his employees as was possible. He remembered the names of the businessmen he entertained and the names of their wives whom he inquired after and never met.

Mr. Hosokawa had not led a static life. As he built his company, he learned. But this was a different sort of learning he did now. This was the learning of childhood. May I sit? May I stand? Thank you. Please. What was the word for apple, for bread? And he remembered what they told him because, unlike the Italian tapes, in this case remembering was all. He could see now the full extent to which he had relied on Gen in the past, how much he relied on him now, though now he often had to wait with his questions while Gen translated something for the Generals. Two days ago Vice President Iglesias had very kindly given Mr. Hosokawa this notebook and a pen from a drawer in the kitchen. "Here," he said. "Consider it a late birthday present." In that notebook Mr. Hosokawa printed the alphabet and had Gen write out the numbers from one to ten and every day he planned to add more words in Spanish. He wrote them over and over, keeping his writing very small because even though paper was plentiful now, it occurred to him that a time could come when he would have to be careful with such things. When had he last written something down? His thoughts were entered, recorded, transmitted. It was in this simple repetition, the rediscovery of his own penmanship, that Mr. Hosokawa found solace. He began to think about Italian again, and thought he might ask Gen to include just a word or two every day from that language as well. There were two Italians in their group and

when he heard them speak he could feel himself straining to understand as if he were listening to a bad phone connection. Italian was so
close to his heart. And English. He would enjoy being able to speak to
Miss Coss.

He sat down and tapped the tip of his pencil against his pad. Too
ambitious. If he took on too many words he would wind up with
nothing. Ten words of Spanish a day, ten nouns actually learned and
then one verb, fully conjugated, was very likely as much as he could
manage if he was to really remember each word and carry them over
from one day to the next.

Garúa. Often when Mr. Hosokawa sat at the window he wondered about the people on the other side of the wall, the police and
the military who were at this point more likely to use the phone than
the bullhorn. Were they constantly damp? Did they sit inside their
cars drinking coffee? The Generals sat in the cars, he would guess,
while the boys with their guns, the foot soldiers, would stand at attention, the chilled rain running freely down the backs of their necks.

Those soldiers, they would not be unlike the children who patrolled
the living room of the vice-presidential estate, though perhaps there
was some minimum age requirement in the military. How young were
these children exactly? The ones who appeared to be the oldest would
then step beneath the bright light of a lamp and it was clear they
weren't older, only bigger. They loped around the room bumping into
things, unaccustomed to the size they had so recently acquired. At
least those boys had Adam's apples, a sprinkling of new hairs mixed
in with the angry pimples. The ones who were actually the youngest
were terrifying in their youth. Their hair had all the weight and gloss
of children's hair. They had the smooth skin and small shoulders of
children. They stretched their little hands around the butts of their
rifles and tried to keep their faces blank. The hostages stared at the
terrorists, and the longer they looked, the younger the terrorists
became. Could these be the same men who burst into their party, the
same marauding animals? They fell asleep on the floor in limp piles
now, their mouths open, their arms twisted. They slept like teenagers.

They slept with a kind of single-minded concentration that every adult in the room had forgotten decades before. Some of them liked being soldiers. They continued to carry their guns. They menaced the adults with the occasional shove and hateful glower. Then it seemed that armed children were a much more dangerous breed than armed adults. They were moody, irrational, anxious for confrontation. The others spent their time staring at the details of the house. They bounced on the beds and tried on the clothes in the dressers. They flushed the toilets again and again for the pleasure of watching the water swirl away. At first there had been a rule that they were not to address their prisoners but even that was growing slack for some of them. Sometimes now they spoke to the hostages, especially when the Generals were busy conferring. "Where are you from?" was the favorite question, though the answers rarely registered. Finally, Ruben Iglesias went to his study and brought back a large atlas so they could show them on maps, and when that didn't seem to make things any clearer he sent a guard to his son's room to bring down the globe on a stand, a pretty blue-and-green planet that spun easily on its stationary axis.

"Paris," Simon Thibault said, pointing to his city. "France."

Lothar Falken showed them Germany and Rasmus Nilson put his finger on Denmark. Akira Yamamoto, who was not interested in playing, turned away, and so Gen showed them Japan. Roxane Coss covered the whole of the United States beneath her palm and then tapped one nail on the dot that represented Chicago. The boys took the globe to the next group of people, who, even if they didn't understand the question, knew the game. "This is Russia," they said. "This is Italy." "This is Argentina." "This is Greece."

"Where are you from?" the boy called Ishmael asked the Vice President. He thought of the Vice President as his own hostage because he had been the one to bring the ice from the kitchen when the Vice President was first injured. He still brought Ruben ice, sometimes three and four times a day, without ever being asked. It gave the Vice President relief as his cheek had become infected and persisted in its swelling.

"Here," the Vice President said, pointing to the floor.

"Show me." Ishmael held up the globe.

"Here." Ruben tapped his foot on the carpet. "This is my house. I live in this city. I am from the same country you are from."

Ishmael looked up at his friend. It had been easier to get the Russians to play. "Show me."

So Ruben sat down on the floor with the boy and the globe and identified the host country, which in this case was flat and pink. "We live here." Ishmael was the very smallest of all of them, so much a boy with a boy's white teeth. Ruben wanted to pull the child into his lap, to keep him.

"You live there."

"No, not just me," Ruben said. Where were his own children? Where were they sleeping now? "Both of us."

Ishmael sighed and pushed himself up from the floor, disappointed in his friend's thickheadedness. "You don't know how to play," he said.

"I don't know how to play," Ruben said, looking at the deplorable condition of the boy's boots. At any minute the right sole would fall off completely. "Now listen to me. Go upstairs to the biggest bedroom you can find and open all the doors until you see a closet full of lady's dresses. In that closet there are a hundred pairs of shoes and if you look you'll find some tennis shoes that might fit you. There could even be some boots."

"I can't wear lady's shoes."

Ruben shook his head. "The tennis shoes and boots are not for ladies. We only keep them there. I know, it makes no sense, but trust me."

"It is ridiculous that we sit here like this," Franz von Schuller said. Gen translated into French for Simon Thibault and Jacques Maitessier and then into Japanese for Mr. Hosokawa. There were two other Germans there as well. The group of them stood by the empty fireplace, drinking grapefruit juice. An enormous treat, the grapefruit juice. It was better than a really good Scotch. The sharpness settled over their.tongues, making them feel alive. Today was the first time it had been brought in. "These people are amateurs. The ones in here as well as the ones outside."

"And you suggest?" Simon Thibault said. Thibault wore his wife's huge blue scarf tied around his neck and hanging down his back, and the presence of this scarf made people less likely to listen to his opinion on serious matters.

Pietro Genovese walked by and asked Gen to translate the conversation to him as well. He knew enough French but no German.

"It isn't as if the guns are hidden from us," von Schuller said, lowering his voice even though no one seemed able to pick up the German. They waited for Gen.

"And so we shoot our way out. Just like television," Pietro Genovese said. "Is that grapefruit juice?" He looked bored by the conversation even though he had just walked into it. He built airports. As a country's industry enlarges, so must its airports.

Gen held up his hand. "One moment, please." He was still translating the German into Japanese.

"We would need a dozen translators and arbitration from the UN before we could decide to overthrow the one teenager with a knife," Jacques Maitessier said, as much to himself as anyone, and he knew what he was talking about, having once been the French ambassador to the United Nations.

"I'm not saying that everyone would have to agree," von Schuller said.

"You'll give it a try on your own?" Thibault said.

"Gentlemen, your patience, please." Gen was trying to translate it all into Japanese. That was his first responsibility. He didn't work for the general convenience of the people, although everyone managed to forget that. He worked for Mr. Hosokawa.

Conversations in more than two languages felt awkward and unreliable, like speaking with a mouthful of cotton and Novocain. No one could hold on to their thoughts long enough and wait their turns. These were not men who were accustomed to waiting or speaking precisely. They preferred to expound, to rant when necessary. Pietro Genovese went off to see if there was more juice in the kitchen. Simon Thibault smoothed down his scarf with the flat of his palm and asked Jacques Maitessier if he would be interested in a hand of cards. "My wife would kill me if I was involved in an overthrow," Thibault said in French.

The three Germans spoke rapidly among themselves and Gen made no attempt to listen.

"I never get tired of the weather," Mr. Hosokawa said to Gen as they walked back to the window. They stood side by side for a while, clearing all those other languages from their heads.

"Do you ever think of rising up?" Gen asked. He could see their reflections. They were standing very close to the glass. Two Japanese men, both wearing glasses, one was taller and twenty-five years younger, but in this room where people had so little in common Gen could see for the first time how they looked very much the same.

Mr. Hosokawa kept his eyes on their reflection, or maybe he was watching the *garúa*. "Something will rise up eventually," he said. "And then there will be nothing we can do to stop it." His voice turned heavy at the thought.

The soldiers spent most of their days exploring the house, eating the pistachio nuts they found in the pantry, sniffing the lavender hand lotion in the bathroom. The house offered up no end of curiosities: closets the size of some houses they had seen, bedrooms where no one slept, cupboards that held nothing but rolls of colored paper and rib- bon. A favorite room was the Vice President's study, which was at the end of a long hallway. Behind the heavy draperies, the windows stopped short at two upholstered bench seats, the kind of place where a person could tuck up his legs and look out into the garden for hours. The study had two leather sofas and two leather chairs and all of the books were covered in leather. Even the desk set, the cup that held the pencils and the edges of the blotter were leather. The room had the comforting and familiar smell of cows standing in the hot sun.

There was a television in this room. A few of them had seen a television before, a wooden box with a curved piece of glass that threw back your reflection in peculiar ways. They were always, always broken. That was the nature of televisions. There was talk, big stories about what a television once had done, but no one believed it because no one had seen it. The boy called Cesar put his face close to the screen, pulled back his lips by hooking a finger into either side of his mouth, and enjoyed the picture. The others were watching. He rolled back his eyes and shook his tongue. Then he took his fingers out of his mouth, crossed his hands over his chest, and began to mimic a song he remembered Roxane Coss singing that first night they were waiting in the air-conditioning vents. He wasn't quite getting the words, but he was close to their sounds and right on their pitch. He wasn't mocking, exactly, he was singing and then he was singing very well. When he couldn't remember what came next, he stopped abruptly and bowed at the waist. He turned and went back to making faces in the television.

It was Simon Thibault who turned the television on. He hadn't meant anything by it. He had come into the room because he heard the singing. He thought that someone was playing some odd and beautiful old record and it made him curious. Then he saw the boy doing the show, a moderately funny boy, and thought he would get a kick out of the picture coming up suddenly where his face had been. Simon picked up the remote control from where it sat balanced on the arm of a comfortable-looking leather chair and pushed the power button.

They screamed. They howled like dogs. They cried out the names of their compatriots, "Gilbert! Francisco! Jesus!" in a voice that would indicate fire, murder, the coming of police. That brought the great metal snap of safeties being removed from guns and the rushing in of the other soldiers and the three Generals who threw Simon Thibault against the wall and cut his lip.

"Nothing foolish," Edith had said, her lips lightly touching his ear. But what was included in foolishness? Turning on a television?

One of the boys who rushed in, a big boy named Gilbert, put the round muzzle of his rifle into Thibault's throat, pressing the blue silk scarf into the soft skin above his trachea. He pinned him there like a butterfly tacked down on a corkboard.

"Television," Thibault said with great difficulty.

Sure enough, in the crowded study the attention had turned away from Simon Thibault. Just as quickly as he had been a threat, a star, they turned their guns away from him, let him slump down the wall in a shuddering crumple of fear. They were all looking at the television now. An attractive woman with dark hair was holding up articles of soiled clothing to the camera with both hands, shaking her head in mild disgust before shoving them into the washing machine. Her lipstick was bright red and the walls behind her a vivid yellow. "This is a real challenge," she said in Spanish. Gilbert crouched down on his toes to watch.

Simon Thibault coughed and rubbed his throat.

Certainly, the Generals had seen television before, though not in the years since they had gone back to the jungle. They were in the room now. This was a very nice television, color with a twenty-eight-inch screen. The remote control had fallen on the floor and now General Alfredo picked it up and began pushing the buttons to take them through the channels: soccer game; a man in a coat and tie sitting at a desk reading; a girl in silver pants singing; a dozen puppies in a basket. There was a fresh burst of excitement, a collective *ah*, at every new picture.

Simon Thibault left the room without being noticed. Cesar's singing did not even cross his mind.

Most days the hostages longed for this whole thing to be over. They longed for their countries, their wives, their privacy. Other days, honestly, they just wanted to be away from all these children, from their sullenness and sleepiness, from their chasing games and appetites. How old could they have been? When asked, they either lied and said twenty-five or they shrugged as if they hadn't the slightest idea what the question meant. Mr. Hosokawa knew he was a poor judge of children. In Japan, he often saw young people who looked to be no more than ten behind the wheels of cars. His own daughters constantly presented him with a mathematical impossibility, one minute running around the house wearing pajamas covered in images of the blankly staring Hello, Kitty, the next minute announcing they had dates who would be picking them up at seven. He believed his daughters were not old enough to date and yet clearly by the standards of this country they were old enough to be members of a terrorist organization. He tried to picture them, their plastic daisy barrettes and short white socks, picking at the door frame with the sharp tip of a knife.

Mr. Hosokawa could not imagine his daughters anyplace but curled in their mother's bed, crying for his return while they watched the news. And yet to everyone's genuine surprise, two of the junior soldiers turned out to be girls. One was revealed quite simply: somewhere around the twelfth day she pulled off her cap to scratch her head and down came a braid. She did not bother to twist it back into place when the scratching was done. She did not seem to think that her being a girl was any secret at all. Her name was Beatriz. She was perfectly happy to tell anyone who asked. She was not blessed with a pretty face or a delicate manner and had passed very well as a boy. She held her gun as ready to shoot as any of the boys and her eyes stayed dull even after it was no longer a necessity. And yet, for all her extraordinary averageness, the hostages watched her as if she were something impossible and rare, a luna moth lighting in a snowfield. How could there be a girl among them? How had they all failed to notice? The other girl was not so hard to figure out. Logic held that if there was one girl then there could just as easily be more than one, and everyone looked immediately towards the silent boy who never answered questions and had seemed in every way unnatural from the start, much too beautiful, too nervous. His hairline dipped onto his forehead and made his face a perfect heart. His mouth was round and soft. His eyes stayed half closed as if the heavy lashes seemed too great a burden to lift. He smelled different from the other boys, a sweet, warm smell, and his neck was long and smooth. He was the one who seemed so particularly in love with Roxane Coss and slept on the hallway floor outside her room at night, using his body to prevent any drafts from coming under the door. Gen looked at him, the one who had made him feel so uneasy, and the anxiousness he had held inside his chest rolled off of him in a long, low wave.

"Beatriz," Simon Thibault said, "that boy over there. Is he your sister?"

Beatriz snorted and shook her head. "Carmen? My sister? You must be crazy."

At the sound of her name, Carmen looked up from across the room. Beatriz speaking her name. There was no such thing as a secret in this world. Carmen threw down the magazine she had been looking at. (It was Italian, with an abundance of glossy pictures of movie stars and royalty. The text undoubtedly contained important information about their most personal lives that she was unable to read. It had been found in the drawer of the nightstand beside the bed where the Vice President's wife slept.) Carmen took her revolver into the kitchen and shut the door and no one followed her, a visibly angry teenaged girl with a gun. There was nowhere to go and everyone assumed that eventually she would come out on her own. They wanted to look at her again, to see her without her cap on, to have the time to contemplate her as a girl, but they were willing to wait. If this was the drama of the afternoon, one of the terrorists taking herself hostage for a few hours, then the suspense was better than single-mindedly watching the drizzle.

"I should have known she was a girl," Ruben said to Oscar Mendoza, the contractor who lived only a few miles away.

Oscar shrugged. "I have five daughters at home. I never saw a girl in this room." He stopped to reconsider his point and then leaned in toward the Vice President. "I just saw one girl in this room, you know? One woman. There can only be one woman in this room." He tilted his head meaningfully towards the far side of the room where Roxane Coss sat.

Ruben nodded. "Of course," he said. "Of course."

"I am thinking there will never be a better opportunity than this to tell her I love her." Oscar rubbed his hand over his chin. "I don't necessarily mean right now. It doesn't have to be today, although it could be today. These days are so long that by supper the time could be exactly right. You never know until it comes to you, you know? Until you are exactly in that place." He was a big man, well over six feet and broad through the shoulders. He had stayed strong because even though he was a contractor he was not above pitching in and carrying boards or putting up Sheetrock. In this way he remained a fine example to the men who worked for him. Oscar Mendoza had to bend forward so as to speak softly into the Vice President's ear. "But I will do it while we are here. You mark my words."

Ruben nodded. Roxane Coss had given up her evening gown days ago and was now wearing a pair of tan slacks that belonged to his wife as well as his wife's favorite cardigan, a navy sweater of extremely fine baby alpaca he had bought for her on their second anniversary. He had requested a guard accompany him upstairs. He went to the closet himself and brought the sweater down to the soprano. "Are you cold?" he had asked, and then draped the cardigan gently around her shoulders. Was it a betrayal, so quickly giving up the sweater his wife loved? The clothing conflated the two women for him in a way that was extraordinarily pleasing, his beautiful guest wearing the clothes of his wife whom he so dearly missed, the traces of his wife's perfume still lingering inside the ribbing of the sweater so that he could smell both women there when he passed the one. If this wasn't enough to ask, Roxane was wearing a pair of familiar slippers that belonged to the governess, Esmeralda, because his wife's shoes had been too small. How delightful it had been to put his head inside Esmeralda's tiny, meticulous closet!

"Are you going to tell her you love her?" the contractor asked. "It is your home. I would certainly defer to your right to go first."

Ruben considered his guest's thoughtful invitation. "It's a possibility." He was trying not to stare at Roxane. He was failing. He imagined taking her hand, suggesting he could show her the stars from the wide stone veranda that wrapped around the back of the house, that is, he would have if they had been allowed to go outside. He was the Vice President, after all, that might impress her. At least she was not a tall woman. She was a pixie, a pocket Venus. He was grateful for that. "It might not be appropriate, given my position here."

"What's appropriate?" Oscar said. His voice was light and unconcerned. "They're bound to kill us in the end. Either the ones inside or the ones outside. The shooting will start. There will be some terrible mistake, you can bank on it. The ones outside can't let it look like we were not mistreated. It will be important to them we wind up dead. Think of the people, the masses. You can't have them getting the wrong idea. You're the government man. You know more about these things than I do."

"It does happen."

"Then what's the point of not telling her? I, for one, want to know that in my last days I made some effort. I'm going to speak to the young Japanese man, the translator. When the time is right, when I know what I want to say. You can't approach a woman like that too quickly."

Ruben liked the contractor. Although they had never met before, the very fact that they both lived in the same city made them feel like neighbors and then old friends and then brothers. "What do you know about women like that?"

Oscar chuckled and put his hand down on his brother's shoulder. "Little Vice President," he said. "There are so many things that I know." It was big talk but in this place big talk seemed appropriate. While he had lost every freedom he was most accustomed to, a new, smaller set of freedoms began to raise a dim light within him: the liberty to think obsessively, the right to remember in detail. Away from his wife and five daughters he was not contradicted or corrected, and without those burdens he found himself able to dream without constant revision. He had lived his life as a good father but now Oscar Mendoza saw again his life as a boy. A daughter was a battle between fathers and boys in which the fathers fought valiantly and always lost. He knew that one by one each of his daughters would be lost, either honorably in the ceremony of marriage or, realistically, in a car pointed out towards the ocean well after dark. In his day, Oscar himself had made too many girls forget their better instincts and fine training by biting them with tender persistence at the base of their skull, just where the hairline grew in downy wisps. Girls were like kittens in this way, if you got them right at the nape of their neck they went easily limp. Then he would whisper his suggestions, all the things they might do together, the wonderful dark explorations for which he was to be their guide. His voice traveled like a drug dripped down the spiraling canals of their ears until they had forgotten everything, until they had forgotten their own names, until they turned and offered themselves up to him, their bodies sweet and soft as marzipan.

Oscar shuddered at the thought. As he was ready to play the part of the boy again he could see the lines of boys forming around his house, boys ready to assuage the awful grief of his daughters now that their father was held hostage. *Pilar, how awful this must be for you. Isabelle, you mustn't stay shut away. Teresa, your father wouldn't want such suffering. Look at this, I brought you some flowers (or a bird, a skein of yarn, a colored pencil.* IT MADE NO DIFFERENCE). Would his wife have the sense to lock the door? She would never have sense enough to believe that the boys meant them any harm. She believed their lies now just as she had believed him then, when she was a girl and he had come to call while her father lay dying from cancer.

What was he thinking of, chasing after an opera singer? Who were those two girls anyway, Beatriz and Carmen? What were they doing here? Where were their fathers? Probably gunned down in some countryside revolution. What could such girls do to keep the boys away without fathers to protect them? Everywhere in this house there were boys, those awful, surly boys with their greasy hair and bitten fingernails, hoping to touch a breast.

"You look bad," the Vice President said. "All this talk of love isn't agreeing with you."

"When will we get out of here?" Oscar said. He sat down on the sofa and dropped his head onto his knees as if dizzy.

"Get out of here? You're the one who said we would be shot."

"I've changed my mind. No one is going to kill me. I may kill someone, but no one is going to kill me."

Ruben sat down beside him and leaned his good cheek against his friend's broad shoulder. "I won't complain about your inconsistencies. I like this talk better anyhow. Let's assume we'll live." He sat up again. "Here, wait here. I'm going to the kitchen to get you some ice. You won't believe how much better ice can make you feel."

"Do you play the piano?" Roxane Coss said to Gen.

He hadn't seen her coming. His back was to the room while he watched the *garúa* from the bay window. He was learning to relax as he watched it, to not strain his eyes. He was beginning to think he could see things. Mr. Hosokawa looked at Gen expectantly, clearly anxious to know what she was saying, and for a minute Gen was confused as to whether he should answer her or translate first as the question was directed to him. He translated and then told her no, he was sorry to say he did not.

"I thought you might," she said. "You seem to know how to do so many things." She looked towards his companion. "What about Mr. Hosokawa?"

Mr. Hosokawa shook his head sadly. Until their capture, he had thought of his life in terms of achievement and success. Now it struck him as a long list of failures: he didn't speak English or Italian or Spanish. He didn't play the piano. He had never even tried to play the piano. He and Gen didn't have a single lesson between them.

Roxane Coss looked across the room as if she were looking for her accompanist, but he was already half a world away, his grave now covered by an early Swedish frost. "I keep telling myself that this is going to be over soon, that I'm just taking a vacation from work." She looked up at Gen. "Not that I think this is a vacation."

"Of course."

"We've been in this miserable place nearly two weeks. I've never gone a week without singing unless I was sick. I'm going to have to start practicing soon." She leaned in towards the two of them and they bent towards her reflexively. "I really don't want to sing here. I don't want to give them the satisfaction. Do you think it would be worth it to wait another couple of days? Do you think they'll let us go by then?" She glanced over the room again to see if there was a par-ticularly elegant pair of hands folded across a lap.

"Surely someone here must play," Gen said, not wanting to address the other issue.

"The piano is very good. I can play a little but not to accompany myself. I somehow doubt they'd go out and kidnap a new accompa-nist for me." Then she spoke directly to Mr. Hosokawa. "I don't know what to do with myself when I'm not singing. I don't have any talent for vacations."

"I feel very much the same way," he said, his voice growing fainter with each word, "when I am not able to listen to opera."

For this Roxane smiled. Such a dignified man. In the others she could see a look of fear, the occasional brush of panic. Not that there was anything wrong with panic given their circumstances, she had cried herself to sleep most nights. But it never seemed to touch Mr. Hosokawa, or he managed not to show it. And when she stood near him she somehow did not feel the panic herself, though she couldn't explain it. Near him, it felt like she was stepping out of a harsh light and into someplace quiet and dark, like she was wrapping herself up in the heavy velvet of the stage curtains where no one could see her. "You should help me find an accompanist," she told him, "and both of our problems will be solved."

All of her makeup was gone now. For the first few days she bothered to go to the lavatory and put on lipstick from the tube she carried in her evening bag. Then her hair went back in a tight elastic and she was wearing someone else's clothes that did not exactly fit. Mr. Hosokawa thought that every day she was lovelier. He had wanted so many times to ask her to sing but he never would have since singing for him was the thing that had brought her all the trouble in the first place. He wasn't able to ask her for a hand of cards or for her thoughts on the *garúa*. He did not seek her out at all and so Gen did not either. In fact both of them had noticed that (with the exception of the priest, whom she could not understand) all the men in their desire to speak to her had decided to leave her alone as if it was some sort of respect, so alone she sat, hour after hour. Sometimes she cried and other times she thumbed through books or took naps on the sofa. It was a pleasure to watch her sleep. Roxane was the only hostage to have the privilege of a bedroom and her own guard, who slept outside her door, though whether that was to keep her in or to keep other people out no one was entirely sure. Now that they knew the guard was Carmen, they wondered if she was only trying to keep herself safe by staying near such an important person.

"Perhaps the Vice President plays," Mr. Hosokawa suggested. "He has a fine piano."

Gen went off to find the Vice President, who was asleep in a chair, his good cheek pressed to his shoulder, his bad cheek turned up, red and blue and still full of Esmeralda's stitches. The skin was growing up around them. They needed to come out. "Sir?" Gen whispered.

"Hmm?" Ruben said, his eyes closed.

"Do you play the piano?"

"Piano?"

"The one in the living room. Do you know how to play it, sir?"

"They brought it in for the party," Ruben said, trying not to let himself wake up completely. He had been dreaming of Esmeralda standing over the sink, peeling a potato. "There was one that was here before but they took it away because it wasn't good enough. It was good, of course, my daughter takes lessons on it, just not good enough for them," he said, his voice full of sleep. "That piano isn't mine. Neither piano is mine, really."

"But do you know how to play it?"

"The piano?" Ruben finally looked at him and then straightened up his neck.

"Yes."

"No," he said, and smiled. "Isn't that a shame?"

Gen agreed that it was. "You should take those stitches out, I think."

Ruben touched his face. "Do you think they're ready?"

"I'd say so."

Ruben smiled as if he had accomplished something by growing his skin back together again. He went off to find Ishmael to ask him to bring the manicure kit from the bathroom upstairs. Hopefully, the cuticle scissors had not been confiscated as a weapon.

Gen went off on his own to try and find a new accompanist. It wasn't a matter of much linguistic finesse, as piano was more or less piano in many languages. Surely Roxane Coss could have gotten the point across herself with a small amount of gesturing, but she stayed with Mr. Hosokawa and together they stared at the nothingness the window offered up to them.

"Do you play?" Gen asked, beginning with the Russians, who were smoking in the dining room. They squinted at him through the blue haze and then shook their heads. "My God," said Victor Fyodorov, covering his heart with his hands. "What I would not give to know! Tell the Red Cross to send in a teacher and I will learn for her." The other two Russians laughed and threw down their cards. "Piano?" Gen asked the next group. He made his way through the house asking all of the guests, skipping over their captors on the assumption that piano lessons were an impossibility in the jungle. Gen imagined lizards on the foot pedals, humidity warping the keyboard, persistent vines winding their way up the heavy wooden legs. One Spaniard, Manuel Flores; one Frenchman, Étienne Boyer; and one Argentinian, Alejandro Rivas, said they could play a little but didn't read music. Andreas Epictetus said he had played quite well in his youth but hadn't touched a piano in years. "Every day my mother made me practice," he said. "The day I moved away from home I piled up all the music in the back of the house and I lit it, right there with her watching. I haven't laid a finger to a piano since." The rest of them said no, they didn't play. People began recounting stories of a couple of lessons or the lessons of their children. Their voices fell over one another and from every corner of the room there came the word, *piano*, *piano*, *piano*. It seemed to Gen (and he included himself in this assessment) that never had a more uncultured group of men been taken hostage. What had they been doing all these years that no one had bothered with such an important instrument? They all wished they could play, if not before then, certainly now. To be able to play for Roxane Coss.

Then Tetsuya Kato, a vice president at Nansei whom Gen had known for years, smiled and walked to the Steinway without a word. He was a slightly built man in his early fifties with graying hair who, in Gen's memory, rarely spoke. He had a reputation for being very good with numbers. The sleeves to his tuxedo shirt were rolled up above his elbows and his jacket was long gone but he sat down on the bench with great formality. The ones in the living room watched him as he lifted the cover of the keyboard and ran his hands once lightly over the keys, soothing them. Some of the others were still talking about the piano, you could hear the Russians' voices coming from the dining room. Then, without making a request for anyone's attention, Tetsuya Kato began to play. He started with Chopin's Nocturne opus 9 in E Flat major no 2. It was the piece he had most often heard in his head since coming to this country, the one he played silently against the edge of the dining-room table when no one was watching. At home he looked at his sheet music and turned the pages. Now he was certain he had known the music all along. He could see the notes in front of him and he followed them with unerring fidelity. In his heart he had never felt closer to Chopin, whom he loved like a father. How strange his fingers felt after two weeks of not playing, as if the skin he wore now was entirely new. He could hear the softest click of his fingernails, two weeks too long, as he touched the keys. The felt-covered hammers tapped the strings gently at first, and the music, even for those who had never heard the piece before, was like a memory. From all over the house, terrorist and hostage alike turned and listened and felt a great easing in their chests. There was a delicacy about Tetsuya Kato's hands, as if they were simply resting in one place on the keyboard and then in another. Then suddenly his right hand spun out notes like water, a sound so light and high that there was a temptation to look beneath the lid for bells. Kato closed his eyes so that he could imagine he was home, playing his own piano. His wife was asleep. His children, two unmarried sons still living with them, were asleep. For them the notes of Kato's playing had become like air, what they depended on and had long since stopped noticing. Playing on this grand piano now Kato could imagine them sleeping and he put that into the nocturne, his sons' steady breathing, his wife clutching her pillow with one hand. All of the tenderness he felt for them went into the keys. He touched them as if he meant not to wake them. It was the love and loneliness that each of them felt, that no one had brought himself to speak of. Had the accompanist played so well? It would have been impossible to remember, his talent was to be invisible, to lift the soprano up, but now the people in the living room of the vice-presidential mansion listened to Kato with hunger and nothing in their lives had ever fed them so well.

Most of the men there did not know him. Most of them had no distinct memory of having noticed him up to this point, so that in a way it felt that he had come in from the outside world to play for them. None of the men who did know him knew that he played, that he continued his lessons and practiced for an hour every morning before boarding the train for work. It had been important to Kato to have another life, a secret life. Now the secrecy of it did not strike him as important at all.

They were all at the piano, Roxane Coss and Mr. Hosokawa and Gen and Simon Thibault and the priest and the Vice President and Oscar Mendoza and little Ishmael and Beatriz and Carmen, who left her gun in the kitchen and came and stood with the rest. All of the Russians were there, and the Germans who had spoken of a revolt, and the Italians, who were weeping, and the two Greeks who were older than the rest of them. The boys were there, Paco and Ranato and Humberto and Bernardo and all the rest, the great and menacing hulk of boy flesh that seemed to soften with every note. Even the Generals came. Every last one of them came, until there were fifty-eight people in the room, and when he finished Tetsuya Kato bowed his head while they applauded. Had there not been a need for a pianist there was little chance that Kato would have sat down that afternoon to play, though he had watched the piano the way the other men watched the door. He would not have chosen to draw attention to himself, and without his playing the story might have missed him altogether. But there was a need, a specific request, and so he stepped forward.

"Fine, fine," General Benjamin said, feeling good to think the accompanist that had been lost was now replaced.

"Very well done," Mr. Hosokawa said, so proud that it was a Nansei man stepping up for the job. Twenty years he had known Kato. He knew his wife and the names of his children. How was it possible he did not know about the piano?

For a moment the room was very quiet and then Carmen, who had so recently become a girl to them, said something in a language that not even Gen was sure of.

"Encore," the priest said to her.

"Encore," Carmen said.

Kato bowed his head to Carmen, who smiled. Who could have ever mistaken her for one of those boys? Even beneath her cap she was wholly lovely. She knew that people were looking at her and she closed her eyes, unable to go back to the kitchen the way she wanted to, unable to leave the nesting curve of the piano's side. When he played she could feel the vibrations of the strings as she leaned one hip against the wood. No one had ever bowed his head to her before. No one had listened to her request. Certainly, no one had ever played a piece of music for her before.

Kato played another and then another until everyone in the room forgot that they badly wanted to be someplace else. When he was finally finished and could not meet the request of another encore because his hands were trembling with exhaustion, Roxane Coss shook his hand and bowed her head, which established a pact that in the future she would sing and he would play.

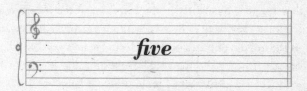

five

*g*en was a busy man. He was needed by Mr. Hosokawa, who wanted another ten words and their pronunciations to add to his book. He was needed by the other hostages, who wanted to know how to say, "Are you finished with that newspaper?" in Greek or German or French, then he was needed to read the newspaper to them if they did not read in Spanish. He was needed by Messner every day to translate the negotiations. Mostly, he was needed by the Generals, who had conveniently mistaken him as Mr. Hosokawa's secretary instead of his translator. They appropriated his services. They liked the idea of having a secretary, and soon they were waking Gen up in the middle of the night, telling him to sit with a pencil and pad while they dictated their latest list of demands for the government. What they wanted seemed to Gen to be unformed. If their plan had been to kidnap the President in order to overthrow the government, they hadn't bothered to think any further than that. Now they talked in generalities about money for the poor. They dredged up the names of every person they had ever known who was in jail, which seemed to Gen to be an inexhaustible list. Late at night, in deliriums of power and generosity, they demanded that everyone be set free. They moved beyond the political prisoners. They remembered the car thieves they had known from boyhood, the petty robbers, men who stole chickens, a handful of drug traffickers who were not entirely bad sorts once you knew them. "Don't forget him," Alfredo said, and gave Gen an irritating poke on the shoulder. "You have no idea how that man has suffered." They admired Gen's neat penmanship, and when they found a typewriter in the bedroom of the Vice President's older daughter, they were impressed with Gen's ability to type. Sometimes, in the middle of transcription, Hector would say, "In English!" and then Alfredo, "In Portuguese!" How amazing it was to watch over his shoulder while he typed on in different languages! It was like having an incredibly fascinating toy. Sometimes, when it was very late, Gen would type up everything in Swedish without benefit of umlauts in an attempt to amuse himself, but he did not feel amused anymore. As far as Gen could tell, there were only two hostages who were not fabulously wealthy and powerful: himself and the priest, and they were the only two who were made to work. Of course, the Vice President worked, but not because anyone had asked him to. He seemed to think that the comfort of his guests was still his responsibility. He was always serving sandwiches and picking up cups. He washed the dishes and swept and twice a day he mopped up the floors in the lavatories. With a dishtowel knotted around his waist, he took on the qualities of a charming hotel concierge. He would ask, would you like some tea? He would ask, would it be too much of an imposition to vacuum beneath the chair in which you were sitting? Everyone was very fond of Ruben. Everyone had completely forgotten that he was the Vice President of the country.

Ruben Iglesias delivered a message to Gen while he waited for the Generals to make up their minds as to what they wanted to say next: he was needed at the piano. Roxane Coss and Kato had a great deal to discuss. Could they spare Gen at this particular moment? They were all in favor of keeping the soprano happy and possibly hearing her sing again, and so they consented to let Gen go. Gen felt like he was a schoolboy called out of class. He remembered his neat box of pencils, the clean pad of paper, the luck of having a desk next to the window simply because of where his name fell in the alphabet. He was a good student, and yet he remembered at every moment how desperately he wished to leave the room. Ruben Iglesias took his arm. "I suppose the problems of the world will have to wait," he whispered, and then he laughed in a way that no one could hear him at all.

Mr. Hosokawa stayed at the piano with Kato and Roxane. It was a pleasure to hear so much talk of opera translated into Japanese, to hear Roxane Coss's conversation in Japanese. It was different to listen to what she said to him and what she said when she was speaking to someone else, speaking to someone about music. There was a regular education to be had from eavesdropping. So much of what was learned was accidentally overheard, just half a sentence caught when walking through the door. Since they had been taken hostage, Mr. Hosokawa had felt the frustration of the deaf. Even as he diligently studied his Spanish, it was only occasionally that he heard a word he recognized. All his life he had wanted more time to listen, and when finally there was time there was nothing to listen to, only the patter of voices he could not understand, the occasional screeching of the police beyond the wall. The Vice President had a stereo system but he seemed only to have a taste for local music. All of his CDs were of bands playing high-pitched pipes and crude drums. The music gave Mr. Hosokawa a headache. The Generals, however, found it inspiring and would not grant requests for new CDs.

But now Mr. Hosokawa pulled his chair up to the piano and listened. Everyone stayed in the living room, hostages and terrorists alike, in hopes that Kato might be persuaded to play again or, better still, that Roxane Coss might sing. Carmen seemed especially intent on watching Roxane. She considered herself to be Roxane's bodyguard, her personal responsibility. She stood in the corner and stared at their party with unwavering concentration. Beatriz chewed on the end of her braid for a while, making talk with the boys her own age. When no music seemed to be immediately forthcoming, she and a few of her cohorts snuck off to watch television.

Only Mr. Hosokawa and Gen were invited to sit with the two

principal players. "I like to sing scales first thing in the morning," Roxane said. "After breakfast. I'll work on some songs, Bellini, Tosti, Schubert. If you can play the Chopin, you can play those." Roxane ran her fingers over the keys, placing her hands for the opening of Schubert's "Die Forelle."

"If we can get the music," Kato said.

"If we can get dinner brought in we can get sheet music. I'll have my manager put a box together and send it down. Someone can fly it down. Tell me what you want." Roxane looked around for a piece of paper and Mr. Hosokawa was able to produce his notebook and pen from the inside pocket of his jacket. He opened it to a blank page towards the back and handed it to her.

"Ah, Mr. Hosokawa," Roxane said. "Imprisonment would be something else altogether without you."

"Surely you've been given nicer gifts than a pad of paper and a pen," Mr. Hosokawa said.

"The quality of the gift depends on the sincerity of the giver. It also helps if the gift is something the receiver actually wants. So far you've given me your handkerchief, your notebook, and your pen. All three things I wanted."

"The little I have here is yours," he said with a sincerity that didn't match her lightness. "You could have my shoes. My watch."

"You have to save something for the future so you can surprise me." Roxane tore off a sheet of paper and handed the notebook back. "Keep up with your studies. If we stay here long enough we'll be able to cut Gen out of the loop."

Gen translated and then added, "I'll put myself out of business."

"You can always go back to the jungle with them," Roxane said, looking over her shoulder at the Generals, who spent their free time watching her. "They seem to want to give you a job."

"I would never give him up," Mr. Hosokawa said.

"Sometimes," Roxane said, touching Mr. Hosokawa's wrist for just a second, "these matters are out of our control."

Mr. Hosokawa smiled at her. He was reeling with the naturalness of their discourse, the sudden ease with which they passed the time. Imagine if it hadn't been Kato who played the piano! It could have been one of the Greeks or a Russian. Then he would have been locked out again, listening to English translated to Greek and Greek into English, knowing that Gen, *his* translator, would not have the time to then repeat every sentence in Japanese. Kato said he would like some Fauré if it wouldn't be too much trouble, and Roxane laughed and said that nothing could be trouble at this point. Wonderful Kato! He scarcely seemed to notice her. It was the piano he couldn't take his eyes off. He had always been a tireless worker and now he was the hero of the day. There would be a healthy raise when all of this was over.

Messner came in as usual at eleven in the morning. Two of the young soldiers patted him down at the door. They made him take off his shoes and they peered inside them, looking for tiny weapons. They patted his legs and frisked beneath his arms. It was a ridiculous habit that had grown not out of suspicion but out of boredom. The Generals struggled to keep their soldiers in the mind-set of battle. More and more the teenagers sprawled on the leather sofa in the Vice President's den and watched television. They took long showers and trimmed each other's hair with a pair of elegant silver scissors they found in the desk. And so the Generals doubled the night watch and guard duty. They made their soldiers patrol the house in pairs and sent two more outside to walk along the edge of the yard in the drizzling rain. When they went, they carried their rifles loaded and held them up as if they were looking to shoot a rabbit.

Messner submitted to this drill with patience. He opened his briefcase and slipped off his shoes. He held his arms out straight to either side and moved his sock feet wide apart so that the strange little hands could rummage around his body as they saw fit. Once, one of them tickled him on the ribs and Messner brought his arm down sharply. "*¡Basta!*" he said. He had never seen such an unprofessional group of terrorists. It was a complete and utter mystery to him how they had ever managed to overtake the house.

General Benjamin swatted Ranato, the boy who had tickled Messner, and took his gun away from him. All he had hoped for was some semblance of military order. "There is no call for that," he said sharply.

Messner sat down in a chair and retied his shoes. He was irritated with the whole lot of them. By now this trip should be forgotten, the snapshots developed, shared, and placed into an album. He should be back in his overpriced apartment in Geneva with the good view and the Danish Modern furniture he had so carefully collected. He should be taking a packet of mail from the cool hands of his secretary in the morning. Instead he went to work, inquiring how the group was doing. He had been practicing his Spanish, and even though he kept Gen close by, for a sense of security as much as a backup for his vocabulary, he was able to conduct much of the informal conversation on his own.

"We are growing tired of this," the General said, and ran his hands back over his head. "We want to know why your people cannot find resolution. Must we start killing hostages to get your attention?"

"Well, first off, they are not *my* people." Messner pulled the laces tight. "Nor is it *my* attention you should be trying for. Don't kill anyone for my benefit. You have my complete attention. I should have gone home a week ago."

"We all should have gone home a week ago," General Benjamin sighed. "But we have to see our brothers released." For General Benjamin, of course, this meant both his philosophical comrades and his literal brother, Luis. Luis, who had committed the crime of distributing flyers for a political protest and was now buried alive in a high-altitude prison. Before his brother's arrest, Benjamin had not been a general at all. He had taught grade school. He had lived in the south of the country near the ocean. He had never had a moment's trouble with his nerves.

"That is the issue," Messner said, looking over the room, doing a quick tally of all present.

"And is there progress?"

"Nothing I've heard of today." He reached into his case and took out a sheaf of papers. "I have these for you. Their demands. If there's anything new you want me to request—"

"Señorita Coss," General Benjamin said, hitching his thumb in her direction. "There's something she wants."

"Ah, yes."

"There is always something for Señorita Coss," the General said. "Kidnapping women is a different business entirely from the kidnapping of men. I hadn't thought of it before. For our people, freedom. For her, something else, dresses possibly."

"I'll see about it," Messner said, and tipped his head, but he didn't get up to leave right away. "Is there anything I can get for you?" He indicated nothing directly but he was wondering about the shingles, which every day seemed to cast their coarse red net another millimeter across the General's face and would soon be dipping their fingers into the cool water of his left eye.

"There is nothing I require."

Messner nodded and excused himself. He preferred Benjamin to the other two. He found him to be a reasonable man, possibly even intelligent. Still, he worked hard to prevent any feeling of real fondness for him, for any of them, captors or hostages. Fondness often prevented one from doing the most effective job. Besides, Messner knew how these stories usually ended. It seemed better to avoid much personal involvement.

But no sensible rules applied to Roxane Coss. Most days there was something she wanted, and while the Generals could care less about the requests of the other hostages they were quick to give in to her. Every time she asked for something, Messner would feel his heart quicken slightly, as if it was him she wanted to see. One day it was dental floss, one day a muffler, then some herbal throat lozenges that Messner was proud to note came from Switzerland. Other hostages had gotten into the habit of asking Roxane when there was something that they needed. When she asked for men's socks or sailing magazines, she never blinked.

"Have you heard the good news?" Roxane said.

"There's good news now?" Messner tried to be rational. He tried to understand what it was about her. Standing next to her, he could look down on the place where her hair parted. She was just like the rest of them, wasn't she? Except, perhaps, for the color of her eyes.

"Mr. Kato plays the piano."

At the mention of his name, Kato stood up from the piano bench and bowed to Messner. They had not been introduced before. All of the hostages greatly admired Messner, both for his calm demeanor and his seemingly magic ability to go in and out of the front door at will.

"At least I'm going to be able to practice again," Roxane said. "On the off chance that we ever get out of here, I still want to be able to sing."

Messner said he hoped he would have an opportunity to hear the rehearsals. For a brief, disquieting moment Messner felt something that was not unlike jealousy. The hostages were there all the time, so if she decided to sing first thing in the morning or in the middle of the night, they would be able to hear her. He had bought himself a portable CD player and as much of her music as he could find. At night he lay in his two-star hotel room paid for by the International Red Cross and listened to her sing *Norma* and *La Sonnambula*. He would be lying alone in his uncomfortable bed looking at the spidery cracks in the ceiling and they would all be there in the grand living room of the vice-presidential estate while she sang "Casta Diva."

Enough, Messner said to himself.

"I've always had closed rehearsals," Roxane said. "I don't believe that anyone is entitled to hear my mistakes. But I doubt there would be much point in trying to arrange that here. I can hardly march them all up to the attic."

"They could hear you in the attic."

"I'd make them stuff cotton in their ears." Roxane laughed at this and Messner was moved. Everything in the house seemed more tolerable since this new accompanist had stepped forward.

"So what can I do for you?" If Gen had been turned into a secretary, then Messner had become the errand boy. In Switzerland he was a member of an elite arbitration team. At forty-two he had had a very successful career with the Red Cross. He had not packed a box of food supplies or driven blankets to a flood sight in almost twenty years. Now he was scouring the city for orange-flavored chocolate and calling a friend in Paris to send an expensive eye cream that came in a small black tub.

"I need music," she said, and handed over her list. "Call my manager and tell him to send this overnight. Tell him to fly it down himself if he thinks there could be any problem. I want this by tomorrow."

"You might have to be a little more reasonable than tomorrow," Messner said. "It's already dark in Italy."

Messner and Roxane spoke in English, with Gen discreetly translating their private conversation into Japanese. Father Arguedas sidled up to the piano, not wanting to interfere but wanting very much to know what was being said.

"Gen," he whispered. "What does she need?"

"Sheet music," Gen said, and then remembered the question had been asked in Spanish. "*Partitura.*"

"Does Messner know who to speak to? Does he know where to go?"

Gen liked the priest and didn't mean to be annoyed but Mr. Hosokawa and Kato clearly meant to follow what was being said in Japanese and he was falling behind on the conversation taking place in English. "They'll contact her people in Italy." Gen turned his back on Father Arguedas and returned to the work at hand.

The priest tugged at Gen's sleeve. Gen held up his hand to ask him to wait.

"But I know where the music is," the priest persisted. "Not two miles from here. There is a man that I know, a music teacher, a deacon in our parish. He loans me records. He has all the music you would need." His voice was becoming loud. Father Arguedas, who had devoted his life to doing good works, was nearly frantic for the want of some good works to do. He helped Ruben with the laundry and in the morning he folded all the blankets and stacked them with the pillows in neat rows against the wall, but he longed to provide assistance and guidance of a more profound nature. He couldn't help but feel he stayed just on the edge of bothering people rather than comforting them, when all that he wanted, the only thing that mattered, was to be helpful.

"What is it he's saying?" Roxane asked.

"What are you saying?" Gen asked the priest.

"The music is here. You could call. Manuel would bring it over, anything you need. If there was something he didn't have, and I can't imagine it, he would find it for you. All you need to say is that it is for Señorita Coss. You wouldn't even have to say that. He is a Christian man. If you tell him you need it for any reason, I promise he will help you." Her eyes were dazzling in their agitation. His hands leapt in front of his chest as if he was trying to offer up his own heart.

"He would have Bellini?" Roxane asked after listening to the translation. "I need songs. I need to have entire opera scores, Rossini, Verdi, Mozart." She leaned towards the priest and asked for the impossible straight on. "Offenbach."

"Offenbach! *Les Contes d'Hoffmann*!" The priest's pronunciation of the French was discernible if not good. He had only seen it written out on the record.

"He would have that?" she said to Gen.

Gen repeated the question and the priest replied, "I have seen his scores. Call him, the name is Manuel. I would be most grateful to place the call if I were allowed."

Because General Benjamin was locked in a room upstairs holding a heating pad to his inflamed face and could not be disturbed,

Messner made the request to the Generals Hector and Alfredo, who granted it with bored indifference.

"For Señorita Coss," Messner explained.

General Hector nodded and waved him away without looking. When Messner was almost out of the room, General Alfredo barked, "Only one call!" thinking they hadn't shown proper authority by agreeing so quickly. They were in the den, watching the President's favorite soap opera. The heroine, Maria, was telling her lover she did not love him anymore in hopes that he would leave town in desperation and thus be protected from his own brother, who, in his love for Maria, sought to murder him. Messner stood in the doorway for a moment to watch the girl on television cry. So completely convincing was her grief that it was difficult for him to turn away.

"Call Manuel," he said, coming back to the living room. Ruben went to the kitchen and brought back the telephone directory and Messner gave the priest his cellular phone and showed him how to dial out.

On the third ring there was an answer. *"Alo!"*

"Manuel?" the priest said. "Manuel, hello?" He felt his voice choke with emotion. Someone outside the house! It was like seeing a ghost from his former life, a silvery shadow walking down the aisle towards the altar. Manuel. He had not been in captivity two full weeks but upon hearing that voice the priest felt as if he were dead to the world.

"Who is this?" The voice was suspicious.

"It is your friend, Father Arguedas." The priest's eyes filled with tears and he held up his hand to excuse himself from the crowd and stepped into the corner, into the lustrous folds of the draperies.

There was a long silence on the other end. "Is this a joke?"

"Manuel, no, I'm calling."

"Father?"

"I am in—" he said, but then faltered. "I have been detained."

"We know all about that. Father, are you well? Do they treat you all right? They let you make phone calls there?"

"I am well. I am fine. The call, no, it is a special circumstance."

"We say the mass for you every day." Now it was his friend's voice that was breaking. "I only came home for lunch. I have only just walked in the door. If you had called five minutes before I wouldn't have been here. Are you safe? We hear terrible things."

"They say the mass for me?" Father Arguedas wrapped his hand around the heavy draperies and rested his cheek against the soft cloth. To the best of his knowledge, he had been remembered in the mass along with twenty-three others on the Sunday before he took his holy orders, and that was all. To think of those people, the people he prayed for, praying for him. To think that God heard his name from so many voices. "They must pray for all of us here, the hostages and captors alike."

"We do," Manuel said. "But the mass is offered in your name."

"I can't believe this," he whispered.

"Does he have the music?" Roxane asked and then Gen asked the priest.

Father Arguedas remembered himself. "Manuel." He coughed to try and clear the emotion from his voice. "I'm calling to ask you for a favor."

"Anything, my friend. Do they want money?"

The priest smiled to think with all these wealthy men around it would be put to him to ask a music teacher for money. "Nothing like that. I need sheet music. There is a singer here—"

"Roxane Coss."

"You know everything," he said, taking comfort in his friend's concern. "She needs music to practice with."

"I heard her accompanist was dead. Murdered by the terrorists. I heard they cut off his hands."

Father Arguedas was shocked. What else did people say about them now that they were gone? "It was nothing like that. He died all on his own. The man was a diabetic." Should he defend the people who kept them? Surely, they should not be falsely accused of cutting the hands off a pianist. "It isn't so bad here. I don't mind it, really. We've found another accompanist. Someone who is here who plays very well, I think," he said, dropping his voice to a whisper. "Perhaps even better than the first one. She wants things in a wide range, opera scores, Bellini songs, Chopin for the accompanist. I have a list."

"There is nothing she needs that I don't have," Manuel said confidently.

The priest could hear his friend rummaging for paper, a pen. "I told her that."

"You spoke of me to Roxane Coss?"

"Of course. That's why I'm calling."

"She's heard my name?"

"She wants to sing from your music," the priest said.

"Even when you are locked away you manage to do good work." Manuel sighed. "What an honor for me. I will bring them now. I will skip lunch completely."

The two men conferred about the list and then Father Arguedas double-checked it with Gen. When everything was settled, the priest asked his friend to hold the line. He hesitated and then he held out the phone to Roxane. "Ask her to say something," he said to Gen.

"What?"

"Anything. It doesn't matter. Ask her to say the names of the operas. Would she do that?"

Gen made the request and Roxane Coss took the small phone from the priest's hand and held it to her ear. "Hello?" she said.

"Hello?" Manuel parroted in English.

She looked at the priest and she smiled. She looked right at him while she said the names into the phone. "*La Bohème,*" she said. "*Così fan tutti.*"

"Dear God," Manuel whispered.

"*La Gioconda, I Capuleti e i Montecchi, Madama Butterfly.*"

It was as if a white light filled up the priest's chest, a hot sort of brightness that made his eyes water and his heart beat like a desperate man pounding on the church door at night. Had he been able to lift up his hands to touch her he could not be sure he could have stopped himself. But it didn't matter. He was paralyzed by her voice, the music of speaking, the rhythmic loops of the names that passed through her lips, into the phone, and then into Manuel's ear some two miles away. The priest knew then for sure that he would survive this. That there would come a day when he would sit at Manuel's kitchen table in his small apartment cluttered with music and they would shamelessly recount the pleasure of this exact moment. He would have to live if only to have that cup of coffee with his friend. And while they would remember, try to place in order the names that she spoke, Father Arguedas would know that he had been the more fortunate of the two because it was he whom she had looked at when she spoke.

"Give me the phone," Simon Thibault said to Messner when they were done.

"He said one call."

"I couldn't care less what he said. Give me the goddamn phone."

"Simon."

"They're watching *television*. Give me the phone." The terrorists had removed all the cords from the phones.

Messner sighed and handed him the phone. "One minute."

"I swear it," Simon said. He was already dialing the number. The phone rang five times and then the answering machine picked up the line. It was his own voice, saying first in Spanish and then again in French that they were out, saying they would return the call. Why hadn't Edith recorded the message? What had he been thinking of? He put his hand over his eyes and began to cry. The sound of his own voice was almost unbearable to him. When it stopped there was a long, dull tone. *"Je t'adore,"* he said. *"Je t'aime, Je t'adore."*

* * *

Everyone was scattering now, wandering off to their chairs to nap or play a hand of solitaire. After Roxane walked away and Kato returned to the letter he had been writing to his sons (he had so much to tell them now!) Gen noticed that Carmen was still in her place on the other side of the room and that she wasn't watching the singer or the accompanist anymore. She was watching him. He felt that same tightness he felt when she had looked at him before. That face, which had seemed pretty to a disadvantage when it was assigned to a boy, did not blink or move or even appear to breathe. Carmen did not wear her cap. Her eyes were large and dark and frozen onto Gen, as if by looking away she would be admitting that she had been looking in the first place.

Gen, in his genius for languages, was often at a loss for what to say when left with only his own words. If Mr. Hosokawa had still been sitting there he might have said to Gen, Go and see what that girl wants, and Gen would go and ask her without hesitation. It had occurred to him in his life that he had the soul of a machine and was only capable of motion when someone else turned the key. He was very good at working and he was very good at being by himself. Sitting alone in his apartment with books and tapes, he would pick up languages the way other men picked up women, with smooth talk and then later, passion. He would scatter books on the floor and pick them up at random. He read Czeslaw Milosz in Polish, Flaubert in French, Chekhov in Russian, Nabokov in English, Mann in German, then he switched them around: Milosz in French, Flaubert in Russian, Mann in English. It was like a game, a showy parlor trick he performed only for himself, in which the constant switching kept his mind sharp, but it was hardly the same thing as being able to approach a person who was looking at you intently from across a room. Perhaps the Generals were right about him after all.

Carmen wore a wide leather belt around her narrow waist and into the right side she had stuck a pistol. Her green fatigues were not dirty the way the fatigues of her compatriots were and the tear in the knee of her pants had been neatly sewn together with the same needle and thread Esmeralda had used to stitch together the Vice President's face. Esmeralda had left the spool with the needle sticking out of it on the side table when she had finished her work and Carmen had surreptitiously dropped them into her pocket the first chance she got. She had been hoping to speak to the translator since she realized what it was he did, but couldn't figure out a way to speak to him without letting him know she was a girl. Then Beatriz took care of that and now there was no secret, no reason to wait, except for the fact that she seemed to be stuck against the wall. He had seen her. He was looking at her now, and that seemed to be as far as things were able to progress. She could not walk away and she was equally unable to walk towards him. Life could very well be lived out in that spot. She tried to remember her aggressiveness, all the things the Generals had taught her in training, but it was one thing to take what you must for the good of the people and quite another to ask for something for yourself. She knew nothing at all about asking.

"Dear Gen," Messner said, clapping a hand down on his shoulder. "I've never seen you sitting alone. You must feel at times that everyone has something to say and no one knows how to say it."

"At times," Gen said absently. He felt if he were to blow in her direction she would be lifted up in the current of air and would simply bob away like a feather.

"We are the handmaidens of circumstance, you and I." Messner spoke to Gen in French, the language he spoke at home in Switzerland. "What would be the male equivalent to handmaiden?"

"*Esclave,*" Gen said.

"Yes, slave, of course, but it doesn't sound as nice. I think I'll stay with handmaidens. I don't mind that." Messner sat down next to Gen on the piano bench and let his eyes follow the course of Gen's stare. "My God," he said quietly. "Isn't that a girl there?"

Gen told him it was.

"Where did she come from? There were no girls. Don't tell me they've found a way to get more of their troops inside."

"She was always here," Gen said. "Two of them. We just didn't notice. That's Carmen. Beatriz, the other one, is in watching television."

"We didn't notice her?"

"Apparently not," Gen said, feeling quite sure he had noticed.

"I was just in the den."

"Then you overlooked Beatriz again."

"Beatriz. And this one is Carmen. Well," Messner said, standing up. "Then there's something wrong with the whole lot of us. Be my translator. I want to speak to her."

"Your Spanish is fine."

"My Spanish is halting and my verbs are improperly conjugated. Get up. Look at her, Gen. She's staring right at you." It was true. So fearful had Carmen become when she saw that Messner meant to come towards her that she had lost her ability to even blink. She was now staring in much the same way a figure stares from a portrait. She prayed to Saint Rose of Lima to grant her that rarest of gifts: to become invisible. "Either she's been commanded to watch you on the penalty of her death or she has something to say."

Gen got up. He was a translator. He would go and translate Messner's conversation. Still, he felt a peculiar fluttering in his chest, a sensation that was not entirely dissimilar to an itch but was located just beneath his ribs.

"Such a remarkable thing and no one even mentioned it," Messner said.

"We were all thinking about the new accompanist," Gen said, his knees feeling looser with every step. Femur, patella, tibia. "We had already forgotten about the girls."

"I suppose it's terribly sexist of me assuming that all of the terrorists were male. It's a modern world, after all. One should suppose a girl can grow up to be a terrorist just as easily as a boy."

"I can't imagine it," Gen said.

When they were three feet away, Carmen found the strength to put her right hand on her gun, which immediately stopped them from coming any closer.

"Do you mean to shoot us?" Messner said in French, a simple sentence he couldn't say in Spanish because he didn't know the word for *shoot*, a word he imagined he should make a point to learn. Gen translated and his voice sounded uncertain. Carmen, wide-eyed, her forehead damp, said nothing.

"Are we certain she speaks Spanish? Are we certain she speaks?" Messner said to Gen.

Gen asked her if she spoke Spanish.

"*Poquito,*" she whispered.

"Don't shoot," Messner said with good nature, and pointed to the gun.

Carmen pulled her hand away and crossed her arms over her chest. "I don't," she said.

"How old are you?"

She said that she was seventeen and they assumed she was telling the truth.

"What is your first language?" Messner asked her.

Gen asked her what she spoke at home.

"Quechua," she said. "We all speak Quechua but we know Spanish." And then, in her first attempt to address what she wanted, she said, "I should know Spanish better." The words came out in a dull croak.

"Your Spanish is good," Gen said.

The expression on her face changed with this compliment. No one could stretch the truth so much as to call it a smile, but her eyebrows lifted and her face tilted up towards them a centimeter or so as if it was drawn towards sunlight. "I am trying to learn better."

"How did a girl like you get tied up with a bunch like this?" Messner said. Gen found the question overly direct but certainly Messner knew enough Spanish to catch him if he were to ask her another question entirely.

"I work to free the people," she said.

Messner scratched the back of his neck. "It's always 'Free the

People.' I never know exactly which people they mean or what it is they want to free them from. I certainly recognize the problems but there is such a vagueness to 'Free the People.' It's easier to negotiate with bank robbers, really. They only want the money. They want to take the money and free themselves and the people be damned. There's something much more straightforward about that, don't you think?"

"Are you asking me or her?"

Messner looked at Carmen and apologized in Spanish. "That is rude of me," he said to Gen. "My Spanish is very poor," Messner said to Carmen, "but I'm trying to improve as well."

"*Sí,*" she said. She should not be talking to them like this. The Generals could come in. Anyone could see her. She was too much out in the open.

"Are you being treated well? Are you in good health?"

"*Sí,*" she said again, although she wasn't sure why he was asking.

"She's really a very lovely girl," he said to Gen in French. "She has a remarkable face. It's almost a perfect heart. Don't tell her that, though. She looks like the kind that could die of embarrassment." Then he turned to Carmen. "If there's anything you need, you let one of us know."

"*Sí,*" she said, just barely able to make a sound come out with the shape of the word.

"You don't see many shy terrorists," Messner said in French. They all stood there as if it was a painful moment at a long, dull cocktail party.

"You like the music," Gen said.

"Very beautiful," she whispered.

"It was Chopin."

"Kato played Chopin?" Messner said. "The nocturnes? I'm sorry I missed that."

"Chopin played," Carmen said.

"No," Gen said. "The man who played was Señor Kato. The music he played was written by Señor Chopin."

"Very beautiful," she said again, and suddenly her eyes welled up with tears and she parted her lips slightly not to speak but to breathe.

"What is the matter?" Messner said. He was going to touch her shoulder and then thought better of it. The big boy named Gilbert called to her from the other side of the room and hearing her name it was as if her power of movement was restored. She quickly rubbed her eyes and stepped around the two men without so much as nodding. They turned and watched her dart off across the wide expanse of the living room and then disappear down the hall with the boy.

"Perhaps the music was getting to her," Messner said.

Gen stood watching the empty place where she had been. "It would be hard on a girl," he said. "All of this."

And while Messner started to say it was hard on them all he knew what Gen meant and frankly, he agreed.

Whenever Messner left there was a lingering sadness in the house that could last for hours. It was very quiet inside and no one listened to the tedious messages the police continued to broadcast from the other side of the wall. *Hopeless, Surrender, Will Not Negotiate.* It droned on until the words simply broke down into a dull buzz, the angry sound of hornets scouring the nest. They imagined what prisoners felt like when the visiting hour was over and there was nothing left to do but sit in their cell and wonder if it was dark yet outside. They were still deep in their afternoon bout of depression, still thinking about all the elderly relatives they never went to visit, when Messner knocked again. Simon Thibault lifted his face from the blue scarf that hung around his neck and General Benjamin motioned for the Vice President to answer the door. Ruben took a moment to untie the dishtowel from his waist. The people with the guns motioned for him to hurry. It was Messner, they knew it. Only Messner came to the door.

"What a lovely surprise," the Vice President said.

Messner was standing on the front steps, struggling to hold a heavy box in his arms.

The Generals had thought that this knock out of schedule indicated a breakthrough, a chance to put this thing to rest. They were that hopeless, that hopeful. When they saw it was only another delivery they felt a crush of disappointment. They wanted none of it. "This isn't his time," General Alfredo said to Gen. "He knows what times he is allowed to come." General Alfredo had fallen asleep in his chair. He had suffered from terrible insomnia ever since their arrival at the Vice President's estate and anyone who woke him from the little sleep he managed would live to regret it. He always dreamed of bullets zipping past his ears. When he woke up his shirt was drenched, his heart was racing, and he was always more exhausted than he had been before he slept.

"It seemed to me to be a special circumstance," Messner said. "The music has arrived."

"We are an army," Alfredo said sharply. "Not a conservatory. Come at your time tomorrow and we will discuss the issue of allowing music."

Roxane Coss asked Gen if it was her music, and when he told her yes she was on her feet. The priest approached the door as well. "These are from Manuel?"

"He's just on the other side of the wall," Messner said. "He sent this all for you."

Father Arguedas pressed his folded hands to his lips. *Everpowerful and merciful God, we do well always and everywhere to give You thanks and praise.*

"Both of you, sit down," General Alfredo said.

"I'll put this inside the door," Messner said, and started to bend down. It was surprising how much music could weigh.

"No," Alfredo said. He had a headache. He was sick to death of giving in on things. There needed to be some order to this business, some respect for authority. Wasn't he the man with the gun? Didn't that count for something? If he said the box would not come inside then the box would not come inside. General Benjamin whispered something in Alfredo's ear but Alfredo simply repeated his point. "No."

Roxane pulled on Gen's arm. "Isn't that mine? Tell them that."

Gen asked if the box belonged to Miss Coss.

"Nothing *belongs* to Señorita Coss! She is a prisoner like the rest of you. This is not her home. There is no special mail service that applies only to her. She does not receive packages." The tone of Alfredo's voice made all the junior terrorists stand up straight and look menacing, for many of them all this took was to put their hands on their guns.

Messner sighed and shifted the weight in his arms. "Then I will come back tomorrow." He spoke in English now, he spoke to Roxane and let Gen translate for the Generals.

He had not left, he had barely started to turn away from the house when Roxane Coss closed her eyes and opened her mouth. In retrospect, it was a risky thing to do, both from the perspective of General Alfredo, who might have seen it as an act of insurrection, and from the care of the instrument of the voice itself. She had not sung in two weeks, nor did she go through a single scale to warm up. Roxane Coss, wearing Mrs. Iglesias's slacks and a white dress shirt belonging to the Vice President, stood in the middle of the vast living room and began to sing "O Mio Babbino Caro" from Puccini's *Gianni Schicchi*. There should have been an orchestra behind her but no one noticed its absence. No one would have said her voice sounded better with an orchestra, or that it was better when the room was immaculately clean and lit by candles. They did not notice the absence of flowers or champagne, in fact, they knew now that flowers and champagne were unnecessary embellishments. Had she really not been singing all along? The sound was no more beautiful when her voice was limber and warm. Their eyes clouded over with tears for so many reasons it would be impossible to list them all. They cried for the beauty of the music, certainly, but also for the failure of their plans. They were thinking of the last time they had heard her sing and longed for the women who had been beside them then. All of the love and the longing a body can contain was spun into not more than two and a half minutes of song, and when she came to the highest notes it seemed that all they had been given in their lives and all they had lost came together and made a weight that was almost impossible to bear. When she was finished, the people around her stood in stunned and shivering silence. Messner leaned into the wall as if struck. He had not been invited to the party. Unlike the others, he had never heard her sing before.

Roxane took a deep breath and rolled her shoulders. "Tell him," she said to Gen, "that's it. Either he gives me that box right now or you will not hear another note out of me or that piano for the duration of this failed social experiment."

"Really?" Gen asked.

"I don't bluff," the soprano said.

So Gen related the message and all eyes turned to General Alfredo. He pinched the bridge of his nose and tried to push down the headache but it didn't work. The music had confused him to the point of senselessness. He could not hold on to his convictions. Now he was thinking of his sister who had died of scarlet fever when he was just a boy. These hostages were like terrible children, always wanting more for themselves. They knew nothing of what it meant to suffer. He would have been glad to walk out of the house at that moment and take whatever fate was waiting for him on the other side of the wall, a lifetime in prison or a bullet in the head. With so little sleep he was in no condition to make decisions. Every possible conclusion seemed like madness. Alfredo turned and left the room, walking down the long hallway towards the Vice President's study. After a time the faint voices of television news could be heard and General Benjamin told Messner to get inside and sharply instructed his soldiers to check thoroughly the contents of the box for anything that was not music. He tried to make it sound as if it was his decision, that he was the one in charge, but even he could see this was no longer true.

The soldiers took the box from Messner and emptied it out on the floor. There were loose scores and bound books, hundreds of pages

covered in the alphabet of song. They sifted through them and separated them, shaking out handfuls as if there might be money caught
between the pages.

"Amazing," Messner said. "I watched the police tear through
them outside and now we have to go through it all again.

Kato went and knelt down beside the boys. Once they had
checked a piece of paper, Kato took it from them. He carefully separated Rossini from Verdi, put Chopin with Chopin. Sometimes he
would stop and read a page as if it were a letter from home, his head
swaying with the timed beat. When he found something of particular
interest he would take it to Roxane and hand it to her, bowing from
the waist. He did not ask for Gen to translate. Everything she needed
to know was there.

"Manuel sends you his best regards," Messner told Father
Arguedas. "He said if there is anything else that is needed he will find
it for you."

The priest knew he committed the sin of pride and still he was
overjoyed at having been able to play a role in bringing in the music.
He was still too dizzy from the sound of Roxane's voice to express
himself properly. He looked to see if the windows were open. He
hoped that Manuel had been able to hear a line, a note, from where
he stood on the sidewalk. What a blessing he had received in his captivity. The mysteries of Christ's love had never been closer to him, not
when he said the mass or received communion, not even on the day he
took holy orders. He realized now he was only just beginning to see
the full extent to which it was his destiny to follow, to walk blindly
into fates he could never understand. In fate there was reward, in
turning over one's heart to God there was a magnificence that lay
beyond description. At the moment one is sure that all is lost, look at
what is gained!

Roxane Coss did not sing again that day. Her voice had been asked
to do enough. Now she contented herself to look through the scores,

sitting on the small couch by the window with Mr. Hosokawa. When one of them had something to say they would call to Gen, but what was surprising was how rarely they needed him. He was a comfort to her. In the absence of language, she believed that he agreed with her completely. She would hum a little of the scores quietly so that he knew what she was looking at and then they would look at the pages together. Mr. Hosokawa could not read music but he accepted that. He did not speak the language of the libretto, the singer, or the host. He was beginning to feel more at ease with all he had lost, all he didn't know. Instead, he was astonished by what he had: the chance to sit beside this woman in the late afternoon light while she read. Her hand brushed his as she set the pages down on the couch between them, and then her hand rested on top of his hand while she continued to read.

After a while Kato approached them. He bowed to Roxane and then bowed again to Mr. Hosokawa. "Do you think it would be all right if I played?" Kato asked his employer.

"I think it would be fine," Mr. Hosokawa said.

"You don't think it would disturb her reading?"

Roxane watched while Mr. Hosokawa pantomimed playing the piano and then nodded to Kato.

"Yes," she said, nodding. She held out her hand for the music.

Kato handed it to her. "Satie," he said.

"Satie." She smiled and nodded again. Kato went to the piano and he played. It wasn't like the last time he had played, when no one could believe that such a talent had been in the room among them without anyone knowing it. It was nothing like Roxane singing, where it seemed that everyone's heart would have to wait until she had finished before it could beat again. The Satie was only music. They could hear its beauty without being paralyzed by it. The men were able to read their books or look out the window while Kato played. Roxane continued to leaf through the scores, though every now and then she stopped and closed her eyes. Only Mr. Hosokawa and the priest completely understood the importance of the music.

Every note was distinct. It was the measurement of the time which had gotten away from them. It was the interpretation of their lives in the very moment they were being lived.

There was one other person there who understood the music, but she was not a guest. Standing in the hallway, looking around the corner to the living room, was Carmen, and Carmen, though she did not have the words for it, understood everything perfectly. This was the happiest time of her life and it was because of the music. When she was a child dreaming on her pallet at night, she never dreamed of pleasures like these. None of her family, left behind in the mountains, could have understood that there was a house made of bricks and sealed glass windows that was never too hot or too cold. She could not have believed that somewhere in the world there was a vast expanse of carpet embroidered to look like a meadow of flowers, or that ceilings came tipped in gold, or that there could be pale marble women who stood on either side of a fireplace and balanced the mantelpiece on their heads. And that would have been enough, the music and the paintings and the garden which she patrolled with her rifle, but in addition there was food that came every day, so much food that some was always wasted no matter how hard they tried to eat it all. There were deep white bathtubs with an endless supply of hot water pouring out of the curved silver spigots. There were stacks of soft white towels and pillows and blankets trimmed in satin and so much space inside that you could wander off and no one would know where you had gone. Yes, the Generals wanted something better for the people, but weren't they the people? Would it be the worst thing in the world if nothing happened at all, if they all stayed together in this generous house? Carmen prayed hard. She prayed while standing near the priest in hopes it would give her request extra credibility. What she prayed for was nothing. She prayed that God would look on them and see the beauty of their existence and leave them alone.

* * *

It was Carmen's night for watch. There was a long wait before everyone had gone to sleep. Some of them read with flashlights, others tossed and stretched in the great room where they all bedded down together. They were like children, up and down for water and then the bathroom. But once they were all still, she crept around their bodies and went to look at Gen. He was in his usual place, sleeping on his back on the floor next to the sofa where his employer slept. Gen had taken his glasses off and in his sleep he held them lightly in one hand. He had a pleasant face, a face that stored a wonderment of knowledge. She could see his eyes moving quickly back and forth beneath the smooth, thin skin of his eyelids, but if he was dreaming, everything else was still. His breathing was quiet and steady. Carmen wished that she could see inside his mind. She wondered if it would look crowded with words, compartments of language carefully fitted on top of each other. Her own brain, by comparison, would be an empty closet. He could refuse her and what would be the harm in that? She wouldn't have anything less than what she had now. All she had to do was ask. All she had to do was say the words and yet the thought of it closed her throat entirely. What experience did she have of piano music and paintings of the Madonna? What experience did she have of asking? Carmen held her breath and stretched out on the floor next to Gen. She was as silent as light on the leaves of trees. She lay on her side and put her mouth near his sleeping ear. She had no talent for asking but she was a genius at being quiet. When they practiced their drills in the woods it was Carmen who could run for a mile without breaking a twig. It was Carmen who could walk up right behind you and tap you on the shoulder without making a sound. She was the one they sent in first to unscrew the covers from the air-conditioning vents because no one would notice her. No one would hear a thing. She said a prayer to Saint Rose of Lima. She asked for courage. After so many prayers offered for the gift of silence, she now asked for sound.

"Gen," she whispered.

Gen was dreaming that he was standing on a beach in Greece looking at the water. Somewhere behind him in the dunes someone was saying his name.

Her heart was stuttering in her chest. The rush of her blood made a roar in her ears. What she heard when she strained to listen was the voice of the saint. "Now or never," Saint Rose told her. "I am with you only for this moment."

"Gen."

And now the voice that was calling was walking away and Gen left the beach to follow it, followed the voice from sleep to waking. It was always so confusing, waking up in the Vice President's house. What hotel room was this? Why was he on the floor? Then he remembered and all at once he opened his eyes, thinking it was Mr. Hosokawa who needed him. He looked up to the sofa but then he felt a hand on his shoulder. When he turned his head, the beautiful boy was there. Not the boy. Carmen. Her nose very nearly touching his nose. He was startled but not afraid. How odd that she was lying down, was all he thought.

The military had recently given up on the floodlights that had raged for so long outside the windows and now the night looked like night again. "Carmen?" he said. Messner should see her like this, in the moonlight. He had been so right about her face, her heart-shaped face.

"Very quiet," she said deep into his ear. "Listen." But where were the words? She was so thankful to be lying down. The racing of her heart was unbearable. Could he see her like this in the darkness, shaking? Could he feel her vibration deep in the wood of the floor? Could he hear her skin rustling inside the clothes she wore?

"Close your eyes," Saint Rose told her. "Say your prayer to me."

All at once there was enough air to fill her lungs. "Teach me to read," she said quickly. "Teach me to make my letters in Spanish."

Gen looked at her. Her eyes were closed. It was as if he had come to lie down beside her and not the other way around. Her lashes were heavy and dark against the blush of her cheek. Was she asleep? Was she talking in her sleep? He could have kissed her without moving an inch and then he struck the thought from his mind.

"You want to read in Spanish," Gen repeated, his voice as small as her own.

Heaven, she thought. He knows how to be quiet. He knows like me how to speak without making a sound. She took a breath and then blinked her dark eyes open. "And English," she whispered. She smiled. She could not contain it. She had managed to ask him for everything she wanted.

Shy Carmen, always hanging back from the others, who knew she could smile? But at the sight of that smile he would have promised her anything. He was just barely awake. Or maybe he was not awake at all. Had he wanted her and not known it? Had he wanted her so much that he dreamed she was lying beside him now? The things our minds keep from us, Gen thought. The secrets we keep even from ourselves. "Yes," he said, "English."

She was reckless and brave, so great was her joy. She took her hand and put it over his eyes. She gently brushed his eyes closed again. Her hand was cool and soft. It smelled of metal. "Go back to sleep," she said. "Go back to sleep."

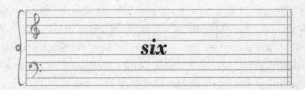

six

Years later when this period of internment was remembered by the people who were actually there, they saw it in two distinct periods: before the box and after the box.

Before the box, the terrorists controlled the Vice President's home. The hostages, even when not being directly threatened, mulled over the inevitability of their own deaths. Even if by some stroke of great good fortune no one shot them in their sleep, they now understood exactly what was in the cards, be it before their release or after. They would each and every one of them die. Surely they had always known this, but now death came and sat on their chests at night, peered cold and hungry into their eyes. The world was a dangerous place, notions of personal safety were a fairy story told to children at bedtime. All anyone had to do was turn the wrong corner and everything would be gone. They thought about the senseless death of the first accompanist. They missed him, and yet look how simply, how brilliantly he had been replaced. They missed their daughters and their wives. They were alive in this house but what difference did it make? Death was already sucking the air from the bottom of their lungs. It left them weak and listless. Powerful heads of corporations collapsed into chairs near the window and stared, diplomats flipped through magazines without noticing the pictures. Some days there was barely enough strength to turn the pages.

But after Messner brought the box into the house everything changed. The terrorists continued to block the doors and carry guns, but now Roxane Coss was in charge. She started the morning at six o'clock because she woke up when the light came in through her window and when she woke up she wanted to work. She took her bath and had two pieces of toast and a cup of tea that Carmen made for her, brought up on a yellow wooden tray that the Vice President had picked out for this purpose. Now that Roxane knew Carmen was a girl she let her sit on the bed with her and drink out of her cup. She liked to braid Carmen's hair, which was as shiny and black as a pool of oil. Some mornings the weight of Carmen's hair between her fingers was the only thing that made any sense at all to her. There was comfort in pretending that she had been detained in order to braid the hair of this young woman. She was Mozart's Susanna. Carmen was the Countess Rosina. The hair folded and looped into heavy black ribbons, perfectly ordered. There was nothing they could say to each other. When Roxane was finished, Carmen would go and stand behind her, brushing Roxane's hair until it shined, then twist it into an identical braid. In this way, only for the little time they had together in the mornings, they were sisters, girlfriends, the same. They were happy together when it was just the two of them alone. They never thought of Beatriz, who shot dice against the pantry door in the kitchen with the boys.

At seven o'clock Kato was waiting for Roxane at the piano, his fingers running silently up and down the keys. She had learned to say good morning, *Ohayo Gozaimasu,* in Japanese, and Kato knew a handful of phrases which included, *good morning, thank you,* and *bye-bye.* That constituted the extent of their abilities in each other's language, so that they said good morning again when it was time to stop for a break or when they passed each other in the hallways before bedtime. They spoke to one another by handing leaves of music back and forth. While their relationship was by no means a democracy, Kato, who read the music the priest's friend had sent while lying on the pile of coats he slept on at night, would sometimes pick out pieces he wanted to hear or pieces that he felt would be well suited to Roxane's voice. He made what he felt to be wild presumptions in handing over his suggestions, but what did it matter? He was a vice president in a giant corporation, a numbers man, suddenly elevated to be the accompanist. He was not himself. He was no one he had ever imagined.

At quarter past seven the scales began. On the first morning there were still people sleeping. Pietro Genovese was sleeping beneath the piano, and when the chords were struck he thought he was hearing the bells of St. Peter's. None of that mattered. It was now time for work. Too much time had been spent weeping on the sofa or staring out the window. Now there was music and an accompanist. Roxane Coss had risked her voice on *Gianni Schicchi* and found that her voice was still there. "We're rotting," she had told Mr. Hosokawa through Gen only the day before. "All of us. I've had enough of it. If anyone is going to shoot me they will have to shoot me while I'm singing." In this way Mr. Hosokawa knew she would be safe, as no one could shoot her while she sang. By extension they were all safe, and so they pressed in close to the piano to listen.

"Step back," Roxane said, and shooed them away with her hands. "I'm going to want that air."

The first thing she sang that morning was the aria from *Rusalka*, which she remembered was the one Mr. Hosokawa had requested that she sing for his birthday, before she knew him, before she knew anything. How she loved that story, the spirit of the water who longs to be a woman who can hold her lover in real arms instead of cool waves. She sang this aria at nearly every performance she gave, though she had never infused it with the compassion and understanding that she gave to it this morning. Mr. Hosokawa heard the difference in her voice, and it brought tears to his eyes.

"She sings Czech like she was born to it," he whispered to Gen.

Gen nodded. He would never refute the beauty of her singing, the warm and liquid quality of her voice that so well matched the watery Rusalka, but there was no point in telling Mr. Hosokawa that this woman did not know a word of Czechoslovakian. She sang the passion of every syllable, but none of the syllables actually managed to form themselves into recognizable words of the language. It was quite obvious that she had memorized the work phonetically, that she sang her love for Dvořák and her love for the translated story, but that the Czech language itself was a stranger which passed her by without a moment's recognition. Not that this was any sort of crime, of course. Who would even know except for him? There were no Czechs among them.

Roxane Coss sang rigorously for three hours in the morning and sometimes sang again in the late afternoon before dinner if her voice felt strong, and for those hours no one gave a single thought to their death. They thought about her singing and about the song, the sweet radiance of her upper register. Soon enough the days were divided into three states: the anticipation of her singing, the pleasure of her singing, and the reflection on her singing.

If the power had shifted away from them, the Generals didn't seem to mind. The utter hopelessness of their mission seemed less overbearing to them now and many nights they slept almost in peace. General Benjamin continued to mark off the days on the dining-room wall. They had more time to concentrate on negotiations. Among themselves they spoke as if the singing had been part of their plan. It calmed the hostages. It focused the soldiers. It also had the remarkable effect of quelling the racket that came from the other side of the wall. They could only assume that with the windows open the people on the streets could hear her because the constant screech of bullhorned messages would stop as soon as she opened her mouth to sing, and after a few days the bullhorn did not come back at all. They imagined the street outside. It was packed with people, not one of them eating chips or coughing, all of them straining to listen to the voice they had heard only on records and in their dreams. It was a daily concert the Generals had arranged, or so they had come to believe. A gift to the people, a diversion to the military. They had kidnapped her for a reason, after all.

"We will make her sing more," General Hector said in the downstairs guest suite that they had taken over as their private offices. He stretched across the canopied bed, his boots nesting on top of the embroidered ivory comforter. Benjamin and Alfredo sat in matching chairs covered in enormous pink peonies. "There is no reason she couldn't sing a few more hours a day. And we will rearrange her times to keep them off their guard."

"We will tell her what to sing as well," Alfredo said. "She should sing in Spanish. All this Italian, it is not what we stand for. Besides, for all we know she could be singing out messages."

But General Benjamin, despite his occasional participation in the delusions at hand, knew that whatever they got from Roxane Coss was something to be grateful for. "I don't think we should ask."

"We won't be asking," Hector said, reaching back to plump the pillows beneath his head. "We will be telling." His voice was even and cold.

General Benjamin waited a moment. She was singing now and he let the sound of her voice wash over him while he sought a way to explain. Isn't it obvious? he wanted to say to his friends. Can't you hear that? "Music, I believe, is different. That's what I understand. We have set this up exactly right, but if we were to push . . ." Benjamin shrugged. He raised a hand to touch his face and then thought better of it. "We could wind up with nothing."

"If we put a gun to her head she would sing all day."

"Try it first with a bird," General Benjamin said gently to Alfredo. "Like our soprano, they have no capacity to understand authority. The bird doesn't know enough to be afraid and the person holding the gun will only end up looking like a lunatic."

When Roxanne was finished singing, Mr. Hosokawa went to get her glass of water himself, cool with no ice, the way she liked it. Ruben

Iglesias had recently mopped the kitchen floor and rubbed it down with a hard wax by hand so that the whole room shimmered like light on the flat surface of a lake. Could Mr. Hosokawa say, picking up the pot of water he had boiled and cooled this morning for this very purpose, that this was the happiest time in his life? Surely that could not be the case. He was being held against his will in a country he did not know and every day he found himself looking down the barrel of some child's gun. He was living on a diet of tough meat sandwiches and soda pop, sleeping in a room with more than fifty men, and although there were irregular privileges at the washing machine, he was thinking of asking the Vice President if he could kindly extend to him a second pair of underwear from his own bureau. Then why this sudden sense of lightness, this great affection for everyone? He looked out the large window over the sink, stared into the mist of bad weather. There had not been poverty in his childhood but there was a great deal of struggle: his mother's death when he was ten; his father holding on, broken, until he joined her the year Katsumi Hosokawa was nineteen; his two sisters disappearing into the distant lives of their marriages. No, that family had not been a greater happiness. The early years he had spent building Nansei were like a hurricane in his memory, a huge, overbearing wind into which every loose thing was sucked. He slept with his head on his desk most nights, he missed holidays, birthdays, entire seasons of the year. From his endless work had come a great industry, great personal gain, but happiness? It was a word he would have puzzled over, unable to understand its importance even while its meaning was evident.

And so that left his own family, his wife and two daughters. They were the question. If he had not drawn happiness from them then the fault was completely his own. His wife had been the daughter of his uncle's friend. The country was past the age of arranged marriages and yet essentially a wife had been found for him because there was no time for him to find his own. They sat in her parents' living room during their courtship, eating candy, speaking little. He was so tired then, always working, and even after they married sometimes he would forget he had a wife at all. He would come home at four in the morning and be startled to see her there in the bed, her long dark hair spilling over his pillows. So this is my wife, he would think to himself, and fall asleep beside her. Not that things had stayed that way. They had come to depend on one another. They were a family. She was an excellent wife, an excellent mother, and surely he had loved her in his own fashion, but happiness? That was not something he thought of when he remembered his wife. Even as he could picture her waiting for him to come home from work, a drink poured, the mail opened and sorted, it was not happiness for either of them that he saw but a kind of efficiency that made their lives run smoothly. She was an honorable woman, a dutiful wife. He had seen her reading mystery novels but she never spoke of them. She wrote beautiful cards. She was a comfort to their children. He wondered suddenly if he knew her at all. He wondered if he had ever made her happy. His happiness was something kept apart, after he had come in from dinner meetings and there was time to spend with his stereo. Happiness, if he was right to use that word, was something that until now he had only experienced in music. He was still experiencing it in music. The difference was that now the music was a person. She sat beside him on the sofa reading. She asked him to sit beside her at the piano. On occasion she took his hand, a gesture so startling and wonderful that he could barely inhale. She asked him, do you like this piece? She asked him, what would you like me to sing? These were things he never could have imagined: the warmth of a person and the music together. Yes, her voice, more than anything her voice, but there were also her fine hands to consider, the bright rope of her hair lying across her shoulder, the pale, soft skin of her neck. There was her enormous power. Had he ever known a businessman who commanded such respect? More than all of it was the mystery of why she had chosen him to sit next to. Could it be possible that such happiness had existed in the world all along and he had never once heard mention of it?

Mr. Hosokawa remembered himself. He filled his glass. When he came back, Roxane was sitting at the piano with Gen. "I've kept you waiting too long," he said.

She took the glass and listened to the translation. "That's because the water is perfect," she said. "Perfect takes a longer time."

Gen exchanged their sentences like a bank teller pushing stacks of currency back and forth over a smooth marble countertop. He only half listened to what they were saying. He was still trying to puzzle out his night. It was not a dream. He didn't have those kinds of dreams. The girl he had watched, the girl named Carmen, had asked him a question and he had agreed, but where was she now? All morning he hadn't seen her. He had tried to look discreetly in the halls but the boys with guns kept corralling him back into the living room. Some days they were open to hostages wandering around and other days they seemed to think life's greatest pleasure was nudging people backwards with a gun. Where was he supposed to meet her and when? He hadn't asked any questions. Despite her clear instructions, he hadn't been able to go back to sleep after she left last night. He couldn't stop wondering how a girl like that had come through the air-conditioner vents with criminals. But what did he know? Maybe she had killed people before. Perhaps she robbed banks or threw Molotov cocktails through embassy windows. Maybe Messner was right, these were modern times.

Beatriz came up and gave Gen two hard taps on the shoulder, interrupting both Mr. Hosokawa's conversation with Roxane and his own private thoughts. "Is it time for Maria yet?" she said, not wanting to be late for the soap opera. As soon as she had spoken, she slipped the damp end of her braid back into her mouth and began the serious business of nibbling again. Gen imagined a knotted tumor of hair growing in her stomach.

"Fifteen minutes," he said, looking at his watch. Like so many other things, the beginning of the soap opera had become his responsibility.

"Come and tell me when."

"Is this about her program?" Roxane asked.

Gen nodded to her and then said to Beatriz in Spanish, "I'll show you on the clock."

"I don't care about the clock," Beatriz said.

"You ask me every day. You ask me five times."

"I ask other people, too," she said sharply. "It's not just you." Her small eyes grew smaller as she puzzled whether or not she was being insulted.

Gen took off his watch. "Hold out your wrist."

"You're going to give it to her?" Mr. Hosokawa asked.

"Why?" Beatriz said suspiciously.

Gen said in Japanese, "I'm better off without it." Then he said to Beatriz, "I'm going to make you a present."

She liked the idea of presents even though she'd had almost no experience of them personally. On the program, Maria's boyfriend gave her a present, a heart-shaped locket with his own picture inside. He put it around her neck before she sent him away. But once he had gone she held it to her lips and cried and cried. A present seemed like a wonderful gesture. Beatriz held out her wrist and Gen fastened on the watch.

"Look at the big hand," he said, tapping the crystal with his nail. "When it gets to the twelve here at the top then you know it's time."

She studied the watch closely. It was beautiful, really, the round glass, the soft brown leather band, the hand that was no bigger than a hair that did a slow and constant sweep across the face. As presents went, she thought this was the nicest, better even than the locket because the watch actually did something. "This one?" she said, pointing out one of the three hands. Three hands, how queer.

"The minute hand on twelve and the hour hand, the little one, on one. That's easy enough."

But it wasn't quite easy enough and Beatriz was afraid she would forget. She was afraid she would read it wrong and then miss the show altogether. She was afraid she would get it wrong and have to ask again, in which case Gen was sure to make fun of her. It was better when he just told her it was time. That was his job. She had a lot of work to do and all the hostages were lazy. "I'm not interested in this," she said, and tried to undo the strap.

"What is the problem?" Mr. Hosokawa said. "Doesn't she like it?"

"She thinks it's too complicated."

"Nonsense." Mr. Hosokawa put his hand over Beatriz's wrist to stop her. "Look at this. It's very simple." He held out his wrist and showed her his own watch, which was dazzling compared to Gen's, a bright coin of rose-colored gold. "Two hands," he said, taking hold of both her hands. "Just like you. Very simple." Gen translated.

"Three hands," Beatriz said, pointing out the only one that seemed to move.

"Those are the seconds. Sixty seconds in a minute, one minute, one circle, pushing the big hand forward one minute." Mr. Hosokawa explained time, seconds to minutes to hours. He could not remember when he had last looked at his watch or wondered about the hour of the day.

Beatriz nodded. She ran her finger around the face of Gen's watch. "It's almost now," she said.

"Seven more minutes," Gen said.

"I'll go and wait." She considered thanking him but she wasn't sure if it was the right thing to do. She could have taken the watch from him. She could have demanded it.

"Does Carmen watch the program?" Gen asked.

"Sometimes," Beatriz said. "But then she forgets. She isn't true to it like I am. She has duty outside today, so she won't be watching it unless she stands at the window. When I have duty outside I stand at the window."

Gen glanced towards the tall French doors at the end of the room that led out onto the garden. There was nothing there. Only the *garúa* and the flowers which were starting to overgrow their beds.

Beatriz knew what he was looking for and she was angry. She liked Gen a little and he should have liked her because he had given her a present. "Take your turn," she said bitterly. "The boys are all waiting at different windows. They're all watching for her, too. Maybe you should go and stand with them." It wasn't true, of course. There was no dating allowed in the ranks and that was a rule that was never broken.

"She had asked me a question," Gen started, but his voice didn't sound natural and so he decided to forget it. It wasn't as if he owed Beatriz any sort of explanation.

"I'll tell her you gave your watch to me." She looked at her wrist. "Four more minutes."

"You should run," Gen said. "You'll lose your spot on the couch."

Beatriz left but she didn't run. She walked away like a girl who knew exactly how much time she had.

"What did she say?" Mr. Hosokawa asked Gen. "Was she happy with the watch?"

Gen translated the question into English for Roxane and then answered them both that there would be no way to tell if she was happy or not.

"I think you're smart to give it to her," Roxane said. "She'll be less likely to shoot someone who's given her such a nice gift."

But who's to say what kept a person from shooting? "Would you excuse me?"

Mr. Hosokawa let Gen go. It used to be that he wanted Gen with him all the time in case he thought of something to say, but he was learning to find some comfort in the quiet. Roxane put her hands on the piano and picked out the opening lines of "Clair de Lune." Then she took one of Mr. Hosokawa's hands and tapped the notes again, very slow and beautiful and sad. He followed her again and again until he could do it quite well on his own.

Gen went to the window and watched. The drizzling rain had stopped but the air was still heavy and gray as if it were dusk. Gen glanced at his watch, knowing it was too early to be dark, and found his watch gone. Why was he waiting for her? Because he wanted to teach her to read? He had plenty to do without taking that on as well. Every person in the room had a thought that was in need of translation. He was lucky to find a minute alone, a minute to look out of the window. He didn't need another job.

"I have watched out this window for hours," a man said to him in Russian. "Nothing ever comes. I can promise you that."

"Sometimes it's enough just to look," Gen said, keeping his eyes straight ahead. He almost never had the opportunity to speak in Russian. It was a language he used for reading Pushkin and Turgenev. It sounded good to hear his own voice managing so many sharp consonants even if he knew his accent was poor. He should practice. It was an opportunity if one chose to see it that way, so many native speakers in one room. Victor Fyodorov was a tall man with large hands and a great wall of a chest. The three Russians, Fyodorov, Ledbed, and Berezovsky, mostly kept to themselves, playing cards and smoking from a seemingly inexhaustible supply of cigarettes, the source of which no one was exactly sure. While the French could make out a few words of Spanish and the Italians remembered some of their school French, Russian, like Japanese, was an island of a language. Even the simplest phrases were met with blank expressions.

"You stay so busy," Fyodorov said. "I envy you at times. We watch you, up and down, up and down, everyone needing your attention. No doubt you envy us doing nothing. You would like a little more time to yourself, yes? Time to look out the window?" What the Russian was saying was that he was sorry to be another bother, another sentence in need of conversion, and that he wouldn't ask were it not important.

Gen smiled. Fyodorov had given up the pleasantries of shaving and in a little more than two weeks had come up with an impressive beard. By the time they were sprung from this place he would look like Tolstoy. "I have plenty of time even when I'm busy. You know yourself these are the longest days in history. Look, I gave up my watch. I thought I was better off not knowing."

"That I admire," the Russian said, staring at Gen's bare wrist. He tapped the skin with one heavy forefinger. "That shows real thinking."

"So don't think you're taking up my time."

Fyodorov took off his own watch and dropped it into his pocket in a gesture of solidarity. He circled his great hand to enjoy the new freedom. "Now we can talk. Now that we have done away with time."

"Absolutely," Gen said, but as soon as he said it, two figures walked near the wall of the garden holding up guns. Their jackets and caps were wet from the earlier rain and they kept their heads down instead of looking around the way Gen imagined they should if they were supposed to be watching for something. It was hard to tell which one was Carmen. From so far away in the rain she was a boy again. He hoped that she would look up and see him, that she might think that he was watching for her even though he recognized the idiocy of this. Still, he had been waiting to see her and he felt better somehow, assuming it was her in the first place and not just another angry teenaged boy.

Fyodorov watched Gen and watched the two figures outside the window until they had passed. "You keep an eye on them," he said in a low voice. "That's smart thinking. I get lazy. In the beginning, I kept account of them, but they are everywhere. Like rabbits. I think they bring in more of them at night."

Gen wanted to point and say, That's Carmen, but he didn't know what he would be explaining. Instead he nodded in agreement.

"But let's not waste our time on them. I have better ways to waste your time. Do you smoke?" he asked, pulling out a small blue package of French cigarettes. "No? Do you mind?"

It seemed that no sooner had he struck his match than the Vice President arrived with an ashtray that he placed on a small table in front of them. "Gen," he said, nodding politely. "Victor." He bowed to them, a pleasantry he had picked up from the Japanese, and then moved on, not wanting to interrupt the conversation he could not understand.

"A wonderful man, Ruben Iglesias. It almost makes me wish I was a citizen of this wretched country so that I could vote for him for President." Fyodorov pulled the smoke through the cigarette and then expelled it slowly. He was trying to find the right way to begin his request. "You can imagine, we have been thinking a great deal about opera," he said.

"Of course," Gen said.

"Who knew that life could be so unexpected? I thought we would be dead by now, or if not dead then regularly begging for our lives, but instead I sit and I consider opera."

"No one could have predicted." Gen leaned forward imperceptibly to see if he could catch sight of Carmen before she passed completely from view, but he was too late.

"I have always been very interested in music. Opera in Russia is very important. You know that. It is virtually a sacred thing."

"I can imagine." Now he wished he had his watch. If he did he would be able to time her, to see how many minutes it took for her to go past the window again. She could become her own sort of clock. He thought about asking Fyodorov but clearly Fyodorov had his mind on other things.

"Opera came to Russia late. In Italy the language lent itself to this kind of singing but for us it took longer. It is, you know, a complicated language. The singers we have now in Russia are very great. I have no complaints about the talent our country possesses, but as I live now there is only one true genius. Many great singers, brilliant voices, but only one genius. She has never been to Russia that I know of. Wouldn't you say the chances of finding oneself trapped in a house with true genius are remarkably small?"

"I would agree," Gen said.

"To find myself here with her and to be unable to say anything it is, well, unfortunate. No, honestly, it is frustrating. What if we were released tomorrow? That is what I pray for and yet, wouldn't I say to myself for the rest of my life, you never spoke to her? She was right there in the room with you and you didn't bother to make arrangements to say something? What would it mean to live with such regret? I suppose it didn't bother me much before she resumed her singing. I was preoccupied with my own thoughts, the circumstances at hand, but now with the music coming so regularly everything has changed. Don't you find that to be true?"

And Gen had to agree. He hadn't thought about it in exactly those terms before but it was true. There was some difference.

"And what are the chances, given that I am a hostage in a country I do not know with a woman I so sincerely admire that there would also be a man such as yourself who has a good heart and speaks both my language and hers? Tell me what the chances are? They are in the millions! This is, of course, why I have come to you. I am interested in engaging your services of translation."

"It's nothing as formal as that," Gen said. "I'm happy to speak to Miss Coss. We can go now. I'll tell her whatever you want to say."

At that the great Russian paled and took three nervous puffs off his cigarette. So massive were this man's lungs that the little cigarette was all but finished off by his sudden burst of attention. "There is no rush for this, my friend."

"Unless we're released tomorrow."

He nodded and smiled. "You let me escape from nothing." He pointed his smoked-out cigarette at Gen. "You are thinking. You are telling me it is time to declare myself."

Gen thought he might have misunderstood the verb *to declare*. It could have other meanings. He could speak Russian, but his understanding lacked nuance. "I'm not telling you anything other than that Miss Coss is right there if you want to speak to her."

"Let's call it tomorrow, shall we? I'll speak in the morning"—he clapped a hand down on Gen's shoulder—"in case we are so fortunate. Is the morning fine with you?"

"I'll be here."

"Just after she sings," he said. Then he added, "But without rushing her any."

Gen told him that sounded reasonable.

"Good, good. That will give me time to prepare my thoughts. I will be awake all night. You are very good. Your Russian is very good."

"Thank you," Gen said. He had hoped that maybe they could talk for a while about Pushkin. There were things he wanted to know about *Eugene Onegin* and *The Queen of Spades,* but Fyodorov was gone, lumbering back to his corner like a fighter ready for the second round. The other two Russians were waiting for him, smoking.

The Vice President was standing in the kitchen looking into a box of vegetables, crookneck squash and dark purple eggplants, tomatoes and sweet yellow onions. He took this as a bad sign that the people who surrounded the house were growing bored with their kidnapping. How long did these crises ever last? Six hours? Two days? After that they lobbed in some tear gas and everyone surrendered. But somehow these cut-rate terrorists had thwarted any rescue. Maybe it was because there were so many hostages. Maybe it was the wall around the vice-presidential house, or their fear of accidentally killing Roxane Coss. For whatever reason, their situation had already crawled past its second week. It was completely conceivable that they were no longer on the front page of the paper or that they had already fallen to the second or even the third story on the evening news. People had gotten on with their lives. A more practical stand was being taken, as evidenced by the food in front of him. The Vice President imagined his group the survivors of a shipwreck who watched helplessly while the last search-and-rescue helicopter spun north towards the mainland. The evidence was in the food. At first it had all been prepared, sandwiches or casseroles of pulled chicken and rice. Then it came in needing some assembly, bread and meat and cheese wrapped on separate trays. But this, this was something else entirely. Fifteen raw chickens, pink and cold, their stomachs greasing the counter, boxes of vegetables, bags of dried beans, tins of shortening. Certainly it was enough food, the chickens appeared to have been robust, but the question was how did one effect the transformation? How did what was here become dinner? Ruben believed the question was his responsibility to answer but he knew nothing of his own kitchen. He did not know where the colander was. He did not know marjoram from thyme. He wondered if his wife would have known. Truthfully, they had been taken care of for too long. He had realized that in these past weeks as he swept the floors and folded up the bedding. Perhaps he had been useful in society, but as far as household matters were concerned he had become some kind of fancy lapdog. As a boy he had received no domestic training. He had never once been asked to set a table or peel a carrot. His sisters made his bed and folded his clothes. It had taken a state of captivity to force him to figure out the operation of his own washer and dryer. Every day there was a never-ending list of things that needed to be attended to. If he worked without stop from the moment he woke up in the morning until he fell into an exhausted heap on his pile of blankets, he could not keep the house in the manner to which he had been accustomed to seeing it. How this house had sung just a short while ago! There was no telling how many girls came and went, dusting and buffing, ironing shirts and handkerchiefs, mopping the most imperceptible cobwebs from the corners of his ceiling. They polished the brass strips at the base of the front door. They kept the pantry filled with sweet cakes and pickled beets. They left the vaguest scent of their own bath powder (which his wife bought each of them for their birthdays every year, a generous round container with a fat down puff on top) behind them in the rooms and so everything smelled like a fistful of hyacinth sprinkled with talc. Not one thing in the house demanded his attention, not one object asked for his intercession. Even his own children were bathed and brushed and put to bed by lovely hired hands. It was perfect, always and completely perfect.

And his guests! Who were these men who never took their dishes to the sink? At least the terrorists he could forgive. They were for the most part children, and besides, they had been raised in the jungle. (At this he thought of his own mother, who would call to him when he forgot to close the front door, "I should send you to live in the jungle where you wouldn't be bothered by things like doors!") The hostages were accustomed to valets and secretaries, and while they had cooks and maids they probably never saw them. Not only were their households run for them, they were run so silently, so efficiently, that they never had to encounter the operations.

Of course Ruben could have let it all go. It wasn't really his house, after all. He could have watched the carpets molder in pools of spilled soda pop and stepped around the trash that circled the overfull wastebaskets, but he was first and foremost the host. He felt a sense of responsibility to keep some semblance of a party running. But what he soon found was that he enjoyed it. Not only did he enjoy it he believed, with all modesty, that he had a certain knack for it. When he got on his hands and knees and waxed the floors, the floors did shine in response to his attentions. Of all the many jobs there were to do, the one he liked the best was ironing. It was amazing to him that they hadn't taken the iron away. If properly wielded he was sure it was as deadly as a gun, so heavy, so incredibly hot. While he pressed the shirts of shirtless men who stood waiting, he thought of the damage he could do. Certainly, he couldn't take them all out (Could an iron deflect bullets? he wondered), but he could clank down two or three before they shot him. With an iron, Ruben could go down fighting and the thought of it made him feel less passive, more like a man. He nosed the pointy silver tip into a pocket and then slid it down a sleeve. He puffed out clouds of steam that made him pour with sweat. The collar, he had quickly come to realize, was the key to everything.

Ironing was one thing. Ironing was within his grasp. But where raw food was concerned he was at a loss, and he stood and he stared at all that now lay before him. He decided to put the chickens in the refrigerator. Avoid warm meat, that much he was sure about. Then he went to look for help.

"Gen," he said. "Gen, I need to speak to Señorita Coss."

"You, too?" Gen asked.

"Me, too," the Vice President said. "What, is there a line? Shall I take a number?"

Gen shook his head and together they walked over to see Roxane. "Gen," she said, and held out her hands as if she hadn't seen them in days. "Mr. Vice President." She had changed since the music had arrived, or she had changed back. She now more closely resembled the famous soprano who had been brought to a party at enormous expense to sing six arias. She once again put out a kind of light that belongs only to the very famous. Ruben always felt slightly weak when he stood this close to her. She was wearing his wife's sweater and his wife's black silk scarf covered in jewel-colored birds tied around her throat. (Oh, how his wife adored that scarf, which had come from Paris. She never wore it more than once or twice a year and she kept it carefully folded in its original box. How quickly Ruben had served up this treasure to Roxane!) He was overcome by the sudden need to tell her how he felt about her. How much her music meant to him. He controlled himself by calling those bare chickens to mind. "You must forgive me," the Vice President said, his voice breaking with emotion. "You do so much for all of us as it is. Your practicing has been a godsend, though how you can call it practicing I don't know. It implies that your singing could improve." He touched his fingers to his eyes and shook his head. He was tired. "This isn't what I came to say to you. I wonder if I may bother you for a favor?"

"Is there something you would like me to sing?" Roxane stroked the edges of the scarf.

"That I would never presume to know. Whatever song you choose is the song I have been wanting to hear."

"Very impressive," Gen said to him in Spanish.

Ruben gave him a look that made it clear he had no interest in editorials. "I need some advice in the kitchen. Some help. Don't mistake me, I would never ask you to do any work, but if you could give me the smallest amount of guidance in the preparation of our dinner, I would be greatly indebted to you."

Roxane looked at Gen and blinked. "You misunderstood him."

"I don't think so."

"Try again."

Spanish was to linguists what hopscotch was to triathletes. If he was managing in Russian and Greek, chances were he would not have misunderstood a sentence of Spanish. A sentence regarding the preparation of food and not the state of the human soul. Spanish was, after all, what he was translating in and out of all day. It was the closest thing available to a common language. "Pardon me," Gen said to Ruben.

"Tell her I need some help with dinner."

"Cooking dinner?" Roxane asked.

Ruben thought about this for a moment, assuming he was not asking for help serving dinner or eating dinner, then yes, cooking dinner was what was left. "Cooking."

"Why would he think I know how to cook?" she asked Gen.

Ruben, whose English was bad but not hopeless, pointed out that she was a woman. "The two girls, I can't imagine they would know a thing except for native dishes that might not be to others' liking," he said through Gen.

"This is some sort of Latin thing, don't you think?" she said to Gen. "I can't even really be offended. It's important to bear the cultural differences in mind." She gave Ruben a smile that was kind but relayed no information.

"I think that's wise," Gen said, and then he told Ruben, "She doesn't cook."

"She cooks a little," Ruben said.

Gen shook his head. "I would think not at all."

"She wasn't born singing opera," the Vice President said. "She must have had a childhood." Even his wife, who had grown up rich, who was a pampered girl with most available luxuries, was taught to cook.

"Possibly, but I imagine someone cooked her food for her."

Roxane, now out of the conversational loop, leaned back against the gold silk cushions of the sofa, held her hands up, and shrugged. It was a charming gesture. Such smooth hands that had never washed a dish or shelled a pea. "Tell him his scar is looking so much better," she said to Gen. "I want to say something nice. Thank God that girl of his was still around when it happened. Otherwise he might have asked me to sew his face up for him, too."

"Should I tell him you don't sew?" Gen said.

"Better he hears it now." The soprano smiled again and waved good-bye to the Vice President.

"Do you know how to cook?" Ruben asked Gen.

Gen ignored the question. "I've heard Simon Thibault complain a great deal about the food. He sounds like he knows what he's talking about. Anyway, he's French. The French know how to cook."

"Two minutes ago I would have said the same thing about women," Ruben said.

But Simon Thibault proved to be a better bet. His face lit up at the mention of raw chickens. "And vegetables?" he said. "Praise God, something that hasn't already been ruined."

"This is your man," Gen said.

Together the three of them walked to the kitchen, making their way through the maze of men and boys who loitered in the great hall of the living room. Thibault immediately went to the vegetables. He took an eggplant out of the box and rolled it in his hands. He could almost make out his own reflection in its shiny skin. He put his nose to the deep purple patent leather. It didn't smell like much and yet there was something vaguely dark and loamy, something alive that made him want to bite down. "This is a good kitchen," he said. "Let me see your pans."

So Ruben opened up the drawers and cabinets and Simon Thibault began his systematic inventory, wire whisks and mixing bowls, lemon squeezers, parchment paper, double boilers. Every imaginable pot in every imaginable size, all the way up to something that weighed thirty pounds empty and could have concealed a small-boned two-year-old child. It was a kitchen that was accustomed to cocktail suppers for five hundred. A kitchen braced to feed the masses. "Where are the knives?" Thibault said.

"The knifes are in the belts of the hoodlums," the Vice President said. "They plan to either hack us up with the meat cleaver or saw us to death with the bread knife."

Thibault drummed his fingers on the steel countertops. It was a nice look, but in their home in Paris he and Edith had marble. What a beautiful pastry crust one could make on marble! "It's not a bad idea," he said, "not bad. I'd just as soon they keep the knives. Gen, go and tell the Generals we will have to cook our food or eat our chickens raw, not that they would balk at a raw chicken. Tell them we understand we are morally unqualified to handle the cutlery and we need some guards, two or three, to slice and dice. Ask them to send the girls and maybe that very small boy."

"Ishmael," Ruben said.

"That's a boy who can take responsibility," Thibault said.

The guards had changed their shifts, or at least he saw two more young soldiers pull on their caps and head outside, but Gen didn't see Carmen. If she had come in she was off somewhere in a part of the house that was off-limits to hostages. Discreetly, he looked for her everyplace he was allowed to go, but he had no luck. "General Benjamin," he said, finding the General going over the newspaper with a pair of scissors in the dining room. He was cutting out the articles that concerned them, as if he could keep them in the dark by editing the paper. The television stayed on all hours but the guests were always driven out of the room when the news came on. Still, they heard bits and pieces from the hall. "There has been a change in the food, sir." Even though Thibault was the diplomat, Gen believed that he probably had a better chance of getting what they wanted. It was the difference in their natures. The French had very little experience in being deferential.

"And that change?" The General did not look up.

"It isn't cooked, sir. They've sent in boxes of vegetables, some chickens." At least the chickens were plucked. At least they were dead. It was probably only a matter of time before dinner walked through the door on its own, that their milk showed up still tucked warmly inside its goat.

"So cook it." He snipped a straight line up the middle of the third page.

"The Vice President and Ambassador Thibault are planning to do that but they need to request some knives."

"No knives," the General said absently.

Gen waited for a moment. General Benjamin crumpled up the articles he had removed and set them in a pile of tight little balls of paper. "Unfortunately, that's a problem. I know very little about cooking myself but I understand that knifes are imperative for the preparation of food."

"No knives."

"Perhaps then if the knives came with people. If you could requisition a few soldiers to do the chopping, then there would be control over the knives. It's a great deal of food. There are fifty-eight people after all."

General Benjamin sighed. "I know how many people are here. I would appreciate not having to hear it from you." He smoothed out what was left of the paper and folded it up again. "Tell me something, Gen. Do you play chess?"

"Chess, sir? I know how to play. I wouldn't say I was very good."

The General tented his fingers and pressed them to his lips. "I'll send you the girls to help in the kitchen," he said. The shingles had just begun to close in on his eye. It was clear, even at this early stage, that the results would be disastrous.

"If we could have one more. Maybe Ishmael. He's a very good boy."

"Two is enough."

"Mr. Hosokawa plays chess," Gen said. He should not be offering his employer up for any services in exchange for an extra boy to chop but the fact was that Mr. Hosokawa was quite brilliant where chess was concerned. He was always asking Gen to play with him on long flights and was always disappointed that Gen could not last more than twenty moves. He thought that Mr. Hosokawa might enjoy the game as much as General Benjamin.

Benjamin looked up, his swollen red face seemed to show plea-sure. "I found a set in the little boy's room. It's good to think that they would teach the game of chess to so young a boy. I think it is a remarkable tool for character. I taught all of my children to play chess."

That was something Gen had never considered, that General Benjamin had children, that he had a home or a wife or any kind of existence outside of the group that was here. Gen had never stopped to think about where they lived, but wouldn't it be in a tent some-where, hammocks strung between the muscular limbs of jungle trees? Or was it a regular job to be a revolutionary? Did he kiss his wife good-bye in the morning, leave her sitting at the table in her bathrobe drinking coca tea? Did he come home in the evening and set up the chessboard while he stretched his legs and smoked a cigarette? "I wish I were better at the game."

"Well, possibly I could teach you something. I can't imagine what I would have to teach you." General Benjamin, all of the soldiers, had an enormous respect for Gen's abilities with languages. They imag-ined that if he could speak in Russian and English and French, he could probably do anything.

"I would appreciate that," Gen said.

Benjamin nodded his head. "Please ask your Mr. Hosokawa if he would come at his convenience. There would be no need for translation. Here, write down the words for *check* and *checkmate* in Japanese. I could trouble myself to learn that much if he would come for a game." General Benjamin took one of the crumpled sheets of newspaper and straightened it out again. He handed Gen a pencil and above the headlines Gen wrote the two words. The headline he saw said *Poco Esperanza*. Little Hope.

"I'll send in some help for dinner," the General said. "They will come directly."

Gen bowed his head. Perhaps it was more respect than was deserved but there was no one there to see him do it.

It would appear that all their choices had been taken away, locked in a house with an armed teenaged boy pressed sullenly against every door. No freedom, no trust, not even enough freedom or trust to deserve a knife with which to cut up a chicken. The simplest things they believed, that they had the right to open a door, that they were free to step outside, were no longer true. But this was true instead: Gen did not go first to Mr. Hosokawa. Gen did not go and tell him about the chess. If he waited instead until tonight what difference could it make? Mr. Hosokawa would never know he had delayed. There certainly was no one else who spoke both Spanish and Japanese to tell him. On the far side of the room, Mr. Hosokawa sat with Roxane Coss on the rosewood piano bench. Leave him there. He was glad to be with her. She was teaching him something on the piano, her hands and then his hands tracing over the keys. The stark, repetitive notes made background music for the room. It was too soon to say anything for sure but he seemed to show more promise for music than he did for learning Spanish. Leave him there for now. Even from this distance Gen could see the way she leaned against him when she reached the lower keys. Mr. Hosokawa was happy, Gen did not need to see his face to know that. He had known his employer to be intelligent, driven, reasonable, and while Gen had never thought him an unhappy man he had never thought he took any particular pleasure in his life. So why not leave this pleasure undisturbed? Gen could simply make the decision himself and then Mr. Hosokawa could practice uninterrupted and Gen could go back to the kitchen where Vice President Iglesias and Ambassador Thibault were discussing sauces.

I'll send you the girls to help in the kitchen, was what General Benjamin had said.

The words looped through Gen's head like the plucked-out refrain of "Clair de Lune." He went to the kitchen and when he pushed through the swinging door he held up both his hands, a prizefighter after an effortless knockout.

"Ah, look at that!" the Vice President cried. "The genius boy returns triumphant."

"We're wasting him on kitchen help and knives," Thibault said in the good Spanish he had acquired when he first thought he would be the French ambassador to Spain. "We should send this young man to Northern Ireland. We should send him to the Gaza Strip."

"We should give him Messner's job. Then maybe we'd get out of here."

"It was only a few knives," Gen said humbly.

"Did you get to speak to Benjamin?" Ruben asked.

"Of course he spoke to Benjamin." Thibault was flipping through a cookbook from the stack in front of him. The way his finger quickly traced back and forth across the lines he appeared to be speed-reading it. "He was successful, wasn't he? You know Alfredo and Hector would have insisted on raw chicken. Better to toughen up the men. What did the good comrade say?"

"That he would send in the girls. He said no to Ishmael but I wouldn't be surprised if he turns up." Gen took a carrot out of the box and rinsed it off in the sink.

"Me they hit in the face with a gun," the Vice President said lightly. "To you they give a staff."

"What about a simple *coq au vin*?" Thibault said.

"They confiscated all the *vin*," Ruben said. "We could always send Gen out for another request. It's probably locked up around here somewhere unless they drank it all."

"No *vin*," Simon Thibault said sadly, as if it were something dangerous, as if it were a knife. How impossible. In Paris one could be careless, one could afford to run out completely because anything you wanted was half a block away, a case, a bottle, a glass. A glass of Burgundy in the autumn at a back table at Brasserie Lipp, the light warm and yellowed where it reflected off the brass railings around the bar. Edith in her navy sweater, her hair pulled back and twisted into a casual knot, her pale hands cupping the bowl of the glass. How clearly he can see it, the light, the sweater, the dark red of the wine beneath Edith's fingers. When they moved to the Heart of Darkness they had the wine shipped two dozen cases at a time, enough wine to quench an entire city through a drought. Thibault tried to make a cellar out of what was merely a wet dirt basement. French wine was the cornerstone of French diplomacy. He handed it out like peppermints. Guests stayed later at their parties. They stood forever on the walk that led down to the gate and said good night, good night, but never seemed to leave. Edith would finally go inside and bring them each a bottle, press it into their resisting hands. Then they scattered into the darkness, each back to his or her car and driver, holding the prize.

"This is my blood." Thibault raised his glass to his wife when the guests had finally gone. "It will be shed for you and for no men." Together they would go through the living room picking up crumpled napkins, stacking plates. They had sent the housekeeper home long ago. This was an act of intimacy, a pure expression of love. They were alone again. They were setting their house to right.

"Isn't there some kind of *coq sans vin*?" Ruben leaned forward to look at the book. All of these books in his home that he had never seen before! He wondered if they belonged to him or to the house.

Thibault pushed Edith's scarf over his shoulder. He said something about roasting and turned his head away to read. No sooner had he looked at the page than the door swung open again and in came three, Beatriz, the tall one, pretty Carmen, and then Ishmael, each of them with two and three knives apiece.

"You asked for us, didn't you?" Beatriz said to Gen. "I'm not on any duty at all now. I was going to watch television."

Gen looked at the clock on the wall. "It's past time for your program," he said, trying to keep his eyes on her.

"There are other things on," she said. "There are lots of good programs. 'Send the girls to do it.' That's always the way."

"They didn't just send the girls," Ishmael said in his own defense.

"Practically," Beatriz said.

Ishmael reddened and he rolled the wooden handle of the knife between his palms.

"The General said we were to come and help with dinner," Carmen said. She spoke to the Vice President. She did not turn her eyes to Gen, who did not look at her, so how did it seem that they were staring at one another?

"We are most grateful," Simon Thibault said. "We know nothing about the operation of knives. If entrusted with something as dangerous as knives there would be a bloodbath here in a matter of minutes. Not that we would be killers, mind you. We'd cut off our own fingers, bleed to death right here on the floor."

"Stop it," Ishmael said, and giggled. He had recently received one of the amateur haircuts that had been going around. Where his head had once been covered in heavy rolls of curls, the hair was now snipped with irregular closeness. It bristled like grass in some places and lay down neatly in others. In a few places it was all but gone and small patches of pink scalp shone through like the skin of a newly born mouse. He was told it would make him look older but really it just made him look ill.

"Do any of you know how to cook?" Ruben asked.

"A little," Carmen said, studying the position of her feet on the black-and-white checkerboard of the floor.

"Of course we can cook," Beatriz snapped. "Who do you think does our cooking for us?"

"Your parents. That's a possibility," the Vice President said.

"We're adults. We take care of ourselves. We don't have parents looking after us like children." Beatriz was only irritated about missing television. She had done all of her work, after all, patrolled the upstairs of the house and stood watch for two hours at the window. She had cleaned and oiled the Generals' guns and her own gun. It wasn't fair that she had been called into the kitchen. There was a wonderful program that came on in the late afternoon, a girl wearing a star-covered vest and a full skirt who sang cowboy songs and danced in high-heeled boots.

Ishmael sighed and set his three knives on the counter in front of him. His parents were dead. His father had been taken from the house one night by a group of men and no one saw him again. His mother went with a simple flu eleven months ago. Ishmael was nearly fifteen, even if his body produced no evidence to support this fact. He was not a child, if being a child meant that one had parents to cook your supper.

"So you know the onion," Thibault said, holding up an onion.

"Better than you do," Beatriz said.

"Then take that dangerous knife and chop up some onions." Thibault passed out cutting boards and bowls. Why weren't cutting boards considered weapons? Hold the two edges firmly in your hands and it was clear that these great slabs of wood were just the right size for hitting someone on the back of the head. And why not bowls, for that matter? The heavy ceramic in the colors of pastel mints seemed harmless enough while holding bananas, but once they were broken how were they much different from the knife? Couldn't one drive a shard of pottery into a human heart just as easily? Thibault asked Carmen to mince the garlic and slice the sweet peppers. To Ishmael he held up an eggplant. "Peeled, seeded, chopped."

Ishmael's knife was heavy and long. Which of them wielded a paring knife for self-defense? Who had taken the grapefruit knife? When he tried to remove the skin he wound up cutting three inches into the spongy yellow flesh. Thibault watched him for a while and then held out his hands. "Not like that," he said. "There will be nothing to eat. Here, give them here."

Ishmael stopped, examined his work, then he held out the butchered vegetable and the knife. He held the blade out to Thibault. What did he know about kitchen manners? Then Thibault had them both, the knife and the eggplant, one in each hand. Deftly, quickly, he began to peel back the skin.

"Drop it!" Beatriz shouted. On calling out she dropped her own knife, the blade slick with onions, a shower of minced onions scattering onto the floor like a wet, heavy snow. She pulled her gun from her belt and raised it up to the Ambassador.

"Jesus!" Ruben said.

Thibault did not understand what he had done. He thought at first she was angry that he had corrected the boy on his peeling. He thought the problem was with the eggplant and so he laid the eggplant down first and then the knife.

"Keep your voice down," Carmen said to Beatriz in Quechua. "You're going to get us all in trouble."

"He took the knife."

Thibault raised up his empty hands, showed his smooth palms to the gun.

"I handed him the knife," Ishmael said. "I gave it to him."

"He was only going to peel," Gen said. He could not recognize a word of this language they spoke to one another.

"He isn't supposed to hold the knife," Beatriz said in Spanish. "The General told us that. Doesn't anyone listen?" She kept her gun aimed, her heavy eyebrows pointed down. Her eyes were starting to water from the fumes of the onions, and soon there were tears washing over her cheeks, which everyone misunderstood.

"What about this?" Thibault began quietly, keeping his hands up. "Everyone can stand away from me and I can show Ishmael how to peel an eggplant. You keep your gun right on me and if it looks like I'm about to do something funny you may shoot me. You may shoot Gen, too, if I do something terrible."

Carmen put down her knife.

"I don't think—" Gen started, but no one was paying attention to him. He felt a small, cold hardness in his chest, like the pit of a cherry had slipped into his heart. He did not want to be shot and he did not want to be offered up to be shot.

"I can shoot you?" Beatriz said. It wasn't his place to give permission, was it? It had not been her intention to shoot anyone anyway.

"Go ahead," Ishmael said, taking out his own gun and pointing it at the Ambassador. He was trying to keep his face serious but he wasn't having much luck. "I'll shoot you, too, if I have to. Show me how to peel the eggplant. I've shot men over less than an eggplant." *Berenjena,* that was the word in Spanish. A beautiful word. It could be a woman's name.

So Thibault picked up the knife and set about his work. His hands stayed remarkably steady as he peeled with two guns pointed on him. Carmen did not participate. She went back to mincing the garlic, hitting her knife against the board in brisk, angry strokes. Thibault kept his eyes on the deep luster of the purple-black skin. "It's difficult to do with a knife this large. You want to slide it just under the surface. Pretend that you're skinning a fish. See that. Very fluid. It's delicate work." All that was lovely about the eggplant fell into ribbons on the floor.

There was something soothing about it, the way it all came out so neatly. "Okay," Ishmael said. "I understand. Give it to me now." He put down his gun and held out his hands. Thibault turned the knife, gave him the smooth wooden handle and another eggplant. What would Edith say when she heard he had been shot over an eggplant or turning on the television? If he was going to die he had hoped for a little bit of honor in his death.

"Well," Ruben said, wiping his face with a dishtowel. "Nothing around here is a small event."

Beatriz mopped up her tears against the dark green sleeve of her jacket. "Onions," she said, pushing the newly oiled gun back into her belt.

"I'd be happy to do them for you if at any point you deem me capable," Thibault said, and went to wash his hands.

Gen stood next to the sink trying to decide the best way to phrase his question. Any way it was put it seemed impolite. He spoke to Thibault in French. He whispered, "Why did you tell her she could shoot me?"

"Because they *wouldn't* shoot you. They all like you too much. It was a harmless gesture on my part. I thought it gave me more credibility. Telling her she could shoot me, now *that* was a risk. They care nothing for me and they think the world of you. It's not like I told them they could shoot poor Ruben. That girl might want to shoot Ruben."

"Still," Gen said. He wanted to be firm on this point but he felt it slipping away from him. Sometimes he suspected he was the weakest person in captivity.

"I hear you gave her your wristwatch."

"Who told you that?"

"Everybody knows. She flashes it around every chance she gets. Would she shoot the man who gave her his watch?"

"Well, that's what we don't know."

Thibault dried his hands and looped a careless arm around Gen's neck. "I would never let them shoot you, no more than I'd let them shoot my own brother. I'll tell you what, Gen, when this is over, you'll come and visit us in Paris. The second this is over I'm resigning my post and Edith and I are moving back to Paris. When you feel like traveling again, you will bring Mr. Hosokawa and Roxane. You can marry one of my daughters if you want to, then you would be my son rather than my brother." He leaned forward and whispered in Gen's ear, "This will all seem very funny to us then."

Gen inhaled Thibault's breath. He tried to take in some of the courage, some of the carelessness. He tried to believe that one day they would all be in Paris in the Thibaults' apartment, but he couldn't picture it. Thibault kissed Gen beside his left eye and then let him go. He went off in search of a roasting pan.

"Speaking in French," Ruben said to Gen. "That's very impolite."

"How is French impolite?"

"Because everyone here speaks Spanish. I can't remember the last time I was in a room where everyone spoke the same language and then you go off speaking some language I failed in high school." And it was true, when they spoke in Spanish no one in the kitchen waited for anything to be explained, no one was forced to stare vacantly while the others tore through unintelligible sentences. No one wondered suspiciously if what was being said was in fact something horrible about them. Of the six people in the room, Spanish was a first language only for Ruben. Gen spoke Japanese, Thibault French, and the three with the knives had first learned Quechua in their village and then a hybrid of Spanish and Quechua together from which they could comb out the Spanish with varying degrees of success.

"You could take the day off," Ishmael said to the translator, a tough rubber spiral of eggplant skin dangling from his knife. "You don't have to stay."

At that Carmen, who had been keeping her eyes on the garlic she was chopping, looked up. The nerve, which she had found so briefly the night before, had been missing all day and all she had managed to do was avoid Gen, but that didn't mean she wanted him to go. She had to believe she had been sent to the kitchen for a reason. She prayed to Saint Rose that the shyness which came down on her like a blinding fog would be lifted as suddenly as it landed.

Gen had no intention of leaving. "I can do more than translate," he said. "I can wash vegetables. I can stir something if something needed stirring."

Thibault came back lugging a huge metal roaster in each hand. He heaved them one at a time up onto the stovetop, where each pan covered three burners. "Did I hear leaving? Is Gen even thinking about leaving?"

"I was thinking about staying."

"No one is leaving! Dinner for fifty-eight, is that what they expect? I will not lose one pair of hands, even if the hands belong to the very valuable translator. Do they think we're going to do this every night, every meal? Do they think I'm a caterer? Has she chopped the onions yet? May I inquire as to the state of the onions or will you threaten to shoot me?"

Beatriz wagged her knife at Thibault. Her face was wet and red from crying. "I would have shot you if I had to but I didn't, so you should be grateful. And I chopped your stupid onions. Are you finished with me now?"

"Does dinner look finished to you?" Thibault said, pouring oil into the pans and turning on the bright blue flames of gas. "Go wash the chickens. Gen, bring me the onions. Sauté these onions."

"Why does he get to cook the onions?" Beatriz said. "They're my onions. And I won't wash the chickens because that does not involve a knife. I was only sent in here to work the knives."

"I will kill her," Thibault said in weary French.

Gen took the bowl of onions and hugged it to his chest. It was never the right time or it was always the right time, depending on how you looked at it. They could stand there for hours, six squares of tile apart from each other and never say anything or one of them, either one, could step forward and begin to speak. Gen was hoping it would be Carmen, but then Gen was hoping they would all be released and neither seemed likely to happen. Gen gave the onions to Thibault, who dumped them into the two pans where they spat and hissed like Beatriz herself. Rallying the very small amount of bravery he still possessed, Gen went to the drawer by the telephone, which hung naked on the wall without its cord. He found a small pad of paper and a pen. He wrote the words *cuchillo*, *ajo*, *chica* each on its own piece of paper and took them to Carmen while Thibault argued with Beatriz over who was to stir the onions. He tried to keep in mind all the languages he had spoken, all the cities he had been to, all the important words of other men that had come through his mouth. What he asked of himself was small and still he could feel his hands shaking. "Knife," he said, and put the first piece down. "Garlic." He set that one on top of the garlic. "Girl." The last piece he handed to Carmen and after she looked at it for a minute she put it in her pocket.

Carmen nodded, she made a sound, something like, "ah," not quite a word.

Gen sighed. It was better now but only slightly. "Do you want to learn?"

Carmen nodded again, her eyes fixed on a drawer handle. She

tried to see Saint Rose of Lima on that handle, a tiny blue-cloaked woman balancing on the curved silver bar. She tried to find her voice through prayer. She thought of Roxane Coss, whose very hands had braided her hair. Shouldn't that give her strength?

"I don't know that I'm much of a teacher. I'm trying to teach Mr. Hosokawa Spanish. He writes down words in a notebook and memorizes them. Maybe we could try the same for you."

After a minute of silence, Carmen offered up that same sound, a little "ah" that gave no real information other than that she had heard him. She was an idiot. A fool.

Gen looked around. Ishmael was watching them but he didn't seem to care.

"The eggplant is perfect!" Ruben said. "Thibault, did you see this eggplant? Every cube is exactly the same size."

"I forgot to take out the seeds," Ishmael said.

"The seeds don't matter," Ruben said. "The seeds are as good for you as anything else."

"Gen, are you going to sauté?" Thibault said.

"One minute," Gen said, and held up his hand. He whispered to Carmen, "Have you changed your mind? Do you want me to help you?"

And then it seemed the saint gave Carmen a sharp blow between her shoulder blades and the word that was so tightly lodged in her throat disengaged like a tough piece of gristle caught in the windpipe. "Yes," she said, gasping. "Yes."

"So we'll practice?"

"Every day." Carmen picked up the words, *knife* and *garlic*, and she put them in her pocket along with *girl*. "I learned my letters. I haven't practiced in a while. I used to make them every day and then we started training for this."

Gen could see her up in the mountains, where it was always cold at night, sitting by the fire, her face flushed from heat and concentration, one piece of dark hair falling from behind her ear the way it was now. She has a cheap tablet, a stubby pencil. In his mind he stands

next to her, praises the straight lines of her *T* and *H,* the delicate
sweep of her *Q.* Outside he can hear the last call of the birds as they
career towards their nests before dusk. He had thought once that she
was a boy and it terrified him, this feeling. "We'll go over the letters,"
he said. "We'll start there."

"Am I the only one who has to work?" Beatriz called loudly.

"When?" Carmen only mouthed the word.

"Tonight," Gen said. What he wanted then was something he
could barely believe. He wanted to fold her in his arms. He wanted to
kiss the parting of her hair. He wanted to touch her lips with the tips
of his fingers. He wanted to whisper things to her in Japanese. Maybe,
if there was time, he could teach her Japanese as well.

"Tonight in the china closet," Carmen said. "Teach me tonight."

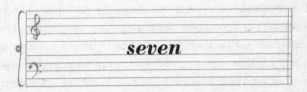

seven

*t*he priest was right about the weather, even though the break came later than he had predicted. By the middle of November, the *garúa* had ended. It did not drift away. It did not lessen. It simply stopped, so that one day everything had the saturated quality of a book dropped into a bathtub and the next day the air was bright and crisp and extremely blue. It reminded Mr. Hosokawa of cherry blossom season in Kyoto and it reminded Roxane Coss of October on Lake Michigan. They stood together in the early morning before she began her singing. He pointed out a pair of yellow birds to her, bright as chrysanthemums, sitting on the branch of some previously unseen tree. They pecked for a while at the spongy bark and then flew off, first one and then the other, up and over the wall. One by one all the hostages and all their keepers went up to the windows around the house, stared and blinked and stared again. So many people put their hands and noses on the glass that Vice President Iglesias had to come out with a rag and a bottle of ammonia and wipe down each pane. "Look at the garden," he said to no one in particular. "The weeds are as tall as the flowers." One would have thought that with so much rain and so little light the forward march of growth would have been suspended, when in fact everything had thrived. The weeds alongside the domesticated bedding plants sniffed at the distant jungle in the air and stretched their roots down and stretched their leaves up in an attempt to turn the vice-presidential garden back into a wild thing. They drank up every bit of the rain. They could have survived another year of wet weather. Left long enough to their own devices, they would overtake the house and pull down the garden wall. After all, this yard had once been a part of the continuum, the dense and twisted interstate of vines that spread right to the sandy edges of the ocean. The only thing that prevented them from taking over the house was the gardener, who pulled up whatever he deemed unworthy, burned it, and then clipped back the rest. But the gardener was now on an indefinite vacation.

The sun had been up and shining no more than an hour and in that time several of the plants had grown half a centimeter.

"I'll have to do something about the yard." Ruben sighed, not that he knew where he would find the time with all that needed to be done in the house. Not that they were likely to let him outside in the first place. Not that they were likely to give him the things he needed: hedge shears, trowels, pruning knives. Everything in the garden shed was a murder weapon.

As Father Arguedas opened the windows in the living room, he thanked God for the light and the sweet quality of the air. Though he was in the house, across the garden, and behind the wall, he could hear more clearly the rustling on the street without the rain to muffle the sound. There were no more messages shouted over the wall, but still he could imagine a large crowd of men and guns. The priest suspected that either they had no plan of action anymore or that they had a plan so complex that it no longer exactly included them. While General Benjamin continued to cut out every mention of their circumstances from the newspaper, they had caught a snippet of talk on the television that a tunnel was being dug, that the police were planning on digging their way up into the house, and so the crisis would end much the way it had started, with strangers crashing into the room and redirecting the course of their lives, but no one believed this. It was too far-fetched, too much like a spy movie to be real. Father Arguedas stared at his feet, his cheap black lace-up shoes settled on such expensive carpet, and he wondered what went on deep beneath the ground. He prayed for their safe delivery, for the safe delivery of each and every one of them, but he did not pray to be rescued through a tunnel. He did not pray to be rescued at all. He only prayed for God's will, His love and protection. He tried to clear his heart of self-ish thoughts while at the same time being grateful for all that God had granted him. Take the mass, as only one example. In his former life (for that was how he thought of it now) he was only allowed to cele-brate the mass with his parishioners when everyone else was on holi-day or sick and then it was the six A.M. mass they gave to him or a mass on Tuesday. Mainly his responsibilities within the church were the same as the ones he had held before he was a priest: he distributed the host he had not blessed on the far left-hand aisle of the church or he lit the candles or he snuffed them out. Here, after much discussion, the Generals agreed to allow Messner to bring in the implements of communion, and last Sunday in the dining room, Father Arguedas celebrated the mass with all of his friends. People who were not Catholic attended and people who did not understand what he was saying got down on their knees. Everyone was more likely to pray when there was something specific they wanted. The young terrorists closed their eyes and bent their chins deeply to their chests, while the Generals stayed in the back of the room. It could have been something else entirely. So many of the terrorist organizations nowadays wanted to abolish all religion, especially Catholicism. Had they been taken over by La Dirección Auténtica instead of the much more reasonable La Familia de Màrtin Suarez, they would never have been allowed to pray. LDA would have dragged one hostage up to the roof every day for the press to see, and then shot him in the head in an attempt to speed negotiations. Father Arguedas considered such things while he lay on the living-room carpet late at night. They were fortunate, really. There was no other way to look at it. Wasn't there still freedom in the deepest sense if there was the freedom to pray? At his mass,

Roxane Coss sang "Ave Maria," an event of such startling beauty that (and he did not wish to sound competitive) it simply could not be topped at any church, anywhere, including Rome. Her voice was so pure, so light, that it opened up the ceiling and carried their petitions directly to God. It swept over them like the feathery dusting of wings, so that even the Catholics who no longer practiced their faith, and the non-Catholics who came along because there was nothing else to do, and all those who had no idea what he was saying, and the stone-cold atheists who wouldn't have cared anyway, because of her singing they all went away feeling moved, feeling comforted, feeling, perhaps, the slightest tremors of faith. The priest stared at the slightly yellowed stucco wall that protected them from whatever was waiting to happen outside. It must have been ten feet high and was covered in some sections with ivy. It was a beautiful wall, not unlike what might have surrounded the Mount of Olives. Perhaps it was not immediately obvious but now he saw how one could consider such a wall a blessing.

Roxane sang Rossini that morning, in keeping with the weather. One song, "Bella crudele," she sang seven times. Clearly, she was trying to perfect something, to find something lodged at the very center of the score that she felt she had not reached. She and Kato communicated in their own way. She pointed at a line of notes. He played it. She tapped her fingers in light rhythm against the top of the piano. He played it again. She sang the line unaccompanied. He played it without her. She sang while he played. They circled each other, each one oblivious to feelings, each caring only for the music. She closed her eyes while he moved through the opening, she nodded her head slightly in approval. He made such easy work of the score. There was no showy bravado in the movements of his arms. He kept things small and light, perfect for her voice. It was one thing when he played for himself, but when he was the accompanist he played like a man who was trying not to wake the neighbors.

Roxane stood so straight that one could easily forget how short she was. She rested her hand on the piano, then she crossed her palms over her heart. She sang. She had taken to following the example of the Japanese and had given up wearing her shoes. Mr. Hosokawa had kept the tradition of his host and had worn his shoes for the first week of their captivity, but as time went on he felt that he could no longer bear it. Wearing shoes in the house was barbaric. There was almost as much indignity in wearing shoes in the house as there was in being kidnapped. When his shoes came off, then so came Gen's, and Kato's, and Mr. Yamamoto's, Mr. Aoi's, Mr. Ogawa's, and Roxane's. She padded around in a pair of athletic socks borrowed from the Vice President, whose feet were not much larger than her own. She sang now in those socks. When she got the song exactly right she took it straight through to the end without a flutter of hesitation. It was impossible to say that her singing had improved, but there was something in her interpretation of the lines that had shifted almost imperceptibly. She sang as if she was saving the life of every person in the room. A breeze made the sheers at the window shiver for a moment but everything else was still. There was not a sound from the street. There was not a sound from the two yellow birds.

On the morning that the rains ended, Gen waited until the last note had been sung and then went to stand beside Carmen. It was a particularly good time to talk without being noticed as everyone wandered around in a state of stunned confusion after Roxane let go of her final note. If anyone had thought to simply walk out the door, they might not have been stopped, but no one was thinking about leaving. When Mr. Hosokawa went to get her water, Roxane stood up to follow him and then looped her arm through his arm.

"She's in love with him," Carmen whispered to Gen. He misunderstood her for the smallest instant, heard only the word *love*. Then he stopped and made himself recall the entire sentence. He could do that. It was as if he had a tape recorder in his head.

"Miss Coss? In love with Mr. Hosokawa?"

Carmen nodded, her head making only the smallest gesture, but he had learned to read her. Love?

What he had seen, and done his best to overlook, was that Mr. Hosokawa was in love with Roxane. The notion that the opposite could be possible had never occurred to him and he asked Carmen what she saw.

"Everything," Carmen whispered. "The way she looks at him, the way she chooses him. She's always sitting with him and they can't even talk. He's so peaceful. She would want to be with him."

"Did she tell you?"

"Maybe." Carmen smiled. "She talks to me sometimes in the morning but I don't know what she says."

Of course, Gen thought. He watched them walk away, his employer and the soprano. "I would think that everyone must be in love with her. How could she even make a choice?"

"Are you in love with her?" Carmen asked. She met his eyes in a way that would never have been possible a week ago. It was Gen who had to look away.

"No," he said. "No." Gen was in love with Carmen. And though he met her every night in the china closet and helped her with her reading and writing, he never revealed as much. They spoke of vowels and consonants. They spoke of diphthongs and possessives. She copied letters into a notebook. As many words as he gave to her, she asked for more. She would have gladly kept him up all night, repeating, practicing, quizzing. He spent his whole life in a confused dream state in which he was never exactly awake or completely asleep. He wondered sometimes if it was love or just a lack of rest that had twisted such a longing in his heart. He stumbled. He drifted off in wing-backed chairs and in the minutes he slept he dreamed of Carmen. Yes, she was shy, and yes, a terrorist from the jungle, but she was as smart as any girl he had met at university. You could tell by the way she picked things up. All she had needed was the smallest amount of instruction. She ate through information like fire licks up hay and asked for more. She took off her gun every night and put it in the glass-front cupboard beside the blue gravy boat. She sat on the floor with her notebook balanced on top of her knees, her pencil sharp. There had been no girls like Carmen at university. There had never been a girl like Carmen. What a sense of humor one would need to believe that the woman you love is not in Tokyo or Paris or New York or Athens. The woman you love is a girl who dresses as a boy and she lives in a village in a jungle, the name of which you are not allowed to know, not that knowing the name would be particularly helpful in trying to find it. The woman you love puts her gun beside a blue gravy boat at night so that you can teach her to read. She came into your life through an air-conditioner vent and how she will leave is the question that keeps you awake in the few free moments you have to sleep.

"Mr. Hosokawa and Miss Coss," Carmen said. "Out of all the people in the world, they found each other. What are the chances of that?"

"What about Mrs. Hosokawa?" Gen said. He did not know his employer's wife well, but he saw her often. She was a dignified woman with cool hands and a calming voice. She called him Mr. Watanabe.

"Mrs. Hosokawa lives in Japan," Carmen said, looking off towards the kitchen, "which is about a million kilometers away from here. Besides, he isn't going home, and while I'm sorry for Mrs. Hosokawa, I don't think that means that Mr. Hosokawa should be alone."

"What do you mean, he isn't going home?"

Carmen gave Gen a very slight smile. She tilted back her head so that he could see her face beneath the bill of her cap. "This is where we live now."

"Not forever," Gen said.

"I think," Carmen said, mouthing the words without making any sound. She was wondering if she had said too much. She knew that her loyalties absolutely must be to the Generals, but telling things to Gen wasn't like telling things to anyone else. Gen could keep a secret because everything about them was a secret, the china closet, the reading. She trusted him absolutely. She plucked at the side of his hand with two fingers and then walked away from him. He waited a minute before following her. She walked silently, her movements small and relaxed. No one noticed her as she passed by. She went into the small lavatory off the hall. All of the pretty rose-scented soaps were gone now and the towels were dingy, but the gold swan was still nesting over the sink and when you turned the wing-shaped handles, water still slid from her long throat. Carmen took off her cap and washed her face. She tried to comb out her hair with her fingers. Her face in the mirror was too coarse, too dark. At home some people had called her beautiful but now she had seen beauty and knew it was something she could never possess. Some mornings, only a few, when Carmen came into the room to bring Roxane her breakfast, the singer had still been asleep and Carmen would put down the tray and touch her shoulder. When Roxane's great, pale eyes blinked open she would smile at Carmen, she would pull the covers back and motion for Carmen to lie down next to her in the warm embroidered sheets. She was careful to dangle her boots over the edge. They would both close their eyes and take an extra five minutes of sleep, Roxane pulling the covers up to Carmen's neck. How quickly Carmen dreamed of her sisters, her mother! In only a few minutes of sleep they all came to visit her. They all wanted to see her there, nestled in the pillows of such a comfortable bed, beside such an unimaginable woman. Yellow hair, blue eyes, skin like white roses brushed in pink. Who would not be in love with Roxane Coss?

"Gen!" Victor Fyodorov said just as he was approaching the bathroom door. "How can you be so difficult to find when there is no place for you to go?"

"I didn't realize—"

"Her voice this morning, didn't you think? Perfection!"

Gen agreed.

"So, this is the time to talk to her."

"Now?"

"Now I know is the perfect time."

"I've asked you every day this week."

"And I have not been completely prepared, that is true, but this morning when she went over and over again on the Rossini, I knew that she would understand my inadequacies. She is a compassionate woman. Today I was assured of that." Fyodorov was twisting his big hands one around the other as if he were washing them beneath some unseen stream of water. Though his voice was calm, there was a distinct look of panic in his eyes, the sharp smell of panic on his skin.

"The time for me is not exactly—"

"The time for *me*," Fyodorov said. Then he added in a low voice, "I will lose my nerve to speak." Fyodorov had shaved off his heavy growth of beard, a process that had been both painful and time-consuming, given the poor quality of the razor blades, and left behind a vast expanse of his own raw, pink face. He had had the Vice President wash and iron his clothes while he stood beside the washing machine, shivering with a towel around his waist. He had bathed and trimmed the hairs from his nose and ears with a pair of cuticle scissors that he had bribed off of Gilbert with a pack of cigarettes. While he had the chance, he cut his nails and tried to do something about his hair, but that proved to be too great a task for cuticle scissors. He had made every effort he knew to make. This was most certainly the day.

Gen nodded towards the bathroom door. "I was on my way."

Fyodorov looked over his shoulder and then held out his hand as if to lead Gen in. "Of course. Of course that is nothing. That long I can wait. However long. You take your time. I will be outside the door. I will make sure that I am first in line for our translator when he is finished." Sweat was creeping down the sides of Fyodorov's shirt, leaving a new dark stain inside a history of much paler stains. Gen wondered if that was what he meant by being unable to wait much longer.

"One minute," he said quietly, and then let himself inside without knocking.

"I wish I knew what you were saying." Carmen laughed. She tried to mimic the words, spoke a Russian nonsense which sounded something close to, "I never cracker table."

Gen put a finger to his lips. The room was small and very dark, black marble walls, black marble floors. One of the lights had burned out next to the mirror. Gen would have to remember to ask Ruben about a new bulb.

She sat up on the sink. "It sounded very important. It was Ledbed, the Russian?" She was whispering.

Gen told her it was Fyodorov.

"Oh, the big one. How do you know Russian, too? How do you know so many languages?"

"It's my job."

"No, no. It's because you understand something and I want to know it, too."

"I only have a minute," he whispered. He was so close to her hair, which was darker, deeper even than the marble. "I have to translate for him. He's waiting right outside the door."

"We can talk tonight."

Gen shook his head. "I want to talk about what you said. What do you mean, this is where we live now?"

Carmen sighed. "You know I can't say. But ask yourself, would it be so awful if we all stayed here in this beautiful house?" This room was a third of the size of the china closet. Her knees touched his legs. If he took even a half step back he would be on the commode. She wished she could take his hand. Why would he want to leave her, leave this place?

"This has to end sooner or later," he said. "These sorts of things never just go on indefinitely, somebody stops them."

"Only if people do terrible things. We haven't hurt anyone. No one is unhappy here."

"*Everyone* is unhappy here." But even as he was saying it Gen was not entirely sure it was true. Carmen's face turned down and she studied her hands in her lap.

"Go on and translate," she said.

"If there's something you should tell me."

Carmen's eyes were watery and she blinked them hard. How ridiculous it would be for her to cry. Would it be such a terrible thing to stay? Be together long enough to speak perfect Spanish, to read it and write, to learn English and then maybe some Japanese? But that was her own selfishness. She knew that. Gen was right to want to get away from her. She offered nothing. She only took his time. "I don't know a thing."

Fyodorov knocked on the door. His mounting nervousness would not allow him to do otherwise. "Trans-laaa-tor?" He sang the word.

"A minute," Gen called through the door.

Time was up and now Carmen had lost a couple of tears. There needed to be whole days together. There needed to be weeks and months of uninterrupted time to say all the things that needed to be said. "Maybe you're right," he told her finally. The way she was sitting on the black marble sink in front of the mirror, he could see both her face and her narrow back at the same time. He could see in the large oval mirror with the frame of gilded gold leaves, his own face over her shoulder, looking at her. He could see in his face a love that was so obviously displayed that she must already know everything there was to know about it. He was so close to her then that they owned every molecule of air in the tiny room and the air grew heavy with their desire and worked to move them together. It was with the smallest step forward that his face was in her hair and then her arms were around his back and they were holding each other. It seemed so simple to get to this place, such a magnificent relief, that he couldn't imagine why he had not been holding her every minute since they first met.

"Translator?" Fyodorov said, his voice a little worried this time.

Carmen leaned forward and kissed him. There was no time for kissing but she wanted him to know that in the future there would be. A kiss in so much loneliness was like a hand pulling you up out of the water, scooping you up from a place of drowning and into the reckless abundance of air. A kiss, another kiss. "Go," she whispered.

And Gen, who wanted no more in the world than this girl and the walls of this bathroom, kissed her again. He was breathless and dizzy and had to lean a moment against her shoulder before he could step away. Carmen got off the sink and stood behind the door, opened the door, and sent him back out into the world.

"Are you unwell?" Fyodorov asked, more in irritation than

concern. Now the back of his shirt was clinging damply to his shoulders. Didn't the translator know this would not be easy for him? All of the time he had spent, first considering whether or not he should speak and then deciding to speak, then after that decision was made there was the decision as to what should be said. In his heart the feelings were clear, but to translate such feelings into words was another matter entirely. Ledbed and Berezovsky were sympathetic, but then they were Russians. They understood the pain of Fyodorov's love. Frankly, they experienced similar pains themselves. It was not impossible that they would eventually find their own nerve and approach the translator to approach the soprano. The more Fyodorov spoke of his heart's desire, the more they were sure it was a malady with which they had all been infected.

"I apologize for the delay," Gen said. The room before him melted and waved like a horizon line in the desert. He leaned back against the closed bathroom door. She was in there, not two and a half centimeters of wood away from him.

"You look unwell," the Russian said, and now he was concerned. He had a fondness for the translator. "Your voice sounds weak."

"I'm sure I'll be fine."

"You are pale, I think. Your eyes are very damp. Perhaps if you are truly ill the Generals will let you go. Since the accompanist, they claim to be very sympathetic in matters of health."

Gen blinked in an attempt to still the swaying furniture, but the bright stripes of an ottoman continued to pulse in the rhythm of his blood. He stood up straight and shook his head. "Look at me," he said uncertainly, "fine now. I have no intention of leaving." He looked at the sun pouring in through the tall windows, the shadows of the leaves falling across the carpet. Finally, standing here with the Russian, Gen could understand what Carmen was saying. Look at this room! The draperies and chandeliers, the soft, deep cushions of the sofas, the colors, gold and green and blue, every shade a jewel. Who would not want to be in this room?

Fyodorov smiled and slapped the translator on the back. "What a man you are! You are all for the people. Ah, how greatly I admire you."

"All for the people," Gen repeated. The Slavic language was pear brandy on his tongue.

"Then we will go to speak to Roxane Coss! There is no time for me to wash again. If I was to stop I would lose my nerve forever."

Gen led the way to the kitchen but he might as well have been walking alone. He had not one thought for Fyodorov, for how he felt or what he might wish to say. Gen's head was filled with Carmen. Carmen up on the sink. He would always remember her there. Years from now when he would think of her it would always be as she was on that day, sitting up on the black marble, her heavy work boots patched with electrical tape, her hands flat out on the cool sink top. Her hair hung loose and straight, parted in the middle, tucked behind such delicate ears. He thought of the kiss, her arms around his back, but the greatest pleasure was seeing her face, the sweet exact shape of a heart, her dark brown eyes and such unruly eyebrows, the round mouth he wanted to touch. Mr. Hosokawa was easily distracted from his studies. Tell him a word one day and he may well have forgotten it the next. He laughed off his mistakes, put tiny check marks by the words he had misspelled. Not Carmen. To tell something to Carmen was to have it sewn forever into the silky folds of her brain. She closed her eyes and said the word, spelled it aloud and on paper, and then she owned it. He did not need to ask her again. They went forward, pressing on through the night as if they were being hunted down by wolves. She wanted more of everything. More vocabulary, more verbs. She wanted him to explain the rules of grammar and punctuation. She wanted gerunds and infinitives and participles. At the end of the lesson, when they were both too tired for another word, she would lean back against the cupboards in the china closet and yawn. "Tell me about commas," she would say, the plates towering over her head, a service in gold for twenty-four, a service with a wide cobalt-blue band around the edge for sixty, each cup hanging still on its own cup hook.

"It's so late. You don't need to know about commas tonight."

She folded her arms across her narrow chest, slid her back towards the floor. "Commas end the sentence," she said, forcing him to correct her, to explain.

Gen closed his eyes, leaned forward, and put his head on his knees. Sleep was a country for which he could not obtain a visa. "Commas," he said through a yawn, "pause the sentence and separate ideas."

"Ah," said Fyodorov, "she is with your employer."

Gen looked up and Carmen was gone and he was in the kitchen with Fyodorov. The china closet was only five feet away. As far as he knew, he and Carmen were the only ones who went in there at all. Mr. Hosokawa and Roxane were standing at the sink. It was odd the way they never spoke and yet always seemed to be engaged in a conversation. Ignacio, Guadalupe, and Humberto were at the breakfast table cleaning guns, a puzzle of disconnected metal spreading out on newspapers before them as they rubbed oil into each part. Thibault sat at the table with them, reading cookbooks.

"I suppose I should try again later," Fyodorov said sadly. "When she isn't so busy."

Roxane Coss did not seem to be in the least bit busy. She was simply standing there, running her finger around the edge of a glass, her face tilted up towards the light. "We should at least ask," Gen said. He wanted to meet his obligation, to not have Fyodorov following him places, saying he was now able to speak and then two minutes later saying he was unable.

Fyodorov took a large handkerchief from his pocket and rubbed at his face as if he were trying to remove a smear of dirt. "There is no reason to do this now. We aren't going anywhere. We will never be released. Is it not enough that I should get to see her every day? That is the greatest luxury. The rest of this is all selfishness on my part. What do I think I have to say to her?"

But Gen wasn't listening. Russian was by no means his best language, and if his concentration lapsed even for a moment it all became a blur of consonants, hard Cyrillic letters bouncing like hail off a tin roof. He smiled at Fyodorov and nodded, a kind of laziness he would never have allowed himself in the real world.

"Isn't the sunlight remarkable?" Mr. Hosokawa said to Gen when he noticed him standing there. "Suddenly I am hungry and the only thing that will feed me is sunlight. All I want to do is stand next to windows. I wonder if it isn't a vitamin deficiency."

"I would think we are all lacking something by now," Gen said. "You know Mr. Fyodorov."

Mr. Hosokawa bowed to him and Fyodorov, confused, bowed in return and then bowed to Roxane, who bowed, though less deeply, to him. In a circle they resembled nothing so much as geese dipping their long necks down to the water. "He wishes to speak to Roxane about the music." Gen said it first in Japanese and then again in English. Mr. Hosokawa and Roxane both smiled at Fyodorov, who then pressed his handkerchief to his mouth as if he might begin to bite it.

"Then I will go for chess." Mr. Hosokawa looked at his watch. "We are to play at eleven. I will not be terribly early."

"I'm sure there's no need for you to go," Gen said.

"But no need to stay." Mr. Hosokawa looked at Roxane and with a certain tenderness of expression seemed to cover all his points in silence: he would be going, he would play chess, she could come and sit with them later if she liked. There was a brief exchange of smiles between the two of them and then Mr. Hosokawa left through the swinging door. There was a lightness in his step Gen did not remember seeing before. He walked with his head up. He wore his shabby tuxedo pants and graying shirt with dignity.

"He is a great man, your friend," she said quietly, watching the empty place where Mr. Hosokawa had been.

"I have always thought so," Gen said. He still felt puzzled, despite what Carmen had explained. The look that passed between the two was one he recognized. Gen was in love and the feeling was so utterly foreign to him that he had a hard time believing that others were experiencing it as well. Except, of course, for Simon Thibault, who sat there with his cookbooks, wearing his wife's blue wrap like a flag. Everyone knew Thibault was in love.

Roxane lifted her head to the great height of Fyodorov. She composed her face in a different way now. She was ready to listen, ready to receive her professional compliments, ready to make the speaker feel that what he was saying actually had some meaning for her. "Mr. Fyodorov, would you be more comfortable sitting in the living room?"

Fyodorov faltered under the weight of a direct question. He appeared to be confused by the translation, and just when Gen was ready to repeat himself he answered. "I am comfortable where you are comfortable. I am very happy to stay in the kitchen. I believe this to be a fine room in which I personally have not spent enough of my time." In fact, as much as he trusted Ledbed and Berezovsky, he would just as soon declare himself in a room where no one could eavesdrop in Russian or English. The occasional clunk of the gun barrels hitting the table or Thibault clucking his tongue over a recipe seemed preferable to being overheard.

"This is certainly fine for me," Roxane said. She sipped her glass of water. The sight of it made Fyodorov tremble, the water, her lips. He had to look away. What was it he wanted to say? He could write a letter instead, wouldn't that be proper? The translator could translate. A word was a word if you spoke it or wrote it down.

"I believe I need a chair," Fyodorov said.

Gen heard the weakness in his voice and rushed forward for a chair. The Russian was slumping down even before it arrived and Gen was barely able to slip it under him in time. With a great exhalation that could have signified the end of everything, the big man tilted his head down towards the floor.

"My God," Roxane said, leaning over him, "is he sick?" She pulled a dishtowel off the refrigerator handle and dipped it into her drinking water. She touched the cool terry cloth to the pink expanse of his neck. He whimpered slightly when she rested her hand against the cloth.

"Do you know what's wrong with him?" Roxane asked Gen. "He looked perfectly fine when he came in here. It's just like Christopf, his color, the faintness. Could he be a diabetic? Touch him, he's cold!"

"Tell me what she says," Fyodorov whispered from between his knees.

"She wants to know what's wrong with you," Gen said.

There was a long silence and Roxane slid her fingers over to his neck to feel the steady thumping of his pulse. Two of her delicate fingers lodged beneath a great flap of his ear. "Tell her it's love," he said.

"Love?"

Fyodorov nodded his head. His hair was thick and wavy and not entirely clean. It had turned quite gray at the temples, but the crown of his head, which Gen and Roxane stared at, was still dark, the crown of a young man.

"You never said anything to me about love," Gen said, feeling tricked, feeling he had been put into an awkward position now.

"I'm not in love with you," Fyodorov said. "Why should I speak to you of love?"

"This is not what I believed I was here to translate."

With real effort, Fyodorov raised himself up. His skin was not just clammy but the color and consistency of actual clams. "What are you here to translate then, what you deem proper? Are we to speak only of the weather? Since when is it for you to decide what it is fitting for people to say to one another?"

Fyodorov was right. Gen had to admit it. The personal feelings of the translator were not the question here. It was not Gen's business to edit the conversation. It was hardly his business to listen at all. "All right," he said. It was easy to sound tired in Russian. "All right then."

"What is he saying?" Roxane said. She moved the cloth to his forehead now that he was sitting up.

"She wants to know what you're saying," Gen told Fyodorov. "I should tell her love?"

Fyodorov gave a weak smile. He would ignore all of this. No real harm had been done as yet, it was just a little faintness. His only hope was to begin at the beginning, to start the speech as he had practiced it a hundred times in front of Ledbed and Berezovsky. He cleared his throat. "In my country, I am the Secretary of Commerce," he opened in a thin voice. "An appointed position, I could be gone just like that." He snapped his fingers but didn't succeed in getting much of a snap out of them. They were sweaty and so slipped by one another without a sound. "But for now it is a very good job and I am grateful. For a man to know what he has when he has it, that is what makes him a fortunate man." He tried to look into her eyes but it was really too much for him. He could feel a grinding sensation in his lower intestine.

Gen translated and tried not to think where all of this was going.

"Ask him if he's feeling better," Roxane said. "I think his color is better." She took the cloth from his head and he looked disappointed.

"She wants to know how you're feeling now."

"Is she listening to the story?"

"You can tell as well as I can."

"Tell her I'm fine. Tell her this: Russia never had any intention of investing capital in this poor country." He kept his eyes for as long as he could on the eyes of Roxane Coss, but when they began to exhaust him too greatly he turned them to Gen. "We have a poor country of our own with many other poor countries to support besides. When the invitation to attend this party came, my friend Mr. Berezovsky, a great businessman, was here and he said I should come down. He told me you would be performing. We were in school together, Berezovsky, Ledbed, and myself. We were dear friends. I am in government now, Berezovsky is in business, and Ledbed, Ledbed you would say deals in loans. We studied in St. Petersburg together a hundred years ago. It is St. Petersburg again. Always we would go to the opera. As young men we would stand in the back for a few rubles, money we did not have at the time. But then jobs came and we had seats, and with better jobs came proper seats. You could mark our rise in the world by our position in the opera house, by what we paid and, later, what we were given. Tchaikovsky, Mussorgsky, Rimsky-Korsakov, Prokofiev, we saw everything that was Russian."

The translation was slow and there was a good deal of waiting for all parties involved. "Russia has beautiful operas," Roxane said. She dropped the dishtowel in the sink and went to get herself a chair, as no one seemed to be bringing one over and this was looking like it might be a long story. When she started to pick one up, the boy called Cesar leapt from the table where he was cleaning his gun and carried it over for her.

"*Gracias,*" she said to him. That much she knew.

"I'm sorry," Gen said, still standing himself. "I don't know what I was thinking of."

"I guess you're thinking of Russian," Roxane said. "That would be a headful. Do you have any idea where this story is going?"

Fyodorov smiled mutely. His cheeks were pink now.

"I have a vague idea."

"Well, don't tell me, I want to be surprised. I think this is today's entertainment." She leaned back and crossed her legs, then held out her hand as a signal for Fyodorov to continue.

Fyodorov waited for a moment. He was rethinking his position entirely. After weeks of planning he was realizing now that the course he had chosen was not at all correct. What he had to tell her did not begin in school. It did not begin at the opera even if that was the place it had brought him to. The story he should be telling started much earlier than this. He began again, putting himself in mind of Russia and his childhood, the dark switchback staircase that led up to the apartment where his family lived. He bent his shoulders forward towards Roxane. He wondered what direction Russia was from where he sat. "When I was a boy the city was called Leningrad, but you know this. For a brief time it was Petrograd but no one was happy with that. Better the city should have its old name or a new name, but nothing that tried to be something of both. In those days we all lived together, Mother and Father, my two brothers, my grandmother, who was my mother's mother. It was my grandmother who had the book of paintings. It was a massive thing." Fyodorov held up his hands to mark the dimensions of the book in the air. If he was to be believed, it was an enormous book. "She told us it was given to her by an admirer from Europe when she was a girl of fifteen, a man she called Julian. If that is true I do not know. My grandmother was one for telling stories. Even more than how she came by the book, how she managed to hold on to it through the war remains a great mystery to me. That she did not try and sell it or burn it for fuel, because there was a time when people would burn anything, that it was not taken from her as it would have been a difficult thing to hide, all of these things are remarkable. But when I was a boy, it was many years past the war and she was an old woman. We did not go to museums to look at paintings in those days. We would walk past the Winter Palace, a marvelous place, but then we did not go inside. I imagine there was not the money for such things. But in the evenings, my grandmother brought out her book and told my brothers and me to go and wash our hands. I was not allowed to even touch the pages until I was ten, but still I washed my hands just for the privilege of looking. She kept it wrapped in a quilt under the sofa in the living room where she slept. She struggled to carry it but would let no one help her. When she was certain the table was clean we would put the quilt with the book inside it on the table and slowly unfold the quilt. Then she would sit down. She was a small woman, and we stood beside her. She was very particular about the light over the table. It couldn't be too strong because she was afraid of fading the colors, and it couldn't be so weak that she felt the paintings could not be fully comprehended. She wore white cotton gloves that were perfectly plain and saved for only this occasion and she turned the pages while we watched. Can you imagine this? I will not say we were terribly poor because we were as rich or poor as everyone else. Our apartment was small, my brothers and I shared a bed. Our family was no different from the other families in our building except for this book. So extraordinary a thing was this book. *Masterworks of the Impressionist Period* it was called. No one knew we had it. We were never allowed to speak of it because my grandmother was afraid someone would come and try and take it away from her. The paintings were by Pissarro, Bonnard, van Gogh, Monet, Manet, Cézanne, hundreds of paintings. The colors we saw at night while she turned the pages were miraculous. Every painting we were to study. Every one she said was something that deserved great consideration. There were nights that she only turned two pages and I'm sure it was a year before I had seen the book in its entirety. It was an extremely good book, I think, expertly done. Certainly, I have not seen the originals of all the paintings, but the ones I saw years later looked very much the way I had remembered them. My grandmother told us she spoke French in her youth and she would read to us as best she could remember the text beneath the plates. Of course she was making it up because the stories would change. Not that it mattered. They were beautiful stories. 'This is the field where van Gogh painted sunflowers,' she would say. 'All day he sat in the hot sun beneath the blue skies. When the white clouds curled past he would remember them for future paintings and here on this canvas he placed those clouds.' This is the way she spoke to us, pretending she was reading. Sometimes she would read for twenty minutes when there were only a few lines of text. She would say that was because French was a much more complicated language than Russian and that every word contained several sentences' worth of meaning. There were so many paintings to consider. It was many, many years before I had memorized them all. Even now I could tell you the number of haystacks in the field and from which direction the light is coming." Fyodorov stopped to give Gen a chance to catch up. He took the opportunity to look at the people around the table: his grandmother, now dead, his mother and father, dead, his youngest brother, Dimitri, drowned in a fishing accident at the age of twenty-one. Only two of them were left now. He wondered about his brother Mikal, who must be following the story of his kidnapping in the news at home. If I was to die here, Fyodorov thought, Mikal would be alone in this world with no other family to comfort him. "Every now and then she wouldn't bring out the book at all. She would say she was tired. She would say that so much beauty hurt her. Sometimes a week or even two could pass. No Seurat! I remember feeling almost frantic, such a dependency I had come to feel for those paintings. But it was the rest from it, the waiting, that made us love the book so madly. I could have had one life but instead I had another because of this book my grandmother protected," he said, his voice quieter now. "What a miracle is that? I was taught to love beautiful things. I had a language in which to consider beauty. Later that extended to the opera, to the ballet, to architecture I saw, and even later still I came to realize that what I had seen in the paintings I could see in the fields or a river. I could see it in people. All of that I attribute to this book. Towards the end of her life she could not pick it up at all and she sent me to get it. Her hands shook so, she was afraid of tearing the paper and so she let us turn the page. My hands were too large for her gloves by then but she showed me how to use them between my fingers like a cloth so I could keep everything clean." Fyodorov sighed, as somehow this was the memory that moved him the most. "My brother has the book now. He is a doctor outside of Moscow. Every few years we hand it off to the other. Neither of us could do without it completely. I have tried to find another copy, but I have been unsuccessful. I believe that there is no other book like this in the world." Through talking, Fyodorov was able to relax. Talking was the thing he was best at. He felt his breath come easily. He had not before this moment made the connection between the book and the point of his story and now he wondered how he hadn't seen it all along. "It was a tragedy to my grandmother that none of us showed a talent for painting. Even at the end of her life, when I was in school studying business, she was telling me to try again. But it wasn't something I was capable of learning. She liked to say my brother Dimitri would have been a great painter but that was only because Dimitri was dead. The dead we can imagine to be anything at all. My brothers and I were all excellent observers. Some people are born to make great art and others are born to appreciate it. Don't you think? It is a kind of talent in itself, to be an audience, whether you are the spectator in the gallery or you are listening to the voice of the world's greatest soprano. Not everyone can be the artist. There have to be those who witness the art, who love and appreciate what they have been privileged to see." Fyodorov spoke slowly. He gave long pauses between his sentences so that Gen would not have to struggle to keep up, but because of this it was difficult to tell whether he was finished speaking.

"It's a lovely story," Roxane said at last.

"But there is a point to it."

Roxane settled back in her chair to hear the point.

"It may not seem immediately evident that I would be a man who has a deep understanding of art and I want you to know that I am. The Secretary of Commerce in Russia, what would that be to you? And yet because of my background I feel I am specifically qualified."

Again, Roxane waited to see if there was more of the sentence coming and when there didn't seem to be she asked him, "Qualified to what?"

"To love you," Fyodorov said. "I love you."

Gen looked at Fyodorov and blinked. He felt the blood drain away from his face.

"What did he say?" Roxane said.

"Go on," Fyodorov said. "Tell her."

Roxane's hair was pulled up tightly from her face and caught in a pink elastic she had been given from the room of the Vice President's oldest daughter. Without makeup or jewelry, without her hair to frame her face, a person might have thought her plain or even tired looking if he didn't know what she was capable of. Gen thought she was patient to have listened for so long, keeping her eyes on Fyodorov, never drifting off to stare out the window. He thought it spoke well of her character that she had chosen Mr. Hosokawa to keep her company when other, lesser men were available, men who spoke English. Gen greatly admired her singing, that went without saying. Every day when she sang he felt deeply moved, but he did not love her. Not that he was being asked to. Not that she would have thought that's what he meant, that he, Gen, loved her, and yet still he struggled. He had never thought of it before but he was quite sure now that he did think of it that he had neither spoken those words or written them, either to someone or for someone else. Birthday cards and letters home were signed *please take good care of yourself*. He had never said I love you to either his parents or his sisters. He had not said it to any of the three women he had slept with in his life or the girls in school with whom he had occasionally walked to class. It simply had not occurred to him to say it and now on the first day of his life when it might have been appropriate to speak of love to a woman, he would be declaring it for another man to another woman.

"Are you going to tell me?" Roxane said. There was only slightly more interest in her voice the second time she asked. Fyodorov waited, hands clasped, a look of great relief already spreading over his face. He had said his piece. He had taken things as far as he could.

Gen swallowed the saliva which had pooled over his tongue and tried to look at Roxane in a businesslike manner. "He is qualified to love you. He says, I love you." Gen framed his translation to make it sound as appropriate as was possible.

"He loves my singing?"

"You," Gen said pointedly. He did not feel the need to consult with Fyodorov on this. The Russian smiled.

Now Roxane did look away. She took a deep breath and stared out the window for a while as if there had been some sort of offer and she was now weighing it out. When she looked back she smiled at Fyodorov. The look on her face was so peaceful, so tender, that for a moment Gen thought perhaps she loved the Russian in return. Was it possible that such a declaration could achieve the desired effect? That she would love him simply for having loved her?

"Victor Fyodorov," she said. "A wonderful story."

"Thank you." Fyodorov bowed his head.

"I wonder what became of the young man from Europe, Julian," she said, though she seemed to be speaking to herself. "It's one thing to give a woman a necklace. It comes in a small box. Even a very expensive necklace isn't much trouble. But to give a woman such a book, to bring it all the way from some other country, I think that's quite extraordinary. I can imagine him carrying it on the train all done up in wrapping paper."

"If we are to believe there was a Julian at all."

"There's no reason not to. It certainly would do no harm to believe the story she told you."

"I'm sure you are right. From now on I will remember it only as the truth."

Gen's head was filled with Carmen again. He wished that she was waiting for him, still sitting on the black marble sink, but he knew this wasn't possible. She was probably on patrol now, walking up and down the hallways of the second floor with a rifle, conjugating verbs under her breath.

"As for the love," Roxane said finally.

"There is nothing to say," Fyodorov interrupted. "It is a gift. There. Something to give to you. If I had the necklace or a book of paintings I would give you that instead. I would give you that in addition to my love."

"Then you are too generous with gifts."

Fyodorov shrugged. "Perhaps you are right. In another setting it would be ridiculous, too grand. In another setting it would not happen because you are a famous woman and at best I would shake your famous hand for one second while you stepped into your car after a performance. But in this place I hear you sing every day. In this place I watch you eat your dinner, and what I feel in my heart is love. There is no point in not telling you that. These people who detain us so pleasantly may decide to shoot us after all. It is a possibility. And if that is the case, then why should I carry this love with me to the other world? Why not give to you what is yours?"

"And what if there is nothing for me to give you?" She seemed to be interested in Fyodorov's argument.

He shook his head. "What a thing to say, after all that you have given to me. But it is never about who has given what. That is not the way to think of gifts. This is not business we are conducting. Would I be pleased if you were to say you loved me as well? That what you wanted was to come to Russia and live with the Secretary of Commerce, attend state dinners, drink your coffee in my bed? A beautiful thought, surely, but my wife would not be pleased. When you think of love you think as an American. You must think like a Russian. It is a more expansive view."

"Americans have a bad habit of thinking like Americans," Roxane said kindly. After that she smiled at Fyodorov and everyone was quiet for a moment. The interview had come to a close and there was nothing left to say.

Then finally Fyodorov stood up from his chair and clapped his hands together. "I, for one, feel much better. What a burden this has been to me! Now I can get some rest. You've been very kind to hear me." He extended his hand to Roxane, and when she stood and gave him hers he kissed it and for a moment stretched it up to hold it against his cheek. "I will remember this day forever, this moment, your hand. No man could want for more than this." He smiled and then he let her go. "A wonderful day. A wonderful thing you have given me in return." He turned and walked out of the kitchen without a word to Gen. In all of his excitement he had forgotten Gen was there at all, the way a person can forget when the translation has gone very smoothly.

Roxane sat down in her chair and Gen sat down where Fyodorov had been. "Well," she said. "That was certainly exhausting."

"I was thinking the same thing."

"Poor Gen." Roxane leaned her head to one side. "All the boring things you have to listen to."

"This was awkward but it wasn't boring."

"Awkward?"

"You don't find strangers declaring themselves to you awkward?" But then she wouldn't, would she? People must fall in love with her hourly. She must keep a staff of translators to interpret the proposals of love and marriage.

"It's easier to love a woman when you can't understand a word she's saying," Roxane said.

"I wish they would bring us some rabbits," Thibault called over to Gen in French. *Des lapins*. He was drumming his fingers on the cookbook. "Are you boys much for rabbit?" he asked the terrorists in Spanish. *Conejo*.

The boys looked up from their work. The guns were mostly reassembled. They had been clean to begin with and now they were only cleaner. When one got used to guns, when the guns weren't pointed at you, one could see them as almost interesting, discreet sculptures for end tables. *"Cabayo,"* said the tall one, Gilbert, who had thought of shooting Thibault not so very long ago in the confusion over the television set.

"Cabayo?" Simon Thibault said. "Gen, what is *cabayo*?"

Gen thought about it for a minute. His mind was still stuck in Russian. "Those furry things, not hamsters . . ." He snapped his fingers. "Guinea pigs!"

"What you want to eat are guinea pigs, not rabbits," Gilbert said. "Very tender."

"Oh," said Cesar, folding his hands over his gun. "What I wouldn't give for a guinea pig now." He gently bit his fingertips at the thought of so much pleasure. Cesar had bad skin that seemed to be clearing up some during their internment.

Thibault closed the book. In Paris, one of his daughters had kept a fat white guinea pig in a large glass aquarium when she was a girl. Milou, it was called, a poor substitute for the dog she wanted. Edith wound up feeding the thing. She felt sorry for it, spending day after day alone, looking out on the life of their family through glass. Sometimes Edith let the guinea pig sit in her lap while she read. There was Milou, curled in a ball against the hem of Edith's sweater, its nose twitching with pleasure. This guinea pig was Thibault's brother, for all he wanted now was the privilege of what this animal had had, the right to lie with his head in his wife's lap, his face turned up to the bottom of her sweater. Must Thibault imagine the animal (who was long since dead but when and how? He couldn't remember) skinned and braised? Milou as dinner. Once something is named it can never be eaten. Once you have called it a brother in your mind it should enjoy the freedoms of a brother. "How do you cook them?"

A conversation ensued about the best way to cook a guinea pig and how it was possible to tell your fortune from cutting open the gut while it was still alive. Gen turned away.

"People love each other for all sorts of different reasons," Roxane said, her lack of Spanish keeping her innocent of the conversation, slow-roasted guinea pigs on a spit. "Most of the time we're loved for what we can do rather than for who we are. It's not such a bad thing, being loved for what you can do."

"But the other is better," Gen said.

Roxane pulled her feet into her chair and hugged her knees to her chest. "Better. I hate to say better, but it is. If someone loves you for what you can do then it's flattering, but why do you love them? If someone loves you for who you are then they have to know you, which means you have to know them." Roxane smiled at Gen.

Once they had left the kitchen, first the other boys, and then Gen and Roxane and Thibault, the people Cesar had come to think of as the grown-ups rather than the hostages, Cesar began to sing the Rossini while he finished up his work. He had the kitchen to himself for a moment and wanted to make use of this rare time alone. The sun came through the windows and shone brightly off his clean rifle and oh, how he loved to hear the words in his mouth. She had sung it so many times this morning he had had the chance to memorize all the words. It didn't matter that he didn't understand the language, he knew what it *meant*. The words and music fused together and became a part of him. Again and again he sang the chorus, almost whispering for fear someone might hear him, mock him, punish him. He felt this too strongly to think that it was something he could get away with. Still, he wished he could open himself up the way she did, bellow it

out, dig inside himself to see what was really there. It thrilled him
when she sang the loudest, the highest. If he didn't have his rifle to
hold in front of him he would have embarrassed himself every time,
her singing brought about such a raging, aching passion that his penis
stiffened before she had finished her first line, growing harder and
harder as the song progressed until he was lost in a confusion of pleasure and terrible pain, the stock of his rifle brushing imperceptibly up
and down, leading him towards relief. He leaned back against the
wall, dizzy and electrified. They were for her, these furious erections.
Every boy there dreamed of crawling on top of her, filling her mouth
with their tongues as they pushed themselves inside her. They loved
her, and in these fantasies that came to them waking and sleeping, she
loved them in return. But for Cesar it was more than that. Cesar knew
he was hard for the music. As if music was a separate thing you could
drive yourself into, make love to, fuck.

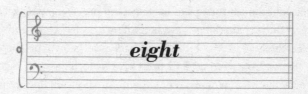

eight

*t*here was a sitting room off of the guest bedroom where the Generals held their meetings and in that room Mr. Hosokawa and General Benjamin played chess for hours at a time. It seemed to be the only thing that took Benjamin's mind off the pain of the shingles. Since they had crept into his eye they had become infected and the infection had led to conjunctivitis, and now the eye was fiercely red and rimmed with pustules. The more completely he concentrated on chess, the more he was able to push the pain aside. He never forgot it, but during the game he did not live exactly in the center of it.

For a long time the guests were only allowed in limited areas of the house but now that things were loosening up the access to other areas was sporadic. Mr. Hosokawa had not even known the room had existed until he was invited back to play. It was a small room, a gaming table and two chairs by the window, a small sofa, a secretary with a writing desk and a glass front filled with leather-bound books. There were yellow draperies on the window, a blue flowered rug on the floor, a framed picture of a clipper ship. It was not an exceptional room in any way, but it was small, and a small room, after three months spent in the vast cavern of the living room, gave Mr. Hosokawa an enormous sense of relief, that comforting tightness a child experiences when bundled into sweaters and a coat. He hadn't thought about it until the third time they played, that in Japan a person was never in such a large room, unless it was a hotel banquet hall or the opera house. He liked the fact that in this room, were he to stand on a chair, he could touch the tips of his fingers to the ceiling. He was especially grateful for anything that made the world feel close and familiar. Everything that Mr. Hosokawa had ever known or suspected about the way life worked had been proven to him to be incorrect these past months. Where before there had been endless hours of work, negotiations and compromises, there were now chess games with a terrorist for whom he felt an unaccountable fondness. Where there had been a respectable family that functioned in the highest order, there were now people he loved and could not speak to. Where there had been a few minutes of opera on a stereo at bedtime, there were now hours of music every day, the living warmth of voice in all its perfection and fallibility, a woman in possession of that voice who sat beside him laughing, holding his hand. The rest of the world believed that Mr. Hosokawa suffered and he would never be able to explain to them how that was not the case. The rest of the world. He could never push it completely from his mind. His understanding that he would eventually lose every sweetness that had come to him only made him hold those very things closer to his chest.

General Benjamin was a good chess player but he was no better than Mr. Hosokawa. Neither of them was the type to play with a speed clock and they took every move as if time had yet to be invented. Because they were both equally talented and equally slow, neither man ever became impatient with the other. Once, Mr. Hosokawa had gone to the small sofa and closed his eyes while he waited for his turn, and when he woke up, General Benjamin was still moving his rook forward and then back across the same three squares, careful to never take his fingers off the horse's head. They had different strategies. General Benjamin tried to control the center of the board. Mr. Hosokawa played defensively: a pawn here, later the knight. One would win, and then the other, and neither one made any comment about it. The game, frankly, was more peaceful without language. Cunning moves need not be congratulated, a danger over-looked was not bemoaned. They would tap a queen, then king, once for check, twice for checkmate, as neither could remember the words Gen had written down for them. Even the endings of games came as quiet affairs, a brief nod of acknowledgment, and then the business of setting it all up again so that when the next day came they would be ready to start over. Neither man would have dreamed of leaving the room with the pieces scattered across the table on the wrong sides of the board.

Even though it was an enormous house by any standard, there was no privacy for people living in the vice-presidential home, not for anyone except Carmen and Gen, who met in the china closet after two A.M. in order to keep their lessons a secret. Opera and cooking and games of chess were there for public consumption. The guest room was on the same side of the house as the study where the tele-vision nattered on hour after hour, so if one of the young terrorists was looking for entertainment he would probably let the chess go. The hostages, when they were allowed down the hallway based on the caprice of whoever happened to be holding the gun at the door, were more likely to stay for ten or fifteen minutes of a game, but in that time they were lucky if they saw a single move. They were used to soc-cer. They tried to consider chess a kind of sport, certainly it was a game, but they wanted to see something happen. The room had the same effect on the spectators as long liturgical services, algebra lec-tures, Halcion.

The two observers who managed to stay and never fall asleep were Ishmael and Roxane. Roxane came to watch the performance of Mr. Hosokawa, who, after all, spent so much of his time watching her, and Ishmael stayed because eventually he wanted to play chess with General Benjamin and Mr. Hosokawa, only he wasn't sure if such a thing was actually allowed. All of the younger terrorists tried to know their limits and not ask for more than they could have. Like all children, they may have pushed on them from time to time, but they were respectful of the Generals and they knew not to ask for too much. They might stay too long watching television, but they never missed their post on guard. They did not tell Messner to bring in gallons of ice cream. Only the Generals could do that and so far they had done it only twice. They did not fight among themselves, though the temptation to do so was overwhelming at times. The Generals punished fighting severely, and General Hector took it upon himself to beat the boys longer and harder than they could ever beat one another to teach them that they had to work together. If there was a terrible need, an argument that could only be settled one way, they met in the basement, took off their shirts, and were careful never to hit each other in the face.

Some things were against the rules, rules that were memorized and repeated in drills. Some rules (speaking respectfully to a superior officer) stood firm. Other rules (never speaking to a hostage unless it was to correct him) weakened and fell away. What the Generals would and would not allow was not always clear. Silently, Ishmael memorized the chessboard. He didn't know the names of the pieces because no one in the room ever spoke. He practiced in his head the most appropriate way of broaching the subject. He considered asking Gen to ask for him. Gen had a way of making things seem especially important. Or he could ask Gen to ask Messner, who was the man who handled the negotiations. But Gen seemed very busy these days and Messner, frankly, didn't seem to be doing such a great job considering that they were all still there. He wished most of all he could ask the Vice President, the man whom he held in the greatest esteem and thought of as his friend, but the Generals made a special point of ridiculing Ruben, and anything he asked for would certainly be denied.

So if Ishmael wanted something, the only logical person to turn to was himself, and after waiting a few more days he found the courage to make the question. One day was just the same as the next and so he reasoned there would never be exactly a right time or a wrong time to ask. General Benjamin had just completed his move and Mr.

Hosokawa was only in the earliest stages of considering his next position. Roxane sat forward on the little sofa, her elbows on her knees, her hands making a comfortable support beneath her chin. She watched the board like something that might try and run away. Ishmael wished he could speak to her. He wondered if she was learning how to play as well.

"Sir," Ishmael began, a sharp chip of ice lodged in his throat.

General Benjamin looked up and blinked. He hadn't noticed the boy in the room. Such a small boy. He was an orphan whose uncle had enlisted him to the cause only a few months before their attack, saying all the boys in the family were small and then came into impressive growth spurts, but Benjamin was beginning to doubt this would ever be true. Ishmael didn't look like a body that was planning on doing anything impressive. Still, he did the best he could to keep up with the others and endure their teasing. And it was helpful to have at least one person who was small, someone who could be hoisted up, pushed through windows. "What is it?"

"I was wondering, sir, if you would consider." He stopped, collected himself, and started again. "I was wondering if there was time later, if I might play the winner." It occurred to him then that there was a fifty-fifty chance that the winner might be Mr. Hosokawa, which might be an inappropriate request. "Or the loser."

"You play chess?" General Benjamin asked.

Mr. Hosokawa and Roxane kept their eyes on the board. There was a time, out of politeness, when they would have at least looked at the person who was speaking, even if they couldn't understand a word of what was being said. Now they both knew a little Spanish and they didn't bother to look up. Mr. Hosokawa was angling for the General's bishop. Roxane could see what he was thinking.

"I guess I do. I've been watching. I think I understand it now."

General Benjamin laughed, but it wasn't such an unkind laugh. He tapped Mr. Hosokawa on the arm. Mr. Hosokawa looked up, pushed his glasses up the bridge of his nose, and watched while General Benjamin took one of Ishmael's small hands beneath his own and put it on a pawn, then he hopped the pawn from place to place on the board. He motioned between the three of them and that was clear enough. Mr. Hosokawa smiled and clapped the boy on the shoulder.

"So you will play the winner," General Benjamin said. "Everything is agreed."

Ishmael, feeling a great rush of luck, took up a place at Roxane's feet and stared at the board the way she did, like it was a living thing. He only had half a game left to learn everything there was to know about chess.

Gen rapped lightly on the frame of the door to the study. Messner stood behind him. Everything about Messner's countenance seemed weary except for his hair, which was as bright as daylight. He still wore a white shirt, black pants, and a black tie, and, like the hostages and terrorists alike, his clothes showed signs of wear. He folded his arms and watched the game. He had been on the chess team in college, rode the bus to play against the French, the Italians. He would have liked to play now, but had he stayed in the house for three hours he would have been expected to have something significant to show for it when he came outside.

General Benjamin held up his hand without looking. He was beginning to sense that his bishop was in peril.

Messner watched the direction of his eyes. He considered telling the General that the bishop wasn't really his problem, but God knows Benjamin never would have listened to him. "Tell him I've brought today's papers," he said to Gen in French. He could have said that much in Spanish but he knew the General would only have glared at him, speaking in the middle of the move.

"I'll tell him."

Roxane Coss lifted one hand and waved to Messner but kept her eyes on the board, as did Ishmael, who felt the creeping bile of fear churning in his esophagus. Maybe he didn't know how to play chess after all.

"Are you planning on springing us anytime soon?" Roxane asked.

"No one moves," Messner said, trying to be light. "I've never seen such a stalemate." He felt oddly jealous of Ishmael, sitting right there by her feet. He would only have to slide his hand two inches to brush against her ankle.

"They could starve us out," Roxane said, her voice steady and calm, as if she didn't want to disrupt the game. "The food isn't so terrible, not as bad as it should be if they were really interested in getting things moving. They can't be so intent on freeing us when they essentially give us everything we want."

Messner scratched the back of his head. "Ah, I'm afraid that's your fault. If you thought you were famous before you came in this place you should read about yourself now. You make Callas look like a spear carrier. If they tried to starve you out the government would be overthrown in an afternoon."

Roxane looked up at him, blinked a pretty stage blink, large and pleased. "So if I get out of here alive I can double my price?"

"You can triple it."

"My God," Roxane said, and there were her teeth, the very sight of which broke Messner's heart. "Do you realize you've told him how to overthrow the government and he doesn't even know it? It's all he's ever wanted and he missed it."

General Benjamin had his hand on his bishop. He was rocking it side to side. The words passed over him, around him, like water passing over a stone.

Messner watched Ishmael. The boy appeared to be holding his breath until the General decided on his move. More than any other negotiation Messner had ever been involved with, he found that he didn't really care who won this one. But that wasn't it exactly, because the governments always won. It was that he wouldn't mind seeing these people get away, the whole lot of them. He wished they could use the tunnel the military was digging, wished they could crawl back into the air vents and down into that tunnel and go back into whatever leafy quarters they came from. Not that they had been a brilliant lot, but maybe for that very reason they didn't deserve the punishment that would eventually catch up with them. He was sorry for them, that was all. He had never felt sorry for the captors before.

Ishmael sighed as General Benjamin took his hand off his bishop and chose the knight instead. It was a bad move. Even Ishmael could see that. He leaned back against the couch, and when he did Roxane draped one arm across his shoulder and put her other hand on the top of his head, touching his hair as absently as she did her own. But Ishmael barely felt it. He kept his eyes on the chess game, which, in six more moves, was over.

"Well, that's enough," General Benjamin said to no one. As soon as the game was finished the floodgate opened again and set all the pain in motion. He shook Mr. Hosokawa's hand in the quick and formal way they did after every game. Mr. Hosokawa bowed several times and Benjamin bowed in return, a weird habit that he had picked up like someone else's nervous tic. After all the bowing he stretched and then motioned for Ishmael to take his seat. "But only if the gentleman wishes to play again. Don't impose yourself on him. Gen, ask Mr. Hosokawa if he would prefer to wait and play tomorrow."

Mr. Hosokawa was glad to play with Ishmael, who was already getting comfortable in General Benjamin's warm chair. He began to set up the board.

"What do you have for me?" the General asked Messner.

"More of the same, really." Messner thumbed through the papers. An imperative letter from the President. An imperative letter from the Chief of Police. "They won't give in. I have to tell you, if anything they seem less inclined now than they did before. The government isn't so uncomfortable with the way things have been going. People are starting to become accustomed to the whole thing. They walk down the street and they don't even stop." He handed over the daily list of demands from the military while Gen translated. Some days they didn't even bother to reword the counterdemands. They just made copies and changed the dates with a pencil.

"Well, they will see, we are geniuses at waiting. We can wait them out forever." General Benjamin gave a halfhearted nod as he looked over the papers. Then he opened the little French secretary and he took out his own set of papers which Gen had typed up the night before. "You'll give them these."

Messner took the papers without looking at them. It would all be the same. The things they were asking for had become reckless in the last month, the release of political prisoners from other countries, men they didn't even know, food distribution to the poor, a change in voting laws. General Hector had come up with that one after reading some of the Vice President's legal books. Instead of curtailing their demands, getting nothing had only made them want more. As usual, they made threats, promises to start killing hostages, but *threat*, *promise*, and *demand*, had become a set of decorative adjectives. They meant no more than the stamps and seals the government affixed to their papers.

Mr. Hosokawa let Ishmael go first. The boy opened with his third pawn. General Benjamin sat down to watch the game.

"We should talk about this," Messner said.

"There's nothing to talk about."

"I think," Messner started. He was feeling a weight of responsibility. He was starting to think that if he were only a more clever man he might have talked this thing through by now. "There are things you must consider."

"Shh," General Benjamin said, and held his finger to his lips. He pointed to the board. "It's starting now."

Messner leaned against the wall, suddenly exhausted. Ishmael removed the tip of his finger from his pawn.

"Let me walk you out," Roxane said to Messner.

"What?" General Benjamin said.

"She said she'll take Mr. Messner to the door," Gen said.

General Benjamin did not care to go along. He was interested in seeing if the boy could actually play.

"Tell me what they're going to do," Roxane said as they walked down the hall. Gen had come along and so the three of them spoke in English.

"I have no idea."

"You have some idea," Roxane said.

He looked at her. Every time he saw her he was surprised all over again by how small she was. At night, in his memory, she was towering, powerful. But standing beside her, she was small enough to slip beneath a coat if he had been wearing one, small enough to sweep out of the house quietly beneath one arm. He had the perfect trench coat at home in Geneva, it had been his father's and his father had been a bigger man. Messner wore it anyway out of a combined sense of love and practicality and it billowed behind him as he walked. "I am a farrier, a delivery service. I bring in the papers, take out the papers, make sure there is plenty of butter for the rolls. They don't tell me anything."

Roxane put her arm through his, not in a flirtatious way, but in the manner of a heroine in a nineteenth-century English novel going for a walk with a gentleman. Messner could feel the warmth of her hand through his shirtsleeve. He did not want to leave her inside. "Tell me," she whispered. "I'm losing track of time. Some days I think this is where I live, where I'm always going to live. If I knew that for sure then I could feel settled. Do you understand that? If it's going to be a very long time, I want to know."

To see her every day, to stand out on the sidewalk in the mornings with the thronging crowd to hear her sing, wasn't that a remarkable thing? "I imagine," Messner said quietly, "that it's going to be a very long time."

As they walked, Gen trailed behind them like a well-trained butler, both discreet and present if he was needed in any way. He listened. Messner said it. *A very long time.* He thought of Carmen, of all the languages there were for a smart girl to learn. They might need a very long time.

When Ruben saw the three of them coming he moved briskly up the hallway before any of the soldiers could cut him off. "Messner!" he said. "It's a miracle! I wait for you and then you manage to slip right by me. How is our government? Have they replaced me yet?"

"Impossible," Messner said. Roxane stepped away, stepped back towards Gen, and Messner felt the air cooling all around him.

"We need soap," the Vice President said. "All sorts of soap, bar soap, dishwashing soap, laundry soap."

Messner was distracted His conversation with Roxane should have lasted longer. They didn't need Gen. Messner often dreamed in English. There was never a moment to be alone. "I'll see what I can do."

Ruben's face darkened. "I'm not asking for anything so complicated."

"I'll bring it tomorrow," he said, his voice growing soft. Why all this sudden tenderness? Messner wanted to go back to Switzerland, where the postman who never recognized him when they passed in the hallway always put mail into the correct slot. He wanted to be unneeded, unknown. "Your face has finally healed up."

The Vice President, sensing the ridiculousness of his anger, the burden on his friend, touched his own cheek. "I never thought it would happen. It's one hell of a scar, don't you think?"

"It will make you a hero of the people," Messner said.

"I'll say I got it from you," Ruben said, looking up into Messner's pale eyes. "A knife fight in a bar."

Messner went to the door and held out his arms and Beatriz and Jesus, the two guards on the door, worked him over until he felt embarrassed by the persistence of Beatriz's hands. It was one thing, the way they shook him down when he came in. He could not understand why the whole process needed to be repeated upon his exit. What was he smuggling out?

"They think you might be taking the soap," the Vice President said, as if he was reading his friend's mind. "They wonder where it has all gone to when they haven't been using any of it themselves."

"Get back to the sofa," Jesus said, and laid two directional fingers on the top of his gun. The Vice President was ready for a nap anyway and went his way without further instruction. Messner went out the door without saying good-bye.

*   *   *

All the time Roxane was thinking. She thought about Messner and how it seemed to her he would have rather been a hostage himself instead of bearing the burden of being the only person in the world who was free to come and go. She thought about Schubert lieder, Puccini's arias, the performances she'd missed in Argentina and the performances she had missed by now in New York that had taken forever to negotiate and had been so important to her, though she had not admitted it at the time. She thought of what she would sing tomorrow in the living room, more Rossini? Mostly, she thought about Mr. Hosokawa, and how she had grown so dependent on him. If he hadn't been there she thought she would have completely lost her mind in the first week, but of course if he hadn't been there she never would have come to this country, she never would have even been asked. Her life would have gone on like a train on schedule: Argentina, New York, a visit to Chicago, then back to Italy. Now she was completely stopped. She thought of Katsumi Hosokawa sitting by the window, listening while she sang, and she wondered how it was possible to love someone you couldn't even speak to. She believed now there was a reason why all of this had happened: his birthday and her invitation to be, in a sense, his birthday present, why they had been stuck here all this time. How else would they have met? How else would there have been any way to get to know someone you couldn't speak to, someone who lived on the other side of the world, unless you were given an enormous amount of empty time to simply sit and wait together? She would have to take care of Carmen, that was the first thing.

"You know Carmen," Roxane said to Gen. They were on their way back to see how the chess game was progressing but she stopped him in the middle of the hall when they were far from any door.

"Carmen?"

"I know you know who she is, but you know her a little, too, don't know? I've seen the two of you speaking."

"Of course." Gen felt a flush rising up in his chest and he willed it not to go any farther, as if one could will such a thing.

But Roxane wasn't looking at him. Her eyes seemed slightly out of focus, like she was tired. It was only noon but she was often tired after she sang in the morning. The guards would let her go upstairs alone to go back to sleep. If Carmen wasn't on watch sometimes she would find her and take her wrist and Carmen would follow her. It was so much easier to sleep when she was there. Carmen was probably twenty years younger than she was, but there was something about her, something that settled Roxane down. "She's a sweet girl. She brings me breakfast in the morning. Sometimes I open the door to my room at night and she's sleeping in the hall," she said. "Not all the time."

Not all the time. Not when she was with him.

Roxane looked back at him and smiled a little. "Poor Gen, you're always in the middle of everything. Anyone who has a secret has to take it through you."

"I'm sure there's plenty I miss."

"I need you to do me a favor, just like everybody else. I need you to do something." Because if Messner was right, if it was still going to be a very long time that they were held hostage, then she deserved to have this. And if, at the end of that long time, they were killed anyway, because that was always the talk, that the military would shoot them to pin it on the terrorists, or that the terrorists would kill them in a moment of desperation (though she found this harder to believe), then she deserved it all the more. And if the third scenario were true, that they would be released quickly and unharmed, that they all would go back to their regular lives and put this behind them, then she would deserve it most of all, because certainly then she would not see Katsumi Hosokawa again. "Find Carmen tonight and tell her to sleep somewhere else. Tell her she shouldn't come up with breakfast in the morning. You'd do that for me?"

Gen nodded.

But that wasn't asking for quite enough. That wasn't asking for everything because she had no way of telling Mr. Hosokawa he should come to her tonight. She wanted to ask him to come to her room but there was only one way of doing that, to ask Gen to go to him and say it in Japanese, and what did she mean to say, exactly? That she meant for him to stay the night? And Gen would have to ask Carmen to find a way to get Mr. Hosokawa upstairs, and what if they were found out, what would happen to Mr. Hosokawa then, and Carmen? It used to be if you met someone and you wanted to see them, maybe you went out to dinner, had a drink. She leaned back against the wall. Two boys with guns walked by but they never teased or poked when Roxane was there. Once they had passed, she took a deep breath and told Gen everything she wanted. He did not tell her this was all insanity. He listened to her as if she wasn't asking for anything unusual at all, nodding while she spoke. Maybe a translator was not unlike a doctor, a lawyer, a priest even. They must have some code of ethics that prevented them from gossiping. And even if she wasn't positive then of his loyalty to her, she knew he would do everything possible to protect Mr. Hosokawa.

Ruben Iglesias went into what he still thought of as the guest room, but was now the Generals' office, in order to empty the wastebaskets. He was going from room to room with a large green trash bag, taking not only what had been thrown away in the cans but what was on the floor as well: pop bottles, banana peels, the bits of the newspaper which had been edited out. Ruben surreptitiously deposited those into his pockets to read late at night with a flashlight. Mr. Hosokawa and Ishmael were playing chess and he stood in the door for a minute to watch. He was very proud of Ishmael, who was so much brighter than the other boys. Ruben had bought that set to teach the game to his son, Marco, but he still felt the boy was too young to learn. General Benjamin was sitting on the couch and after a while he looked up at Ruben. The sight of his eye, so badly infected, took Ruben's breath away.

"That Ishmael, he's a fast learner," General Benjamin said. "Nobody taught him the game, you know. He just picked it up from watching." The boy's accomplishment had put him in a good mood. It reminded him of when he used to be a schoolteacher.

"Come into the hall for a moment," Ruben said to him quietly. "I must speak to you about something."

"Then speak to me here."

Ruben cast his eyes towards the boy, indicating that this was a private matter between men. Benjamin sighed and pushed himself off the couch. "Everyone has a problem," he said.

Outside the doorway, Ruben put down his bag of trash. He did not like to speak to the Generals. His first encounter with them had set a precedent which he followed, but no decent man could pretend not to notice such a thing.

"What is it you need?" Benjamin said, his voice heavy.

"What you need," Ruben said. He reached into his pocket and took out a bottle of pills with his name on them. "Antibiotics. Look, they gave me more than I would ever need. They stopped the infection in my face."

"Good for you," General Benjamin said.

"And you. There are plenty here. Take them. You be will surprised by the difference they make."

"You are a doctor?"

"You don't need to be a doctor to see an infection. I'm telling you."

Benjamin smiled at him. "How do I know you don't mean to poison me, little Vice President?"

"Yes, yes." Ruben sighed. "I mean to poison you. I mean for us to die together." He opened the bottle and shook one of the pills into his mouth and after making sure to show Benjamin how it sat there on his tongue, he swallowed it. Then he handed the bottle over to the General. "I will not ask you what you mean to do with them, but there, they are yours."

After that, Benjamin returned to the chess game and Ruben picked up the trash and headed on to the next room in the hall.

It was Saturday, but since all the days were essentially the same, the only two people who gave this any thought at all were Father Arguedas, who heard confession on Saturday and planned for his Sunday mass, and Beatriz, who found the weekends to be an unbearable wasteland because the program she liked, *The Story of Maria,* was only on Monday through Friday.

"It is a healthy thing to wait," General Alfredo told her, because he enjoyed the show himself. "It gives you a sense of anticipation."

"I don't want to wait," she said, and suddenly thought that she might cry with frustration, the dull white stretch of the afternoon pushing out endlessly in every direction. She had already cleaned her gun and passed inspection and she didn't have to stand guard until night. She could have taken a nap or looked at one of the magazines she had seen and not understood a hundred times before, but the thought of it all seemed unbearable. She wanted out of this place. She wanted to walk down the streets in the city like any other girl and have men tap their horns as they drove by her. She wanted to do something. "I'm going to see the priest," she said to Alfredo. She quickly turned her face away. To cry was strictly forbidden. She thought of it as the worst thing she could do.

Father Arguedas adopted a "translator optional" policy in regard to confession. If people chose to confess in a language other than Spanish, then he would be happy to sit and listen and assume their sins were filtered through him and washed away by God exactly as they would have been if he had understood what they were saying. If people would rather be understood in a more traditional way, then they were welcome to bring Gen along if it worked out with his schedule. Gen was perfect for the job, as he seemed to have a remarkable ability not to listen to the words coming out of his own mouth. But that didn't matter because today Oscar Mendoza was confessing in the language they both grew up speaking. They sat face-to-face on two dining-room chairs pulled over to the corner. People respected the arrangement and avoided the dining room when they saw the priest was sitting down with someone there. At first, Father Arguedas had brought up the idea of trying to rig up some sort of proper confessional in the coat closet but the Generals would not allow it. All of the hostages must be out in the open where they could be clearly seen at all times.

"Bless me, Father, for I have sinned. It's been three weeks since my last confession. At home I go every week, I promise you that, but there isn't a great deal of opportunity to sin in our present circumstances," Oscar Mendoza said. "No drinking, no gambling, only three women. Even to try and sin with yourself is nearly impossible. There is so little privacy."

"There are rewards to the way we live."

Mendoza nodded, though he could hardly see it as such. "I am having dreams, though. Can certain types of dreams constitute a sin, Father?"

The priest shrugged. He enjoyed confession, the chance to talk to people, possibly to relieve them of their burden. He could count on one hand the number of times he had been allowed to hear confession before the kidnapping, but since then there had been instances when there had been several people waiting to speak to him. Perhaps he would have chosen slightly more sin, if only because it would have kept the people with him longer. "Dreams are a matter of the subconscious. That's unclear territory. Still, I think it would be best if you told me. Then maybe I can help you."

Beatriz leaned her head into the doorway, her heavy braid swung down against the light. "Are you finished yet?"

"Not yet," the priest said.

"Soon?"

"Go and play for a while. I can see you next."

Play. Did he think she was a child? She looked at Gen's big watch on her wrist. It was seventeen minutes after one o'clock. She understood the watch perfectly now, though it dogged her a little. She couldn't go for more than three minutes without checking the time no matter how hard she tried to ignore it. Beatriz lay down on a small red Oriental carpet just outside the door where Father couldn't see her but she could comfortably hear confession. She slipped the end of her braid into her mouth. Oscar Mendoza had a voice as big as his shoulders and it carried easily, even when he whispered.

"It is more or less the same dream every night." Oscar Mendoza stopped, not entirely sure he wanted to say anything too horrible to such a young priest. "Dreams of terrible violence."

"Against our captors?" the priest said quietly.

Out in the hall, Beatriz lifted up her head.

"Oh no, nothing like that. I wish they would leave us alone but I don't wish them any particular violence, at least not usually. No, the dreams that I have are about my daughters. I come home from this place. I escape or am freed, it's different in different dreams, and when I get to my house it is full of boys. It's like some sort of boys' academy. Boys of every size, light-skinned, dark-skinned, some fat, some lanky. They're everywhere. They are eating out of my refrigerator and smoking cigarettes on my porch. They are in my bathroom, using my razor. When I pass them they glance up, give me a dull look, like they couldn't really be bothered, and then they go back to whatever it was they were doing. But that's not the terrible part. These boys, what they are mostly doing, they are . . . they are, having knowledge of my daughters. They are lined up outside their bedrooms, even the rooms of my two little girls. It is a terrible thing, Father. From some of the doors I hear laughing and from others I hear sobbing and I start to kill the boys, one by one, I go down the hall and I break them apart like matches. They don't even step away from me. Each one looks so surprised just before I reach up to snap his neck in my hands." Oscar's hands were shaking and he knotted them together and pressed them between his knees.

Beatriz tried to look discreetly around the corner to see if the big man was crying. She thought she could detect a trembling in his voice. Were these the sorts of things other people dreamed about? Was this what they confessed? She checked the watch: 1:20.

"Ah, Oscar. Oscar." Father Arguedas patted his shoulder. "It is just the pressure. It's not a sin. We pray that our minds won't turn towards terrible things but sometimes they do and it is beyond our control."

"It feels very real at the time," Oscar said, and then he added reluctantly, "I'm not so unhappy in the dreams. I feel a rage, but I'm glad to be killing them."

This piece of information was perhaps more troubling. "The thing to do then is to learn. Pray for God's strength, for His justice. Then when the time comes for you to go back to your home there will be peace in your heart."

"I suppose." Oscar nodded slowly, feeling unconvinced. He realized now that what he had wanted the priest to do was not to absolve him but to reassure him that it was impossible, the things he dreamed about. That his daughters were safe and unmolested in their home.

Father Arguedas looked at him very closely. He leaned in towards him, his voice full of portent. "Pray to the Virgin. Three rosaries. Do you understand me?" He took his own rosary out of his pocket and pressed it into Oscar's big hands.

"Three rosaries," Oscar said, and sure enough, there was a loosening of pressure in his chest as he began to work the beads through his fingers. He left the room thanking Father. At least if he could pray he would be doing something.

The priest took a few minutes to pray for the sins of Oscar Mendoza and when he was finished he cleared his throat and called out, "Beatriz, was that fun for you?"

She waited, dried her braid on her sleeve, then she simply rolled over onto her stomach so that now she was facing into the room. "I don't know what you mean."

"You shouldn't be listening."

"You are a prisoner," she said, but without much conviction. She would never raise her gun to a priest and so she pointed her finger at him instead. "I have every right to hear what you are saying."

Father Arguedas leaned back in his chair. "To make sure we weren't in here plotting to kill you in your sleep."

"Exactly."

"Come in now and make your confession. You have something to confess already. That will make it easier." Father Arguedas was bluffing. None of the terrorists made confession, although many of them came to mass and he let them take communion just the same. He thought it was probably a rule of the Generals, no confession.

But Beatriz had never made confession before. In her village, the priest came through irregularly, only when his schedule permitted it. The priest was a very busy man who served a large region in the mountains. Sometimes months would pass between visits and then when he came his time was crowded up with not only the mass itself but baptisms and marriages, funerals, land disputes, communion. Confession was saved for murderers and the terminally ill, not idle girls who had done nothing worse then pinch their sisters or disobey their mothers. It was something for the very grown up and for the very wicked, and if she were to tell the truth, Beatriz considered herself to be neither of those things.

Father Arguedas held out his hand and he spoke to her softly. Really, he was the only one who ever spoke to her in that tone. "Come here," he said. "I'll make this very easy for you."

It was so simple to go to him, to sit down in the chair. He told her to bow her head and then he put a hand on either side of the straight part of her hair and began to pray for her. She didn't listen to the prayer. She only heard words here and there, beautiful words, *father* and *blessed* and *forgiveness*. It was just such a pleasant sensation, the weight of his hands on her head. When he finally took his hands away after what seemed to be a very long time, she felt delightfully weightless, free. She lifted up her face and smiled at him.

"Now you call your sins to mind," he said. "Usually you do that before you come. You pray to God to give you the courage to remember your sins and the courage to release them. And when you come to the confessional you say, 'Bless me, Father, for I have sinned. This is my first confession.'"

"Bless me, Father, for I have sinned. This is my first confession."

Father Arguedas waited for a while but Beatriz only continued to smile at him. "Now you tell me your sins."

"What are they?"

"Well," he said, "to start with, you listened in on Mr. Mendoza's confession when you knew it was the wrong thing to do."

She shook her head. "That wasn't a sin. I told you, I was doing my job."

Father Arguedas put his hands on her shoulders this time and it had the same wonderfully calming effect on her. "While you are in confession you must tell the absolute truth. You are telling that truth to God through me, and I will never tell another living soul. What this is is between you and me and God. It is a sacred rite and you must never, never lie when you make your confession. Do you understand that?"

"I do," Beatriz whispered. He had the nicest face of anyone here, nicer even than Gen's, who she had liked a little bit before. All the other hostages were too old, and the boys in her troop were too young, and the Generals were the Generals.

"Pray," the priest said. "Try very hard to understand this."

Because she liked him, she tried to make herself think about it. With the feel of his hands on her shoulders she closed her eyes and she prayed, and suddenly it seemed very clear to her. Yes, she knew she was not supposed to listen. She knew it like something she could see behind her closed eyes and it made her happy. "I confess having listened." All she had to do was say it and there it went, floating away from her. It wasn't her sin anymore.

"And something else?"

Something else. She thought again. She stared hard into the darkness of her closed eyes, the place where she knew the sins stacked up like kindling, dry and ready for a fire. There was something else, lots of something else. She began to see them all. But it was too much and she didn't know what to call it, how to form so many sins into words.

"I shouldn't have pointed the gun," she said finally, because there was no way to make sense of all of it. She felt like if she stayed forever she would never be able to confess them all. Not that she meant to stop doing any of those things. She couldn't stop. It wouldn't be allowed and she didn't even want to. She could see her sins now and knew that she would make more and more of them.

"God forgives you," the priest said.

Beatriz opened her eyes and blinked at the priest. "So it will go away?"

"You'll have to pray. You'll have to be sorry."

"I can do that." Maybe that was the answer, a sort of cycle of sinning and sorriness. She could come every Saturday, maybe more often than that, and he would keep having God forgive her, and then she would be free to go to heaven.

"I want you to say some prayers now."

"I don't know all the words."

Father Arguedas nodded his head. "We can say them together. I can teach them to you. But, Beatriz, I need you to be kind, to be helpful. That is part of your contrition. I want you to try it just for today."

Carmen was in the living room, but so was General Hector and a half-dozen of the bigger boys. Four of them played cards and the rest of them watched. They had stuck their knives into the table they played on, something that drove the Vice President to the brink of insanity. The table was from the early 1800s, hand-carved by Spanish artisans who never envisioned that knives would bristle from the wood's smooth top like so many porcupine quills. Gen walked past them slowly. He could not even attempt to catch Carmen's eye. All he could do was hope that she saw him and would think to follow. Gen stopped and spoke to Simon Thibault, who was stretched across a nearby sofa reading *One Hundred Years of Solitude* in Spanish.

"This will take me forever," Thibault said to Gen in French. "Maybe a hundred years. At least I know I have the time."

"Who knew that being kidnapped was so much like attending university?" Gen said.

Thibault laughed and turned a page. Had she heard them talking? Did she see him walking away? He went on to the kitchen, which was mercifully empty, slipped inside the china closet, and waited. Whenever he had come to the china closet, Carmen was already there, waiting for him. He had never been in there alone and the sight of all those plates stacked up above his head filled his heart with love for Carmen. Plates on which two people could eat a year's worth of dinners and never have to wash a dish. There was never a minute alone, a minute when someone wasn't asking him to say something. Always his head was cluttered with other people's overly expressed sentiments, and now it was quiet and he could imagine Carmen sitting next to him, her long, slender legs folded up in front of her while she conjugated verbs. She had asked him for favors and now he would ask her for her help. Together they would help Mr. Hosokawa and Miss Coss. Normally he would say that the private life of one's employer was in no manner his business, but no one pretended anymore that this was a normal life. He could not think of Mrs. Hosokawa or Nansei or Japan. Those things had receded so far behind them that it was almost impossible to believe they had ever existed. What he believed in was this china closet, saucers and soup bowls, towering stacks of bread-and-butter plates. He believed in this night. It struck him that he had looked for Carmen first, that he had not gone back to speak to Mr. Hosokawa, who was most likely still playing chess with Ishmael. He could not be two places at once and finally he felt himself settling, felt the kitchen floor hard and cold beneath his buttocks, felt the slightest ache in his back. He was here, only here, in this country he did not know, waiting on the girl he taught and loved, waiting to help Mr. Hosokawa, whom he loved as well. There was Gen, who had gone from nothing to loving two people.

He didn't know how much time was passing without his watch. He couldn't even guess anymore. Five minutes felt so much like an hour. *L'amour est un oiseau rebelle que nul ne peut apprivoiser, et c'est bien en vain qu'on l'appelle, s'il lui convient de refuser.* He only said the words to himself, humming lightly. He wished that he could sing them but Gen couldn't sing.

And then Carmen came, flushed as if she had been running when in fact she had walked to the kitchen as slowly as such a walk was possible to make. She closed the door behind her and sank down on the floor. "I thought this was what you meant," she whispered, pressing in close beside him as if it were cold. "I thought you would be waiting for me."

Gen took her hands, which were so small. How did he ever think she was only a beautiful boy? "I need to ask you something." *Love is a rebellious bird that no one can tame,* he thought again, and he kissed her.

She kissed him for the kiss, touched his hair, whose gloss and weight she found to be an endless source of fascination. "I didn't want to get up right away. I thought I should wait awhile before I followed you."

He kissed her. There was such an incredible logic to kissing, such a metal-to-magnet pull between two people that it was a wonder that they found the strength to prevent themselves from succumbing every second. Rightfully, the world should be a whirlpool of kissing into which we sank and never found the strength to rise up again. "Roxane Coss came to speak to me today. She said she wants you to sleep somewhere else tonight, to not bring her breakfast in the morning."

Carmen pushed away from him, keeping one hand on his chest. Roxane Coss didn't want her to bring breakfast? "Did I do something wrong?"

"Oh, no," Gen said. "She thinks very highly of you. She told me so." He tucked her into the crook of his arm and she breathed into his shoulder. This was what it felt like, to be a man with a woman. This was the thing Gen had missed in all the translation of language. "You were right, what you thought about, her feelings for Mr. Hosokawa. She wants to be with him tonight."

Carmen raised her head. "How will he get upstairs?"

"Roxane wants you to help him."

Gen lived one life and in that life he was always a prisoner and his friends were the other prisoners, and even though he loved Carmen and got along politely with some of the terrorists, he never got confused and thought he wanted to join LFDMS. But for Carmen it was different. She had clearly two lives. She did her push-ups in the morning and stood for inspection. She carried her rifle on guard. She kept a boning knife in her boot and she knew how to use it. She obeyed orders. She was, as it had been explained to her, part of the force that would bring about change. But she was also the girl who went to the china closet at night, who was learning to read in Spanish and could already say several things in English. *Good morning. I am very well, thank you. Where is the restaurant?* Some mornings, Roxane Coss let her climb into the impossibly soft sheets on her big bed, let her close her eyes for a few minutes and pretend she belonged there. She would pretend she was one of the prisoners, that she lived in a world with so many privileges that there was nothing to fight for. But no matter how the two sides got along, they were always two sides, and when she went from one to the other it was a matter of crossing over something. Either she told Gen she couldn't get Mr. Hosokawa upstairs, in which case she disappointed Gen and Mr. Hosokawa and Miss Coss, who had all been so kind to her, or she told him she could, in which case she broke every oath she had sworn to her party and put herself at risk of a punishment she would not imagine. If Gen had understood any of this he never would have asked her. For him it was merely about helping out, being a friend. It was as if he only wanted to borrow a book. Carmen closed her eyes and pretended to be tired. She prayed to Saint Rose of Lima. "Saint Rose, give me guidance. Saint Rose, give me clarity." She pressed her eyes closed and pleaded for the intercession of the only saint she knew personally, but a saint is very little help when it comes to smuggling a married man into an opera singer's bedroom. On this matter, Carmen was on her own.

"Sure," Carmen whispered, her eyes still closed, her ear pressed to the steady thump of Gen's heart. Gen's hand came up and smoothed her hair, over and over again, the way her mother had done when Carmen was a child and had a fever.

In the vice-presidential mansion, none of the guests, not even Ruben Iglesias himself, knew the house as well as the members of LFDMS. Part of their daily work was the memorization of windows and which ones were wide enough to jump through. They calculated the falls, estimated the damage in terms of their own bones. They each knew the length of the hallways, rooms from which one could make a clear shot to the outside, the fastest exits to the roof, to the garden. So naturally, Carmen knew there was a back stairwell in the hallway off the kitchen that led to the servants' quarters, and that in the very room that Esmeralda had once slept there was a door that went to the nursery, and the nursery had a door onto the main hallway of the second floor, and that hallway led to the bedroom where Roxane Coss slept. Of course, other people slept on the second floor as well. Generals Benjamin and Hector had rooms on the second floor. (General Alfredo, the worst sleeper, found a little rest in the guest suite on the first floor.) Many of the boys slept on the second floor and not always in the same place, which is why Carmen chose to sleep in the hallway outside of Roxane Coss's room, just in case one of those boys woke up in the middle of the night, restless. Carmen herself had used this route to the china closet every night, her stocking feet silent on the polished wood floor. She knew the location of every creaky board, every potentially light sleeper. She knew how to flatten herself into the shadows when someone came around the corner headed for the bathroom. She could skate those floors as quiet as a blade drawing over ice. Carmen was trained, an expert at remaining silent. Still, she could sense the depth of Mr. Hosokawa's ability to be quiet. Thank God Roxane Coss had not fallen in love with one of the Russians. She doubted they could make it up the stairs without stopping for a cigarette and telling at least one loud story that no one could understand.

Gen was to bring Mr. Hosokawa to the back hallway at two A.M. and she would take him to Roxane Coss's room. Two hours later she would come to the door to lead him back. They would say nothing to each other, but that part was easy enough. Even if in this case they were allies, there was nothing they knew to say.

Once the plans were made, Carmen left Gen to watch television with the other soldiers. There she saw a repeat broadcast of *The Story of Maria*. Maria had gone to the city to search for her lover, whom she had sent away. She wandered the crowded streets with her little suitcase in her hand and on every corner strangers lurked in the shadows, conspiring to ruin her. Everyone in the Vice President's study wept. Carmen played checkers when the program was over and she helped with supply lists and volunteered to cover afternoon watch if anyone was feeling tired. She would be exemplary in her helpfulness and willing participation. She did not want to see Gen or Mr. Hosokawa or Roxane Coss for fear she would blush and give herself away, for fear that she would become angry at them for asking so much of her.

How much does a house know? There could not have been gossip and yet there was a slight tension in the air, the vaguest electricity that made men lift their heads and look and find nothing. The salted fish and rice that came for dinner did not go down well and one after the other they put their shares on the table half eaten and walked away. Kato picked out Cole Porter on the piano and the evening fell into a low, blue light. Maybe it was the fine weather, the irritation of once again not being able to walk outside. A half-dozen men stood near an open window and tried to breathe the night air as darkness settled in, taking away the view of the overgrown garden one twisted flower at a time. From the other side of the wall they could hear the faint race of engines, cars that were possibly blocks away from their street, and for a moment the men at the window remembered that there was a world out there, and then just as quickly they let the thought go.

Roxane Coss had gone to bed early. Like Carmen, she didn't want to be there once she had made her decision. Mr. Hosokawa sat next to Gen on the love seat nearest the piano. "Tell me again," he said.

"She wants to see you tonight."

"That's what she said?"

"Carmen will take you to her room."

Mr. Hosokawa looked at his hands. They were old hands. His father's hands. His nails were long. "It's very awkward that Carmen should know this. That you should know."

"There was no other way."

"What if it is dangerous for the girl?"

"Carmen knows what she's doing." Gen said. Dangerous? She went down the stairs every night to come to the china closet. He wouldn't ask her to do something that wasn't safe.

Mr. Hosokawa nodded slowly. He had the distinct sensation that the living room was tilting, that the living room had become a boat in a gently tilting sea. He had stopped thinking of what he wanted most so many years ago, even when he was a child perhaps. He disciplined himself to only want the things that were possible to have: an enormous industry, a productive family, an understanding of music. And now, a few months after his fifty-third birthday, in a country he had never really seen, he felt desire in the deepest part of himself, the kind of wanting that can only come when the thing you want is very close to you. When he was a child he dreamed of love, not only to witness it, the way he saw love in the opera, but to feel it himself. But that, he decided, was madness. That was wanting too much. Tonight he wished for little things, the chance to take a hot bath, a reasonable suit of clothing, a gift to bring, at the very least some flowers, but then the room tilted slightly in the other direction and he opened up his hands and all of that fell away from him and he wanted nothing. He had been asked to come to her room at two A.M. and there was nothing more in the world to want, ever.

When the time came to sleep, Mr. Hosokawa lay flat on his back and looked at his watch by the bright light of the moon. He was afraid he would fall asleep and he knew he would never fall asleep. He marveled at Gen, who took measured, peaceful breaths on the floor beside him. What he didn't know was that Gen woke up every morning at two A.M., as regular as a baby waking for food, and slipped out of the living room without ever being missed. Mr. Hosokawa watched the night guard circle, Beatriz and Sergio, and lowered his eyelids whenever they came near. They stopped to watch certain members of his group sleep. They whispered to one another and nodded. By one o'clock they had disappeared exactly the way Gen said they would. This was the world of the night of which he knew nothing. Mr. Hosokawa could feel his pulse pushing in his temples, his wrists, his neck. He pointed his toes. This was the hour. He had been sleeping forever. He had been dead. Now he was suddenly, completely alive.

At five minutes until two, Gen sat up as if an alarm had gone off. He stood, looked at his employer, and together they crossed the living room, placing their feet down gently between their sleeping friends and acquaintances. There were the Argentinians. There were the Portuguese. The Germans slept near the Italians. The Russians were safe in the dining room. There was Kato, his dear hands folded on his chest, his fingers twitching almost imperceptibly in his sleep, like a dog dreaming of Schubert. There was the priest, rolled over on his side, both hands under one cheek. Scattered among them were a handful of soldiers sprawled on their backs as if sleep was a car that had hit them dead on, their necks twisted sideways, their mouths wrenched open, their rifles resting in their open hands like ripe fruit.

In a hallway off the kitchen, Carmen was waiting exactly as Gen said she would be, her dark hair tied into a braid, her feet bare. She looked at Gen first, and he touched her shoulder lightly instead of speaking, and everything was understood among the three of them. There was no sense in waiting, as waiting would have only made it worse. Carmen would have liked to have been in the china closet now, her legs across Gen's lap, reading aloud the practice paragraph he had written up for her, but she had made her choice. She had agreed. She said a quick prayer to the saint who ignored her now and crossed herself as quickly, lightly, as a hummingbird touching down four times. Then she turned and went down the hall, Mr. Hosokawa moving silently behind her. Gen watched them as they turned away, never having realized it would be worse to be left behind.

When they got to the staircase, a narrow, twisting affair whose boards were cheap and only good enough to carry servants from one floor to the other, Carmen turned and looked at Mr. Hosokawa. She leaned over and touched his ankle and then touched her own, she moved their feet together, and when she stood up he nodded to her. It was very dark and as they took the stairs it would get darker. Never had her prayers failed her completely. She tried to believe this was only a lesson, a necessary delay, and that if they were to get caught she would not be alone forever.

All Mr. Hosokawa could see now was the outline of her narrow back. He tried to do what she told him, to place his foot exactly in the place her foot had left, but he couldn't help think about how much smaller she was. Captivity had made him thinner, and as he took the stairs he was grateful for every pound he had lost. He held his breath and listened. Truly, they were silent. He had never been so aware of the complete absence of sound. He had not climbed a set of stairs in the months he had been inside this house and the very act felt brave and daring. How right it was to climb! How happy he was to finally have the chance to risk himself. When they reached the top, Carmen pushed open the door with her fingertips and a little light fell onto her face, a reassurance that at least part of the trip was behind them now. She turned and smiled at him. She was a beautiful girl. She was his own daughter.

They took the slim hallway to the nanny's room, and when she opened that door there was the slightest hint of a whine. Still no noise from the two of them, but a small sound from the door. There was also someone in the bed. It didn't happen often. The girl who watched the children had the least comfortable bed in the whole house and rarely would anyone fall asleep there, but it did happen, tonight it happened. Carmen put her hand against Mr. Hosokawa's chest so they could wait for a minute for the room to forget the sound the door had made. She could feel his heart beating so clearly it was as if she were holding it in her hand. Carmen took a breath and waited, then she nodded without looking back and moved one foot forward. Maybe this was hard but it was not impossible. It was nothing compared to breaking into the mansion through the air vents. There had been other nights when she had found people sleeping in this bed.

It was Beatriz. She had lain down in the middle of night watch. Everyone did it. Carmen certainly had. It was too long to stay awake. Sergio would be in some other room, slumped over in a hard and guilty sleep. Beatriz did not have a blanket over her and her boots were on. In her sleep she cradled her rifle in her arms like a child. Mr. Hosokawa tried to make his feet move forward, but now he was afraid. He closed his eyes and thought of Roxane Coss, he thought of love and tried to say a prayer to love, and when he opened his eyes, Beatriz sat up in bed and just as quickly raised her gun. Just as quickly, Carmen stepped between them. These two things Mr. Hosokawa was sure of: Beatriz pointed the rifle at him and Carmen came in front of the gun. She went to Beatriz, who should have been her friend, the only other girl in a troop of so many men, and grabbed her and held her tight, leaving the rifle to point at the ceiling.

"What are you doing?" Beatriz hissed. Even she knew this was a quiet business. "Get away from me."

But Carmen held her. She practically fell into her she was so frightened and so oddly relieved now that she had been caught. "Don't tell," she whispered in the other girl's ear.

"You're taking him upstairs? You are in so much trouble." Beatriz struggled and found Carmen stronger than she had imagined. Or maybe it was just that she had been so deeply asleep. Asleep on guard, and maybe Carmen meant to tell.

"Shh," Carmen said. She buried her nose in the loose hair where

258   *Ann Patchett*

Beatriz's braid had unraveled in her sleep and kept her grip tight. For a second she forgot about Mr. Hosokawa and it was only the two of them, only this immediate problem. She could feel Beatriz's back was still warm from the bed and the barrel of the gun pressed cold into her cheek, and even though she had not thought to ask for help, she heard the beloved voice of Saint Rose of Lima say to her, "Tell the truth."

"He's in love with the opera singer," Carmen said. She didn't care about secrets now. Her only hope was to do what she was told. "They wanted to be alone together."

"They would kill you for this," Beatriz said, though she thought that probably wasn't true.

"Help me," Carmen said. She meant to say it only to her saint, but the words slipped from her lips in desperation. Beatriz thought for a moment she heard the voice of the priest. He had forgiven her. He had instructed her towards kindness. She thought of her own sins and the chance to forgive the sins of others, and she raised up what she could of her pinned-down arm and put it lightly on Carmen's back.

"She loves him?" Beatriz said.

"I'm going to bring him back in two hours."

Beatriz shifted herself in Carmen's arms and this time Carmen let her go. She could barely make out Carmen's face. She could not be entirely sure it was Mr. Hosokawa there in the darkness. He had taught her to tell time. He had always smiled at her. Once, when they reached the door to the kitchen at the same time, he bowed to her. Beatriz closed her eyes, searched the darkness for her own pile of sins. "I won't tell," she whispered. And again, for the second time that day, she felt a loosening as some of her burden was lifted from her.

Carmen kissed her cheek. She was full of gratitude. She felt for the first time that she was lucky. Then she stepped back into the shadows. Beatriz had meant to extract a promise from her in return, that she wouldn't tell that she had seen her sleeping, but of course she wouldn't tell, she couldn't. Beatriz lay back on the bed, though she hadn't meant to, and in a minute she was asleep and the whole business was over with as suddenly as it had all begun.

Through the nursery, where a moon-shaped night-light still glowed faintly from a wall socket illuminating a cast of lonesome dolls, past yet another bathroom with a white porcelain tub that was bigger than some canoes Carmen had ridden in, and out into the main hall, where the house became again the house that they knew, wide and gracious and grand. Carmen led Mr. Hosokawa to the third door and then she stopped. This was where she slept most nights, the little sleeping she did. She had been holding on to his hand ever since she had led him away from Beatriz and she was holding it now. It seemed they had come a very long way, but the Vice President's children could make it from their mother's bedroom, through the nursery, cutting through Esmeralda's room and down the back stairs to the kitchen in well under a minute, even though they had been told to never run in the house. Carmen liked Mr. Hosokawa. She wished she could tell him so, but if she had had the language she wouldn't have had the courage. Instead she pressed his hand once and then let it go.

Mr. Hosokawa bowed to her, his face pointing down towards his knees, and he held this position for what seemed to Carmen to be too long. Then he stood again and opened the door.

There was a high window in the upstairs hallway and the main staircase was flooded with the bright light of the moon, but Carmen didn't take the front stairs. She navigated her course backwards, through the nursery and past the bed where Beatriz was sleeping deeply. Carmen stopped to untangle the rifle's trigger from her fingers. She leaned the gun against the wall and pulled a coverlet up over her shoulders. She hoped that Beatriz would not decide to tell in the morning, or better yet that she would wake up thinking it was all a dream. Coming down the kitchen stairs, Carmen felt a different kind of wild heartbeat. She imagined Roxane Coss on the other side of the door, anxious from all the waiting. She imagined Mr. Hosokawa, silent and dignified, taking her into his arms. The sweetness of that touch, the security inside the embrace, Carmen raised her hand to the thin pricking of sweat on the back of her neck. She was silent, but still the stairs came faster now, four, three, two, one, then she was through the hallway, the kitchen. She skidded to a stop just inside the wondrous world of the china closet, where Gen sat on the floor, an unopened book on his knees. When he looked up she put her fingers to her lips. So much brightness in her face, her cheeks flushed, her eyes open wide. When she turned away, of course he would stand and follow her.

How much luck is one person entitled to in a night? Does it come in a limited allotment, like milk in a bottle, and when so much has been poured out then only so much is left? Or was luck a matter of the day, and on the day you're lucky you are limitlessly lucky? If it was the former, then surely Carmen had used up all her luck getting Mr. Hosokawa safely into Roxane Coss's bedroom. But if it was the latter, and in her bones she felt this was the truth, then this was her night. If all the saints in heaven were behind her now, then her luck must be good for a few more hours. Carmen took Gen's hand and led him through the kitchen and onto the back porch, where he had never been before. She opened up the door, simply put her hand on the knob and turned it, and together they walked out into the night.

Look at this night: the moon a floodlight washing over what had once been an orderly garden, the moonlight pouring over the high stucco wall like water. The air smelled of the thick jasmine vines and the evening lilies that had long ago finished their work and closed up for the day. The grass was high, past their ankles and brushing heavy against their calves, and it made a shushing sound as they walked so they stopped to look up at the stars, forgetting that they were right in the middle of a city block. There weren't more than half a dozen stars to see.

Carmen went outside all the time. Even in the rain she had gone out every day to walk on guard or simply to stretch her legs, but for Gen the night seemed miraculous, the air and the sky, the soft crush of grass beneath his heel. He was back in the world and the world looked, on that night, to be an incomprehensibly beautiful place. Such a limited view he was given yet still he would swear to it, the world was beautiful.

For the rest of Gen's life he will remember this night in two completely different ways.

First, he will imagine what he did not do:

In this version, he takes Carmen's hand and leads her out the gate at the end of the front walkway. There are military guards on the other side of the wall but they, too, are young and asleep, and together they pass them and simply walk out into the capital city of the host country. Nobody knows to stop them. They are not famous and nobody cares. They go to an airport and find a flight back to Japan and they live there, together, happily and forever.

Then he will imagine exactly what did happen:

It did not occur to him to leave, as it does not occur to a dog to leave once he has been trained to stay in the yard. He only feels blessed for the little freedom he is given. Carmen takes his hand and together they walk to the place where Esmeralda held picnics for the Vice President's children, a place where the wall curves back and makes a pocket of grass and slender trees and there is no clear view of the house. Carmen kisses him and he kisses her and from then on he will never be able to separate the smell of her from the smell of night. They are deep in the lush growth of grass, in a part of the yard that is covered in shadows thrown down by the wall, and Gen can see nothing. Later, he would remember that his friend, Mr. Hosokawa, was inside that house on the second floor, in bed with the singer, but on that night he does not think of them at all. Carmen has pulled off her jacket even though there's a cool breeze. She unbuttons his shirt while he covers her breasts with his hands. In the dark they are not themselves at all. They are confident. Gen pulls her down and she pulls him down. They defy gravity in their slow tumble to earth. Neither of them wear shoes and their pants slip off, too big for them anyway, and that feeling, that first luxury of skin touching skin.

Sometimes Gen will stop his memory there.

Her skin, the night, the grass, to be outside and then to be inside Carmen. He doesn't know to want for more because nothing in his life has been as much as this. At the very moment he could have been taking her away, he is pulling her closer. Her hair is tangled around his neck. On that night he thinks that no one has ever had so much and only later will he know that he should have asked for more. His fingers slip into the soft indentations between her ribs, the delicate gullies carved out by hunger. He feels her teeth, takes her tongue. Carmen, Carmen, Carmen, Carmen. In the future, he will try to say her name enough, but he never can.

Inside, the house slept, the guests and guards, and no one knew the difference. The Japanese man and his beloved soprano upstairs in bed, the translator and Carmen beneath the six stars outside, nobody missed them. Only Simon Thibault was awake, and he woke up from dreaming of Edith, his wife. When he was fully awake and could see where he was and remember that she wasn't there with him, he began to cry. He tried to stop himself but he could see her so vividly. They had been in bed in the dream. They had been making love and in that love each had gently said the other's name. When it was over, Edith had sat up in the tangle of blankets and wrapped her blue scarf around his shoulders to keep him warm. Simon Thibault buried his face in that scarf now but the crying only came harder. Nothing he could think of would stop it, and after a while he didn't even try.

nine

*i*n the morning everything was right. The sun came pouring in through the windows and showed up a series of irregular stains on the carpet. Outside, the birds whistled and called. Two of the boys, Jesus and Sergio, circled the house, their boots heavy with dew, their rifles raised. At home, they might have shot a bird or two but here shooting was Strictly Prohibited Unless Absolutely Necessary. The birds darted past them, their wings making a breeze in the boys' hair. They looked in the window and saw Carmen and Beatriz in the kitchen together, taking rolls out of large plastic packages while eggs boiled to hard-cooked on the stove. They looked at each other and Carmen smiled a little and Beatriz pretended not to see it, which Carmen thought was probably a good sign, or good enough. The room smelled of strong coffee. Carmen disappeared into the china closet and came back carrying a stack of blue-and-gold plates with the word *Wedgwood* stamped on the bottom, because what was the good of having them if they were never used?

Everything was like it was every other morning. Except Roxane Coss did not come down to the piano. Kato had been waiting. After a while he stood up from the piano bench and stretched his legs. He leaned over and picked out a piece of Schumann, the simple one that everybody knows, music to pass the time. He didn't even look at the keys. It was as if he was talking to himself and didn't seem to know that everyone could hear him. Roxane was sleeping in. Carmen had not taken up her breakfast. It was not such a terrible thing. She sang every day, after all, didn't she deserve to rest?

But wasn't it strange that Mr. Hosokawa was asleep as well? There on the couch, with everyone milling around him, he was still on his back, his glasses folded closed on his chest, his lips parted. No one ever saw him sleeping. He was always the first one up in the morning. Maybe he was sick. Two of the boys, Guadalupe and Humberto, the inside morning guards, leaned over the back of the couch and watched him to see if he was still breathing, which he was, so they left him alone.

Quarter past eight, Beatriz knew because she had the watch. Too much fucking, she thought, but didn't say it to Carmen. She was letting Carmen think she had forgotten when no such thing was true. She didn't know how she would use this information, but she savored it like unspent money. There were so many possibilities for such knowledge.

People get used to their little routines. They drank their coffee, brushed their teeth, and then they came into the living room and Roxane Coss sang. That was morning. But now they watched the stairs. Where was she? If she wasn't sick then shouldn't she be downstairs? Was consistency too much to ask for? They gave her so much respect, glory, wasn't it right to think she would respect them in return? They watched Kato, who stood there like the man at the train station who looks at the open train door long after all the passengers have gotten off. The man who you know has been jilted long before he realizes it himself. He tapped at the keys absently, still standing. He was wondering at what point he could sit down and really play without her. It was the first time Kato had to ask himself: What was he without her? What would happen when all of this was over and he no longer spent entire days at the piano, his nights reading over music?

He was a pianist now. He had rows of fine blue tendons in his fingers to prove it. Could he go back to that other life in which he got up at four A.M. to play furtively for an hour before work? What would happen when he was reinstated as a senior vice president at Nansei and once again became the numbers man, the man without a soprano? That's all he would be. He remembered what had happened to the first accompanist, how he chose to die rather than to go out in the world alone. The chilling emptiness of Kato's future made his fingers tighten and slip off the keys without a sound.

And then something remarkable happened:

Someone else began to sing, an a cappella voice from the far side of the room, a lovely, familiar voice. People were confused at first and then one by one all the boys started laughing, Humberto and Jesus, Sergio and Francisco, Gilbert, there were others coming from down the hall, big belly laughs, laughs in which they were forced to drape their arms around each other's necks just to stand up, but Cesar kept singing, *"Vissi d'arte, vissi d'amore, non feci mai,"* from *Tosca*. And it *was* funny, because he so completely mimicked Roxane. It was as if while the rest of them slept he had become her, the way she held out her hand when she sang, *Ever a fervent believer, I have laid flowers on the altar*. It was uncanny, for certainly Cesar looked nothing like the Diva. He was a spindly boy with blemished skin and two dozen silky black whiskers, but seeing him was so much like seeing her, the way he tilted his head and then, just at the very moment she would, closed his eyes. He didn't seem to hear them laughing. His gaze was unfocused. He was singing to no one in particular. It wasn't that he was mocking her so much as he was just trying to fill up the space where she should have been. It would have been mocking if it had only been her gestures he was repeating, but it wasn't. It was her voice. The legendary voice of Roxane Coss. He held his notes long and clear. He reached down into the depths of his lungs for the power, the volume he had not allowed himself when singing alone under his breath. He was singing now, a part that was too high for him and yet he jumped up and grabbed onto the edge of the note. He pulled himself up and held it. He had no idea what he was saying, but he knew he was saying it correctly. He had paid too much attention to get it wrong. He rolled the pronunciation of every word in a perfect arch over his tongue. He was not a soprano. He did not know Italian. And yet somehow he gave the illusion of both things and for a moment the room believed in him. The boys' laughter dissipated then vanished. Everyone, the guests, the boys, the Generals, they were all looking at Cesar now. Carmen and Beatriz were drawn out of the kitchen, their ears cocked, not at all sure if what was happening was good or bad. Mr. Hosokawa, who knew the music better than all of them, woke up thinking he was waking up to singing he knew, woke up thinking her voice was strange this morning, and wondered if maybe she was tired, look, he was still asleep himself. But he woke up thinking it was her voice.

It is not such a long piece and when it was over Cesar barely took in breath. He went ahead because what if this was his only chance to sing? He hadn't meant to exactly, but when he saw that she wasn't coming down, that everyone was waiting, the notes welled up in his throat like a wave and nothing he could do would have held them down. How brilliant it was to sing! How wonderful to hear his own voice now. He went on to the aria from *La Wally*. He could only sing the pieces that were Roxane's favorites, the ones she sang over and over again. Those were the only ones whose words he could be absolutely sure of, and if he faked the words, made some sounds that were close but might mean something else entirely, then everyone would see him as a fraud. Cesar did not know that only four people in the house spoke Italian. It would have been easier to sing something that they didn't all associate with her, because how could he not fail by comparison? But he had no choice, no other material to chose from. He didn't know that there were songs for men and songs for women, that different pieces were tailored to the abilities of different voices. All he had heard were the parts for soprano, so why should they not be his parts? He did not compare himself to her. There was no comparison. She was the singer. He was only a boy who loved her by singing. Or was it singing he loved? He could no longer remember. He was too far inside. He closed his eyes and followed his voice. Somewhere far away he heard the piano tailing him, then catching up, then leading him ahead. The end of the aria was very high and he had no idea if he would make it. It was like falling, no, like diving, twisting your body through the air without a single thought as to how it might land.

Mr. Hosokawa was standing at the piano now in a confusion of sleep, his hair disheveled, his shirttails crumpled behind him. He simply didn't know what to make of it. Part of him thought he should stop the boy in case he was being disrespectful, but it was all too remarkable, really, he loved *La Wally*. Still, there was something unnerving about watching this boy who now folded his hands over his heart the way Roxane did; what came out of his mouth was not her but so oddly reminiscent, as if it was only a poor recording of her voice that he was hearing. He closed his eyes. Yes, there was a considerable difference. There was no mistaking it now, but somehow this boy brought on the rocking sensation of love. Mr. Hosokawa loved Roxane Coss. Perhaps the boy wasn't even singing. Perhaps his love was capable of turning the most ordinary objects into her.

Roxane Coss was standing among them listening. How was it that no one saw her coming down the stairs? She had not stopped to dress and was wearing a pair of white silk pajamas and the Vice President's wife's blue alpaca robe even though it was too warm for this weather. Her feet were bare and her hair was loose down her back. After so many months her roots had grown out and it was easy to see that her hair was in fact a duller shade of pale brown and thatched with shimmering silver. The boy was singing. His singing had drawn her out of such a deep sleep. She would have slept for several more hours but the singing woke her and she followed it down the stairs in a state of confusion. A recording? A cappella? But then she saw him, Cesar, a boy who had done nothing to set himself apart until now. When did he learn to sing? Her mind was racing in every direction. He was good. He was excellent. If someone was to run across such raw talent in Milan, in New York, the boy would be bundled off to a conservatory in a minute. He would be a star, because now he was nothing, not a minute of training and listen to the depth in his tone! Listen to the power that shook his narrow shoulders. He was careening towards the end, towards a high C that he could not be prepared for. She knew the music as well as she knew her own breath and she rushed towards him, as if he were a child in the road, as if the note was a speeding car bearing down on him. She grabbed his wrist. *"Detengase! Basta!"* She didn't know Spanish, yet those two words she heard every day. Stop. Enough.

Cesar stopped his singing dead but sadly left his mouth open, shaped to the last word he had sung. And when she did not say, "Begin again!" his lips betrayed the slightest tremor.

Roxane Coss was touching his arm. She was speaking so fast and he didn't understand a word of what she was saying. He stared at her blankly and he could see that she was frustrated, panicked even. The more panicked she became the louder and faster her senseless words came out and when he still didn't respond she called out, "Gen!"

But the whole room was watching them and it was too awful. Cesar felt the trembling everywhere now, and even though she was standing right beside him, touching him, he turned away and ran out of the room. They all stood there in embarrassed silence, as if the boy had run out suddenly naked. It was Kato who thought to put his hands together and the Italians, Gianni Davansate and Pietro Genovese, who called out, *"Bravo!"* And then everyone in the room was clapping and calling for the boy, but he was gone, out the back door and up into a tree where he often kept watch of the goings-on of the world. He could hear them, the dull buzz from inside, but who's to say they weren't mocking him terribly? Maybe she was in there now doing her own imitation: pretending to be him pretending to be her.

"Gen!" Roxane took Gen's hand. "Go after him. Tell someone to go after him."

And when Gen turned around, there stood Carmen. Always there was Carmen, her bright dark eyes turned up to him, ready to help him like a person whose life you've saved. He didn't even have to say it. That was how they understood each other. She turned and then she was gone.

Having kept such close quarters for so long, everybody knew what everybody else liked. Ishmael, for example, followed the Vice President like a dog. Looking for Ishmael? Find the Vice President and chances were the boy would be tangled up in his feet. Beatriz would always be in front of the television unless compelled by a direct order to be elsewhere. Gilbert was mad for the bathtub, especially the one in the master bathroom that roared into a raging boil when you flipped a switch (wasn't that a surprise the first time it happened!). Cesar liked the tree, a sturdy oak that leaned into the wall, a tree with low, strong branches for easy climbing, high, wide branches for comfortable sitting. The other soldiers thought he was especially stupid or brave because sometimes he climbed up high enough that he was actually over the wall, where any military personnel could have popped him off like a squirrel. Sometimes the Generals asked him to look out over the city and report back, and off he would go into the tree. So there was no great puzzle as to where Carmen should look. She went out into the yard, a place that seemed completely different to her after last night. She took the long way around so that she could pass by the spot where the wall pocketed out into a private cove and look, the grass was still flattened, pressed down in the shape of her back. She felt every drop of her blood race to her head and she put her fingers to the wall, dizzy. Dear God, what if somebody noticed? Should she stop now, take the time to try and set it right? Could grass be fluffed up again? Would it stay that way? But then Carmen realized that she planned to pound down that same spot of grass again tonight, that she wanted to press down every blade of grass in the garden with her hips, her shoulders, the bare soles of her feet. If there had been a way she would have taken Gen then and there, wrapped her legs around him and climbed him like a tree. Who would ever think that such man would want to be with her? She was so distracted by the certainty of love that for a moment she forgot why she had come outside in the first place or who she was looking for. Then, in the distance, she saw a boot dangling like a large, ugly fruit from the high leaves and the world came rushing back to her. Carmen went to the oak tree, grabbed a branch above her head, and climbed.

There was Cesar, shaking, crying. Anyone else who climbed this tree he would have thrown out on his head. He would have kicked him hard under the chin and sent him flying. But the head that pulled itself up to him was Carmen's and Carmen he liked. He thought she understood him because of how she clearly loved Roxane Coss. She was the luckiest of them all, getting to take up her breakfast, getting to sleep outside her door. (Because Carmen was completely discreet he knew nothing about the rest of it: that she had slept in Roxane's bed, brushed her hair, that Carmen had smuggled Roxane's lover to her in the middle of the night and held her confidence. Had he known all of that he might have imploded with jealousy.) And while no one should see him cry like he was still a child, it would be less than terrible if the person who saw him was Carmen. Before he fell in love with Roxane Coss, back before they ever came to the city, he thought constantly about how much he would have liked to kiss Carmen, kissed her and more, but he gave up on the idea after a sharp smack from General Hector. Such business was completely forbidden between soldiers.

"You sing so beautifully," she said.

Cesar turned his face away from her. A small branch scraped lightly against his cheek. "I'm a fool," he said into the leaves.

Carmen swung onto a branch across from him and clamped her legs around it. "Not a fool! You had to do it. You didn't have any choice." She could see the battered-down portion of grass from where she was now. It was different from this vantage point, larger and almost perfectly round, as if they had spun each other in great circles, which seemed possible. She could smell the grass in her hair. Love was action. It came to you. It was not a choice.

But Cesar would not look back at her. From where she was she could have seen over the wall if she had just stretched up a little bit. She did not.

"Roxane Coss sent me out to get you," Carmen said. It was close enough to the truth. "She wants to talk to you about your singing. She thinks you're very good." She could say this because she knew he was very good and of course Roxane would tell him so. She did not understand anywhere near enough English to have deciphered what had been said in the living room, but she was developing a knack of figuring things out without having to know all the actual words.

"You don't know that."

"I do, too. The translator was there."

"She said, *stop*. She said, *enough*. I understood what she said." A bird swooped once past the tree, hoping to land, and then shot on.

"She wanted to talk to you. What does she know to say? You have to ask Gen for help. He's the only way to understand anything."

Cesar sniffed, blotted his eyes with his cuff. In the perfect world it would not be Carmen in this tree. It would be Roxane Coss herself who had followed him up there. She would be touching his cheek, speaking to him in perfect Spanish. They would sing together. The word for that was *duet*. They would travel all over the world.

"Well, you're not a squirrel," Carmen said. "You aren't going to stay up here forever. You'll have to come down for guard duty and when you do she'll tell you herself with the translator. She'll tell you how good you are and then you will feel like an idiot for sulking up here. Everyone wants to celebrate with you. You'll miss out on everything."

Cesar slid his hand over the rough bark. Carmen had never talked like this before. When they were in training together she was almost too shy to speak at all, that was one of the things that had made her so appealing. He had never heard her string two full sentences together. "How do you know all of this?"

"I told you, the translator."

"And how do you know he tells you the truth?"

Carmen looked at him like he was crazy, but she didn't say a word. She reached down for the branch beneath her, held on, let her feet fall, and then opened her hands to drop to the ground. She was an expert at jumping. She kept her knees soft and sprang straight up after her feet hit the grass. She did not lose her balance at all. She walked away from Cesar without so much as a glance over her shoulder. Let him rot up there. On her way back into the house she passed one of the windows that looked into the great living room. How strange it was to see it all from that side. She stopped for a while and stood beside a bush that had been so neatly shaped when they first arrived and now was almost as tall as she was. She could see Gen near the piano, talking to Roxane Coss and Mr. Hosokawa. Kato was there. She could see Gen, his straight back and tender mouth, his hands which had helped her out of her clothes and then folded her neatly back inside them again. She wished she could tap on the glass and wave to him, but it was a miraculous thing to be able to watch the person you love undetected, as if you were a stranger seeing them for the first time. She could see his beauty as someone who took nothing for granted. Look at that beautiful man, that brilliant man, he loves me. She said a prayer to Saint Rose of Lima. Safety for Gen. Happiness and a long life. Watch over him and guide him. She looked through the window. He was speaking to Roxane now, Roxane who had been so good to her, and so Carmen included her in the prayer. Then she bowed her head for a minute and quickly crossed herself, thus hurrying the prayer on its way.

"I shouldn't have told him to stop," Roxane said. Gen translated it into Japanese.

"There is no place for the boy to go," Mr. Hosokawa said. "He will have to come back. You mustn't worry about that." In Japan, he was often made uneasy by this modern age of affection, young men and women holding hands in public, kissing good-bye on subway trains. There was nothing about these gestures he had understood. He had believed that what a man felt in his heart was a private matter and so should remain with him, but he had never had so much in his heart before. There wasn't enough room for this much love and it left an aching sensation in his chest. Heartache! Who would have thought it was true? Now all he wanted was to take her hand or curve his arm around her shoulder.

Roxane Coss leaned towards him, dipped her head down to his shoulder just for a second, just long enough for her cheek to touch his shirt.

"Ah," said Mr. Hosokawa softly. "You are everything in the world to me."

Gen looked at him. Was that meant to be translated, the tenderness his employer whispered? Mr. Hosokawa took one of Roxane's hands. He held it up to his chest, touched it to his shirt in the place above his heart. He nodded. Was he nodding to Gen? Was he telling Gen to go ahead? Or was he nodding to her? Gen felt a terrible discomfort. He wanted to turn away. It was a private matter. He knew what that meant now.

"Everything in the world," Mr. Hosokawa said again, but this time he looked at Gen.

And so Gen told her. He tried to make his voice soft. "Respectfully," he said to Roxane, "Mr. Hosokawa would like you to know that you are everything in the world to him." He remembered saying something very similar to her from the Russian.

It was to her credit that Roxane never looked at Gen. She kept her eyes exactly on Mr. Hosokawa's eyes and took the words from him.

Carmen came back. She was flustered and everyone thought it had to do with Cesar, when she had almost forgotten about Cesar. She wanted to go to Gen but she went first to General Benjamin. "Cesar is up in the tree," she said. She started to say more but then she remembered herself. It was always wiser to wait.

"What is he doing there?" the General asked her. He couldn't help but notice how pretty this girl was becoming. Had she been this pretty before, he never would have let her sign up. He should tell her to keep her hair under her cap. He should let her go just as soon as they were home.

"Sulking."

"I don't understand."

"He feels embarrassed."

Maybe it was wrong to let a pretty girl go after him. One of the boys should have gone and simply shaken the tree until Cesar fell out. General Benjamin sighed. He had been impressed with Cesar's singing. He wondered if the talent would make the boy high-strung, the way the soprano was high-strung. If that was the case he would be forced to dismiss Cesar as well, and then he would have lost two soldiers. Even as he was thinking this he remembered where he was, and the thought of ever getting home, of ever having a choice so simple as to let someone go or to keep them, seemed impossible. Why was he even wasting his time with this? Cesar in a tree? What did it matter? "Leave him up there." General Benjamin looked over Carmen's head to the far side of the room, which was his way of saying that the conversation was over.

"May I tell Miss Coss?"

He looked back down at her and blinked. She was obedient, well mannered. It was a shame that things hadn't turned out better. Certainly there would be a role for pretty girls in a revolution. There was no sense being hard on her. "I think she would want to know."

Carmen, happy, grateful, bowed to him.

He said to her sharply, "Salute!"

Carmen saluted him, her face as serious as any soldier's, and then skated away.

"Cesar's in the tree," Carmen said. She stood between Mr. Hosokawa and Mr. Kato. She stood across from Gen, where she would not be tempted to hold on to his sleeve in front of everyone. She loved the sound of his voice, translating.

"Won't he come in?" Roxane said. Her blue eyes were shadowed in purple. Never had Carmen seen her look so tired, except at the very beginning.

"Oh, he'll come in. He's just embarrassed. He thinks he made a fool of himself. He thinks you think he's an idiot for trying to sing." She looked at Roxane, her friend. "I told him you didn't think that at all."

Gen translated her words into English and Japanese. Both the men and Roxane Coss were nodding. Carmen's words translated into Japanese. They had such a beautiful sound.

"Would you ask the General if I could go outside?" Roxane said to Carmen. "Do you think it would be possible?"

Carmen listened. She was included. It was thought that she would be the best person to make the request. Her opinion was sought out. It was more than she could believe, of all the people in the room with all their money and education and talent, they thought that she was the one. She wanted to say to Roxane Coss in her most polite voice, No, they will never let you outside, but I am very pleased that you asked me. Not that she had any idea how to say that in English. The Generals were ignoring her conversation, the Generals Hector and Alfredo had left the room altogether, none of the boys cared, but Beatriz was listening. Carmen could see her out of the corner of one eye. She wanted to trust Beatriz. She had trusted her. And anyway, she wasn't doing anything wrong now. "Tell her I would be glad to ask for her," she said to Gen. She was aware of her posture and she tried to hold her back straight like Roxane Coss. She tried to train her shoulders to go back though the effect was mostly lost inside the dark green shirt that hung over her like a piece of tarp.

They thanked her in English and Japanese and then in Spanish. Gen was proud of her, she could tell. Gen, if circumstances allowed, would have put his hand on her shoulder and told her so in front of his friends.

There was no way Roxane Coss would be allowed to go outside to speak to Cesar in the tree. Keeping the hostages inside was a top priority. Certainly, no one knew that better than Carmen, who had broken this important rule just last night. But it wasn't her place to refuse the request. No one had asked Carmen for an answer, they had only asked her to approach the General with the question. In truth, she would have rather not done it. What was the point in asking for something that you knew would be denied? Carmen wondered if she could ask the General something else, say, if he wanted a fresh cup of coffee, then everyone would see her asking without being able to hear her. She could come back with the news that they had been turned down. But she didn't want to lie to Roxane Coss and Mr. Hosokawa, people who valued her opinion and treated her as a friend, and certainly she couldn't lie to Gen. She would have to ask because she said she would. It would have been better if she could have waited an hour or two. The generals did not like being approached when they had so recently been bothered. But there wasn't an hour or two to wait. Cesar would be long out of the tree by then. Carmen had sat in that tree herself and she knew it to be both lovely and uncomfortable. The amount of time anyone could sulk while sitting in a tree was limited, and the point was that Roxane Coss wanted the opportunity to coax him down. There was no sense trying to explain the General's inner workings to her dearest hostages, any more than she would bother to try and explain Roxane Coss's motives to General Benjamin, who certainly would not have cared. All she could do was ask. Carmen smiled and left her group, crossed back over the room where General Benjamin was sitting in a wing-backed chair near the empty fireplace. He was reading papers. She couldn't tell what the papers were, although she saw that they were written in Spanish. She could read a little now but not so well as that. His eyebrows were pointed down towards the bridge of his nose and his eyes were squinting. His shingles ran across the side of his face and into his eye like a slash of molten lava but they no longer appeared to be so infected. He lifted a finger and touched them once gently, then he winced and went back to his reading. Truly, Carmen knew better than to disturb him.

"Sir?" she whispered.

They had been speaking not five minutes before but now

he looked at her as if he was confused. His eyes were red and watery, especially his left eye, which was rimmed in blisters no bigger than pinheads.

Carmen waited for him to speak to her but he said nothing. It was up to her to start the conversation. "Forgive me for bothering you again, General, but Roxane Coss asked me to ask you . . ." She paused, thinking surely he would cut her off, tell her to go away, but he didn't. He did nothing. Had he turned away and gone back to reading his papers, she would have understood that. She would have known how to act if he shouted at her, but General Benjamin only stared. She took in her breath, straightened up her shoulders, and started again. "Roxane Coss would like to go outside to speak to Cesar. Cesar in the tree? She wants to tell him he did well." Again she waited but nothing happened. "I think the translator would have to go, too, if Cesar was to understand what she was saying. We could send some guards out with them. I could get my gun." She stopped and waited patiently for him to deny the request. She had never considered any other possibility, but he didn't say anything, and for a minute he closed his eyes so as not to look at her anymore. She glanced down at the papers he was holding and felt a chill pass through her thin chest. She was suddenly afraid that the General had received bad news, that there was something in those papers that would ruin her happiness.

"General Benjamin," she said, leaning over so that only he could hear her. "Sir, are things all right?" Her hair fell loose from behind one ear and it brushed against his shoulder. It smelled like lemons. Roxane had washed Carmen's hair in some of the lemon shampoo Messner had had flown in for her all the way from Italy.

The smell of lemons. He is a boy in the city, a quarter lemon clenched between his teeth as he runs to school, the bright lemon yellow of the peel showing between his open lips, the impossible tartness, the utter clarity of taste that he was addicted to. His brother, Luis, is with him, running along beside him, a little boy. He is younger than Benjamin and so he is Benjamin's responsibility. He, too, has a lemon in his mouth and they look at one another and begin to laugh so hard they have to raise their hands to their mouths to catch the now empty rinds. The smell of lemons snaps him back. Carmen wanted something else. He was still in the living room. Why was it only now that he understood that things would end badly? It didn't seem strange that he knew it, but that he hadn't known it from the very start, that he hadn't turned his troops around and run them straight back into the air vents the second it was established that President Masuda was not at the party. That mistake was almost impossible to comprehend now. It was all the fault of hope. Hope was a murderer.

"She wants to go outside?" he said.

"Yes, sir."

"Cesar is still out there?"

"I believe so, sir."

General Benjamin nodded his head. "The weather is good now." He looked out the window for a long time to make sure that what he was saying to her was true. "Take them all outside. Tell Hector and Alfredo. Put some soldiers along the wall." He looked at Carmen. If he had known anything he would have paid more attention to her. "We need some air in here, don't you think? Get some sun on them."

"Everyone, sir? Do you mean Miss Coss and the translator?"

"I mean all of them." He swept a hand across the room. "Get them out of here."

That was how it happened that on the very day after Carmen had taken Gen outside, the rest of the party was allowed to go as well. She did not want to be the one to tell the Generals Hector and Alfredo, but she did so as a direct order. She stood at the door of the study still stunned by the news. Outside. The Generals were watching soccer. They sat on the edge of the sofa, their hands gripping their knees, yelling at the television set. There was an abandoned card game half played on the table in front of them, two automatic pistols sticking out from between the cushions. When she was able to get their attention, she did not tell them that she had asked that anyone be allowed to go outside, or that Roxane Coss wished to speak to Cesar in the tree, she only said that General Benjamin had made a decision and she was instructed to inform them of that decision. She used as few words as was possible.

"Outside!" General Alfredo said. "Insanity! How are we supposed to control them outside?" He gesticulated with the hand that was short two fingers, a sight that always filled Carmen with pity.

"What is there to control?" General Hector said, stretching his arms above his head. "As if they would go anywhere now."

It was a surprise. Hector was usually against every idea. If he had disagreed strongly they could have probably made General Benjamin change his mind, but the sun was pouring through every window and there was a staleness that had grown up around them. Why not open the doors? Why not today if every day was exactly the same? They went into the living room and the three Generals called the troops together and told them to get their guns and load them. Even after so many months of lying on couches the boys, along with Beatriz and Carmen, could still move quickly. They didn't know why they were loading their guns, they didn't ask. They obeyed their orders, and in doing so their eyes took on a certain coldness. General Benjamin could not help but think, If I told them to kill everyone now, they would still do it. They would do what I told them to. The idea of taking everyone outside was a good one. It would put the soldiers to work. It would remind the hostages of both his authority and his benevolence. It was time to get out of the house.

Roxane Coss had Mr. Hosokawa's arm to lean on, but Gen was left alone to watch his lover running across the room with the soldiers, her rifle held high against her chest.

"I do not understand this," Mr. Hosokawa whispered. He could feel Roxane trembling beside him and he pressed her hand between his own. It was as if a switch had been thrown and the people they knew were suddenly people they had never seen before.

"Can you understand what they're saying?" Roxane whispered to Gen. "What's happened?"

Of course he could understand what they were saying. They were shouting it, after all. *Load your weapons. Prepare formations.* But there was no sense in telling Roxane that. The other hostages were standing with them now. They pushed together like sheep in an open field of hard rain. Thirty-nine men and one woman, the sudden nervousness rising off of them like steam.

Then General Benjamin stepped forward and said, *"Traductor!"*

Mr. Hosokawa touched the translator's arm as he stepped forward. Gen wished he was a brave man. Even though Carmen wasn't with them now, he wished she could see him as brave.

"I have decided that everyone should go outside," General Benjamin said. "Tell the people they are to go outside now."

But Gen didn't translate. That was no longer his profession. Instead he asked, "For what purpose?" If there was to be an execution he would not be the one to lead these sheep out to be lined up against the wall. It wasn't enough to translate what was said, you had to know the truth.

"What purpose?" General Benjamin said. He stepped towards Gen, so close that Gen could see red lines half the thickness of sewing threads webbing across his face. "I was told Roxane Coss requested to go outside."

"And you're letting everyone out?"

"You object to this?" General Benjamin was about to change his mind. What had he ever shown these people but decency and now they stared him down like a murderer? "You think I will take you outside and shoot the lot of you?"

"The guns—" Gen had made a mistake. He could see that.

"Protection," the General said, his teeth clamped together.

Gen turned away from him and faced the people he thought of as his people. He watched their faces soften at the sound of his voice. "We are going outside," Gen said in English, in Japanese, in Russian, Italian, French. "We are going outside," he said in Spanish and Danish. Only four words but in every language he was able to convey that they would not be shot, this was not a trick. The group laughed and sighed and shook away from one another. The priest crossed himself quickly in gratitude for an answered prayer. Ishmael went and opened the door and hostages filed out into the light.

Glorious light.

Vice President Ruben Iglesias, who thought he would not live to feel once again the sensation of grass beneath his feet, stepped off the shale stone walkway and sank into the luxury of his own yard. He had stared at it every day from the living-room window but now that he was actually there it seemed like a new world. Had he ever walked around his own lawn in the evening? Had he made a mental note of the trees, the miraculous flowering bushes that grew up around the wall? What were they called? He dropped his face into the nest of deep purple blossoms and inhaled. Dear God, if he were to get out of this alive he would be attentive to his plants. Maybe he would work as a gardener. The new leaves were bright green and velvety to touch. He stroked them between his thumb and forefinger, careful not to bruise. Too many evenings he had come home after dark. He saw the life in his garden as a series of shadows and silhouettes. If there was ever such a thing as a second chance he would have his coffee outside in the morning. He would come home to have lunch with his wife in the afternoons on a blanket beneath the trees. His two girls would be in school, but he would hold his son on his knees and teach him the names of birds. How had he come to live in such a beautiful place? He walked through the grass towards the west side of the house and the grass was so heavy he knew it would be difficult to cut. He liked it that way. Maybe he would never have the grass mown again. If a man had a ten-foot wall then he could do whatever he wanted with his yard. He could make love to his wife late at night in the place where the wall made a pocket of lawn and three slender trees grew in a semi-circle. They could come out after the children were in bed, after the servants were asleep, and who would see them? The earth they lie down on is as soft as their bed. He pictured her long dark hair undone and spread over the heavy grass. He would be a better husband in the future, a better father. He got on his knees and reached between the tall yellow lilies. He pulled up a weed that was as high as the flowers, its stem as thick as a finger, then another, and another. He filled his hands with green stems, roots and dirt. There was a great deal of work to be done.

The soldiers did not push the people or direct them in any way. They simply stood against the wall, spacing themselves apart at regular intervals. They leaned against the wall and took in the sun. It was good to do something different. It was good even to all be armed again, to be a line of soldiers holding guns. The hostages raised their arms above their heads and stretched. Some of them lay down in the grass, others examined the flowers. Gen was not looking at the plants, he was looking at the soldiers, and when he found Carmen she gave him a very small nod and pointed the tip of her rifle ever so slightly in the direction of Cesar's tree. Everyone looked so glad to be out in the daylight. Carmen wanted to say, I did this for you. I'm the one who asked, but she kept perfectly quiet. She had to look away from Gen to keep from smiling.

Gen found Roxane with Mr. Hosokawa, walking hand in hand, as if this was some other garden and they were alone. They looked different this morning, not so improbable together, and Gen wondered if he looked different as well. He thought perhaps he shouldn't bother them, but he had no idea how long they would be allowed to stay outside.

"I've located the boy," Gen said.

"The boy?" Mr. Hosokawa said.

"The singer."

"Oh, yes, the boy, of course."

Gen said it again in English and together the three of them walked to a tree near the very back section of wall.

"He's up there?" Roxane said, but she could barely concentrate, the breeze distracted her, the lush intertwining plants. She felt the sun curving over her cheeks. She wanted to touch the wall, she wanted to tangle her fingers up in the grass. She had never given a thought to grass before in her life.

"This is his tree."

Roxane cocked her head back and sure enough she saw the bottom soles of two boots dangling in the branchs. She could make out his shirt, the underside of his chin. "Cesar?"

A face looked down between the leaves.

"Tell him he sings beautifully," she said to Gen. "Tell him I want to be his teacher."

"She's fooling me," Cesar called down.

"Why do you think we're all outside?" Gen said. "Does this look like fooling to you? She wanted to come outside and talk to you, and the Generals decided that everyone could come along. Doesn't that seem important enough to you?"

It was true. Cesar could see everything from where he sat. All three of the Generals and every one of the soldiers except Gilbert and Jesus were outside. They must have been left behind to guard the house. Every one of the hostages was walking around the yard like he was drunk or blind, touching and sniffing, weaving and then suddenly sitting down. They were in love with the place. They wouldn't leave if you tore the wall down. If you poked them in the back with your gun and told them to get going they would still run to you. "So you're outside," Cesar said.

"He isn't planning on staying in that tree, is he?" Roxane asked.

It was remarkable even to Cesar that he had not been called down for duty. He would have gone. He could only imagine that in the excitement of deciding to let everyone outside he had been forgotten. He had been forgotten by everyone but Roxane Coss.

"She doesn't think I'm a fool?"

"He wants to know if you think he's a fool," Gen said.

She sighed at the self-indulgence of children. "Staying up in the tree seems foolish, but the singing, not at all."

"Foolish for the tree and not the singing," Gen reported. "Come down and talk to her."

"I'm not sure," Cesar said. But he was sure. He had already pictured the two of them singing together, their voices rising, their hands clasped.

"What are you going to do, live in the tree?" Gen called. His neck was aching from dropping his head back.

"How do you sound so much like Carmen?" Cesar said. He reached down and took hold of the branch beneath him. He had been up there a long time. One of his legs was stiff and the other was completely asleep. When his feet hit the ground they did nothing to support him and he fell into a pile at their feet, striking his head against the trunk of the tree that had held him.

Roxane Coss dropped to her knees and put her hands on either side of the boy's head. She could feel the blood jumping in his temples. "My God, I didn't mean for him to throw himself out of the tree."

Mr. Hosokawa caught a flash of a smile cross Cesar's face. It was released and then just as quickly suppressed, though the boy never opened his eyes. "Tell her he's fine," Mr. Hosokawa said to Gen. "And tell the boy he can get up now."

Gen helped Cesar into a sitting position, leaned him like a floppy doll against the tree. Though Cesar's head was splitting he didn't mind opening his eyes. Roxane Coss was crouching down so close to him it was as if he could see inside her. Look at the blue of her eyes! They were so much deeper, more complicated than he could have imagined from a distance. She still had on a bathrobe and white pajamas and not twelve centimeters from his nose her pajamas formed a V where he could see the place her breasts came together. Who was this old Japanese man who was always with her? He looked too much like the President. In fact, Cesar suspected that maybe he *was* the President, regardless of any lies he might have told, right in front of them the whole time.

"Pay attention," she said, and then the translator said it in Spanish. She sang five notes. She wanted him to listen and repeat, to follow the notes. He could see right inside her mouth, a damp, pink cave. It was the most intimate thing of all.

He opened his mouth and croaked a little, then he touched his head with his fingertips.

"That's all right," she said. "You can sing later. Did you sing at home, before you came here?"

Certainly he sang the way people will sing, not thinking about it when he was doing something else. He could mimic the people they heard sometimes when the radio worked, but that wasn't about singing so much as it was about making people laugh.

"Does he want to learn? Would he be willing to practice very hard to see if he has a real voice?"

"To practice with her?" Cesar asked Gen. "Just the two of us?"

"I imagine there would be other people there."

Cesar touched Gen's sleeve. "Tell her I'm shy. Tell her I'd work much better if we could be alone."

"Once you learn English you can tell her that yourself," Gen said.

"What does he want?" Mr. Hosokawa said. He was standing over them, trying to keep the sun out of Roxane's eyes.

"Impossible things," Gen said. Then he said to the boy in Spanish, "Yes or no, do you want her to teach you to sing?"

"Of course I do," Cesar said.

"We'll start this afternoon," Roxane said. "We'll start with scales." She picked up Cesar's hand and patted it. He turned pale again and closed his eyes.

"Let him rest," Mr. Hosokawa said. "The boy wants to sleep."

Lothar Falken put his hands flat against the wall and stretched his hamstrings, pressing one heel down and then the other. He touched his toes and rocked his hips from side to side and when he felt his legs were warm and limber he began to run barefoot through the grass. The soldiers bristled at first, leaned forward, aimed their rifles half-heartedly in his general direction, but he kept running. It was a large yard in terms of the size of lawns in cities, but it was still small in terms of a track, and a few minutes after Lothar had gone outside the sight of any one person, he had looped back around again, his head up, his arms pumping by his chest. He was a slender man with long, graceful legs, and while it might have gone unnoticed while he was lying on the couch, here in the sun, running rings around the vice-presidential mansion, it was easy to see that the manufacturer of German pharmaceuticals had once been an athlete. With every lap he felt his body again, the relation of muscle to bone, the oxygen stirring his blood. He kicked his feet high behind him, every step going deep into the thick grass. After a while Manuel Flores of Spain began to run alongside him, keeping pace at first and then falling back. Simon Thibault began to run and proved himself to be almost Falken's match. Victor Fyodorov handed his cigarette to his friend Yegor and joined in for two rounds. Such a beautiful day, to run seemed only fitting. He collapsed exactly where he had started, his heart beating at the cage of his ribs with a manic fury.

While the others ran, Ruben Iglesias weeded one of the many flower beds. It was a small gesture in the face of so much work but all he knew to do was start. Oscar Mendoza and the young priest knelt to help him.

"Ishmael," the Vice President called out to his friend. "Why are you standing there holding up the wall? Come over here and get to work. We can use that rifle you're so proud of to aerate the soil."

"Don't pick on the boy," Oscar Mendoza said. "He's the only one I like."

"You know I can't come over," Ishmael said, shifting his rifle to his other shoulder.

"Ah, you could come over," Ruben said. "You just don't want to get your hands dirty. You're keeping them nice for the chess games. You don't want to work." Ruben smiled at the boy. Truly, he wished he could come over. He would teach him which of the plants were weeds. He found himself thinking that Ishmael could be his son, his other son. They were both on the small side, and anyway, people would believe whatever you told them. There would be plenty of room for one more small boy.

"I work," Ishmael said.

"I've seen him," Oscar Mendoza said, rubbing the dirt from his hands. "He does more than all the others. Not so big perhaps, but he's strong as an ox, and smart. You have to be smart to win chess games." The big man leaned towards the wall, towards the boy. "Ishmael, I would give you a job, if you wanted one. When this is over you could come and work for me."

Ishmael was used to being teased. He had been teased cruelly by his brothers. He had been teased plenty by the other soldiers. Once they called him a bucket and tied his feet together and lowered him upside down into the well until the top of his head sank into cold water. He liked the Vice President's way of teasing because it made him feel singled out as someone special. But Oscar Mendoza he wasn't sure of. There was nothing in his expression that gave the joke away.

"Do you want a job?" Oscar said.

"He doesn't need a job," Ruben said, pulling a stack of weeds into his lap. He saw his chance. Oscar had given him the opening. "He'll live with me. He'll have everything he needs."

Oscar looked at his friend and each man saw that the other one was serious. "Every man needs a job," he said. "He will live with you and work for me. Does that sound fine, Ishmael?"

Ishmael put his gun between his feet and looked at them. He would live in this house? He would stay on? He would have a job and earn his own money? He knew he should laugh and tell them to leave him alone. He should make a joke of it himself: No, he would never be caught dead living in such a place. That was the only way to manage if you were the person being teased. Laugh back at them. But he couldn't. He wanted too much to believe they were telling him the truth. "Yes." That was all he could say.

Oscar Mendoza held out his dirty hand to Ruben Iglesias and they shook. "We're shaking for you," Ruben said, his voice betraying his happiness. "This seals the deal." He would have another son. The boy would be legally adopted. The boy would be known after that as Ishmael Iglesias.

The priest, who had only been watching, now sat back on his heels, his grimy hands resting on his thighs. He felt something cold and startling move through his heart. The men should not be talking to Ishmael this way. They were forgetting the circumstances. The only way things could work would be for everything to stay exactly as it was, for no one to speak of the future as if speaking of it could bring it on.

"Father Arguedas here will teach you catechism. Won't you, Father? You can come back to the house for the lessons and we'll all have lunch together." Ruben was lost in his story now. He wished he could call his wife and tell her the news. He would tell Messner and Messner would call her. Once she met the boy she would fall in love with him.

"Of course I will." The priest's voice was weak, but no one noticed it at all.

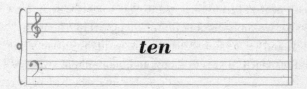

ten

*M*r. Hosokawa could find his way in the dark. Some nights he closed his eyes rather than strain them trying to see. He knew the schedule and habits of every guard, where they walked and when they slept. He knew who made their bed on the floor and how to step over them carefully. He felt the corners of walls with his fingertips, avoided boards that creaked, could turn a doorknob as silently as a leaf falls. He was so proficient at moving through the house that he thought that even if he had no place to go he might be tempted to get up and stretch his legs, go from room to room just because he could. It even occurred to him that he might be able to escape now if he wanted to, simply walk down the front path to the gate at night and set himself free. He did not want to.

Everything he knew he learned from Carmen, who taught him without benefit of a translator. To teach someone how to be perfectly quiet you don't need to speak to them. Everything Mr. Hosokawa needed desperately to know Carmen taught him over two days. He still carried around his notebook, added ten new vocabulary words to his list every morning, but he struggled against the tide of memorization. For silence, though, he had a gift. He could tell from the approval in Carmen's eyes, from the light touch of her fingers on the back of his hand. She taught him how to get from place to place in the house in plain sight of everyone and yet no one saw them because she was teaching him to be invisible. It was learning humility, to no longer assume that anyone would notice who you were or where you were going. It wasn't until she began to teach him that Mr. Hosokawa saw Carmen's genius, because her genius was to not be seen. How much harder that would be for a beautiful young girl in a house full of restless men, and yet he found that she drew almost no attention at all. She had managed to pass as a boy, and, more impressively, had managed to make herself utterly forgettable after she had been revealed as a beautiful girl. When Carmen walked through the room without wanting to be seen she hardly moved the air around her. She didn't sneak. She did not dart to hide behind the piano and then a chair. She walked through the middle of the room, asking for nothing, keeping her head level, making no sound. In fact, she had been teaching him this lesson since the day they were first in the house together, but it was only now that he could understand it.

She would have accompanied him upstairs every night. She told that to Gen. But it was better that he know how to go on his own. Nothing made people as clumsy as fear, and she could show him how not to be afraid.

"She is an extraordinary girl," Mr. Hosokawa said to Gen.

"She seems to be," Gen said.

Mr. Hosokawa gave him a small, avuncular smile and pretended that there was nothing else to say. That was part of it, too. The private life. Mr. Hosokawa had a private life now. He had always thought of himself as a private man, but now he saw that there was nothing in his life before that had been private. It didn't mean that he had no secrets then and now he did. It was that now there was something that was strictly between himself and one other person, that it was so completely their own that it would have been pointless to even try to speak of it to someone else. He wondered now if everyone had a private life. He wondered if his wife had one. It was possible that all those years he had been alone, never knowing that a complete world existed and no one spoke of it.

During their entire captivity he had slept through the night, but now he knew how to sleep and how to wake up in the pitch-black darkness without the aid of a clock. Often when he woke up Gen was gone. Then he would stand and walk, so peacefully, so above suspicion, that if someone were to wake and see him they would have only thought he was going to get a drink of water. He stepped over his neighbors, his compatriots, and made his way to the back stairs behind the kitchen. Once he saw a light on beneath a closet door and thought he heard whispering, but he didn't stop to see what it might be. It didn't concern him, which was part of being invisible. He floated up the back steps. He had never been so easy inside his own skin. He thought at once he had never been so alive and so much a ghost. It would have been fine if he were to climb these steps forever, always the lover going to meet his beloved. He was happy then, and every step he climbed he was happier. He wished he could stop time. As much as Mr. Hosokawa was overwhelmed by love, he could never completely shake what he knew to be the truth: that every night they were together could be seen as a miracle for a hundred different reasons, not the least of which was that at some point these days would end, would be ended for them. He tried not to give himself over to fantasies: he would get a divorce; he would follow her from city to city, sitting in the front row of every opera house in the world. Happily, he would have done this, given up everything for her. But he understood that these were extraordinary times, and if their old life was ever restored to them, nothing would be the same.

When he opened the door to her room there were tears in his eyes more often than not, and he was grateful for the darkness. He didn't want her to think that anything had gone wrong. She came to him and he pressed his damp face into the fall of lemon-scented hair. He was in love, and never had he felt such kindness towards another person. Never had he received such kindness. Maybe the private life wasn't forever. Maybe everyone got it for a little while and then spent the rest of their lives remembering.

In the china closet, Carmen and Gen made a decision: two full hours of studying before they made love. Carmen was still every bit as serious about learning to read and write in Spanish, look at all the progress she'd made! Haltingly, she could read an entire paragraph without asking for help. She was completely committed to learning English. She could fully conjugate ten verbs and knew at least a hundred nouns and other parts of speech. She held out hopes for Japanese so she could speak to Gen in his own language when all of this was over and they would be in bed together at night. Gen was equally firm on their resolve to continue Carmen's lessons. It would be pointless to have come so far and then just abandon everything because they were in love. Wasn't this exactly what love was? To want what was best for someone, to help them along as Carmen and Gen helped each other? No, they would study and practice for two hours, no less than they had done before. After that, yes, their time was their own and they could do whatever they wanted. Carmen stole the egg timer from the kitchen. They settled in to work.

Spanish first. Carmen had found a satchel of schoolbooks stuffed in the closet of the Vice President's daughter, skinny books with pictures of rolling puppies on the front, a fatter book of paper with solid lines and dotted lines to practice penmanship. The girl had only used five pages. She had written the alphabet and her numbers. She had written her name, *Imelda Iglesias*, over and over again in sweetly curved letters. Carmen wrote her name beneath that. She wrote out the words Gen told her: *pescado, calcetín, sopa.* Fish, sock, soup. All he wanted was to press his lips against the side of her neck. He would not stop the lesson. She was leaning over her notebook, working so hard to make her letters as nice as those of the Vice President's eight-year-old daughter. Two thick strands of hair fell forward onto the notebook. Carmen ignored them and folded her lower lip into her mouth to concentrate. He wondered if it was possible to die from wanting someone so much. In this narrow hall of plates all he could smell was her, lemons and the dusty, sun-bleached smell of her uniform, the softer, more complicated smell of Carmen's skin. Thirty seconds to kiss her neck, that wasn't asking so much. He would not even mind if she kept on writing. He would kiss her that gently, her pencil need never leave the page.

When she looked up his face was very close to hers and she could no longer remember the word he said and if he was to say it again she would not know how to spell it or how to bend a single letter out of a straight line. All she needed was a kiss, a single kiss to clear her head and then she would be all business again, right back to work. She could not make herself swallow or blink. She was sure that with one kiss she could study all night. It would not make her less of a student. She had no mind for letters anyway, all she could think of was the grass, the grass and trees and dark night sky, the smell of the jasmine the first time he slid her shirt over her head and fell to his knees to kiss her stomach, her breasts.

"*Pastel,*" Gen said, his voice unsteady.

Perhaps she was trained in ways she didn't understand, like a police dog, and *cake* was the word that released her, because as soon as he said it she fell on him, book and pencil skittering across the floor. She ate off of him, huge, devouring gulps, pressed her tongue against his tongue, rolled against the lower cupboards where soup bowls were stacked, one nestled perfectly inside the other.

They did not go back to work that night.

So the next night they agreed: an hour of studying before giving in. They applied themselves with great seriousness. But in fact that plan was three minutes less successful than the one they'd had the night before. They were hopeless, starving, reckless, and everything they did, they did again.

They experimented with shorter lengths of time but in every attempt they were unsuccessful until Gen came up with the following plan: they would make love immediately, the second they had securely closed the door behind them, and then after that they would study, and it was this plan that was by far the most successful. Sometimes they fell asleep for a while, Carmen curled against Gen's chest, Gen inside the crook of Carmen's arm. Like soldiers shot in battle, they lay where they fell. Other times they had to make love again, the first time forgotten as soon as it was finished, but for the most part they managed to get some work done. Before it was anywhere near getting light they would kiss good night and Carmen would go back to sleep in the hallway in front of Roxane's door and Gen would go back to the floor next to Mr. Hosokawa's couch. Sometimes they detected the slightest sound of his movement as he came down the stairs. Sometimes Carmen passed him in the hall.

Did the others know? Possibly, but they wouldn't have said anything. They suspected only Roxane Coss and Mr. Hosokawa, who did not hesitate to hold hands or exchange a brief kiss during the day. If anyone suspected Gen and Carmen of anything it was only that perhaps they helped the first couple in their meetings. Roxane Coss and Mr. Hosokawa, however improbable to those around them, were members of the same tribe, the tribe of the hostages. So many people were in love with her that of course, it was only natural that she should fall in love with one of them. But Gen and Carmen were another matter. Even if the Generals relied on Gen's translations and polished secretarial skills, even if they found him extremely bright and pleasant enough, they never forgot who he was. And even though the hostages had a soft spot for Carmen, the way she kept her eyes down, her unwillingness to point her gun at anyone directly, when there was any call from the Generals, she went and stood with them.

Recently life had improved for all the hostages, not just those who were in love. Once the front door had been opened, it opened regularly. Every day they went outside and stood in the hot sun. Lothar Falken encouraged other men to take up running. He led them through a series of exercises every day and then they went in a pack around and around the house. The soldiers played soccer with a ball they had found in the basement and some days there was an actual game, the terrorists against the hostages, though the terrorists were so much younger and trained into better shape that they almost always won.

When Messner came now he often found everyone in the yard. The priest got up from his digging and waved.

"How is the world?" Father Arguedas said to him.

"Impatient," Messner said. His Spanish kept improving, but still he asked for Gen.

Father Arguedas pointed to the sprawled-out figure beneath a tree. "Sleeping. It is a terrible thing the way they work him so hard. And you. They work you too hard as well. If you don't mind my saying, you look tired."

It was true that recently Messner had lost the sangfroid that everyone had found so reassuring in the beginning. He had aged ten years in the four and a half months they had been living here, and while everyone else seemed to mind it less and less, Messner clearly minded it more. "All this sunlight is no good for me," Messner said. "All Swiss citizens were meant to live in the shade."

"It's very warm," the priest said. "But the plants do wonderfully, rain, sun, drought, there's no holding them back."

"I won't keep you from your work." Messner patted the priest on the shoulder, remembering how they had tried several times to let him go and how the priest would have none of it. He wondered if, in the end, Father Arguedas would be sorry to have stayed. Probably not. Regret didn't seem to be in his nature the way it was in Messner's.

Paco and Ranato ran up from the side lawn, which they now called the playing field, and made an extremely halfhearted effort to frisk him that consisted of nothing more than a few brisk slaps near his pockets. Then they ran back to join the game, which had been stopped for this purpose.

"Gen," Messner said, and tapped the sleeping body on the shoulder with the toe of his shoe. "For God's sake, get up."

Gen was sleeping the sleep of the heavily drugged. His mouth was open and slack and his arms flung straight out to the side. A small, rippling snore came up from his throat.

"Hey, translator." He leaned over and picked up one of Gen's eyelids between his thumb and forefinger. Gen shook him off and opened his eyes slowly.

"You speak Spanish," Gen said thickly. "You have from the beginning. Now leave me alone." He rolled over on his side and pulled his knees up to his chest.

"I don't speak Spanish. I don't speak anything. Get up." Messner thought he felt a shaking in the earth. Surely Gen must feel it, lying with his cheek pressed down to the grass. Was it his imagination that the earth might actually cave in beneath them? How much did these engineers know? Who's to say that the ground wouldn't swallow them up, opera diva and common criminal in the same fatal bite. Messner got down on his knees. He pressed his palms to the grass and when he had decided that he was only experiencing a temporary madness, he shook Gen again. "Listen to me," he said in French. "We have to talk them into surrendering. Today. This can't go on. Do you understand me?"

Gen rolled onto his back, stretched like a cat, and then folded his arms beneath his head. "And then we'll talk the trees into growing blue feathers. Haven't you paid attention at all, Messner? They aren't going to be talked into anything. Especially not by the likes of us."

The likes of us. Messner wondered if Gen was implying that he had not done his job well enough. Four and a half months living in a hotel room half the world away from Geneva when all he had come here for in the first place was a holiday. Both parties were intractable and what the party inside this wall didn't understand was that the government was always intractable, no matter what the country, what the circumstances. The government did not give in, and when they said they were giving in they were lying, every time, you could count on it. As Messner saw it, it was his job not to hammer out a compromise but merely to steer them clear of a tragedy. There wasn't much time left for this work. Despite the rhythmic thud of the runners and the boys playing soccer, he could definitely feel something happening in the ground.

The sign of the Red Cross, like the very sign of Switzerland, stood for peaceful neutrality. Messner had stopped wearing his armband a long time ago but he didn't believe in it any less. Members of the Red Cross brought food and medicine, sometimes they would ferry papers for arbitration, but they were not moles. They did not spy. Joachim Messner would have no more told the terrorists what the military had planned than he would tell the military what was happening on the other side of the wall.

"Get up," he said again.

Sluggishly, Gen sat up and raised an arm to Messner to be pulled to his feet. Was this a picnic? Had they been drinking so early? No one seemed to be suffering in the least. In fact they all looked pink-cheeked and energetic. "The Generals are probably still over at the playing field," Gen said. "They might be in the game."

"You have to help me," Messner said.

Gen pushed his hair back into some semblance of order with his fingers and then, finally awake, threw his arm across his friend's shoulder. "When have I not helped you?"

The Generals were not playing ball but they were sitting at the edge of the field in three wrought-iron chairs pulled over from the patio. General Alfredo was shouting instructions at the players, General Hector was watching with intent silence, and General Benjamin had his face tilted up to make an even plane for the sun. All three had their feet buried in the high grass.

Gilbert kicked a beautiful shot and Gen waited until the play was over to announce their guest. "Sir," he said, meaning whoever looked up. "Messner is here."

"Another day," General Hector said. The second arm of his glasses had broken off that morning and now he held them up to his face like a pince-nez.

"I need to speak to you," Messner said. If his voice had taken on some new urgency none of them heard it over the whooping and shouting of the boys in the game.

"Permission to speak," General Hector said. General Alfredo hadn't taken his eyes off the game and General Benjamin hadn't opened his eyes at all.

"I need to speak to you inside. We need to talk about negotiations."

Then General Alfredo turned his head in Messner's direction. "They are ready to negotiate?"

"Your negotiations."

General Hector waved his hand at Messner as if he had never been so bored in all his life. "You're taking up our time." He turned his attention back to the game and called out, "Francisco! The ball!"

"Listen to me with seriousness," Messner said quietly in French. "One time. I have done a great deal for you. I have brought in your food, your cigarettes. I have carried your messages. I am asking that you sit down with me now and talk." Even in the bright sun Messner's face was drained of color. Gen looked at him and then he translated the message, trying to keep Messner's tone of voice. The two of them stood there but the Generals did not look up again. Usually this was Messner's sign to go but he stood there with his arms folded across his chest and waited.

"Enough?" Gen whispered in English, but Messner didn't look at him. They waited for more than half an hour.

Finally, General Benjamin opened his eyes. "All right," he said, his voice as tired as Messner's. "We'll go to my office."

Cesar, who had been so fearless when he sang from *Tosca* in front of the full house, really did prefer to practice in the afternoons when everyone else was outside, especially since practicing so often meant scales, which he found degrading. And he and Roxane Coss were never alone, there was no such thing as alone. Kato was there to play the piano and Mr. Hosokawa was there because he was always there. Today, Ishmael, who was regularly humiliated in soccer, had set up the chess set on a low table near the piano and played with Mr. Hosokawa. He and Cesar both had guns because if they both chose to stay in the house then they were the default house guards. If Cesar complained about other people staying to listen and if there was someone there to translate from Spanish to English and back into Spanish again (and several people could do this), Roxane Coss would tell him that singing was intended to be heard by other people and he might as well get used to it. He wanted to learn songs, arias, entire operas, but mostly she made him sing scales and nonsense lines. She made him roar and pucker his lips and hold his breath until he had to sit down quickly and put his head between his knees. He would have invited everyone in if she had let him sing a song with the piano, but that, she said, was something to be earned.

"There's a boy who sings now?" Messner asked. "Is that Cesar?" He stopped in the living room to listen and General Benjamin and Gen stopped with him. Cesar's jacket was too short in the sleeves and his wrists hung out like broomsticks with hands loosely attached.

General Benjamin was clearly proud of the boy. "He's been singing for weeks now. You've simply come at the wrong time. Cesar is always singing. Señorita Coss says he has the potential to be truly great, as she is great."

"Remember your breath," Roxane said, and inhaled deeply to show Cesar what she meant.

Cesar stumbled over a note, suddenly nervous to see the General there.

"Ask her how he's doing," Benjamin said to Gen.

Roxane put her hand on Kato's shoulder and he lifted his fingers from the keys as if she had touched an off switch. Cesar sang three more notes and then stopped when he realized the music was gone.

"We've only been at this a very short time, but I think he has enormous potential."

"Have him sing his song for Messner," General Benjamin said. "Messner is in need of a song today."

Roxane Coss agreed. "Listen to this," she said. "We've been working on this."

She sang a few words under her breath so that Cesar knew what he was to sing. He could not read or write in Spanish and certainly he didn't understand Italian, but his ability to memorize and repeat a sound, to repeat it with such pathos the listener could only imagine he understood what he was saying completely, was uncanny. Once she had prompted Cesar, Kato began to play the opening of Bellini's "Malinconia, Ninfa Gentile," the first, short song from *Sei Ariette*. Gen recognized the music. He had heard it floating through the windows in the afternoons. The boy closed his eyes and then looked towards the ceiling, *Oh, Melancholy, you graceful nymph, I devote my life to you.* When he forgot a line, Roxane Coss sang it in a surprising tenor voice: *I asked the Gods for hills and springs; they listened to me at last.* Then Cesar repeated the line. It was not unlike watching a calf rise up for the first time on spindly legs, at the same time awkward and beautiful. With every step he learned the business of walking, with every note he sang with more assurance. It was a very short song, finished almost as soon as it was started. General Benjamin clapped and Messner whistled.

"Don't praise him too much," Roxane said. "He'll be ruined."

Cesar, his face flushed from pride or lack of breath, bowed his head to them.

"Well, you can't tell it from looking at him," General Benjamin said as he walked down the back hallway to his office with Messner and Gen. It was true. The only thing more crooked than Cesar's teeth was Cesar's nose. "It makes you wonder. All the brilliant things we might have done with our lives if only we suspected we knew how."

"I know I will never sing," Messner said.

"I know that much as well." General Benjamin flipped the light on in the room and the three men sat down.

"I want to tell you that soon now they will not let me come here anymore," Messner said.

Gen was startled. Life without Messner?

"You are losing your job," the General said.

"The government feels that they've put enough effort into negotiations."

"I have seen no effort at all. They have made us no reasonable offers."

"I am telling you this as someone who likes you," Messner said. "I will not pretend that we are friends, but I want what is best for everyone here. Give this up. Do it today. Walk outside where everyone can see you and surrender." Messner knew this was not convincing and still he had no idea how to make it so. In his confusion he wandered back and forth between the languages he knew: German, which he had spoken as a boy at home; French, which he had spoken in school; English, which he had spoken for the four years he lived in Canada when he was a young man; and Spanish, which he knew better every day. Gen tried his best to keep up with the patchwork, but with every sentence he had to stop and think. It was Messner's inability to stay with one country that frightened Gen more than what he was saying. There was no time to concentrate on what he was saying.

"What about our demands? Have you spoken to them in a similar way? Have you spoken to them as friends?"

"They will give up nothing," Messner said. "There is no chance, no matter how long you wait. You have to trust me on this."

"Then we will kill the hostages."

"No, you won't," Messner said, rubbing his eyes with his fingers. "I said it the first time we met, you are reasonable men. Even if you did kill them it wouldn't change the outcome. The government would be even less inclined to bargain with you then."

From down the long hallway in the living room they could hear

Roxane sing a phrase and then Cesar repeat the phrase. They went over it again and again and the repetition was beautiful.

Benjamin listened to the music for a while and then, as if he had heard a note that didn't agree with him, he struck the table they used for chess with his fist. Not that it mattered, the game was in the other room. "Why is it our responsibility to make every concession? Are we expected to give up just because we have such a long history of giving things up? I am trying to free the men I know from prison. I am not trying to join them. It is not my intention to put my soldiers down in those caves. I would sooner see them dead and buried."

You might see them dead, Messner thought, but you won't have the chance to see them buried. He sighed. There was no such place as Switzerland. Truly, time had stopped. He had always been here and he would always be here. "I'm afraid those are your two choices," he said.

"The meeting is over." General Benjamin stood up. You could chart the course of this story on his skin, which was burning now. The shingles flared with every word he spoke and every word he listened to.

"It cannot be over. We have to keep talking until we reach some agreement, that is imperative. I am begging you to think about this."

"Messner, what else do I do all day?" the General said, and then he left the room.

Messner and Gen sat alone in the guest bedroom suite, where hostages were not allowed to sit without guards. They listened to the small French enamel clock strike the hour of noon. "I don't think I can stand this anymore," Messner said after several minutes had passed.

Stand what? Gen knew that everything was getting better and not just for him. People were happier. Look, they were outside right now. He could see them from the windows, running. "It is a standoff," Gen said. "Maybe a permanent one. If they keep us here forever, we'll manage."

"Are you insane?" Messner said. "You were the brightest one here once, and now you're as crazy as the rest of them. What do you think, that they'll just keep the wall up and pretend this is a zoo, bring in your food, charge money for tickets? 'See defenseless hostages and vicious terrorists live together in peaceful coexistence.' It doesn't just go on. Someone puts a stop to it and there needs to be a decision as to who will be in charge of the stopping."

"Do you think the military has plans?"

Messner stared at him. "Just because you're in here doesn't mean the rest of the world just shut down."

"So they will arrest them?"

"At best."

"The Generals?"

"All of them."

But all of them could not possibly include Carmen. It could not include Beatriz or Ishmael or Cesar. When Gen scanned the list he couldn't think of one he would be willing to give up, even the bullies and the fools. He would marry Carmen. He would have Father Arguedas marry them and it would be legal and binding, so that when they came for them he could say she was his wife. But that would only save one, albeit the most important one. For the others he had no ideas. How had he come to want to save all of them? The people who followed him around with loaded guns. How had he fallen in love with so many people? "What do we do?" Gen said.

"You can try to talk them into giving up," Messner said. "But honestly, I'm not even sure what good it would do them."

All his life, Gen had worked to learn, the deep rolling *R* in Italian, the clutter of vowels in Danish. As a child in Nagano, he sat in the kitchen on a high stool, repeating his mother's American accent while she chopped vegetables for dinner. She had gone to school in Boston and spoke French as well as English. His father's father worked in China as a young man and so his father spoke Chinese and had studied Russian in college. In his childhood, it seemed that language changed on the hour and no one was better at keeping up than Gen. He and his sisters played with words instead of toys. He studied and read, printed nouns onto index cards, listened to language tapes on the subway. He did not stop. Even if he was a natural polyglot, he never relied solely on talent. He learned. Gen was born to learn.

But these last months had turned him around and now Gen saw there could be as much virtue in letting go of what you knew as there had ever been in gathering new information. He worked as hard at forgetting as he had ever worked to learn. He managed to forget that Carmen was a soldier in the terrorist organization that had kidnapped him. That was not an easy task. Every day he forced himself to practice until he was able to look at Carmen and only see the woman he loved. He forgot about the future and past. He forgot about his country, his work, and what would become of him when all of this was over. He forgot that the way he lived now would ever be over. And Gen wasn't the only one. Carmen forgot, too. She did not remember her direct orders to form no emotional bonds to the hostages. When she found it was a struggle to let such important knowledge slip from her memory, the other soldiers helped her forget. Ishmael forgot because he wanted to be the other son of Ruben Iglesias and an employee of Oscar Mendoza. He could picture himself sharing a bedroom with Ruben's son, Marco, and being a helpful older brother to the boy. Cesar forgot because Roxane Coss had said he could come with her to Milan and learn to sing. How easy it was to imagine himself on a stage with her, a rain of tender blossoms pouring down on their feet. The Generals helped them to forget by turning a blind eye to all the affection and slackness that surrounded them, and they could do that because there was so much they were forgetting themselves. They had to forget that they had been the ones to recruit these young people from their families by promising them work and opportunity and a cause to fight for. They had to forget that the President of the country had neglected to attend the party from which they had so elaborately planned to kidnap him and so they changed their plans and took everyone else hostage. Mostly, they had to forget that they had not come up with a way to leave. They had to think that one might present itself if they waited long enough. Why should they think about the future? No one else seemed to remember it. Father Arguedas refused to think about it. Everyone came to Sunday mass. He performed the sacraments: communion, confession, even last rites. He had put the souls in this house in order and that was the only thing that mattered, so why should he think about the future? The future never even occurred to Roxane Coss. She had become so proficient at forgetting that she never considered the wife of her lover anymore. She was not concerned that he ran a corporation in Japan, or that they did not speak the same language. Even the ones who had no real reason to forget had done so. They lived their lives only for the hour that lay ahead of them. Lothar Falken thought only of running around the house. Victor Fyodorov thought of nothing but playing cards with his friends and gossiping about their love for Roxane Coss. Tetsuya Kato thought of his responsibilities as an accompanist and forgot about the rest. It was too much work to remember things you might not have again, and so one by one they opened up their hands and them let go. Except for Messner, whose job it was to remember. And Simon Thibault, who even in his sleep thought of nothing but his wife.

So even though Gen understood that there was something real and dangerous waiting for them, he began to forget it almost as soon as Messner left the house that afternoon. He busied himself typing up fresh lists of demands for the Generals and when it got later he helped serve dinner. He went to sleep that night and woke up at two A.M. to meet Carmen in the china closet and he told her, but not with the urgency he had felt in the afternoon. It was the sense of urgency he had managed to forget.

"What Messner was saying worried me," Gen said. Carmen was sitting in his lap, both of her legs to the left of him, both of her arms around his neck. *Worried me.* Shouldn't he have said something stronger than that?

And Carmen, who should have listened, who should have asked

him questions for her own safety and the safety of the other soldiers, her friends, only kissed him, because the important thing was to forget. It was their business, their job. That kiss was like a lake, deep and clear and they swam into it, forgetting. "We'll have to wait and see," Carmen said.

Should they do something, try to escape? There must be a way by now, everyone was lax. Hardly anyone was watching anymore. Gen asked her, his hands up under her shirt, feeling her shoulder blades flex beneath his fingertips.

"We could think about escaping," she said. But the military would catch her and torture her, that's what the Generals told them in training, and under the pains of torture she would tell them something. She could not remember what it was that she shouldn't tell but that would be the thing that would get everyone else killed. There were only two places in the world to go: inside and outside, and the question was where were you safer? Inside this house, in this china closet, she had never felt so safe in all her life. Clearly, Saint Rose of Lima lived inside this house. She was protected here. She was rewarded for her prayers with abundance. It was always better to stay with your saint. She kissed Gen's throat. All girls dreamed of being in love like this.

"So we'll talk about it?" Gen said, but now her shirt was off and it stretched out like a carpet for them to lie on. They closed the angle between their bodies and the floor.

"Let's talk about it," she said, sweetly shutting her eyes.

As soon as Roxane Coss fell in love, she fell in love again. The two experiences were completely different and yet coming as they did, one right on top of the other, she could not help but link them together in her mind. Katsumi Hosokawa came to her room in the middle of the night and for the longest time he just stood there inside her bedroom door and held her. It was as if he had returned from something no one is meant to survive, a plane crash, a ship lost at sea, and he could imagine nothing more than this: her in his arms. There was nothing they could say to one another but Roxane was far beyond thinking that speaking the same language was the only way to communicate with people. Besides, what was there to say, really? He knew her. She leaned against him, her arms around his neck, his hands flat against her back. Sometimes she nodded or he rocked her back and forth. From the way he was breathing she thought he might be crying and she understood that, too. She cried herself, she cried for the relief that came in being with him in that dark room, the relief that came from loving someone and from being loved. They would have stood there all night, he would have left without ever asking for anything else if she hadn't reached behind her at some point and taken one of his hands, led him there to her bed. There were so many ways to talk. He kissed her as she was leaning back, the curtains closed, the room completely dark.

In the morning she woke up for a minute, stretched, rolled over, and went back to sleep. She didn't know how long she slept, but then she heard singing and for the second time she was struck by the thought that she wasn't alone. It wasn't that she was in love with Cesar, but she was in love with his singing.

It was like this: every night Mr. Hosokawa came back to her bedroom and every morning Cesar waited to practice. If there was something else to want she forgot what it might be.

"Breathe," she said. "Like this." Roxane filled up her lungs, took in more air and then some more, and then held it. It didn't matter that he didn't understand the words she used. She stepped behind him and put her hand flat on his diaphragm. What she was saying was clear. She pushed all of the breath from his body and then filled him up again. She sang a line of Tosti, moving her hand back and forth like a metronome, and he sang it back to her. He was not a conservatory student who thought that to please was to be careful. He did not have a lifetime of mediocre instruction to overcome. He was not afraid. He was a boy, full of a boy's bravado, and when the line came back it was loud and passionate. He sang every line, every scale, as if the singing would save his life. He was settling into his own voice now and it was a voice that amazed her. It would have lived and died in a jungle, this voice, if she hadn't come along to rescue it.

It was a fine time, except for the fact that Messner didn't linger anymore. He was thinner now. His clothes hung from his shoulders as if they were sitting alone on a wire coat hanger. He only dropped things off and then was in a hurry to get away.

Cesar had his lesson in the morning, and no matter how hard he begged them to go outside, everyone sat down and listened. He was improving so quickly, even the other boys knew that what they were seeing was more interesting than television. He didn't sound a thing like Roxane anymore. He was finding his own depth. Every morning, he unfolded his voice before them like a rare jeweled fan; the more you listened, the more intricate it became. The crowd assembled in the living room could always count on the fact that he would be even better than he had been the day before. That was what was so astonishing about it. He had yet to show the slightest hint of finding the edges of what he was capable of. He sang with hypnotic passion and then with passionate lust. How impossible it seemed, so much voice pouring out of such an average boy. His arms still hung useless at his sides.

When Cesar released his final note, they were raucous, stamping their feet and whistling. "Hail, Cesar!" they called, hostage and terrorist alike. He was their boy. There was not a man or woman there who did not acclaim his greatness.

Thibault leaned over and whispered in the Vice President's ear. "One must wonder how our diva is taking this."

"With a brave face, no doubt," Ruben whispered back, and then he put two fingers in his mouth and blew a long, high whistle.

Cesar took a few nervous bows and when he was through the crowd began to call for Roxane. "Sing! Sing!" they demanded. She shook her head several times, but they did not accept this. It only made them call out more. When she finally stood she was laughing, because who did not feel the joy in such music? She raised her hands to try and silence them.

"Only one!" she said. "I can't compete with this." She leaned over and whispered in Kato's ear and he nodded. What was she whispering? They did not speak the same language.

Kato had transcribed the music from *Il Barbiere di Siviglia* for the piano and his fingers sprang high off the keys as if they were scorching to the touch. There was a time when she had missed the orchestra, the sweet weight of so many violins in front of her, but she never thought about it now. She stepped into the music as if it was a cool stream on a hot day and began "Una Voce Poco Fa." The music sounded exactly right to her now, and she thought this was the way Rossini had always intended it to be. Despite what anyone might whisper, she could certainly compete, and she could win. Her singing was a meringue, and when she trilled past the highest notes she put her hands on her hips and rocked them back and forth, smiling wickedly at the audience. She was an actress, too. She must teach that part to Cesar. *A thousand wayward tricks, and subtle wiles, I'd play before they should guide my will.* They cheered for her. Oh, how they loved those ridiculously high notes, the impossible acrobatics that she tossed off as if they were nothing at all. At the end she made them dizzy, and then she threw up her hands and said, "Outside, all of you," and even though they didn't know what she was saying, they followed her command and went out into the sunlight.

Mr. Hosokawa laughed and kissed her cheek. Who could believe such a woman existed? He went to the kitchen to make her a cup of tea and Cesar sat beside her on the piano bench, hoping that his lesson might be extended now that everyone was gone.

The rest went outside to play soccer or sit in the grass and watch the soccer game. Ruben had been able to petition a spade and a small hand rake from the gardener's shed, which was locked, and he turned over the soil in the flower beds, which he had meticulously cleared of weeds and grass. Ishmael skipped the game in order to help him. He didn't mind. He never liked to play. Ruben gave him a silver serving spoon with which to dig. "My father had a wonderful way with plants," Ruben told him. "All he had to do was say a few kind words to the ground and here they would come. He had meant to be a farmer, like his father, but the drought caught them all." Ruben shrugged and slipped his spade into the hard soil, turned it over.

"He would be proud of us now," Ishmael said.

The boys who were on guard climbed into the ivy banks at the edge of the yard, leaned their guns against the stucco wall, and joined the game. The runners gave up their running to play. "Una Voce Poco Fa" still bounced around in their heads, and even though they could not hum it, they chased the ball to the rhythm of the song. Beatriz had gotten the ball away from Simon Thibault and kicked it over to Jesus, who had a clear shot to take it past two chairs that were set up as the goal, and the Generals yelled to him, "Now! Now!" The light was cut to lace by the trees that had grown so thick with leaves in the last few months but still the light was everywhere. It was early, hours before lunch. Kato left the piano and came outside to sit on the grass in the sun beside Gen, so the only sound was the kick of the ball, the calling of names, Gilbert, Francisco, Paco, as they ran.

When Roxane Coss screamed it was because she saw a man she didn't recognize walking quickly into the room. She wasn't startled by his uniform or by his gun, she was used to those, but the way he came towards them was terrifying. He walked like no wall could stop him. Whatever he meant to do, his mind was made up, and nothing she could say or sing would ever make a difference. Cesar jumped up from the piano bench where he had been sitting and before he had gotten anywhere close to the door he was shot. He fell straight forward, not putting out his hands to save himself, not calling for anyone to help. Roxane crouched beneath the piano, her voice sounding out the alarm. She crawled towards the boy who she was sure was meant to be the greatest singer of his time, and covered his body with her own, lest something else should happen to him. She could feel his warm blood soaking her shirt, wetting her skin. She took his head in her hands and kissed his cheeks.

At the sound of the shot it seemed the man with the gun divided, first into two and then four, eight, sixteen, thirty-two, sixty-four. With every loud pop more came and they spread through the house and jumped through the windows, poured through the doors into the garden. No one could see where they had come from, only that they were everywhere. Their boots seemed to kick the house apart, to open up every entrance. They covered the playing field while the ball was still rolling away from the game. The guns fired over and over and it was impossible to say if the ones who were dropping were trying to protect themselves or if they had been hit. It was an instant and in that instant everything that had been known about the world was forgotten and relearned. The men were shouting something, but with the rushing of blood in his ears, the sickening spin of adrenaline, the deafness left over from the gunfire, not even Gen could understand them. He saw General Benjamin look back towards the wall, possibly gauging its height, and then with a shot Benjamin was down, the bullet catching him squarely in the side of his head. In one shot he lost both his life and the life of his brother, Luis, who would soon be taken from prison and executed for conspiracy. General Alfredo had already fallen. Humberto, Ignacio, Guadalupe, dead. Then Lothar Falken put his hands up and Father Arguedas put his hands up, Bernardo and Sergio and Beatriz put their hands up. *"Ort und Stelle bleiben!"* Lothar said, *stay put,* but where was the translator? German was useless to him now. General Hector started to put up his hands but he was shot before they had passed his chest.

The strangers cut the group apart as if they knew every member intimately. There was not a second's hesitation as to who was to be pulled away, handed down the line of men towards the back of the house where the sounds of guns being fired reported back to them without any pause. There were not that many people in the house. Even if they meant to shoot every one of them a hundred times, they would not have fired so many shots. Ranato was off his feet, twisting and screaming like a wild animal as he was pulled away by two men, each holding one of his arms. Father Arguedas rushed forward to help the boy and then just as quickly he was hit. He thought he had been shot, a bullet bearing in to the back of his neck, and in that moment he remembered his God. But when he was on the grass he knew he was wrong. He was very much alive. He opened his eyes and found himself looking at Ishmael, his friend, not two minutes dead. The Vice President was crying into the boy's neck, his eyes pressed closed, his mouth stretched open wide. He was holding his child's lovely head in his hands. In Ishmael's hands was the spoon with which he had been digging.

Beatriz held her hands up straight above her head and the sun hit the crystal of Gen's watch and threw a perfect circle of light against the wall. All around her were the people she knew. There was General Hector lying on his side, his glasses gone, his shirt a soggy mess. There was Gilbert, who once she had kissed out of boredom. He was flat on his back, his arms stretched out to the sides as if he meant to fly. Then there was someone else, but that was awful. She couldn't tell who it was. She felt afraid of them now, the people she knew. She had more in common with the strangers who were shooting because she and they were all alive. She would keep her arms the straightest of them all. That was the difference. She would do exactly what she was told and she would be spared. She closed her eyes and looked for her dark pile of sins, hoping she could release a few more on her own without the help of the priest, thinking that fewer sins would give her a lightness that these new men would recognize. But the sins were gone. She looked and looked behind the darkness of her eyelids but there was not a single sin left and she was amazed. She heard Oscar Mendoza calling her name, "Beatriz! Beatriz!" and she opened her eyes. He was coming towards her, his arms stretched out. He was running towards her like a lover and she smiled at him. Then she heard another gunshot but this time it knocked her off her feet. A pain exploded up high in her chest and spit her out of this terrible world.

Gen saw Beatriz fall and called for Carmen. Where was Carmen?

He did not know if she was outside. He could not see her anywhere. No one was more clever than Carmen. No one was more likely to escape, unless she did something stupid. What if she had some idea of saving him? "She is my wife! She is my wife!" he cried into the bedlam, because that was the only plan he had ever devised, even though he had never asked her to marry him, or asked the priest to bless them. She was his wife in every way that mattered and that would save her.

But nothing could save her. Carmen was already dead, killed right at the start. She had been in the kitchen putting the dishes back into the china closet when Mr. Hosokawa came in to make the tea. He bowed to her, which always made her smile shyly. He had not reached the kettle when they heard Roxane Coss. Not a song but a scream and then a long, wolflike howl. Together they turned towards the door, Mr. Hosokawa and Carmen. They ran together down the hallway, Carmen, younger, faster, in front of him. They were through the dining room when they heard the shot that brought down Cesar. They stepped into the living room just as a man with a gun turned to face them, just as Roxane took the body of her student in her arms. Time, so long suspended, now came back with such force that it overlapped and everything happened at once. Roxane saw them as the man with the gun saw them, Carmen saw Cesar, and Mr. Hosokawa saw Carmen and he scooped her from the space in front of him, the force of his arm hitting the side of her waist like a blow. He was in front of her the instant she was being thrown behind him, the instant the man who saw her standing in front, separate from Mr. Hosokawa, fired his gun. From six feet away there would have been no missing her except for the confusion, the firing of guns, the frenzy of voices, the man who was on the list to save stepping in front of her. One shot fixed them together in a pairing no one had considered before: Carmen and Mr. Hosokawa, her head just to the left of his as if she was looking over his shoulder.

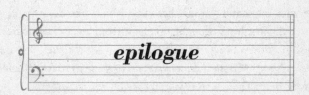

epilogue

When the ceremony was over, the wedding party walked out into the late afternoon sun. Edith Thibault kissed the bride and groom and then kissed her own husband for good measure. There was a brightness in her that the other three lacked. She still believed she was lucky. She had been the one who insisted that she and Simon come to Lucca for the day to be witnesses for Gen and Roxane. It was only right to wish them well. "I thought it was beautiful," she said in French. The four of them spoke French.

Thibault held his wife's arm as if he was dizzy. It would have been nice if someone had thought to fly Father Arguedas up to perform the ceremony, but no one had thought of it and now the thing was done. The French government fully expected Thibault would resume his post after an adequate period of rest, but when the Thibaults left the house for Paris they took all of their personal belongings with them. Simon and Edith would never set foot in that godforsaken country again. *Quel bled,* they said now.

It was early May and the tourist season had not yet begun in Lucca. The old stone streets would soon be packed solid with college students holding guidebooks, but for now it was completely empty. It felt like their own private city, which was exactly what the bride wanted, a very quiet wedding in the birthplace of Giacomo Puccini. A breeze came up and she held down her hat with her hand.

"I'm happy," Roxane said, and then she looked at Gen and said it again. He kissed her.

"The restaurants won't be open yet," Edith said. She scanned the square with one hand shading her eyes. It was like an ancient, abandoned city, something brought up clean from an archaeological dig. No part of Paris was ever like this. "Go and see if there's a bar somewhere, will you? We should have a glass of wine to toast. Roxane and I can wait here. These streets weren't meant for heels."

Thibault felt a small flush of panic, but just as quickly he got hold of it. The square was too open, too quiet. He had felt better inside the church. "A drink, absolutely." He kissed her once near her eye and then kissed her again on the lips. It was a wedding day, after all, a wedding day in Italy.

"You don't mind waiting?" Gen asked Roxane.

She smiled at him. "Married women don't mind waiting."

Edith Thibault took her hand and admired the bright new ring. "They mind it terribly, but they would still like a glass of wine."

The two women sat down on the edge of a fountain, Roxane with a bouquet of flowers in her lap, and watched as the men wandered off down one of the narrow, identical streets. When they turned out of sight Edith thought she had made a mistake. She and Roxane should have taken off their shoes and gone along.

Gen and Thibault crossed two piazzas before either of them said anything and their silence made the clap of their heels echo up the high walls. "So you'll live in Milan," Thibault said.

"It's a beautiful city."

"And your work?" Because Gen's work had been Mr. Hosokawa.

"I mostly translate books now. It leaves my schedule more flexible. I like to go to rehearsals with Roxane."

"Yes, of course," Thibault said absently, and pushed his hands deep into his pockets as they walked. "I miss hearing her sing."

"You should come visit."

A boy on a bright red moped sped past and then two men with dachshunds came out of a bakery and walked towards them. The city wasn't deserted after all. "Will you miss Japan?"

Gen shook his head. "It's better for her here, better for me, too, I'm sure. All opera singers should live in Italy." He pointed to the building on the corner. "There's a bar that's open."

Thibault stopped. He would have missed it. He hadn't been paying attention. "Good, then we've done our job. Let's go back for our wives."

But Gen didn't turn. He stared at the bar for a long time as if it were a place he had once lived years before.

Thibault asked him if something was wrong. He froze up like that from time to time himself.

"I wanted to ask you," Gen said, but it took him another minute to find the words. "Carmen and Beatriz are never mentioned in the papers. Everything I've read says there were fifty-nine men and one woman. Is that the way they reported it in France?"

Thibault said there had been no mention of the girls.

Gen nodded. "I suppose it makes a better story that way, fifty-nine and one." He wore a white rose boutonniere on his wedding suit. Edith had brought it for him in a cardboard box along with the bouquet of white roses for Roxane to carry. She had pinned the flower on his lapel herself. "I've called the papers and asked them to publish a correction, but no one is interested. It's almost as if they never existed."

"Nothing you read in the papers is true," Thibault said. He was thinking about the first time they had to cook dinner, all those chickens, and the girls and Ishmael coming in with the knives.

Still Gen wouldn't look at him. He talked as if he were telling the story to the bar. "I called Ruben, did I tell you that? I called to tell him about the wedding. He said that he thought we should wait, that we would be wrong to rush into anything. He was very kind about it, you know how Ruben would be. But we didn't want to wait. I love Roxane."

"No," Thibault said. "You did the right thing. Getting married was the best thing that ever happened to me." Though now he was wondering about Carmen. Why had he never thought of it before? He could plainly remember them together, time after time standing at the back of the room, whispering, the way her face brightened when she turned it to Gen. Thibault did not wish to see her face again.

"When I hear Roxane sing I am still able to think well of the world," Gen said. "This is a world in which someone could have written such music, a world in which she can still sing that music with so much compassion. That's proof of something, isn't it? I don't think I would last a day without that now."

Even when Thibault closed his eyes and rubbed them with his thumb and forefinger he could still see Carmen. Her hair in a braid on the back of her slender neck. She is laughing. "She is a beautiful girl," he said. They had found the bar. He needed to get back to Edith now. He looped his arm around his friend's shoulder and guided him back in the direction of the Piazza San Martino. He felt himself growing breathless, and he had to concentrate on the muscles in his legs to keep from running. He was sure that Gen and Roxane had married for love, the love of each other and the love of all the people they remembered.

When they turned the corner the street opened into the bright square and there the wives were, still sitting on the edge of the fountain. They were looking in the direction of the cathedral but then Edith turned and when she saw him, the joy in her face! They stood up and walked towards the two men, Edith with her dark hair shining, Roxane still in her hat. Either one of them could have been the bride. Thibault was sure there had never been such beautiful women, and the beautiful women came to them and held out their arms.

My love and gratitude to my editor Robert Jones.

Your chance to win

The Times and Harper Collins are offering you the opportunity to win £500 worth of books.

For more details and to enter, visit
www.timesonline.co.uk/bookcomp

**Don't miss the next book
by your favourite author**
www.authortracker.co.uk

Full terms and conditions online